Book 4
of the
Cornish Chronicles Series

The Path We Take

Ann E Brockbank

To Pam

My treasured and much-loved friend who brought about something wonderful in my life that I will forever thank you for.

By Ann E Brockbank

Cornish Chronicles Series

1. A Gift from the Sea – 1901 - 1902
2. Waiting for the Harvest Moon - 1907-1908
3. My Song of the Sea -1911 -1912
4. The Path We Take – 1912
5. The Glittering Sea – 1912 – 1919

Historical Novels

Mr de Sousa's Legacy – 1939 – 1960

Contemporary Novels

The Blue Bay Café
On a Distant Shore

ACKNOWLEDGMENTS

My grateful thanks go to all you lovely people who buy and read my books. I so appreciate your continual support. You are all wonderful I am enormously privileged that you believe in me and chose my books to read.

There is always a list of wonderful people to thank for helping me get this book to publication and here they are.

My upmost thanks go to Angie, for her historical guidance, reining in my creative spelling and for improving this book no end. You have no idea how much I appreciate your generous time, friendship and expertise.

To Pam, a much-loved friend who I haven't seen for a long time. You made something wonderful happen in my life that I will forever thank you for – you know what it was. This book is dedicated to you.

To my partner, Rob, for every single wonderful thing you do, your love and encouragement has kept me writing, and as always, your beautiful artwork adds a special quality to my novels.

To the amazing staff at Poldhu Café - I thank you for your continued support and being the inspiration for this novel.

To my darling late husband, Peter, who encourage me to write, you are forever in my heart.

My heartfelt gratitude goes to Sarah and Martin Caton and their lovely family for allowing me to use their beautiful home Bochym Manor as a setting for four of my novels in the 'Cornish Chronicles' series.

If you enjoyed this book, please could you leave a short review on Amazon? You can do this even if you didn't buy the book on Amazon! If you loved this book, please spread the love and tell your friends, hopefully they too will support me by buying the book.

ABOUT THE AUTHOR

Ann E Brockbank was born in Yorkshire, but has lived in Cornwall for many years. The Path We Take is Ann's eighth book and the fourth in the Cornish Chronicles Series. Ann lives with her artist partner on the beautiful banks of the Helford River in Cornwall - an integral setting for all of her novels. Ann is currently writing her ninth novel. Ann loves to chat with her readers so please visit her Facebook Author page and follow her on Twitter and Instagram

Facebook: @AnnEBrockbank.Author
Twitter: @AnnEBrockbank1
Instagram: annebrockbank

The Path We Take

Though it was late in the month of September, the Cornish summer seemed to be holding the autumn at bay for a while longer. It was Monday, and Betsy Tamblin, the senior maid at Bochym Manor, was using her half day off to take a walk in her favourite field - probably for the last time before the harvesters came to cut it. Climbing the stile, she stood gazing at the golden field of wheat which was sprinkled liberally with wild flowers. The field swayed in the breeze like the waves on the ocean. The slightly medicinal aroma of meadowsweet, mixed with the honey scent from the frothy yellow flowers of lady's bedstraw, filled the air with the fragrance of late summer. It was a sight to behold, and lifted Betsy's spirits, as they'd been sorely dashed since hearing that her best friend Jessie Blackthorn had left the county yesterday - without saying goodbye to her! Jessie had left her a letter though - which was safely tucked in her skirt pocket, hopefully it would explain the rumours circulating about her departure.

Stepping down from the stile, she walked into the wheat, but no sooner had she unfolded the letter, the most horrendous pain seared her leg. Howling in agony, unable to comprehend what had happened, her heart was hammering with adrenalin – had she been bitten by an adder? Deeply alarmed at the thought she staggered backwards, only to find the pain intensify, and the realisation that she'd been pinioned to the ground. Frantically dragging her skirts up, she was horrified to find the rusty spikes of a rabbit trap puncturing her foot, and blood oozing through her best grey stockings. A cold sweat slicked her body and her ears began to ring alarmingly - a moment later everything turned black, she lost consciousness and the much-anticipated letter she'd been reading fell from her hands.

Moments later, she became aware again of her surroundings and the pain which had made her faint, and was gratified to find a man, albeit a stranger, tending to her.

Ryan Penrose had been nearby when he'd heard her scream, and without hesitation he'd come to her aid. He cursed under his breath as he curled his fingers in-between the vicious claws to pull them apart.

Betsy squealed in agony and was about to faint again - the extraction being far worse than the initial impact.

'Stay with me, Miss. I need you to pull your foot away.' But Betsy was too traumatised to understand him. *'Please move your foot* - I can't hold the trap open for long!' he yelled.

His abrupt manner brought her to her senses and she somehow slithered her wounded foot from the teeth of the trap.

'Thank god!' he muttered. Wiping his blood–stained hands down his trousers, he scooped Betsy effortlessly into his arms. 'Where do you live?'

'At the manor,' she whimpered, 'I'm a maid there.' Through the fug of pain, she felt sure he'd hesitated for a split-second, but then thankfully they set off. He sat her down atop of the stile while he climbed over, and then ever so gently, gathered her back into his arms.

Being in such close proximity to her rescuer, Betsy realised he was definitely a stranger to these parts - a rough sleeper by the look of him. His straw-coloured hair was long and untidy, and in desperate need of a wash - as were his clothes by the smell of them. The stink was not helping in her struggle to fight the nausea rising in her throat. His face looked kind though and, whoever he was, she was ever so grateful for his help.

The man must have noted her scrutiny, because he gave her a gentle, albeit crooked, smile. 'We'll soon have you home, Miss.'

'Hey, hey, you!' A shout came from behind them.

Ryan turned to see an angry, odd looking man running towards them, and when Betsy saw who it was, she groaned audibly and clung to Ryan.

'Put her *down* this instant,' the man yelled.

'Christ man, she's injured her foot....' But before Ryan could finish his sentence, the man had thumped him hard on the nose. Ryan staggered from the blow and Betsy screamed, but he kept a tight hold on her.

Someone came running from the other direction shouting, 'Trencrom, what's happening here?'

After steadying himself, Ryan hitched Betsy closer, and said, 'This maniac has just thumped me!'

'Only on account that he's got his filthy hands all over Betsy, Mr Oliver,' Trencrom shouted. 'I'll bloody thump him again if he doesn't put her down right now!'

Betsy whimpered. 'It's all right,' Ryan soothed, looking towards Mr Oliver for help. 'The young woman has injured herself.' He sniffed back the blood beginning to trickle from his nose and added, 'I'm taking her home.'

'You're taking her nowhere,' Trencrom yelled as he tried to pull Betsy from his arms.

Betsy shrieked and buried her face into Ryan's smelly shirt.

'Trencrom, leave them alone.' Mr Oliver pulled him away from Ryan. 'I'll sort this out from here,' he said authoritatively.

Trencrom cursed as he reluctantly let go.

'Bring her this way,' Mr Oliver ordered Ryan, but when Trencrom began to follow them, he turned on him. 'Trencrom - get back to work.'

'But...'

'Now!'

Mrs Blair, the Bochym cook, had seen them from the window as they crossed the kitchen courtyard and was at the door in a state of high agitation to greet them.

'Oh, lordy me!' she shrieked when she saw Betsy, and the man holding her, covered in blood. 'What on earth has happened?'

*

Ruby Sanders - the Bochym housekeeper for the last ten years - was sat at her desk in the housekeeper's room. It was as tidy and orderly as she kept herself. She was thirty-four-years-old, a spinster, and believed that her best years were behind her now. Love and marriage had passed her by - as was so often the case if you worked in service. But Ruby was happily ensconced in the Bochym household - they were her family - she could ask for no better. She was busy working on the rotas for the maids, in preparation for the busy week ahead of them. Her ladyship's artist brother, Justin Devereux was arriving from Italy on Wednesday for an extended stay, and to welcome him, Lord and Lady de Bochym were hosting a dinner party with overnight guests on Friday. Ruby prided herself that she had everything under control, she, along with Joe Treen the butler, ran an efficient and happy household between them.

With the rota complete, she'd begun to organise the linen for the overnight guests when she heard the commotion in the kitchen. Both she and Joe emerged from their respective offices to exchange curious glances.

They found the kitchen in chaos. Mr Oliver the gamekeeper was tending the blood splattered nose of a stranger - who looked remarkably like a vagrant! Betsy was sitting down, ashen-faced and bleeding profusely from her foot, while Mrs Blair was flapping her teacloth, fretting about the amount of blood on her kitchen floor.

While Mr Oliver gave Joe an account of what had happened, Ruby tended to Betsy. Juliet Gwyn, the newest maid to join Bochym, was standing pale-faced and open-mouthed. It was not Betsy she was looking at, but the man who had brought her in.

'Juliet…. *Juliet.*' Mrs Sanders shouted, 'fetch a bowl of salt water. Thomas, Mr Treen, I think we need to get Betsy upstairs. I'll go and call the doctor.'

No sooner had Joe and Thomas, the footman stood Betsy up, Sarah Dunstan - the Countess de Bochym appeared in the kitchen, a waft of expensive perfume preceding her. Everyone bowed and curtseyed – even Betsy tried to do so.

'My goodness, what can be happening in here? I heard the commotion from the library.'

'I'm dreadfully sorry for the noise, my lady,' Ruby spoke, 'but it appears that poor Betsy has stood in a rabbit trap. This young man here brought her home,' she gestured towards Ryan.

Horrified, Sarah asked, 'Where did this happen, Betsy?'

'The wheat field, my lady,' she answered, hiccupping back a painful sob.

'Goodness me!' Sarah gasped, 'who on earth would set such a trap - and on private ground?'

Juliet, who was stood frozen at the scullery sink, shot a look at Ryan, who was stood anxiously twisting his hat in his hands.

Ever the compassionate mistress, Sarah put a comforting hand on Betsy's shoulder. 'We'll soon have you comfortable, Betsy,' she said gently and nodded for Joe and Thomas to help her up to her room.

While Ruby went to call the doctor, Sarah turned to Mr Oliver. 'Could you liaise with my husband's steward to have this matter looked into. We cannot have this sort of thing happening on our land.'

'Yes, my lady,' he said doffing his cap.

*

Realising he was no longer needed, now he'd delivered Betsy home, nor that he was a particularly welcome sight by the look on Juliet and the cook's face, Ryan turned to leave, only to be called back by the Countess.

'Excuse me, good morning.' Sarah smiled at him. 'And, you are?'

'Ryan Penrose, my lady,' he said, bowing his head. 'I found the maid trapped, and brought her home.'

'Well, thank goodness that you did, but tell me, how did you come to be wounded yourself?'

'Someone thumped me, my lady, when I was carrying

the young woman. I couldn't defend myself.'

'Goodness, who on earth would do such a thing?'

'Mr Oliver said it was Trencrom, my lady,' the cook answered with a nod. 'Apparently Trencrom was defending Betsy's honour,' she added derisively.

'I was just bringing her home, that's all!' Ryan said in his defence. He watched uncomfortably as Sarah's eyes scrutinised his dirty attire, and if she could smell the odour from him, she did not show it.

'You're a stranger in these parts?' It was a statement rather than a question.

'Yes, my lady. I'm looking for work.'

'Where are you from?'

Juliet, emitted a small squeak of alarm at the question as she emerged from the scullery carrying the bowl of water, but quickly coughed to mask it.

Ryan hesitated slightly before answering. 'Gweek, my lady.'

'Gweek!' Sarah turned to Juliet, who had paled significantly. 'Are you not from Gweek too, Juliet?'

'Yes, my lady,' she answered almost inaudibly.

'Do you know each other then?'

'No,' they said in unison, and then Ryan added, 'I haven't lived there long – I moved there from Manaccan.'

'I see.' Sarah raised an eyebrow. 'And now you are here! Are you staying locally?'

'Yes, my lady - quite local,' he answered evasively.

Sarah smiled. 'Mrs Blair, could we get this young man a cup of tea for his troubles - and perhaps a bite to eat?'

'Of course, my lady,' Mrs Blair answered crisply.

Ryan's stomach rumbled audibly at the mention of food – he hadn't eaten properly for days. He clutched his stomach apologetically.

'That's very kind of you, my lady. Thank you,' but noting the cook's displeasure, he added, 'I'll wait outside - I'm not dressed appropriately to be inside a clean kitchen. Please convey my good wishes to the young woman - I hope for a speedy recovery for her.' He bowed to take his leave.

*

Betsy's shoe was ruined, and as Ruby peeled the stocking off her foot, she winced through gritted teeth as the material pulled at the dried blood on her skin. Juliet was waiting with a bowl of warm salty water to bathe her wounds, and all three women gasped when the terrible state of her foot was revealed.

'It looks terribly angry, Betsy,' Ruby said.

'It's flipping painful, Mrs Sanders!' She grimaced as she dipped her foot into the bowl Juliet had put down.

When Ruby left them for a moment to fetch a towel, Juliet asked tentatively, 'That man who brought you in, Betsy - did he say anything?'

'Like what?' she said wincing as the salt water stung her wounds.

'Did he say who he was, and why he was in the vicinity?'

Betsy shook her head. 'I was a little too preoccupied with the pain, and then that stupid Mr Trencrom thumped the poor man! He was claiming that he had his hands all over me! For goodness' sake he was only carrying me! As to your question though, no, he didn't say anything and I don't know who he was, but he smelt like a vagrant - the pong was terrible. He had a nice smile though and a kind, handsome face.' Her mood brightened at the thought of him. 'I hope horrible Mr Trencrom's thump hasn't altered his good looks,' she grinned through her pain.

Ruby returned with a towel, and after a good soak, lifted Betsy's foot out of the salt bath a moment before Sarah swept into their room.

'Mr Penrose sends his good wishes up to you, Betsy.'

Puzzled, Betsy asked, 'I'm sorry, but who is Mr Penrose, my lady?'

'The young man who brought you in - he's going to have a cup of tea and something to eat outside in the courtyard for his troubles.'

Juliet's eyes widened and quickly picked up the bowl to take it away. 'Shall I go and thank him for you, Betsy?' she asked.

'Oh, yes please, Juliet. Thank you.'

*

Joe Treen watched curiously as Juliet delivered a tray of tea and sandwiches to Betsy's rescuer who was sitting in the kitchen courtyard. There was no denying – he felt a pang of jealousy, watching her speak so animatedly to the man. *Oh, Joe!* He thought. *You've done it again, haven't you? For the second time in your life, you've fallen for a woman who does not reciprocate your feelings.* It puzzled him as to how he had read her so wrongly. When Juliet had joined them here in August, Joe found himself immediately infatuated by her. She was a true natural beauty, with clear skin, pale blue eyes and thick golden hair which shone like spun gold in the sunshine. At first Juliet had welcomed his friendship, but then last week, he'd made the fundamental mistake in conveying his growing feelings for her. Since then, she'd shied away from him and now would barely make eye contact. He peeled his eyes away from Juliet and then glanced at Mrs Blair, who in turn was watching him. The cook smiled sympathetically, clearly understanding his consternation.

2

Ryan licked his lips when he saw the generous ham sandwich which Juliet had delivered to him. Unfortunately, it was accompanied by a brisk, intense and extremely emotional conversation, cut short only when the Earl's steward, Mr Parson, emerged from the back door of his cottage to walk briskly across the cobbled courtyard towards the manor kitchen. Juliet swiftly left Ryan to his thoughts and his meal.

Although enjoying the sun and surroundings of the Bochym kitchen courtyard, Ryan was troubled by their conversation. His appearance had clearly upset Juliet - and that had never been his intention. He had hoped to have kept his presence hereabouts a secret, but with the young woman injuring herself, events had overtaken his good intentions. Well, he couldn't just leave Betsy there in agony, could he? He cursed himself, sickened to think of the injury she'd sustained. To his infinite regret, he'd been the one to lay the trap. It was his only source of catching rabbits – he'd tried snaring them without success, and living on a diet of mushrooms and berries was taking its toll. He'd never thought for one moment that anyone would walk through the wheat - he had certainly never meant to harm anyone. However, the incident had now brought to Juliet's attention that he was living close by *and* the reason why! He thought, in fact hoped, his presence would settle her mind, but he was not so sure now. He'd endeavour to keep a low profile from now on – the last thing he wanted was to upset her any more than necessary.

He took a bite of the sandwich - audibly groaning with delight as he savoured the delicious salty ham liberally spread with hot mustard. His taste-buds being so devoid of anything flavoursome, he'd eagerly taken a second bite when the steward stepped out of the kitchen with another gentleman.

Although the Earl de Bochym did not introduce

himself, one glance at his fine attire urged Ryan to stand and bow.

'Now then, Penrose,' the Earl addressed him. 'We understand you're the chap who found Betsy?'

Ryan swallowed the mouthful of sandwich as fast as he could. 'Yes, my lord.'

'Good, you can come with us and show us where this dreadful contraption is – they're no better than mantraps.'

Realising they were not about to wait for him to finish his meal, Ryan took a quick drink of tea, pushed the half-eaten sandwich inside his shirt and followed them.

The gamekeeper had joined them in the wheat field, and Ryan pointed out where the trap was. He was sensible enough not to admit any other knowledge of it, and agreed wholeheartedly with them, that whoever had set the trap should be horsewhipped. It was while the steward, gamekeeper and the Earl were inspecting the trap, Ryan noticed a letter and envelope lying in the long grass. He picked it up and swiftly pushed it into his pocket.

'Penrose, can you spare us a little more of your time to sweep this field for more traps,' the steward asked.

'Of course, sir,' Ryan replied, knowing full well there were no more traps. This was the only one he had set!

It took a good hour to sweep the field enough for them to be happy with the outcome, and by the time they'd finished, Ryan's stomach was rumbling cavernously for want of the rest of the sandwich.

While the Earl and steward were deep in conversation, the gamekeeper stepped forward. 'How is your nose?' he asked.

'Smarting a bit - but thankfully not broken.' He wiggled it a little.

'I've reported the incident to Mr Parson - he'll give him an official warning.'

'Good! If I hadn't had my arms full, I'd have thumped him back! Was he the young woman's sweetheart then?'

Mr Oliver roared with laughter. 'I shouldn't think so -

no one likes the man, least of all the maids.'

Ryan smiled - heartened at this news.

'Tell me, Penrose, do you live nearby?'

'Um, quite near, yes,' he answered evasively - hoping he wasn't going to ask more questions. 'I'm looking for work.'

'I see, well then, I'll bid you good day, and thank you for your help. I'll be keeping a watchful eye out for the culprit. I've no doubt the blaggard will be back to check the trap, and then he'll be up before the magistrates before he knows what's hit him.'

Ryan swallowed hard as he watched the three men walk away, and then he turned to walk back to the wood shack he'd commandeered in the woods. The encampment, hid him from sight, but also gave him a good vantage of the drive to the manor – something he felt was necessary at the moment. Settling down on a tree stump, he pulled his sandwich from his shirt and ate hungrily, before turning his attention to the letter he'd found. He would always be grateful to his teacher, Mr Floyd, at the school he'd attended in Manaccan. That man had a mission in life to never let a child leave the school without having the ability to read, write and do sums - all the while making the learning of them fun. Not a single child had left his school without knowing their times tables. He wiped his hands down his shirt and looked first at the envelope - It was addressed to Betsy. The poor woman must have been reading this when she stood in the trap. He didn't read the letter, but put it back in the envelope and decided to take it back up to the manor, even though it would upset Juliet to see him again.

*

When the doctor arrived to see Betsy, he smiled kindly before taking a closer look at her foot.

'Oh dear, you've certainly been in the wars, but fortunately it looks clean.'

'We've bathed it in salt water, Dr Martin,' Betsy said trying not to wince as the doctor carefully touched the skin surrounding the wounds.

'I'm glad to hear it - you can get a nasty infection with a wound like this. Now, I'm not going to stitch anything. We need to let the wounds weep and heal naturally, so I'll just loosely bandage it, but I'm afraid you'll be out of action for a few days - longer, if an infection takes hold.'

'But I can't lay here for a few days!' Betsy shot a worried glance at Mrs Sanders. 'We have such a lot to do!'

'I'm sure we'll manage, Betsy.' Ruby smiled

The doctor nodded, reassured that she would get the best of care and reiterated, 'Rest! If the pain gets worse or your foot becomes very hot, someone must call for me. I'll pop back tomorrow anyway to see how you are getting on.'

Left alone now, the bedroom fell silent. Betsy allowed the tears she'd bravely held in to fall. In truth, she'd never felt pain like this, but it wasn't just the pain upsetting her - she feared she would never dare to take her favourite walk in that field again - and she'd lost the letter Jessie had sent her. There was an old wives' tale that said bad things happen in threes. There had already been a fatal shooting down at Poldhu Cove recently, involving people she knew very well, and now she had caught her foot in a trap – she was fearful now, wondering what else was going to happen? Wiping her tears, she sank back into her pillow and turned her thoughts to Ryan Penrose. She gave a ghost of a smile - she'd never been in a man's arms before – it had been the one highlight of her dreadful ordeal, until stupid Mr Trencrom had hit him! She would definitely put in a formal complaint about that horrible man.

*

With a maid down, it fell on Juliet and Dorothy to do the lion's share of the work. Juliet didn't mind though – it took her mind off why Ryan was in the vicinity.

It was just as Juliet and Dorothy were filling buckets of water to wash the guest bedroom windows, that Mrs Blair thumped her fists into her ample hips.

'*Now*, what does he want again?' she said, spotting Ryan walking back through the kitchen courtyard. 'He smells to high heaven and I really don't want him in my kitchen again. Go see what he wants, Dorothy.'

'Me?' the girl looked aghast.

'No, the kitchen chair! Of course, I mean you. You're the only one called Dorothy!'

Juliet's heart quickened when she saw Ryan and put her bucket down. 'I'll go,' she said, stepping out to meet him before he knocked. She closed the door swiftly behind her so that no one could hear them speak.

'What's happened - why are you here again?'

'It's all right, Juliet, everything is fine.' He smiled gently, hoping to ease her distress. 'I found this letter near where the trap was.'

Juliet clenched her teeth. 'It was *your* trap, wasn't it?'

Ryan looked shamefaced. 'I have to eat, Juliet!' he said in his defence.

'Betsy could lose her foot you know!'

'Oh, don't say that,' he said raking his fingers through his dirty hair.

'Give me the letter,' she took it from his hand, 'I'll see she gets it.'

'Is she all right?' His eyes searched hers.

'Hopefully, yes, the doctor has seen to her. You'd better go now.'

'I'm so sorry, Juliet, I don't mean to upset you,' he said earnestly. 'I wouldn't be here, if not for……'

'I know, Ryan, and I wish it would not be so …..' Her face softened. 'Thank you though, but please, no more traps.'

'I promise – and I'm that sorry I hurt Betsy.'

'I know you are.' She glanced back to make sure no one could hear her, and whispered, 'Look, I'll try to get some food down to you. I'll leave it in the hay barn behind the boating lake.'

He smiled gratefully. 'I wish I could get some work. If

you hear of any….'

She nodded. 'I'll let you know.'

Back in the kitchen, Mrs Blair narrowed her eyes curiously. 'You look a little ruffled – do I detect a love interest here?'

Juliet's breath caught in her throat. 'Absolutely not!'

Mrs Blair raised an eyebrow. 'Well, something has pinked your cheeks.'

Juliet flushed furiously. 'Only on account of having to speak to a stranger!' she parried.

'Mmm.' Mrs Blair was unconvinced. 'What did he want?'

'To ask after Betsy and to give her this letter - she must have dropped it when she got her foot caught.'

Mrs Blair glanced at the grubby letter. 'Take it to Mrs Sanders - she'll give it to Betsy.'

*

Betsy was bored laid up in bed, she felt so helpless listening to the sounds of the busy household below her getting ready for the expected guests. Having tried to read for a while, she eventually gave up, unable to concentrate for the dreadful throbbing pain in her foot. The spoonful of laudanum the doctor administered was clearly wearing off. She brightened a little when Ruby swept into her bedroom just before the staff tea bell was rung, and placed the tray holding a cup of tea and a slice of cake by her bed. Betsy shifted her weight up the bed and sat up.

'Goodness, Mrs Sanders, I feel like the lady of the manor laid here while you bring me tea,' she joked.

'It's good that you still have a sense of humour. I've also brought you a letter.'

'Oh, thank goodness!' She clutched it to her chest. 'I thought I'd lost this!'

'The young man who rescued you, found the letter in the field where you had your accident. It's a bit grubby I'm afraid, but at least you have it now. So, how are you feeling? Are you still in pain?' Betsy nodded. 'Dr Martin has left you some laudanum should the pain get too much for you,' she put the bottle on the bedside table, 'but its powerful stuff, so take it with care.'

'I will thank you, Mrs Sanders. I'm so sorry about this. I know we have such a busy week.'

'You just concentrate on getting better, Betsy. We'll cope.' She smiled and nodded at the letter Betsy was clutching. 'Is your letter from Jessie?'

'Yes.'

'Well, I'll leave you to read it then. When you write back to Jessie, send my good wishes to her.'

'Thank you, Mrs Sanders, I will,' she said, heartened that she'd made no reference to the rumours which were flying around about Jessie.

As soon as she'd gone Betsy unfolded the letter. She'd only just read the first line when the accident happened – the thought made her shudder.

Sunday 22ⁿᵈ of September, 1912.

My dearest friend, Betsy,

I have left this letter with Ellie, who assures me she will forward it onto you as soon as possible. First let me apologise for leaving without saying goodbye to you. Events last week happened so quickly; I don't know where to start to explain. You will no doubt have heard by now that I've left Cornwall to start a new life with Daniel Chandler, who, I can now tell you, was the father of my poor dead baby, Cordelia. I truly believed that Daniel had perished when his ship sank en route to America, and because of that, I vowed never to disclose or sully his name. I'm not even sure if you would have believed me if I'd told you at the time – I hardly believed it myself when we fell in love last year – he seemed so far above my station in life. Daniel quite unexpectedly returned to me late last Wednesday, and even though I've been estranged from Silas since May, I knew he would cause trouble for us when he found Daniel had returned. We had planned to leave on that Thursday evening, but then of course Silas died so tragically in the dreadful shooting incident at Poldhu. Although, Silas's death had nothing to do with Daniel or myself, understandably our lives and plans were thrown into chaos. With the aftermath and shock of what happened - and Silas's funeral, I didn't have time to tell you my plans with Daniel. Silas's brother, Guy, is understandably bereft at his death, and has not looked on our union favourably. He believes that as I'm Silas's wife, albeit an estranged one, I should stay and morn Silas for decency's sake. But Betsy, you of all people know the dreadful sorrow I've endured this year. First thinking I'd lost the love of my life and latterly losing our precious baby, so I feel that as my friend, you'll understand my reluctance to delay my chance of a happy life with Daniel any longer. For this reason, and so as not to cause a fuss about leaving so soon after Silas's death, we've decided to slip away quietly today. I regret only one thing, and that is that I haven't had the chance to say a proper goodbye to you, and to all my friends. I also want to apologise for the many secrets I've kept from you over this past year – I hope you will forgive me and understand a little of why they were necessary. My goodbye to Ellie, which, after working with her at the tea room for all these years, and latterly being part of the Blackthorn family, was deeply emotional, but she understood my urgency to get away to start a new life. I suspect though that Guy will probably never forgive me for it. I shall miss you, dear Betsy, with all my heart - we have been friends for such a long time. I pray that very soon someone wonderful will walk into your life, and you will know the happiness I am feeling. Send my love to everyone at the manor, especially Joe and Sarah. I will write to them all soon. Take care and look after yourself. As soon as I'm settled in London, I will write again and send my address. If you find the time to go to Cordelia's grave – put a flower on it for me and tell her that her mama and papa will never forget her, and that we love her very much. The stonemason has been instructed to finish the headstone now. Please let me know when it's erected. I'll write again very soon. With love always, Jessie x

Betsy dropped the letter on the bed. She sighed heavily - she would miss Jessie desperately. With the letter, the dreadful pain in her foot, and the fact that at the age of twenty-one Betsy very much doubted that anyone wonderful would walk into her life, she had another little weep.

3

Henry Trencrom seethed with indignation as the estate steward reprimanded him for hitting Ryan Penrose.

'The Earl will not tolerate such behaviour. One more step out of line and you'll be out on your ear.'

Trencrom raised his eyebrows.

'And you can take that look off your face. Nobody is indispensable – no matter what skills you *claim* to have regarding manuka honeybee management.' He narrowed his eyes to scan the enclosed apiary. 'There had better be a good yield of manuka honey from these bees, or else you'll be out on your ear.'

Trencrom's mouth twitched involuntarily, as he pushed the single jar of honey – the sum total of this season's yield, out of sight.

'The Earl wants to see you at ten tomorrow morning with it.'

Once the steward had gone, Trencrom glanced pensively at the jar, berating himself for eating so much of it. He'd thought there would be enough at the end of the season, but then, damn it, he'd lost half the workforce when his bees swarmed in June. He hadn't a clue why they'd swarmed, or what to do about it! He certainly dared not ask anyone - otherwise it would have exposed his lack of knowledge about honeybee management. He wished now that he'd taken more interest in what his father had tried to teach him, but it was all too late now that his father had died. He couldn't even teach himself from a book because he couldn't read! His father had been an apiarist, lately specialising in Manuka honey bee management on several of the grand estates on the Lizard Peninsular - and his excellent reputation had gone before him. He'd been brought in to Bochym earlier that spring to set up the Manuka apery in the disused walled kitchen garden, but no sooner had the hives been established, his father had died unexpectedly. His death gave Trencrom an idea, to better his own position on the estate. He'd been employed as a ditch digger on the estate for the last two years – a lowly filthy job, and if he was to step into his father's shoes, his position on the estate would elevate, and he could then perhaps secure one of the tied cottages. He was sick of living in the cramped accommodation at the nearby Wheal Inn. So, he'd spun a yarn to the Earl, misleading him about his own knowledge of beekeeping, and managed to procure this position on the back of his father's reputation. It was only an hour a day, but it brought in a little more money, and though he still had to dig ditches, he gave himself airs because of his new position, which made him deeply unpopular. Trencrom had no qualms about falsifying his claim to be an apiarist – after all, how hard could it be to keep a few bees? He glanced again at the meagre jar of honey – harder than he thought it seems. He was in trouble if he didn't think of something to excuse the lack of honey. He glanced over at Mr Hubbard, the gardener who had planted the newly propagated manuka bushes imported from New Zealand, and gave a wry smile. What was that saying? *He who smiles in a crisis has found someone to blame.* He'd blame Hubbard for putting the bushes in the wrong place!

*

The servants had gathered around the kitchen dining table for tea, discussing, amongst other things, poor Betsy's accident, when the cook emitted a low angry growl.

'Are you all right Mrs Blair?' Joe asked.

'I was until I saw who was coming, Mr Treen?' Everyone turned to the window and groaned in unison. Trencrom, completely kitted out in his beekeeping attire, was striding across the courtyard like a cock turkey.

'The last time that idiot came in my kitchen with that outfit on, he brought a bee in with him,' Mrs Blair grumbled. 'Damn thing had got under his mesh hat and stung him, sending him into such a frenzied panic he flailed his arms about and knocked every single one of my clean pans off my rack and onto the floor.'

'It looks like he's holding a jar of that special honey, Mrs Blair – probably the first batch since His Lordship acquired those manuka bushes,' Joe offered up.

Mrs Blair hummed in her throat 'I've no idea why His Lordship has given him that job – he's only fit to dig ditches. Mr Hubbard is more than capable of looking after the new apery, as well as his own.'

Joe smiled - Mrs Blair had always had a soft spot for the gardener.

'And Mr Hubbard says Trencrom hasn't got a clue how to look after those bees!' she added. 'He reckons he only got the job because of his father's reputation!'

The conversation halted when Trencrom stepped into the kitchen.

'Oh, no you don't!' Mrs Blair flapped her teacloth at him. 'You can take that lot off before you come in my kitchen this time.'

'I'll only be here a few minutes,' Trencrom protested.

'Out, and take it off!' Mrs Blair stood her ground.

Grumbling audibly, he shed the suit at the door, but as soon as he stepped back in, Mrs Blair set into him again.

'You've a nerve coming in here, especially after thumping that poor man who brought our Betsy home!'

Trencrom curled his lip. 'He deserved a thumping - his filthy hands were all over Betsy like a rash.'

'No, they weren't!' Juliet snapped. 'Ryan is not that sort of man!'

Unaccustomed to Juliet ever speaking up, everyone turned to her in astonishment. Joe especially felt a pang of discord, because Juliet clearly felt the need to defend Ryan Penrose.

'How do *you* know?' Trencrom parried, 'You weren't there.'

Juliet flushed to the roots of her hair. 'Betsy told me!' she snapped back.

Mrs Blair turned back to Trencrom. 'Yes, and you need

to watch your back. He's a big strong lad, and would have pulverised you, if he hadn't had Betsy in his arms. I'd make myself scarce, if I were you.'

'I work here! Besides, I'm not afraid of him, I was a prize boxer you know, and I'll not put up with some vagrant molesting my wom......' He paused, and Mrs Blair raised an eyebrow, so he didn't say what he was going to say.

'What do you want in my kitchen anyway?'

'I brought this for the Earl,' he said, proudly producing the jar of honey with a chunk of honeycomb inside to bulk it out.

Mrs Blair glanced at the jar and then at Trencrom. 'Is that it?' she scoffed.

'Granted,' he grumbled, 'I thought there would be more, but well, it's only been one season and the bees are getting used to the manuka bushes.'

'You're not due to see His Lordship until the morning, Mr Trencrom,' Joe pointed out.

'I know. I just brought this in out of harm's way – I don't trust that gardener, and this is liquid gold!' He nodded to the jar.

Mrs Blair bristled. 'Now don't you go badmouthing Mr Hubbard to us – he's as trustworthy as the day is long.'

'He badmouths me enough!' Trencrom muttered under his breath.

Mrs Blair picked up the jar. 'Anyway, what makes this honey so precious that it's better than Mr Hubbard's honey then?'

'It has real beneficial healing qualities,' he answered authoritatively.

'Does it?' she quipped, holding the sticky jar aloft. 'It's to be hoped we don't need a great deal of healing in the household if this is all we get!'

'I assure you, Mrs Blair,' he snatched the jar from her grasp, 'the yield will be better next year.'

An awkward silence followed and everyone hoped

Trencrom would now take his leave - he was a disagreeable presence at the best of time, but Trencrom had spied the cake on the table.

'Nice looking cake,' he said angling for an invite to sit down.

'Yes,' said Mrs Blair scooping it away from the table, 'I make it especially for the domestic staff.'

Trencrom snorted, and then his small beady eyes scanned the table for Betsy.

'Where is Betsy anyway?' His tongue flicked in and out as he mentioned her name.

'Probably keeping out of your way,' Mrs Blair said, 'she didn't take too kindly to you thumping the man who was helping her!'

Twitching his nose in annoyance, Trencrom put down the jar of honey with a thump and said, 'I'll be obliged if you'll put that somewhere safe. I'll be seeing you all tomorrow.' He grabbed his bee suit and slammed the door after him.

'Not if we see you first,' Mrs Blair muttered as she put the cake back on the table.

*

It was almost half-past-ten before Juliet finally flopped down on her bed.

'Blimey, I'm worn out,' she declared. 'We've been sweeping floors, beating rugs, washing windows and polishing furniture in all the guest bedrooms, and this evening I had the mucky job of polishing the fire grates while my lord and lady were having dinner.'

'I'm so sorry, Juliet,' Betsy said apologetically, 'all the work is falling on you with me being laid up - and with such a busy week ahead of us.'

'Oh, don't worry. Mary and Dorothy have both been roped in to cleaning the silverware, though with the harvest starting on Wednesday, Mrs Blair needs Mary back in the kitchen to help bake the pasties for the harvesters. How are you feeling anyway - how's your foot?'

'Throbbing, like mad,' Betsy gently touched her bandage, 'and so is my head!'

'Do you need something for the pain?'

Betsy shook her head, immediately regretting the action. 'I've taken a little laudanum, but it's made me nauseous. I'm a little warm too - could I ask you to open the window, please?' She slapped her hands down on the eiderdown in frustration. 'You know, I could crown whoever set that trap. I've walked in that meadow for years without mishap. There is nothing nicer than walking through a field knee deep in wild flowers. Now because of someone's thoughtlessness I'll always be wary. I hope they find whoever is responsible and punish them.'

Juliet blanched. 'Was your letter from Jessie?' she asked changing the subject.

'Yes, it was.'

'Has she really gone away with that orchestral musician, Daniel Chandler?'

'Yes,' Betsy said evasively.

'Well, I think being swept away to London to start a new life, is so romantic. I never met Mr Chandler, but by all accounts, he sounds perfectly charming,' Juliet said, as she washed, donned her nightdress and climbed into bed.

'He was - and always so kind and courteous with us when he stayed at the manor.'

'Did you really not know about them?'

'No, Jessie never told me - but I understand why,' she said adamantly, *even though she didn't really*. 'She perhaps thought I wouldn't approve, because she was still married to Silas!'

'And do you approve?'

Betsy nodded. 'She was terribly unhappy with Silas. I'm sure she would never have wanted Silas to die, but in truth, his death has set her free. I just hope they fare well together - Jessie and Daniel are from very different worlds. You never know, Juliet, we both might meet our Prince Charming amongst one of our guests.'

'Well, I think your Prince Charming might have to fight that horrible Mr Trencrom for you. He came in at teatime looking for you.'

Betsy shuddered. 'That reptile seems to have taken a shine to me – goodness knows why – I've never given him the time of day. I'm going to lodge a complaint about him.'

Juliet smiled at the reptile reference – with Trencrom's long thin legs and ugly face, he closely resembled a toad. 'Well, we've heard he's received an official warning from the steward!'

'Good!' Betsy sighed. 'Oh, why can't someone lovely come into my life? I could do with a bit of romance like Jessie's.'

Juliet fell quiet.

'What about you, Juliet? Do you not want some romance in your life? Everyone knows Joe Treen is sweet on you, you know?'

'Yes, I know,' Juliet said tentatively, pulling the sheets up to her chin.

'Joe is a good man, and he's smitten with you. We could all see that the moment he set eyes on you. We all thought you felt the same, but you seemed to have pulled away from him – to a point that you're avoiding him nowadays.'

Juliet remained silent.

'Don't you like him?'

'Yes - I like him very much,' she whispered.

'What is it then?' Juliet shook her head. 'Please don't hurt Joe. If there is something, or someone stopping you from liking Joe more, you must tell him. Is there someone?'

'No,' she said emphatically.

'Something then?'

'Not that I want to speak about,' she answered and turned away from Betsy.

After watching her for a moment, Betsy said, 'Sorry, Juliet.'

'It's all right,' Juliet said quietly. 'Goodnight.'

'Goodnight.' Betsy sank down into her pillow, feeling a curl of unrest for her friend, but if she would not say - she could not help her. She blew her cheeks out, and pushed the sheets away from her hot body - she really did feel odd, she hoped she'd feel better in the morning.

*

Ryan wrapped his arms around himself as he lay on his uncomfortable bed of hessian sacks. The shack was cold and damp, and the musty air permeated his nostrils. He longed to light a fire for warmth, but dared not for fear of alerting his presence to anyone. An owl nearby called to another. The rooks in the trees above him squabbled and hawked as they jostled for roosting space. His hearing sharpened as a rat scurried across the earth floor looking for any scraps of food – it would be sorely disappointed. He shuddered, not only from his nocturnal visitor, but from the cold and hunger. He needed to work, in order to find lodgings, but also he needed to be close to Juliet – it was the least he could do. His thoughts drifted to Betsy. He could still feel the ache in his arms from carrying her, even though she'd been slight of build, it had been an effort all the same. It was a nice ache though that he would like to repeat. He'd never been in such close contact to a woman before and despite his shame that he was only carrying her because he'd inadvertently hurt her, he'd enjoyed the closeness. She was lovely - truly lovely, especially those startling blue eyes - intensified by her tears which had gazed right at him. He marvelled remembering her fresh pale complexion, speckled with freckles, and her lovely brunette hair which had come loose from its pins to curl and glisten in the sunshine. Oh, and she smelt so clean! He wondered if he would ever see her again, but because he'd made a promise to himself to keep away from the manor, he thought it was unlikely. He really didn't want to upset Juliet!

*

Once everyone had gone to bed, Joe Treen made his last check on the manor before retiring himself. Confident that all the doors were locked, he stood for a moment in the kitchen and gazed out into the darkness of the courtyard. His thoughts turned to having seen Juliet deep in conversation with Ryan Penrose out there. Mrs Blair had informed him they'd both lived in Gweek once. Had they known each other then? Had he turned up to claim Juliet? She'd certainly been quick to defend him to Trencrom. He blinked to stop himself staring into thin air. Whatever was going on, it just increased the gulf between them. *Enough Joe, enough*, he told himself as he climbed the stairs to bed.

4

Juliet woke with a start, to a strange sound in the bedroom. It was still dark so she fumbled to light the oil lamp – electricity had not been put in the servants' quarters yet! She squinted at the clock – twenty past three, and then realised the noise was coming from Betsy.

Juliet shook Betsy, but she just rolled her head, moaning incoherently.

'You're shivering,' she said, pulling the eiderdown over her, but Betsy pushed it away and moaned again. Realising Betsy was burning up, she ran to fetch Mrs Sanders.

They were fortunate that the manor had telephones installed during the summer. They were even more fortunate that the new doctor in the village had also seen the importance of one, which meant that the doctor was at the door within the hour.

'She's running a fever, doctor, and her foot has swollen to almost twice its size,' Ruby said as she and Juliet tried desperately to cool Betsy's hot body with damp cloths.

Dr Martin unwrapped the foot. 'Hmm! The puncture wounds looked very clean when I saw it earlier. There must have been some dirt still in the wound for this to happen.' He turned and looked at Juliet, 'I'm sorry I don't know your name?'

'Juliet.'

'I'm going to need you to fetch a bowl of hot salty water. We'll bathe the foot again and try to drain the pus.'

When she returned with the bowl they sat Betsy up, though her head lolled like a damp rag doll, as they plunged her foot into the water.

'Now ladies, if you're squeamish I'd advise you to look away now,' the doctor said, pressing the swelling gently. Green pus squirted on his trousers, but quite undeterred, he continued to press gently until the angry swelling around the wound had reduced considerably. 'I need some honey to draw any impurities out that might be left in the wound - do you have any?' he asked Ruby,

Ruby nodded. 'Juliet, go back down to the larder and bring the pot up here for the good doctor.'

Juliet ran down the back steps, almost colliding with Joe, who was waiting in the downstairs corridor to escort the doctor out of the manor when he'd finished. For a split second, she was in his arms, until she shrieked and pulled quickly away to cower in the laundry hallway.

'Juliet, forgive me, I didn't mean to startle you,' Joe said, equally alarmed at her reaction. 'But perhaps if you slowed down a little?'

Pulling herself together she covered her nightgown with her shawl. 'I'm so sorry, Mr Treen.'

'No harm done.' He reached his hand out to help her up, but retracted it when she did not take it. 'How is Betsy?'

'The doctor needs some honey from the kitchen to help bring the infection under control,' she said edging nervously away from him.

'Off you go then, but take care not to run - those stairs can be slippery sometimes.'

'Yes, Mr Treen,' she said, dreadfully embarrassed to have reacted so in front of him.

In the kitchen, she spotted the jar of honey on the table, yanked the piece of honeycomb out of it and ran back upstairs.

Patting Betsy's foot dry, the doctor prepared a new bandage. He smeared the honey liberally over a folded piece of linen and placed it on the angry wound.

Juliet watched anxiously. 'Will she lose her foot, doctor?'

He shook his head. 'The honey should bring the swelling down, but it might take a couple of days. She'll need nursing through the next few hours though - she has a raging temperature.'

'I'll look after her, Mrs Sanders,' Juliet said, 'I'll be fine - I've had a few hours' sleep!'

'Well, if you're sure, Juliet. I'll come and take over when it's time for you to start work.'

The doctor smiled. 'I can see my patient is in good hands. I'll come back in the morning, to see how she's faring.'

*

Betsy was aware of people moving about in her room. Hushed voices sounded concerned. Her throat felt scratchy and parched, but when a glass of water was brought to her lips, she believed someone was trying to drown her. 'Will she lose her foot?' someone asked, but she did not hear the answer. Panicked - what will I do without my foot? I'd be useless to anyone, homeless, and unemployable if I'm disabled. If they take my foot, I'll bleed to death! Please don't take my foot. She remembered the blood on the kitchen floor. Oh no! Have I lost it already, am I bleeding to death? I'm too young to die - don't let me die. She felt cold cloths on her skin. Oh god, I'm being washed down ready for burial! I must have died already.

'It's all right Betsy, you'll be fine.' Soothing words were whispered in her ear, but she didn't feel fine, she didn't feel fine at all! Her world was spiralling into a misty darkness and then to oblivion.

*

Ruby, checked in on Betsy at six the next morning and found Juliet slumped over Betsy's bed, gently snoring.

Aware of someone in the room, Juliet stirred, and lifted her head.

'How is she?' Ruby smiled.

'She's calmer now, Mrs Sanders,' Juliet said, trying to moisten her dry mouth. 'She tossed and turned until about an hour ago, but then I noticed she felt a lot cooler and began to sleep more peacefully.'

Ruby tipped her head. 'You didn't get much sleep then?'

'I got a little, when Betsy settled - not much though - but I'm fine.' Juliet glanced at the tower clock across the courtyard. 'If you're going to take over, I'll get ready for work, but in all honesty, I think Betsy will just sleep it off now.'

'Has the swelling gone down on her foot?' Ruby asked inspected the dressing.

'It has a bit – it's not as hot as it was anyway. I think the honey did the trick.'

They both glanced at the almost empty honey jar.

Ruby frowned. 'Juliet, where did you get that jar of honey from?'

'It was on Mrs Blair's table.'

'Was there a honeycomb in it?'

'Yes, I left that on a plate.'

'Oh dear! I didn't notice last night - I was so worried about Betsy.'

'What is it?' Juliet asked uneasily. 'Have I done something wrong?'

'I think the doctor has just healed Betsy's wounds with the special manuka honey Mr Trencrom brought in yesterday.'

Juliet glanced back at the pot. 'Oh, crumbs, I never thought in the panic. I just grabbed it because it was honey.'

Ruby suppressed a smile. 'Mr Trencrom is coming back today to see His Lordship – he's hoping to present his meagre collection of honey – which is even more meagre now!'

Juliet panicked. 'Oh, no, what shall I do?'

'Take the jar down with you, Juliet, and explain to Mrs Blair what has happened.'

'Will she be really angry with me?'

Knowing there was no love lost between Mrs Blair and Henry Trencrom. Ruby smiled. 'I don't think so. Now, I'll stay with Betsy until breakfast. If she remains stable, I'll decide as to whether we can leave her in peace. We have much to do this week. Remember, Mr Devereux will be with us early Thursday morning. I believe he's coming down on the Night Riviera train.'

'I'll make sure Mr Devereux's room is finished today and I'll make the bed up tomorrow.'

'Thank you, Juliet – you really are an asset to us here.'

*

Ruby settled beside Betsy, enjoying a welcome break from the hustle and bustle of a household making ready for guests. As Betsy was breathing and sleeping peacefully now, Ruby turned her thoughts to the elusive Justin Devereux. The notice of him coming had come quite out of the blue, and had been shortly after a beautiful life-size canvas he'd painted of Her Ladyship, had arrived. Her ladyship had been astounded when the painting had been unwrapped – apparently, she'd only sat for her brother during one afternoon, when they'd made a brief visit to him in Tuscany while touring Italy. This only confirmed his merit as a talented artist. Ruby appreciated fine art when she saw it, and whenever she passed the painting, which hung in pride of place over the fireplace in the Jacobean drawing room, the beauty of it took her breath away. She was looking forward to seeing the man who could produce such a work of art – though she'd probably never get a chance to speak to him about it! This was to be Mr Devereux's first visit to Bochym. By all accounts he came over from Italy when Her Ladyship married the Earl eleven years ago. The wedding had been in Devon at the Devereux's family seat, and by all accounts Mr Devereux had gone straight back to Italy after the wedding – the English weather not being to his liking. He'd certainly picked the wrong season to visit now if that was the case - Autumn was biting at the heels of summer. She hoped that he would be as kind and gentle as Her Ladyship, and not snappy and demanding like Carole – the Countess de Auberive - His Lordship's sister, who was staying with the Dowager Countess in the Dower Lodge at the moment. Ah well, she folded her hands on her lap - they would all find out soon enough.

*

Downstairs, Juliet tentatively presented the honey jar with the remnants of the manuka honey to Mrs Blair, explaining her mistake in taking it.

Mrs Blair's lip curled in amusement. 'I wondered where it had gone,' she said glancing at the honeycomb sitting in a pool of honey on the plate.

'What shall we say to Mr Trencrom, Mrs Blair?'

'Mr Trencrom will never know,' she whispered, tapping the side of her nose. She bustled into the larder and came back with another jar of honey. She poured it into the manuka jar, popped the honeycomb back in and screwed the lid tight and winked at Juliet. 'How is Betsy this morning? Dorothy said the doctor was brought for her during the night.'

'Sleeping peacefully now, but she had a raging temperature and her foot was like a football!'

'And Mr Trencrom's honey is slathered all over her foot, is it?' she grinned.

'It is, and it seems to have done the trick, yes.'

'Well, it's been good for something then.'

*

Mist lay entwined within the branches of the trees overhanging Ryan's makeshift dwelling in Bochym woods early that morning. Everywhere felt damp. He shivered, feeling stiff and chilled to the bone. Last night had been decidedly colder than the previous nights he'd spent here. It was only the end of September, but it wouldn't be long before he'd need somewhere warmer to sleep, or at the very least some blankets. At the moment he slept fully clothed with his overcoat draped over him, and was deeply aware that he did not smell very clean. He'd managed to wash a couple of shirts and his underwear in the stream, but they'd taken ages to dry, hung up, out of sight at the back of the wood shack. He really didn't want to bring attention to himself by hanging washing out for all and sundry to see - especially knowing that he was trespassing.

He'd been desperate for something hot to eat, to warm his belly, and he'd been foraging for food since first light. He'd checked the snares he'd laid, unfortunately they'd been empty, but had managed to collect beech nuts, a few tiny, wild raspberries, and had an abundance of blackberries in his neckerchief. He also had several field mushrooms in his battered leather bag, so at least he'd have something to cook and wouldn't go too hungry. He hoped, as promised, Juliet would bring him some food from the Bochym larder and leave it in the hay barn – though the last thing he wanted was for her to get into trouble for doing so. He'd just begun to prime his paraffin stove to cook the mushrooms, when he stilled on hearing the crack of a twig behind him. His heart sank when he turned and saw the gamekeeper walking up to his shelter.

'Good morning, Mr Penrose,' he said, giving nothing away for his reason for visiting.

'Good morning, sir.' Ryan stood up and touched his brow.

The gamekeeper glanced at the foraged food and hitched his gun strap more securely on his shoulder. He cast his eyes around the shelter.

'How long are you intending to stay here? It can't be comfortable.'

'Until I can find some work, and pay for some lodgings, sir.'

'These woods belong to the Bochym Estate you know – you're trespassing.'

Ryan sighed dejectedly. 'I'll move on then. Could you allow me another day here though, so I can find somewhere else to sleep?'

The gamekeeper's face softened. 'Don't worry, His Lordship is happy to turn the other cheek to your trespass, in light of you helping the young maid yesterday, and helping to sweep the field afterwards.'

'Gosh!' Ryan gasped. 'That's very kind of him - please convey my thanks.'

'So, you need work, do you?'

'I do.'

'Where are you from?'

'Gweek, sir.'

'I should think there's work over there – the wood yard, the port, custom house and so forth.'

'Yes, but I thought I'd try my hand over here, sir.'

'Well, there's always work at Mullion on the fishing boats, wouldn't that suit?'

'No, sir, I like to feel the ground under my feet.'

He nodded. 'Aye, I know what you mean. So, we start the harvest tomorrow on the estate. Can you scythe?'

Ryan felt his heart lift. 'Yes, sir.'

'Good, report to me tomorrow morning at six-o-clock, sharp, then.' He pulled his leather bag around, opened it and produced a blood-stained rabbit. 'Here,' he said handing it to Ryan.

Astonished, Ryan took the rabbit from him.

'I found it in a poacher's snare,' he said. 'You'll need more than a few berries and mushrooms to sustain you. Harvesting is heavy work,' he winked.

'Thank you, sir.'

'My office is behind the stables. Oh, and make sure you contain your fire when you cook that - we don't want the harvest fields to catch light, they're tinder dry.'

Ryan nodded, grateful for the endorsement that he could light a fire. 'I'll be careful, thank you.'

Ryan watched him go, and though the rabbit was still to be skinned and gutted, his stomach rumbled cavernously at the promise of a decent meal.

5

Trencrom arrived at the Bochym kitchen door to see the Earl ten minutes early, in a hope of being offered some refreshment – but was sorely disappointed when Mrs Blair told him they were too busy. He picked up the honey jar and narrowed his eyes.

'Why is there more in this jar than when I left it yesterday?'

'Perhaps it's drained from the honeycomb,' Mrs Blair answered nonchalantly.

Narrowing his eyes he said, 'It's a different colour as well.'

'Honey changes colour by the temperature of a room - you should know that being a *honey expert.*'

Trencrom snorted. 'Where's Betsy, is she about? I'd like a word with her,' he asked, scratching some sort of irritation at the seat of his pants.

'She's still avoiding you I should think. Now, I'd be obliged if you would please vacate my kitchen space.' She flicked her hand as she would an irritating fly.

*

The Earl's study smelt of rich leather and polish. Books and ledgers lined the shelves and everything was neat, tidy and in order – exactly how Peter Dunstan liked it to be.

Trencrom felt a curl of unease as the Earl held the jar of honey aloft.

'Is this it?' Peter said pursing his lips.

Trencrom wrung his hands nervously. 'Yes, my lord. The yield will be higher next year - I promise. The first year of hive keeping is all about building it up. The bees may or may not produce a good yield, and of course it didn't help when Mr Hubbard planted the manuka bushes too far from the hives. The bees couldn't find them. I told him, I said…..'

Peter held his hand up to stop him. 'Mr Hubbard consulted the Kynance Estate as to where to locate the bushes and hives, and they are in the walled garden, so, I do *not* accept that as an excuse.'

This put Trencrom on the back foot. 'Well, err, of course, I… had to leave the bees some of the honey - otherwise I'd risk starving them through the winter.' *That reminded him - he'd have to leave a sugar solution for them, because he had decimated the hive.*

'I am disappointed, Trencrom - if this paltry amount is all they produced in one season. The first yield from our other bees gave us much more. Hubbard presented at least thirty pounds of honey to me.' He screwed the top off the jar, dipped his spoon in to taste, rolled it around his mouth and frowned. 'I've tasted manuka honey – it has a distinct flavour - this tastes no different to the honey my other bees make!'

'W…What?' he stammered.

'Try it.' The Earl pushed another spoon in his direction.

Trencrom nostrils flared - there *was* no difference! 'Someone must have tampered with this in the kitchen! This is not the honey I brought in yesterday.'

'I will thank you not to accuse my staff of such things. Now, Trencrom, I'm not happy - not happy at all. I went to a great deal of expense in acquiring those manuka bushes, and this,' he shook the jar, 'is what you present me with! Go on, get out of my sight. I'll give you one more season to show an improvement in the yield. If things do not improve, you'll be back digging ditches full time. Good day to you.'

Livid, Trencrom turned on his heel and stomped down the corridor into the kitchen and glared at Mrs Blair. 'I'll get to the bottom of this, you see if I don't.'

'And a good day to you too, Mr Trencrom,' she answered casually as she went about making the pies for the dinner.

*

Betsy woke, with a start. Unsure of where she was at first,

the sounds of the busy kitchen below panicked her into thinking she'd slept in. Her foot throbbed, as did her head, and she had a raging thirst. She glanced at the clock tower while she drank from her glass of water, but could not define what time of day it might be. The clock said ten-past-five – morning or afternoon - she did not know? Juliet's bed was empty and made – so it must be the afternoon! Reaching down to ease the throb in her foot, she noted with alarm a sticky substance oozing through the bandage. Fortunately, Ruby walked in as she was un-wrapping it.

'No, Betsy, the doctor said to leave the bandage for a couple of days.'

'But there's something horrible oozing out of it, Mrs Sanders.'

'It's honey. Dr Martin was called here last night. Your foot had swollen to twice its size, so he put the honey on to heal the wound - it looks like it's doing the trick though. You had a high temperature and were quite delirious for several hours. You had us all terribly worried. Juliet sat with you all night, until you settled around about five this morning. You've slept peacefully the whole day - I've been checking in with you every hour.'

'Gosh, I don't remember a thing!' Betsy said falling back on her pillow.

'How does your foot feel?'

'It throbs a bit.'

'Are you hungry?'

'Yes, a little.'

'I'll get Mrs Blair to make you a plate up for you.'

'I'm sorry to be so much trouble.'

'You're no trouble, Betsy.' Ruby smiled. 'Just rest and get better.'

*

Betsy woke again as the tower clock chimed six, and watched Juliet climb wearily out of bed. That could only mean it was Wednesday morning! Not only had she slept the best part of Tuesday, but had also slept right through the night.

Poor Juliet, she looked tired out. She'd come up to bed the previous night, barely able to stand. She'd almost been asleep before her head touched the pillow.

Juliet turned when she realised Betsy was awake.

'Sorry,' she whispered, 'I didn't mean to wake you.'

'You didn't, it was my body clock. It's telling me I should be up and ready for work.' She swung her legs over the edge of the bed.

'No, Betsy! Don't get up. I think you're meant to rest a while longer.'

'I know, but I hate to be so idle when there is so much to do.' She stood up unsteadily - her head felt woozy from lying down for so long.

'How's your foot?'

Uncomfortable, but as the wounds are on the upper part of my foot, I'm sure I could walk a little if I tried.'

As Juliet pinned her cap on, she looked uncertain. 'Just take it easy. We can manage without you - don't worry.'

Noting the unconvincing tone in Juliet's voice, she waited until Juliet had left, before walking tentatively around the room. The bandage pulled tight on the top of her foot where the puncture wounds were making her wince slightly, so she un-wrapped the bandage to inspect her foot. The sticky honey residue, smeared with blood underneath, made her grimace, but at least her wounds looked less angry now. She bandaged her foot again, only looser, to give a little as she walked. Once she had washed and dressed, she put one of her shoes on and wrapped the other foot in a thick scarf to enable her to get around. As she was making her bed, she glanced out of the window and there, beyond the kitchen courtyard, stood Ryan Penrose - her rescuer! Her heart quickened with excitement - she thought she would never see him again! Soon he was joined by a group of other men and she realised he'd been employed for the harvest. Betsy's stomach gave a little flutter - if he was working here, perhaps she'd be able to thank him for what he'd done in person.

*

By the time she'd bumped her way downstairs on her bottom, Mrs Blair was preparing breakfast for the staff.

'Oh, lordy me!' Mrs Blair flapped her teacloth. 'What on earth are you doing down here? You're meant to be resting. You were at deaths door yesterday.'

Betsy sat at the table. 'I had a fever that's all. I'm fine now - just sore.'

'Betsy!' Ruby said walking into the kitchen, 'what on earth….?'

'I'm fine, Mrs Sanders, really. I've come down to help. I could polish the glassware and silver while I'm sat here.'

'Well… thank you - if you're absolutely sure?' Ruby's relief was palpable.

*

Twenty-four-hours had passed, but still Trencrom was fuming about his honey. He knew everyone was conspiring against him - they wanted him to fail because without doubt they *had* swapped that honey! God knows he'd tasted enough of the manuka honey to know the jar he'd brought back from the manor was not the honey he left the night before. He sucked at his rotting teeth - he'd have to be more vigilant, because he was determined to stay in this job. A tied cottage had become vacant on the estate and he intended to have it! First though, he must marry - preferably someone who worked on the estate, it would give them a better chance of acquiring it. He felt a stirring in his groin, knowing who he'd chosen to warm his marital bed and *nothing* and *no one* was going to scupper his plans. He turned to watch the harvesters busy working the field to his left, and felt his bile rise. There, scything at the edge of the field was that damn vagrant who'd been carrying Betsy the day she injured her foot. What the devil was he doing here, and how had he secured that job? He thumped the hive so hard with his fist an angry bee flew right at him to defend its home.

*

The kitchen had filled with the rich meaty aroma of beef pasties when Juliet came into the kitchen and flopped down at the table.

'Gosh, I'm pooped. I'm just having a moment.'

Mrs Blair smiled sympathetically. 'I don't suppose you fancy a spot of fresh air do you, Juliet? We're up to our elbows making pasties for the harvester's dinner.'

Her face brightened. 'I'd love a spot of fresh air - the weather looks so lovely out there. What would you like me to do?'

'Francis, bless her little hen heart, has escaped the coop and taken up residence in the hay barn. No one can catch her, so I need someone to collect her eggs.'

'The hay barn!' Juliet's eyes lit from within. 'I'll gladly go.'

Betsy watched curiously as Juliet disappeared into the larder with her basket, noting it looked heavier when she came back out. When she left it on the table to put on her outdoor boots, Betsy surreptitiously lifted the gingham cloth, to find a slice of bread, a wedge of cheese and two apples from the larder nestled there. She quickly covered them as Juliet emerged from the boot room.

Juliet glanced at the basket and then at Betsy, but neither said anything.

'I won't be long - can someone please tell Mrs Sanders where I am?'

When the door closed, Mrs Blair glanced up at Betsy from crimping her pasties and said, 'She's a nice girl, but it's a shame she's changed allegiance from Mr Treen though. I thought there was a budding romance there – and, so did Mr Treen.'

'What do you mean changed allegiance?' Betsy asked, but the cook's attention was diverted when Henry Trencrom came running across the kitchen courtyard.

'What on earth does *he* want now?' she groaned.

Trencrom burst into the kitchen, his ugly face drenched in sweat, mucus and tears – a huge, swollen lump on his nostril shone red like a beacon.

'Help me someone, help me,' he demanded, cupping his nose as he danced about the kitchen.

Horrified, Betsy looked towards Mrs Blair and Mary for help, but they were both elbow-deep in flour. Resignedly, she limped over to him, dragging a chair for him to sit on. She grimaced to see great bubbles of green mucus emerging from both his nostrils.

'Hurry up, woman,' he ordered, but Betsy refusing to rush, limped to the scullery for a bowl of water to bathe the sting with.

Mrs Blair shot him a derisory look. 'For a beekeeper you get an awful lot of stings,' she scoffed, to which Trencrom muttered something derogatory back.

'Hurry up, it stings like hell,' he shouted as Betsy emerged from the scullery.

'You're lucky I'm tending to you at all, after what you did to that poor man who was helping me the other day,' Betsy snapped.

'Aye and I'll do it again if I see him anywhere near you.'

'It's no concern of yours, who I see, and what I do,' she answered firmly as she cleaned his face. Betsy held her breath to avoid his, whilst dabbing the sting with a thick paste of baking powder and water to neutralize the bee venom. According to his boasts he'd eaten honey almost every day, and by the sight of his rotting teeth, he'd never cleaned the sugary residue from them - hence his appalling halitosis. Relieved when she'd finished the task, she stood back quickly to get away from him, but he grabbed her wrist.

'Ah but you *are* my concern, Betsy Tamblin,' he whispered and flicked his tongue in and out - openly excited to have hold of her.

Betsy's skin crawled at his touch - everything about this

man was odious. She tried to wrench her arm from his hand, but he would not let go.

'I've a mind to make you my wife, you see.'

Betsy gasped in horror, but thankfully Mrs Blair had seen what was happening and came over.

'Let her go,' she warned, wielding her wooden spoon.

He reluctantly released her and she backed away horrified.

'What's the matter?' he growled at Betsy, 'You'd be lucky to have me - you're not a young girl anymore, you must be past twenty – you've clearly been left on the shelf.'

'*I beg your pardon?*' she said, appalled at his audacity.

'You heard. You'll not get another proposal at your age, and you'll do for me very nicely. So, I'll expect you to consider it.'

'I'll consider nothing of the sort,' she snapped and limped away to the scullery as fast as her sore foot would carry her.

Trencrom glanced at the cook. 'Whatever's ailing her foot is making her bad-tempered, because she'll be lucky to have me as a husband.'

'You heard - she's not interested, so leave her alone and be off with you now.'

Trencrom sneered, and then winced, as it made the sting smart. 'I'll be taking one of those pasties with me then,' he said reaching over for one.

'You will not!' She walloped his hand with the wooden spoon. 'These are for good, decent people who do an *honest* day's work!'

Betsy, who was hiding in the scullery, wishing him gone, froze when Trencrom appeared at the scullery door.

'I'll be back and I'll expect a favourable answer from you on my proposal.'

Thankfully he was swiftly yanked away by Mrs Blair. 'I said leave her alone or I'll send for Mr Treen.'

When the back door slammed, Betsy emerged ashen-faced from the scullery.

'Oh, my goodness, I thought catching my foot in a rabbit trap was the worst thing that could happen to me this week, until *that* proposal! I feel quite queasy now.'

*

When Mary and Dorothy returned from delivering pasties to the harvesters and sat down to dinner in the Bochym kitchen, they were both excited at the prospect of lots of new young men working on the estate.

'Guess what, Betsy?' Dorothy said brightly. 'That handsome man, who rescued you from the rabbit trap, is working with the harvesters! I've just seen him scything.'

'Is he?' Juliet said sharply, before Betsy could comment, and her eyes opened wide with interest. The gesture did not go unnoticed by either Betsy or Joe.

As Joe looked down at his dinner and Betsy felt her own appetite wane - all hopes of renewing her acquaintance with Ryan had dissipated for it seemed that Juliet had a vested interest in Ryan too.

6

Thursday dawned bright and breezy - small white clouds scudded across the pale blue sky so the gardens at Bochym were basking in the morning sunshine. The French drawing room was luminous in the refracted light from the stained-glass windows when Sarah met with Peter at the breakfast table.

'Good morning, darling,' Peter greeted her warmly before helping himself to breakfast. 'We have a young man arriving today, Lyndon FitzSimmons - he's a master hedger – the best of his kind, so Matthew Bickford tells me. Matthew has known the chap all his life apparently – they grew up together on the Trevarno Estate. I thought as we advocate skilled workmanship, we could use him here.'

'Absolutely,' Sarah answered buttering her toast. 'Which hedges are you planning on repairing?'

'The ones down by the arboretum - the cows broke through the fences again last week - the third time this year. Matthew assures me that Fitzsimmons's hedges are sturdy enough to keep any livestock where they should be.' Peter glanced at the butler. 'Treen, please inform Mrs Blair that Fitzsimmons is to eat with the staff.'

'Yes, my lord. Will he need accommodation?'

'No, I'm told he prefers to stay in his wagon when he is on the road. If you could ask the grooms to see to his horse and wagon when he gets here – they can be settled near the gamekeeper's cottage.'

'Yes, my lord.'

'What time is Justin due, Sarah?'

'About ten this morning - I've sent the car to the station for him. I simply can't wait to see my gorgeous brother again. I do wonder what is bringing him home to England though - and for an indefinite time! He seemed so settled in Tuscany when we saw him a couple of years ago.'

'Perhaps he's curious, as to where we've hung the painting, he sent us.' Peter dabbed his mouth with his napkin and got up.

'I hope he approves - It does look rather lovely in the Jacobean drawing room.'

'It would look lovely anywhere, Sarah – It's a painting of you.' He kissed her tenderly on the head. 'I'll be in my study until Justin comes.'

*

After a last flurry of attention to the bedroom being prepared for the Countess's brother, everyone sat at the kitchen dining table taking a short and very welcome tea break, until they heard the car coming up the drive.

'Make haste, everyone. Mr Devereux is here,' Joe rallied the staff.

The maids checked their reflection to make sure they were neat and tidy before scurrying, or limping in Betsy's case, to the front door. Theo and Lowenna Trevail - the Earl's valet and the Countess's lady's maid were already there waiting, Thomas too was ready to open the car door, while Joe and Ruby took up their positions in the line.

Ruby noted that Mr Devereux was unmistakably Sarah Dunstan's brother when he alighted from the car. He had the same golden blond hair and patrician good looks as her. He was dressed casually in a cream linen suit which was crumpled from travelling, his shirt was open at the neck and he wore his hair unusually long for a gentleman. He brought with him a large trunk, which Thomas, allocated as his temporary valet, later told the others contained little in the way of clothes - only artists equipment.

'Sarah!' Justin pulled his sister into his arms to kiss her warmly. He pulled away and took hold of Peter's hand with both of his and shook it enthusiastically. 'It's so good to see you both again. Thank you for allowing me to impose on you like this.'

'Your being here could never be an imposition,' Peter answered warmly.

Dabbing tears of happiness, Sarah added, 'I cannot tell

you what a joy it is to have my beloved brother here with me at last, but you look so tired, my darling.'

'I am a little – it's a long journey.'

'Come in and rest then.' She linked arms with him, and as they walked past the staff waiting in line to greet him, Justin gave a friendly nod to everyone, and then his eyes settled on Ruby – he held her gaze for a few seconds, before a smile crinkled his eyes and then he walked into the manor.

As everyone made their way back indoors, Ruby felt quite flustered, deeply aware that everyone was looking askance at her – it seemed that no one had missed the look Mr Devereux had given her.

'He looks a nice, affable fellow,' Joe whispered as he fell into step with Ruby.

'Yes, yes he does,' she whispered. 'Excuse me.' She retreated to the housekeeper's room, closed the door, and stood with her back to it. *Did that really just happen?* For those few short seconds, Ruby felt that there was no one else in the world other than Mr Devereux and herself. *Don't be silly, Ruby*, she berated. *Why would he be remotely interested in you? You've probably got some dusty smudge or something on your face.* She inspected her reflection in the mirror, but nothing was amiss, all she noted was a flush in her cheeks, a sparkle in her eyes and a delightful tingle running through her veins.

*

A leisurely, lively luncheon was held in the French drawing room.

While Joe and Thomas presided over the meal, Joe noted that Mr Devereux only picked selectively at the glorious buffet Mrs Blair had made. There had been cold beef, chicken and lobster, salads and pickles. He chose only a small plate of chicken and lobster accompanied with a slice of bread and butter, and drank little of the wine on the table, preferring only water. He was curiously evasive as to what had prompted this unexpected visit apart from admitting that he'd become weary of the constant Italian heat and needed to feel the cool British breeze on his face.

When luncheon was finished and the table cleared away, Joe knocked on the Earl's study door to address the matter of Mr Devereux's lack of formal clothes.

'I was wondering, my lord, if I should send for the tailor? Mr Devereux seems not to have any suitable attire for dining in.'

Peter Dunstan sat back in his chair and smiled. 'No, thank you, Treen, Mr Devereux is family and will not need to dress for dinner.'

'Very well, my lord,' he said bowing as he left the room, thinking this very odd - normally everyone dressed for dinner! When he turned, he practically bumped into Justin.

'Ah, hello there,' Justin smiled broadly. Could you perhaps tell me where I can find Sarah?'

'Sir?'

'My sister, Sarah - I'm trying to locate her.'

'Oh, of course, sir - Her Ladyship is out in the front garden.'

'Thank you,' he said walking swiftly to the front door before Joe could get there to open it for him.

*

Sarah smiled, put down her secateurs and kissed Justin warmly on the cheek.

'Do you have everything you need?'

'I do, and it seems to me, dear sister, you do too,' his arm gestured across the grounds and buildings, 'I always knew you'd be queen of your own castle one day.'

She laughed softly. 'So, to what *do* we owe this unexpected honour of your visit? You were very evasive at luncheon.'

'I wanted to see my sister - is that not allowed?'

'I'm flattered and delighted that you should come all this way, though I'm puzzled. You always said that England was too wet and chilly!'

Justin turned his face to the sun. 'I may have been wrong. The weather looks perfectly agreeable at the moment.'

'Yes,' she looked up into the perfect blue sky, 'I hope it holds until after the harvest. Are you not working on anything at the moment then?'

'No, but I'm itching to paint, I wondered, do you have anywhere private where I can set up my easel?'

'The attic is empty but for a few trunks. If there is enough light for you there you are welcome to use it, but there is no electric up there, I'm afraid.'

He smiled. 'I've no electricity in Italy either, so that isn't a problem.'

'The servant's quarters are to one side of the attic, but it's partitioned off, so you will be quite private there. I'll show you later.'

'It sounds perfect.'

'Speaking of dinner, we have a few friends coming over tomorrow to meet you.'

Justin's face dropped.

'Don't look so troubled. They're good friends - interesting people - I think you'll like them. Kit and Sophie Trevellick are members of our Arts and Craft Association - I'll take you around the workshops later. Kit is a master carpenter, and Sophie is a beautiful embroiderer. We have the author, James Blackwell, coming with his house guests - who are always an eclectic crowd. There will also be Matthew Bickford. Matthew is a fine fellow and is in the process of taking over the running of the Trevarno Estate in Helston from his father, and there will also be my sister-in-law, Carole, the Countess de Auberive. Be warned though - she's a terrible flirt,' she whispered, 'and newly widowed, so watch your step or you might be taking a wife back home to Tuscany.'

He laughed.

'Well, having said that, you'll only have to dodge her advances for a couple of days. On Monday, she and the

Dowager Countess are heading back to the late Comte's château, for the winter months.'

'Ah, I think I'm safe, then. Living in a château sounds like she's used to the high life, so she'll not be interested in me, or living in my mere Italian artist's studio!'

'Don't think she won't try,' Sarah warned. 'Sorry, that was rude of me, but she can be very challenging at times.'

Justin patted her hand. 'So, she's looking for a second husband then?'

'Third actually - she was married before the Comte, to Philip Goldsworthy! The old Earl, Peter's father, arranged that marriage, and Carole was a willing participant due to the substantial marriage dowry it came with. It was a marriage of convenience – a business arrangement, that's all. It didn't last. He turned out to be a rather unsavoury character right from the start.'

'Oh, do I detect a little scandal?'

'You do.'

'Do tell.' Justin sat on a bench and beckoned her to join him.

'I suppose you will hear about it anyway.' She settled beside him. 'Philip took a shine to a good friend of mine - Elise 'Ellie' Blackthorn. Elise owns The Poldhu Tea Room – you'll meet her very soon,' she smiled, 'sorry I digress. At the time, Elise was unaware that Philip was married, so when she found out that he meant her to be his mistress she naturally dropped him like a stone. Philip was used to getting exactly what he wanted, and didn't take too kindly to her rebuff, so, when Elise eventually took up with her now husband, Guy, Philip tried to kill him.'

'You're jesting?'

'No. Philip escaped justice and became a fugitive for almost ten years, that's how Carole managed to divorce him, but….' her eyes clouded, 'he turned up again last week with the most dreadful consequences. He shot and killed Guy's brother, thinking it was Guy – they looked so alike you see. He's in Exeter jail waiting to be hanged now.'

'Good god!'

'That is why Carole is leaving on Monday,' she whispered. 'She'd planned on staying until after Christmas, but Carole's name has been mentioned in the papers reporting the incident, and she's not happy about being tainted by association with Philip. Anyway, enough horribleness, do you want to help me in the garden?' she offered him her secateurs.

'No, I'll just watch you work for a while.'

After a pleasant hour chatting and watching Sarah dead head the flowers, Justin, weary from his travels, returned indoors to lie down for a much-needed siesta.

*

If all chores were finished, members of staff were allowed a couple of hours off from two in the afternoon, before tea was served to the family at four.

Betsy went to her room to read and to take the strain off her foot. She limped across to open the window and allow some fresh air in, just as Juliet was striding across the kitchen courtyard with her egg collecting basket. Once again there seemed to be a small mound under the gingham cloth. Betsy's suspicions were well founded, when Juliet, thinking she was out of view, pulled the cloth back to inspect the goods in her basket. *Where are you going with that food, Juliet?* Betsy glanced down at her foot – if she only had something she could wear outdoors she could follow her! Stealing food from the manor kitchen was a misdemeanour Juliet could be dismissed for. She'd have to have a word with her if it continued.

*

Joe, having just finished his stock check of wine, sought Ruby's company in the housekeeper's room. Ruby, as always, was busy at her desk, but smiled and put down her pen, always ready for a chat with Joe.

'Mr Devereux has a very casual manner about him!' Joe declared, relaying his encounter with him on the stairs.

'Yes,' she breathed.

Joe tipped his head – *did he detect a twinkle in Ruby's eyes?*

'The Earl doesn't think it necessary for me to send for the tailor for him.'

Ruby frowned. 'That's a shame. He'd cut a fine figure in a dinner suit. We have to remember though – he's an artist! You've seen the attire our Arts and Craftsmen here wear - they're a bohemian lot. I suspect he is too.'

'The thing is though – he doesn't seem to have many clothes other than those he's stood up in, especially considering he plans an extended visit with us.'

Ruby hummed. 'That may prove problematic for Izzy if she has to launder and dry his clothes overnight. Perhaps, Thomas, as his valet, could urge him to purchase some new clothes?' She glanced up at the clock. 'Sorry, Joe, I must go – I have a meeting with Her Ladyship about tomorrow's guests.'

*

After finalising the menus and accommodation with Ruby and Mrs Blair around the kitchen table, Sarah was about to take her leave when the kitchen door opened and a young man walked in. The man glanced at Sarah's fine attire, bowed, apologised and began to back out of the door.

'That's Lyndon FitzSimmons, the hedger my lady,' Ruby offered.

'Good afternoon, Mr FitzSimmons,' Sarah called him.

'Good afternoon, my lady.' Lyndon stood awkwardly in the kitchen with his hat in hand. 'Begging your pardon, I was told to come in for some tea.'

Sarah smiled at the tall, young, handsome man. He was dressed in a white shirt with rolled up sleeves, a black waistcoat and heavy serge breeches. A brightly coloured neckerchief was tied at his neck and he sported an abundance of auburn hair. Sarah suspected the maids would be rather happy with this addition to their fold.

'I'm very pleased to meet you, Mr FitzSimmons. Our good friend Matthew Bickford speaks very highly of you. I understand you're a master hedger?'

Lyndon smiled and patted the billhook in his belt. 'Yes, my lady - it's a tradition my grandfather taught me.'

'I shall be very interested to see your hedge once you have crafted it.'

'Thank you, my lady. It will be an honour to show it to you.' He bowed.

'I shall leave you all to your tea now,' she said sweeping out of the kitchen.

7

Mary and Dorothy were beside themselves with glee when their new table guest Lyndon settled down with them for tea. Dorothy being the oldest at seventeen was openly displaying all the signs of pure infatuation.

'So, Lyndon,' Joe started, 'I understand you come highly recommended by Matthew Bickford?'

'Yes, I grew up on the Trevarno Estate where my father is head gardener. I've known Matthew all my life, and though he's the master's son, being of similar age, we often played together. I can safely say we're the greatest of friends. It's thanks to that friendship that I manage to secure much of my work in and around the other grand estates in Cornwall – and for that I'm truly grateful.'

'Where were you working before you came to us?'

'I was at Gweek, and before that, Trelowarren - another of Matthew's recommendations.'

'Oh! Juliet is from Gweek,' Ruby said, immediately wishing she hadn't mentioned it when she saw Juliet blanch.

Lyndon smiled. 'Ah, well, I mostly meet with the farmers thereabouts and only occasionally drop into the village. I'm please to meet you, Juliet.'

Juliet smiled shakily before casting her eyes downward.

Dorothy, on the other hand, fluttered her eyelashes at him. 'How long will you be with us, Lyndon?'

'About ten days, and then I've secured work on the Tehidy Estate on the north coast for a few weeks.'

'Are you married?' Dorothy asked, and though Mary laughed at her forwardness, Ruby scolded her for her impertinent question.

'Not yet,' he smiled, 'but I have a sweetheart and hope to marry in the spring.'

Dorothy gave an audible groan.

'Hard luck, Dorothy, but full marks for trying,' Thomas joked.

Lyndon smiled at her. 'I'm sorry to disappoint you, Dorothy, but never fear, for a lovely girl like you, your time will surely come.'

'Huh! Some hope, working in service,' Dorothy grumbled.

The other maids nodded in agreement.

'I married, and I'm in service,' Lowenna gazed lovingly at her husband Theo.

'You two met because you both work in the same house! If that's going to be the case, I'm to marry either Mr Treen or you, Thomas.' Dorothy sighed resignedly.

Joe Treen nearly choked on his tea, as the whole table erupted with laughter.

'Well,' Thomas teased, 'I can't speak for Mr Treen, but I'm up for it, Dorothy.'

Dorothy pulled a face. 'No offence intended, Thomas, but you're a million years older than me.'

Again, the table erupted with mirth.

'Charming, I'm sure.' Thomas feigned hurt. 'And for your information, I'm only ten years older than you.'

'Well, that might as well be a million,' Dorothy parried.

*

Justin woke and blinked as he looked around the sumptuous bedroom that was to be his for, well, he had no idea how long for. The windows were dressed in duck egg blue brocade curtains which matched the drapes on the bedposts and the ornate ceiling architraves and wall mouldings would happily adorn any Italian renaissance building. He felt settled and quite at home here, though it was a far cry from his Tuscan villa studio – not that that wasn't beautiful – it was just not magnificent like Bochym Manor! He consulted his pocket watch - he'd slept for a couple of hours after coming in from the garden, and had probably missed tea. So, after freshening up, he made his way down the stairs to look for company and possibly something to eat as his stomach was protesting loudly. He could hear laughter from somewhere in the house and went in search of the source, but as he walked into the kitchen dining room, there was a sudden loud scuffle of chairs being pushed back as everyone stood up.

Alarmed that he'd made everyone uncomfortable, Justin held his hands out. 'Oh, goodness, please don't get up on my account.'

'Is there something I can do for you, sir,' Joe asked.

'Well, if it's not too much bother, I'd rather like a cup of tea and a piece of that cake. I appear to have missed tea and it seems an age until dinner - my stomach is rumbling like thunder.' On cue his stomach made a cavernous groan and everyone smiled. 'See what I mean?'

'Of course, sir, I'll have a tray sent to the Jacobean drawing room at once.'

'Oh, no, I don't want to put anyone to any bother. I thought perhaps, if you don't mind, I could join you all,' he asked hopefully. 'You look like you're having a jolly old time.'

'Oh, well, err.' Joe glanced at Ruby for guidance, when she nodded, he said, 'Of course. Betsy, move up a little so we can fit a chair between you and Mrs Sanders.'

*

Ryan was making his way back to his shelter after a hard day scything in the fields. He was hot and sweaty, but at least he could wash his clothes and hang them out to dry in the sunshine, now that his presence in the woods was known to the Earl. The muscles on his arms ached considerably, but it felt so good to be working again. He'd never shied away from hard work. He was starving – the pasty, bread and cheese they were given at lunchtime, seemed like a distant memory, and hoped, as he approached the hay barn, that Juliet had managed to leave him a little something. He emerged from the barn, happily tucking the fare Juliet had left him into his shirt. He stopped for a moment and glanced up at the manor, wondering how Betsy was feeling. He'd hoped to see her, but of course she'd probably be lame for a few days, by which time the harvest would be over and he'd have no reason to venture onto the Bochym Estate any longer. Once he had some money in his pocket though, a regular job and somewhere to stay, perhaps he would call on her – not that Juliet would be too happy with that prospect!

*

Ruby's heart was hammering in her chest when Justin settled beside her. She had to contain herself not to blush as Mrs Blair put a cup and saucer down and Betsy cut Justin a generous slice of Victoria sandwich.

'Thank you,' he said, carefully scraping the cream from the inside of the cake before taking a hungry bite. 'Mmm - delicious cake! This is just the ticket,' he said licking the jam residue off the side of his mouth.

Ruby dared not look at Justin, for chance of revealing how thrilled she was to sit in such close proximity.

'Do you not eat cream, Mr Devereux?' Mrs Blair asked, thumping her fists into her ample sides - clearly fretting about the dinner menu.

Abashed, Justin looked at his plate smeared with the residue cream.

'Forgive me - I believe I ate something in the summer which did not agree with me. Since then, my stomach protests if I eat anything rich.'

'Oh, lordy me!' Mrs Blair's hands flew upwards. 'I'll have to change the menu,' she declared.

'Mrs Blair.' Joe gave her a wide-eyed warning, and then turned to Justin. 'This is Mrs Blair, our cook,' he explained. 'If you have a special dietary requirement, I'm sure she can accommodate it - can't you Mrs Blair?'

The cook pursed her lips and nodded.

'Oh, no, please don't think you have to cook anything special for me. I don't want to be any trouble. I select what I can eat from what I'm given, but I do like plain cake,' he grinned boyishly.

Mrs Blair relaxed and smiled, but everyone knew she *was* planning a new menu in her head.

'So,' Justin said taking a sip of tea, 'would you all like to introduce yourselves to me – I need to know all your names if I'm to stay amongst you for a while.'

Joe cleared his throat. 'I'm Mr Treen, the butler and this is Mrs Sanders, the housekeeper.'

Justin turned his blue eyes on Ruby. 'And does Mrs Sanders have a Christian name?' he asked softly.

Ruby felt a quiver run through her. 'It's Ruby,' she said almost inaudibly.

'Ruby.' He rolled her name on his tongue and his eyes crinkled as they had before, and then he turned to Betsy. 'And you are?'

'Betsy Tamblin, senior maid, sir,' she said assertively. Justin smiled and then looked at Juliet.

'Juliet, sir,' she said lowering her eyes shyly.

'And I'm Izzy Bennett – the laundry maid,' Izzy said proudly.

'Lyndon FitzSimmons. It's my first day here, but I'm not staff - I'm just here mending hedges.'

Justin smiled at Thomas Jennings. 'We've met, haven't we, Thomas?'

'Yes, sir, besides being your temporary valet, I'm the footman.'

'This is Theo Trevail and his wife Lowenna - valet and lady's maid to the Earl and Countess,' Joe introduced them, 'and this is Mary Tonkin the kitchen maid.'

'And that just leaves you?' Justin glanced at Dorothy who was sitting open-mouthed.

'This is Dorothy Ellis– the scullery maid,' Thomas said, 'it's not often she has nothing to say for herself, so enjoy the silence while it's happening.'

Dorothy scowled at Thomas and thumped him on the leg.

He turned to smile at the cook. 'And does the lovely Mrs Blair have a Christian name?'

Everyone around the table stilled as they waited for her response – no one had ever found out what her first name was. Mrs Blair took a large intake of breath, as they all waited uncomfortably for her short, but polite rebuff. Instead, her lips curled into an enigmatic smile.

'Persephone - I'm very pleased to meet you, Mr Devereux,' she said holding her hand out to him.

Mouths dropped in astonishment when the cook took herself back to the kitchen to fetch another pot of tea.

'Persephone! Wow, what a name!' Dorothy whispered to Mary. 'Who would have thought?'

'Shush, Dorothy,' Ruby warned.

'Well,' Justin said, 'I'm very pleased to meet you all. I do hope I won't be too much bother to any of you. I have little in the way of needs. I'm used to looking after myself.'

'We're all happy to serve you, sir, should you need anything,' Joe said.

'Sorry, Mr Treen, I didn't catch your Christian name.'

Joe cleared his throat uncomfortably. 'Joseph, Joe, sir.'

'Well, Joe, all my friends call me Justin – of which, I include you all. So, could you drop the term, sir? I do so dislike it - it takes me back to boarding school and gives me the shudders.'

Joe shifted uncomfortably. 'I'm not sure, my lord and ladyship may not approve.'

'Well, they're not here now, are they?' He winked.

'No, sir,' Joe said wincing.

'Would you like another slice of cake, Justin,' Mary said bravely, but received a sharp look from Joe.

'I would, but I won't. I assume dinner will be served soon. Will it?' He looked directly at Ruby for guidance.

'Dinner is served at eight,' she answered.

Justin glanced at the clock as it ticked a quarter-past-five.

'Good lord, I'll die of hunger by then! So, yes, Mary, another slice of cake will do nicely.'

*

Later that evening, Ruby was checking the household accounts in the housekeeper's room when a knock came to the door. Thinking it was one of the maids calling to say goodnight, she beckoned them in, but did not look up immediately.

'I'm terribly sorry to bother you, Ruby...'

When she realised who her visitor was, Ruby quickly stood up almost knocking her chair over. 'Mr Devereux! What can I do for you?'

'Please, Ruby, don't stand on my account and *do* call me Justin,' he pleaded. 'I just wondered if I could possibly have another blanket.'

'Of course, Mr..., I'll have one sent up in a moment. You should have rung for someone.'

'I don't want to bother anyone. If you could just let me have one, I'll take it up with me now. Coming from Tuscany, I feel the chill of a British autumn.'

'Having never been abroad, I can only imagine you do.' She opened her blanket cupboard and selected a thick woollen one for him. As she passed it to his outstretched hands, she was struck by the intensity of his blue eyes, gazing at her. Ruby was not unfamiliar with the gaze of men, before securing her job as housekeeper at Bochym, she'd been a bar-maid for several years, and deflected many a flirty glance, but Justin's gaze was not full of lust – it was a searching gaze - that seemed to reach deep into her soul. It was quite unnerving!

'Thank you, Ruby. You're very kind.'

Goose-bumps appeared on her skin at the use of her name so casually. Having laid the blanket on his hands, for a moment, they were both holding it, and when her hands brushed his, she was alarmed at how cold he felt.

'Goodness, but your hands feel frozen, let me send up a warming pan and a cup of hot chocolate and have someone tend your fire.'

'No, really, I'll be fine with just this, thank you.'

'Well, please ring down if you should need anything else.'

'Thank you, I will. Goodnight, Ruby.'

'Goodnight,' she whispered. Closing the door, she stood still for a good few seconds after he'd left. Forgetting all about her accounts for the moment, she realised that a very strange, but not unwelcome, frisson was again searing through her.

A knock came at her door, causing a squeak of delight, but it was only Joe who popped his head around the door this time.

'Everything all right, Ruby? I just saw Mr Devereux coming out of your room.'

'Yes, he needed a blanket, but didn't want to bother any of us.'

'He is a strange one, isn't he? Anyway, I'll say goodnight then.'

'Goodnight, Joe,' she answered breathlessly.

'Are you sure you're all right, Ruby – you look,' he tipped his head,' a little flushed.'

'Absolutely fine,' she said, trying to still her heart from hammering in her chest.

8

Matthew Bickford was the first of the dinner guests to arrive at Bochym Manor. He arrived on horseback just after three on Friday afternoon, having just ridden over from the Trelowarren Estate, where he'd been staying with Lord and Lady Vyvyan. As he trotted up through the arboretum, he came across Peter Dunstan speaking to Lyndon FitzSimmons as he was hedge-laying.

'Matthew, good to see you again.' Peter shook his hand when he dismounted. 'This is well met - I've just come to watch a master hedger at work.'

'He's good, isn't he?' Matthew said greeting Lyndon with all the warmth he would a brother.

Lyndon turned to Peter. 'I'm eternally grateful that Matthew recommended me to you, my lord.'

'We are lucky to have you, Mr FitzSimmons – I've heard excellent reports from the landowners hereabouts who have used your skills. May we watch a moment?'

'Certainly.' Lyndon wielded his billhook and began the task of pleaching the branch in hand. He spoke as he worked. 'It's incredibly important for a hedgerow to be a thick, bushy, impenetrable barrier to sheep and cattle. A well-managed hedgerow will do that. It's also a haven for wildlife. If you leave a hedge unmanaged, it will continue to grow upwards and outwards and will eventually just become a line of trees – which is what happened here! Once I've laid this hedge, regular trimming will keep it in good order for years.'

'Well, I'm impressed by the amount you have done already.'

Lyndon smiled. 'It should take me no more than ten days, my lord.'

'Good man. I trust you're taking advantage of cook's fine meals.'

'I am, my lord, thank you. I haven't eaten so well since Matthew and I used to raid the Trevarno larder.'

Matthew laughed. 'Our cook couldn't tell me off because I was the master's son - it meant we ate like lords while playing out in the fields.'

Peter smiled at the banter. 'We'll leave you to your work then.'

As they walked away, Matthew leading his horse, Peter said, 'You two really *are* good friends, aren't you?'

'The best.'

'I feel I should have invited Lyndon to dinner tonight.'

'He wouldn't accept. He's a man happy in the outside world. He'd be out of his depth around your dining table – as informal as it is. He'd tell you the same if you asked him.'

When they approached the manor, a groom came out to take Matthew's horse just as the car Peter had sent for James Blackwell and his house guests, Hillary Stanton and Glen Diamond, passed them.

'Ah! I see Hillary is in the party again,' Matthew mused watching her emerge from the vehicle.

'She's a fine young woman - you could do a lot worse.'

'Please, Peter, no matchmaking - I have an estate to learn to run.'

'Estates run better with a good woman by your side.'

'Yes, but I don't think Hillary is ready to settle down yet – she's rather wild don't you think?'

They both looked over as Hillary laughed loudly at something James had said.

'I might try to tame her one day though – in a few years, if she's still interested.' He winked at Peter.

*

Justin watched from his attic studio, as various people arrived at the manor for the dinner that night. In truth, he'd have been happier staying here with the four-by-four linen canvas he'd just stretched over a wooden frame. Having said that, the pungent smell of the hot rabbit skin glue he'd prepared the canvas with, would probably force him out into the social scene developing downstairs. He rubbed his fingers together – Oh, but he was itching to paint. It had crossed his mind that a change of country would tamper his desire to make art – how wrong could he have been!

'Justin,' Sarah knocked softly on the attic door, 'our guests are arriving. There is tea laid out in the drawing room.'

Justin exhaled resignedly. 'I'm coming.'

Dressed in a fresh shirt, casually unbuttoned at the neck, he prepared himself to meet his dinner guests. He was not an unsociable man – far from it with his own kind of people, but he'd really rather be having tea with the lovely people in the kitchen. He was smiling at this thought when he came face to face with Ruby on the first-floor landing and couldn't help but note how her face lit up when she saw him.

'Hello, Ruby.'

Quickly glancing around to make sure they were alone, she whispered, 'Hello, Justin. Can I get you anything?'

He laughed briefly. 'Not unless you can find me an excuse to escape from dinner with a crowd of people I don't know.'

'Don't worry - the majority are very nice. They're arty people, like you,' she assured him.

'And the minority?'

Ruby's lips curled into a smile, but said nothing.

'I suspect you're busy with all this going on? I fear it is my fault, as they are here to welcome me to Bochym.'

'It's all in a day's work, and it's nice to have the house full of guests.'

They fell silent for a moment, but held each other's gaze without embarrassment. Justin knew he was stalling from going downstairs, but it was not time wasted. In the short timeframe of this conversation, his mind had processed and stored so many things about this woman standing before him. Their gaze was broken when laughter filtered up the stairs from the drawing room.

'I think they're waiting for you,' Ruby said.

He sighed deeply and nodded.

'I hope you find someone you can relate to.'

He smiled and nodded. *I already have.*

*

Most of the guests had arrived, only Kit and Sophie Trevellick were still to come from Gweek, and they were due around half-past-five. Everyone was so busy - no one noticed Juliet's agitation the nearer it got to the Trevellick's arrival. No sooner had their wagon been spotted coming up the drive, Juliet was struck down by a sudden 'blinding' headache, and Ruby was forced to send her to bed immediately.

Sophie was heavy with her second child, so Ruby helped her to settle their daughter Selene in the nursery with Peter and Sarah's children.

'When are you due?' Ruby asked as Sophie slumped in the chair, fanning herself furiously.

'About four weeks. I was in two minds whether to come tonight. It's not the most comfortable journey by wagon, but I'm rather curious to meet Justin. What is he like?'

Ruby couldn't help but smile as Justin's handsome face flashed before her. 'He's absolutely charming.'

'Worth the effort then,' Sophie said struggling to get up and leave her daughter in the capable hands of Nanny.

Once Sophie had gone up to change, Ruby joined Joe to make sure everything was shipshape and everyone had everything they needed.

Cook and Mary were busy preparing the finishing touches to the hors d'oeuvres, while Betsy, despite her foot being bound in hessian, stepped into the breach to cover for Juliet.

James Blackwell was the first to come down the stairs, but instead of making for the drawing room, he wandered into the kitchen, causing everyone to stop what they were doing to give a little bow or curtsy.

'I'm sorry to disturb you all,' James said scanning the room.

Joe stepped forward 'What can I do for you, sir.'

'I'm looking for one of the maids called Betsy.'

Puzzled as to what on earth James Blackwell wanted with her, Betsy's mouth dropped as everyone turned to her. 'I'm Betsy, sir.'

'Ah, splendid, I've a letter for you - Jessie asked me to pass it onto you.'

'Oh!' she clasped her hands together. 'You've seen Jessie then?'

'I have, I believe the letter explains all.'

'Thank you.' She took the letter.

'I'll leave you all in peace now,' he said turning to leave.

Almost immediately the other guests started to come downstairs, so there was no time for Betsy to read the letter. She tucked it away in her pocket to read later. There was work to do - she and Dorothy had been assigned to check on the bathrooms for damp towels and tidy the rooms while the guests were in the drawing room enjoying a pre-dinner drink.

*

When the dinner gong sounded at eight, a flurry of trays and tureens were ferried from the kitchen, to present a meal consisting of a first course of clear veal consommé garnished with scallops. A second course of poached salmon with mousseline sauce, followed by roast lamb, redcurrant sauce and stuffed vegetables. The kitchen staff watched enviously as the delicious food went through on the platters, hoping some of it would come back for their own dinner tomorrow. If not, it would be boiled beef, carrots and potatoes.

*

Upstairs, Juliet sat in bed cradling her knees with her arms, listening to the hectic kitchen noises below, feeling dreadful about leaving all the work to the others, but she simply could not let Kit and Sophie Trevellick see her.

She'd fretted constantly since hearing they were on the dinner guest list, and hoped she could feign this headache until they'd gone tomorrow. She cast her eyes skywards - what with Lyndon FitzSimmons here, and now the Trevellick's – how many more people associated with Gweek would she have to try to avoid?

*

After dinner, the male guests retired with the ladies to the drawing room, for coffee and brandy, allowing Joe and Thomas to clear the table.

Justin, desperate to avoid sitting next to Carole, took himself off to the water closet – hoping the place she said she was saving him would be taken. He'd been placed beside the very dour Dowager Countess on one side of him at dinner – Sarah had apologised in advance that her mother-in-law had insisted on it. To his other side though, he had the hugely entertaining Hillary Stanton. The latter's wit had more than made up for the dullness of the former. Thankfully the Dowager Countess had gone straight home after dinner, and Justin wished that she'd taken her annoying daughter Carole with her. Carole had pouted and made eyes at him across the table all evening – all very embarrassing. She was a woman who very much liked to be the centre of attention, and her vacuous conversation made her so - for all the wrong reasons. En route to the water closet, Justin paused for a moment in the deserted library and stood at the window looking out into the darkness. He could hear the dining room being cleared of the dinner remnants, so waited a few moments until everything fell silent. When he thought the coast was clear he stepped out into the hall to find Ruby emerging backwards from the dining room as she switched off the light and closed the door. When she turned, she held her hand to her heart, startled at his presence.

'Good god, I thought you were a ghost.'

Justin apologised and then laughed heartily. 'What do you mean - a ghost?'

'Oh, we have a few here, believe me,' she said, smoothing down her dress.

His face paled, though his interest piqued. 'Really?' he said warily. 'To tell you the truth, I'm more interested in avoiding the living at the moment – how long do these get-togethers go on for? I'm ready for my bed now.'

Ruby smiled sympathetically. 'Another hour or so I suspect.'

'Oh!' He rolled his eyes. 'But you'll be able to retire now, won't you?'

'No, I'll wait with Joe to make sure everyone has everything they need.'

'I'm sorry.' Justin's heart went out to her.

'It's fine - it's what we do.'

More than anything, he'd like to have stayed and talked to Ruby for the rest of the night, but he knew he could not.

'I'd better go back - they'll wonder where I am.' He smiled softly. 'Goodnight then, Ruby.'

'Goodnight, Justin.'

*

Betsy climbed the stairs wearily after the last of the dishes were washed, to find Juliet sleeping. After washing and dressing for bed, she rubbed the ache in her foot – she'd practically worn the hessian foot covering through at the sole. She'd have to find something more supportive if she was to go without her shoe for much longer - and she was desperate to take a walk outside. Plumping her pillows behind her, she got herself comfortable and opened the letter, hesitant and excited in equal measure to hear Jessie's news.

No. 3 Bellevue Gardens
North London
Dear Betsy,
As promised, here is the address above where you can write to me. Although Daniel and I are residing in London, he is at his home, and I'm staying in James Blackwell's house in Bellevue Gardens – a

very fine house indeed. I've sent my address to Ellie and Meg by post, but as James was coming down to Cornwall and is to dine at Bochym, he very kindly offered to hand deliver this letter for me. I will stay at James's house while the banns are read for our wedding – which I hope will be mid-October.

Please write to me now and tell me all your news and I'll write back once we have a wedding date.

I miss you. Love to you always. Your friend, Jessie xx

Betsy let the letter fall on her eiderdown. So, getting married, living in London in James Blackwell's house no less, it seemed her friend had well and truly left her old life behind. She looked around the stark attic bedroom, how she wished something exciting would happen in *her* life, but the chances were she'd still be staring at these four walls when her hair was threaded with silver. Picking up the end of her long-pleated hair to inspect its rich chestnut colour, she sighed, flicked it over her shoulder, and turned off the oil lamp.

9

When Justin walked back into the drawing room, all the seats were taken except for the one Carole was patting beside her. He poured himself a coffee, mourning the fact that he couldn't even dull his senses with a stiff brandy nowadays.

'Well, we have some news,' Kit said, raising his brandy glass. 'We're going to be away for a while. I've taken a commission in Yorkshire to refurbish a panelled dining room and make some bespoke furniture for a fine house there. We've decided to take a house up there while I complete the work.'

'Oh, goodness,' Sarah clasped her hand to her face, 'how long will you be gone?'

'Twelve months, perhaps fourteen. We'll go after Sophie has safely delivered our baby.'

'But what will you do about your work for the Arts and Craft Association?'

'It'll be fine. Everything Sophie embroiders, we'll be able to send down to you, and I've two pieces of carved furniture, and a jewellery box, which I'll finish and leave with you before we go.'

'What will you do about Quay House?' Peter enquired.

'Well, that all depends on you, Peter, as you own the house. We're hoping that you don't want to re-let it. We're willing to pay rent on it while we're away, though I know it's not good for a house to lay empty, it will get damp being so close to the Helford River.'

'You need not pay the rent - we have no need of the money. I'll arrange for someone - a housekeeper perhaps, to air the place regularly.'

Kit smiled with relief. 'Thank you, Peter that saves us from moving our furniture into storage.'

Carole pouted her painted lips. 'And what about you, Justin? Sarah tells me you're staying in England for a while. Are you to reside here, or are you going to take a house somewhere?'

Justin took a sip of coffee. 'I've no plans to take a house. Sarah and Peter have generously offered me a room and the use of the attic here - which is all I need.' He glanced happily at his sister and brother-in-law.

'And you are welcome to it for as long as you wish,' Sarah added with a smile.

'You could always come and stay at my château,' Carole purred. 'I have many rooms, all a great deal nicer than the musty attic here and the company will be less boring. It would be oodles of fun – *we* could have oodles of fun.' She gave a vampish look.

Justin smiled tightly. 'Thank you for the invite, but I think not, the attic is perfect, and I rather *enjoy* the company I have *here*.' He turned away from her and glanced at Sarah.

Carole frowned, clearly unsure if she'd been slighted or not, she carried on undeterred. 'I rather wish I wasn't leaving on Monday now. I could delay my departure, you know, Justin. You could give me some private art lessons,' she said walking her fingers gently up his sleeve.

Justin took a deep breath in order to form a measured response. 'Your delay would be wasted. Art lessons I do *not* do. There is a saying, those who can't do, teach.'

Carole's mouth twitched. 'I see you have a very high opinion of yourself,' she said scathingly.

'And with good reason,' Sarah said jumping to Justin's defence whilst directing Carole to his painting of her hanging above the fireplace.

Carole's eyes flickered with only a degree of interest at the painting. 'Granted, it's good. I suppose I could allow you to do some sketches of me before I leave.'

'Why would I want to do that?'

She frowned. 'So, you can paint me of course! You can send the painting to me and I'll hang it in the château for all my rich friends to see – you never know, it *might* even bring you a few commissions,' she said, pretending to inspect one of her fingernails.

'Ah, well, I'm rather choosy who I paint, I only paint beautiful things I love - and I have no need for your commissions, thank you.'

Carole's cheeks pinked as a scowl darkened her face.

'Justin's paintings fetch a lot of money, Carole,' Peter intervened.

Carole lifted her chin. 'And yet he resides here, free of charge, instead of taking a house – which, if what you tell me is correct, he could well afford.' She shifted slightly and lowered her gaze at Justin. 'Perhaps you're taking advantage of my brother's generosity.'

'*Carol!*' Peter warned, as everyone shifted uneasily, but Justin was ready for battle.

'I understand you know a great deal about the generosity of others! Forgive me, but did you not marry twice for money.' Justin raised his coffee cup to her.

'Touché,' Hillary said sotto voce.

Sarah bit her lip, clearly enjoying the fact that Carole had met her match, but as hostess, she needed to bring this conversation to a halt.

'Justin, Carol, I think that's enough, thank you.'

'Yes, Sarah,' Carole smarted, 'I think that is *more* than enough. It's late - I think I'll retire to the Dower Lodge. I need to get ready to return to my own home in France. I simply can't abide outstaying my welcome anywhere. Can you send for the car, Peter?'

Peter duly rang the bell, and as Sarah and Peter followed her out, Carole bid her goodnights to everyone, making a note to scowl at Justin, who in turn raised his cup to her departure.

'Oh, Justin darling, never argue with an idiot. They will just drag you down to their level and beat you with experience,' Hillary whispered

Justin's lip curled into a smile.

'I swear that woman's only flair is in her nostrils,' she added with an exasperated sigh.

'Hillary! Behave!' James warned.

There was a short embarrassed silence when Peter and Sarah came back in. 'Sorry about Carole she can be very tactless at times,' Peter apologised.

Everyone dismissed it, and her, as drinks were refilled.

'I must say, it's strange not having Guy and Ellie here, isn't it?' Kit said to change the subject.

'Yes,' Sarah answered, 'they were invited of course, but it is a little too soon after the shooting tragedy, and Guy is naturally heart-sore by it. Elise believes he will never get over the loss of his brother, Silas.'

'Terrible business,' James said shaking his head.

'As Guy and Elise are not here tonight, James, may I ask if you've seen anything of Daniel Chandler and Jessie?' Sarah asked, and then turned to explain to Justin, 'Daniel is an orchestral musician, he was James's house guest and visited us a couple of times over the last twelve months – while he was here, he stole the heart of a friend of ours.'

'How romantic,' Justin mused.

'I don't think Guy sees it that way,' Peter muttered.

Justin gave Peter a questioning look.

'Daniel took off with Silas's wife, Jessie, quite soon after his death,' he added.

'Peter,' Sarah scolded, 'everyone knew she was leaving with Daniel and she'd been estranged from Silas for many months - It was just so unfortunate that Silas was killed.'

'And she was terribly unhappy with Silas,' Sophie added.

'As it happens,' James said taking a sip of brandy, 'I have seen them, and it's perhaps fortunate that Guy isn't amongst us tonight, so I can speak freely. Jessie is residing in my London residence until they can get married, so everything is being done in the correct manner.'

'As he was your regular house guest, James, did you know about Daniel and Jessie?' Kit asked curiously.

'Not a whisper – I thought he was just coming back down to enjoy more of the Cornish scenery! I really had no idea there was anything between them - they both hid it well, but I must say, they are very happy together. And for what it's worth, Peter, Silas's death does not sit easily with Jessie.'

Peter hummed, unconvinced.

'Changing the subject,' Kit said, 'Is Guy thatching again yet? We haven't seen him since Silas's funeral.'

'Yes, I don't think he can waste this good weather,' Peter answered. 'He's a man down now though, but I should think he will be hard pushed to think about a replacement for Silas just yet.'

'What about the tea room?' Sophie enquired. 'We're planning on going down tomorrow after leaving here.'

'You'll be in luck, Elise is opening again tomorrow,' Sarah answered. 'As they say, life goes on. I plan to go down on Sunday myself to show my support. Poldhu Cove has become something of a macabre interest to many in the surrounding area, and I think Elise needs my help, so I'll gather some of my friends to visit and bring some sort of normality to the tea room.

As they were all discussing people Justin did not know, he failed to stifle a yawn. 'I'm so sorry. The journey from Italy is taking its toll I'm afraid. Would any of you mind if I retired to my bed.'

'Not at all,' Kit said. 'I think we're ready to retire as well.' He looked at Sophie, who nodded thankfully.

There followed a general chorus of agreement and the party broke up. As they all said their goodnights, Justin smiled inwardly - at least Ruby and Joe could get to bed at a decent hour now.

*

Ruby was just making the last checks on all the bedrooms - turning down the bed sheets and closing the curtains.

In Justin's bedroom she found the windows were open, and smiled – he must be acclimatising to the English weather now. His room had a marked quietness about it and smelt of his lemon cologne. Moving towards his bed, she found his bedside table was tidy. Beside the electric lamp, he had a decanter of water and glass, a pair of spectacles - which she didn't know he wore, and a leather-bound book of poems by Lord Byron.

Sitting down on the bed, she reached out her hand until her fingers softly touched his pillow where his head had laid.

'Justin,' she whispered his name softly, but a movement at the door made her quickly stand. 'Hello?' she called, but no sound came. She straightened the eiderdown and walked swiftly to the door, but there was no one about.

As she descended the stairs, she scolded herself. *That was madness, Ruby. To sit on a gentleman's bed, caressing his pillow, what on earth are you thinking?* She rushed towards the housekeeping room feeling dreadfully shameful – this was no way for a woman in her position to act.

*

Justin waited until Ruby's footsteps had disappeared before emerging from where he'd hidden behind the bathroom door. A moment ago, he'd stood at his bedroom door and seen her touch his pillow whispering his name. He flung his head back and smiled joyously – she clearly felt something for him, as he did for her.

*

Once satisfied that everyone was settled, and Joe had said goodnight to Ruby, he began to make the last checks in the household before bed. Once all doors and windows were secure, he switched the light off at the kitchen door and noticed a scarf on the floor which had fallen from the cloak peg. He bent down to pick it up and caught the unmistakable fragrance of the rose water Juliet used. In fact, all the maids used a slight dab of rose water, especially on their half days off, but strangely enough, although they all shared the same bottle, it smelt different on each of them, and this was clearly Juliet's scarf. He folded the soft woollen scarf, inhaled her fragrance and sighed. *Why do you always fall for the wrong woman, Joe?* His thoughts turned to

73

Jessie who he'd fallen secretly in love with many years ago. She too had been a maid once at Bochym, when he was a mere footman, but she'd gone to work at The Poldhu Tea Room and married Silas Blackthorn. When her marriage failed and she found solace in the arms of another, who for a while seemed to have deserted her, Joe had been prepared to risk his fine reputation as a butler, to help her, but even that didn't go to plan! Now Jessie had gone away forever! It seemed that he was destined, as many people in service were, to live a single life. He looked at the scarf again, and hung it on the peg. He really must stop torturing himself like this – it was clear that Juliet did not care for him as he did for her – perhaps it was time to give up on finding a soul mate in life. He switched the lights off and climbed the stairs to bed.

10

When the clock tower chimed six, Betsy yawned and stretched as she pushed the covers away. There would be a lot to do this morning, especially when the guests had all gone.

Juliet,' she whispered, 'are you feeling better?'

Juliet turned but kept her eyes closed. 'No, my head is still bad.'

'Gosh, do you suffer much from headaches much then?'

'No! Hopefully it will go soon.'

'I hope so - for your sake. I'll get dressed and bring you a headache draft – hopefully that will shift it.'

*

Juliet curled herself into a ball after Betsy left, wretched at having to lie to everyone. She duly took the remedy Betsy brought her and laid in bed until the clock struck ten. She watched from her bedroom window as the Trevellick's horse and wagon were made ready to leave. Almost as soon as they left, she dressed quickly and ventured downstairs.

'I'm feeling a little better now, Mrs Sanders,' she said, her hand touching her brow. Seeing the relief on Ruby's face made her feel less guilty for what she had done.

*

The early part of the morning had been extremely busy without the initial help of Juliet, but Ruby was thankful for that and threw herself into her work in an attempt to erase the memory of what she'd done last night. Just touching Justin's pillow had evoked such wild dreams about him - it really would not do. She was in a position of trust in this house – falling for a guest, such as Justin, would be madness.

By mid-morning the maids had finished cleaning the French drawing room, and the house was settling back into its normal routine. Ruby breezed into the room, and after a quick inspection, she reached to open the window. Her gaze fell on Justin, sitting under the shade of the fig tree drawing, in the far corner of the front lawn. Her heart stilled and all her resolutions earlier not to fall for him fell by the wayside. A ghost of a smile passed her lips, knowing that for a few moments she could secretly observe him. Despite his demonstrative nature, there was such calmness about him while he was engrossed in his art. There had been many bohemian types at the manor – many of them occupying the workshops of the Bochym Arts and Craft Association, but Justin was enigmatic.

*

Unbeknown to Ruby, Joe was standing at the threshold of the French drawing room door watching her. In all the time he'd known Ruby, he'd never known her stand so silent and motionless. She was always busy, breezing here and there, keeping the manor running like clockwork. He took a step back from where he stood, so as not to disturb her, but the movement must have pulled her from her reverie, because a moment later he heard the jangle of the keys she kept on her belt as she moved.

She smiled and nodded a greeting at him on leaving the dining room, before moving to the library to check all was well there. He waited for a moment and then went to stand where Ruby had been standing. He drew a puzzled frown - all he could see was Mr Devereux sketching.

He turned and smiled when Juliet entered the room with a vase of flowers. He was heartened when she returned a shy smile.

'Do you feel better, Juliet?' he asked.

'Yes, thank you, Mr Treen,' she answered, rushing away before he could say more to her. He hoped her haste was so that Ruby didn't catch her loitering, but deep down he knew she was avoiding him.

*

Later that evening, Ruby should have been updating the household accounts, but instead she was staring into thin air - her thoughts were both disturbing and pleasant. Last evening's madness of stroking his pillow, and this morning of watching Justin from every front-facing window like a love-sick schoolgirl, deeply unsettled her. She must stop all thoughts of him - they were interfering with her work, oh, but he was so fascinating. Her thoughts were quickly gathered back to the present when a knock came on her door.

'Good evening, Ruby.'

'Oh, good evening.' Ruby felt the heat burn on her face when Justin appeared - It was as though she'd conjured him up with her thoughts. 'What can I do for you?' she said, fighting the furious fluttering in her stomach.

'I'm returning the blanket. Thank you. I've acclimatised now.'

Ruby smiled and took the blanket from him. 'Really, Justin,' she whispered, 'my maids would have collected it from you.'

'Well, that's it you see, I'm not used to having people fetch and carry for me. May I?' He gestured to be allowed to take a seat.

'Of course,' she answered happily as he sat down and crossed his legs casually - seemingly unperturbed that being alone in the room with her would be frowned on if anyone should find out.

'I live alone in Tuscany and do everything for myself, you see. It's hard to 'teach an old dog new tricks', as they say.' He smiled, crinkling the lines at his eyes.

'Forgive me, but you're from an aristocratic family! Surely you were used to having servants?' Ruby enquired.

'You're correct. My family have a great estate in Devon, which my father rather hoped I would take over the running of, but....'

Ruby tipped her head ready to hear more.

'I left boarding school and instead of going to university, I took myself off to live my own life in Italy. Father cut me off without a penny, but I knew what I wanted in life, and it wasn't to struggle keeping the family pile standing.'

'And so, you became an artist?'

He folded his arms. 'And so, I became an artist!' he smiled, 'and a rather successful one at that - if I might be so bold as to say.'

'Yes, we've all admired the painting of Her Ladyship. It really is rather magnificent.'

'Why, thank you.' He bowed he head graciously. 'I rather thought it was one of my best too. My sister is very beautiful, so it was a pleasure to paint her. I like painting beautiful things. I took a few sketches of her when she came over to see me a couple of years ago, and that's all I had to go on, so I'm happy it turned out as well as it did.'

'Do you not miss Italy? We're under the impression that you're in no rush to return. *Are* you planning to return?'

'I do miss the place, and I'd like to return, but,' he inspected his fingernails which had traces of paint under them, 'that all depends on certain things - which I won't bore you with at the moment. Tell me, Ruby, are you married? I see you wear no wedding ring, but your title suggests otherwise.'

'No, I'm not. We in service seemed to be married to our job. Many of us never marry.'

'So, the title, Mrs?'

'All senior women in the domestic household take on that title. I would have thought you'd know that growing up in a large estate.'

'No, as I said, I didn't stay around to find out the ways and workings of a grand house. I always believed our housekeeper and cook were widowed!'

Justin had such an easy way with him - Ruby began to relax in his presence.

'What about you, Justin,' she enjoyed saying his name, 'are you married?'

'I am, as you are, Ruby, married to my work. When I

was a young impoverished artist, no woman would take me on, and now I'm rich and famous, it seems the ladies are only interested in my money, and to be honest, at forty years of age, I think I am a little set in my ways. We're a strange breed, artists. We spend long hours alone with only a painting for company, and when we finally emerge from the studio, we want to have fun. I suspect only a rather special lady, who understands my ways, will tame me.'

'Gosh, I hope whoever you choose doesn't try to tame you, Justin. You are who you are. It gets lonely though, doesn't it?' Ruby spoke without thinking, immediately wanting to retract her words.

Justin considered her question and then gently nodded in agreement. 'It does, but this evening, you have eased my loneliness with your generous time.' He uncrossed his legs and arms, stood up and tipped his head to the side. 'Ruby,' he smiled, 'it's such a jewel of a name.'

Ruby's heart caught.

'Thank you, for your time. It's so nice to be able to call on a friend for a little chat. I'll look forward to the next time - which I hope will be very soon,' he whispered.

Ruby's knees weakened, elated and alarmed in equal measure that there would be other occasions she might risk being found alone in her office with him.

'I'll bid you goodnight, Ruby.'

'Goodnight, Justin.'

His eyes twinkled at her as he turned to leave.

Ruby sat for a long time trying to settle the flutter in her stomach, before taking herself to bed. She called in on Joe in his office to bid him goodnight. He too, she thought, had more than work on his mind. On the top landing, Juliet - Joe's enigma - was just letting herself into her bedroom. Ruby bid her good night before stepping into her own stark bedroom. Looking around the room, she had little in the way of nice things, the odd cushion and a bone comb and brush set —nothing that said she was anything other than a housekeeper. She pulled the chair towards the wardrobe and retrieved the childhood box of memories she kept on top of it. It contained a doll, her mother's wedding ring, a paint book and a pallet of watercolour paints. Her fingers caressed the pallet – there was a time many years ago when she too painted pictures, albeit naively. Putting the box back, she walked to the mirror, and with her fingertips, traced the fine lines on her thirty-four-year-old face. Although she noted there were a couple of silver hairs amongst her brown locks, Justin made her feel young again. Shaking her head to rid these silly thoughts – *he'd called you a friend, that's all*. She could never be anything else to him - it would not be permitted in any case by the household rules. She sighed - she could *not* permit anything else. She'd never secure another position like this if she were to be dismissed, but oh, goodness - to be more than his friend, would make her very happy.

*

It was early Sunday morning and Ryan was sharpening his scythe ready for the day's harvest. He'd been working the fields these last four days – dry, thirsty work, but it felt good to be working the land. He had money in his pocket, but no time at the moment to buy anything. Juliet, god bless her, had sneaked away apples, bread and a few eggs from the manor, so he would not starve. Lifting the blade to inspect it, he heard a commotion in the far corner of the high meadow.

'Whoa there, Beauty, steady boy.'

Shading the sun from his eyes, he witnessed a woman struggling to control her horse. It bucked and whinnied, stomping around in a great big circle before suddenly taking off. The woman riding it shrieked, but held on. Ryan dropped the scythe and ran towards the bolting horse with his arms outstretched. He said nothing – no shouting or waving, he just stood in its path. Miraculously the horse slowed to a canter and then a trot, but as it neared Ryan, it faltered and sidestepped. White foam soaped its withers and its large liquid brown eyes looked wild and terrified as he stepped forward.

'There now, there now, boy,' Ryan soothed, slowly reaching up for the bridle. He whispered calming words, until the horse leant its head against Ryan and they shared a moment of peace.

'Thank you so much,' Sarah said, 'I could have taken a nasty fall, had you not intervened.'

Ryan, so preoccupied with the horse, had failed to see who the horse's rider was, and quickly touched his brow when he realised. 'You're welcome, my lady.'

'I've never known him to bolt before. We were just about to jump the fence back there when a man, dressed in white, stepped out from behind a tree. I've no idea who it was, but Beau shied and reared up. He set off so fast I could not stop him.'

'I think he's settled now, my lady.'

'It's Mr Penrose, isn't it - the young man who carried Betsy to the house when she was injured?'

He nodded - amazed she'd remembered his name. 'Yes, my lady. I trust she's recovering?'

'Yes, she is. She's able to move about a little better now, and we've instructed our leather man to construct a makeshift boot for her until she can wear her own. The poor girl is desperate to get out into the fresh air, but her foot is healing nicely, all thanks to you and your quick thinking. You seemed to be where people need you at the right time.'

Ryan smiled sheepishly.

'You're very good with horses, Mr Penrose. Have you had training with them?'

'No, my lady, I just find them gentle creatures - I seem to have a way with them.'

'Tell me, have you found yourself employment yet?'

'I'm helping with the harvest. I have a few more days work, but apart from that, no one around here seems to be taking anyone on at the moment.'

Sarah nodded. 'Have you tried elsewhere?'

'I'd rather settle nearby.'

She tipped her head. 'Any reason?'

'I just like it here,' he answered truthfully.

'Well, thank you for helping with the harvest, and I am sure something will soon turn up for you.'

'I hope so, my lady.'

*

Henry Trencrom was adjusting the fly on his trousers, before pulling his bee suit back on. He'd been relieving himself behind a tree and felt quite shaken up after that stupid woman on horseback nearly killed him when her horse reared like it did. She should learn to control the beast if she was going to ride it around the estate! He peered down the meadow – it looked like she was speaking to that vagrant who had been working with the harvesters. His lip curled – he'd not settle until he'd got that wastrel out of the way. He didn't want him sniffing around his intended. Speaking of which, he'd heard that Jim Riley the leather maker was making a boot for Betsy so she could get out and about. He snorted derisively at the thought of Jim, privy to seeing Betsy's foot and ankle. She belonged to him damn it, and by god, as soon as she was out and about, away from that meddling cook who did everything she could to block him from seeing Betsy, he'd force her hand for an acceptance to his proposal. That tied cottage wouldn't stay vacant for long.

11

The horse bolting had not deterred Sarah from riding out to visit the tea room as planned, but she now also had another agenda for visiting that day. She arrived a little before most of the ladies she took tea with, and found Ellie sitting outside on the veranda with Guy and their children.

'Good morning, to you all,' Sarah said, kissing them warmly. 'I'm here to give moral support. The other ladies will be along shortly.'

Ellie stood up to speak to her. 'Thank you, Sarah, I appreciate it, we could do with the custom. We opened yesterday, but apart from Kit and Sophie there were very few customers.' Ellie lowered her voice so Guy could not hear, and added, 'Having said that, there is no shortage of people coming down to the cove, but they only have some macabre interest in seeing the spot where poor Silas died. God knows, but there is nothing to see! The wind has blown the sand over the bloodstain and for anyone other than we, who witnessed the shooting - it is just another sand dune.'

Meg, Ellie's assistant came out to take Sarah's order, but Sarah declined until the other ladies could join her. 'Are you staying on full time, Meg?' she asked.

'With Jessie gone, I've decided to stay until a replacement waitress can be found. I don't really want to work full-time - I'm jiggered by the end of the day!'

'Have you found anyone suitable to replace Jessie yet, Elise?'

Ellie smiled ruefully. 'Jessie is going to be a hard act to follow.'

Sarah turned to look at Guy when he snorted at the mention of Jessie's name, then glanced back at Ellie, who pulled a tight smile.

Sarah observed Guy - he looked thin and gaunt - the loss of his brother lying heavy on his shoulders. She wondered now whether to broach the subject she wanted to speak to him about, and then thought - now was as good a time as ever!

'We have a young man living rough in the woods at Bochym, Guy.'

Guy looked up at Sarah, but said nothing.

'He's looking for work,' she said cautiously glancing between him and Ellie.

'As a waitress?' Guy raised an eyebrow.

'No, Guy, not as a waitress,' she chided him, 'outdoor work.'

Guy remained quiet and began to brush cake crumbs from his youngest daughter's dress.

'I wondered if you could help him. He's working on the harvest at the manor at the moment, but that will end on Tuesday.' She watched as Guy took a deep tremulous breath, but still kept his head down.

Sarah glanced at Ellie who shrugged and was just about to leave the conversation there, when Guy looked up and asked, 'Where is he from?'

'Gweek, I believe.'

Being from the Helford River village of Gweek himself, Guy's interest was piqued. 'What's his name?'

'Ryan Penrose.'

Guy frowned – he thought he knew everyone in Gweek. 'It's not a name I'm familiar with.'

'I don't think he lived there long.'

'Is he a drifter then?'

'I don't know, Guy.'

He folded his arms. 'Why do you want to help him?'

'He was kind enough to help Betsy last week when she got her foot caught in a rabbit trap.' The very mention of the event made her shudder. 'He carried her to the house and has shown an interest in her welfare since. He seems like a genuine sort of chap. He also saved me when Beau bolted earlier today.'

Guy nodded, but remained silent and Sarah decided to

leave it at that. In any case she noticed the rest of her party of ladies was making their way down the boardwalk to the tea room.

*

Guy watched thoughtfully as Sarah and her friends engaged in lively chatter. One or two other people drifted into the tea room after a walk on the beach – life was returning to some sort of normality - well, for some it was! He too had returned to work, and although Silas had been a volatile man, at odds with everything in the world, Guy missed his brother. It felt as though he'd lost a limb with Silas's passing. Jake Treen, his co-worker, had been a godsend, but without doubt they were in need of another pair of hands to help with the thatching. Guy just didn't know if he had the will or energy to train someone else to thatch at the moment.

'Papa.' Agnes, Guy's eldest daughter pulled on his shirt sleeve. He looked down at her. 'Now Uncle Silas has gone to heaven, can I come and work for you?'

Guy's heart almost broke at the thought of Silas in heaven. He dragged a smile from the depths of somewhere. 'When you are older, Agnes, I promise there will be a job for you thatching. You will be the first girl thatcher.'

'Why don't all girls want to be thatchers, Papa?'

'Because, they're not special like you, my darling girl.'

'How old were you when you became a thatcher, Papa?'

'I was fourteen when I started to work for my pa.'

Agnes counted on her fingers, sighing dramatically. 'That's five more years!'

'Don't wish your life away, Agnes,' his voice cracked with emotion, 'enjoy being my little girl.'

'I thought *I* was your little girl, Papa!' Sophie sulked.

Guy looked affectionately at his youngest daughter. 'You are both my precious little girls, and I need you to stay that way for as long as possible.' He looked down at

Zack, his seven-year-old son, quiet as always, happy to play with his toys rather than engage in any wish to grow up or join his father on a roof. He was as shy and reserved as his sisters were loud and boisterous and Guy wondered, not for the first-time, what path his son would take when he grew up.

Guy was in quiet turmoil when Ellie came out of the tea room to refresh his teapot and put a bowl of water down for their dogs Blue and Brandy. The conversation with Sarah had troubled him. He knew in his heart that they needed an extra pair of hands to do the amount of thatching they had on their books, but...... it just felt so final to give Silas's job away. His eyes watered yet again for his younger brother – he'd never felt a wrench on his heart like this.

Ellie, seeing his distress, smiled and kissed him.

'I'm sorry - it's not a manly thing to do to be so emotional.'

'Don't apologise, my darling, grief is a long process.'

He pulled his mouth downwards - Ellie did not seem to be grieving for Silas as he thought she should! Yes, Silas had been a troubled soul and thoughtless in his dealings with his wife Jessie, but, he glanced down at Silas's dog, Blue - it seemed only to be himself and the dog truly grieving for him. He bent down to pat Blue. The poor creature was thin and pining away, he would neither eat nor drink a thing. They had to keep him on a leash now because if they let him off, he would make straight for Cury churchyard and lay on Silas's grave. The dog was clearly going to die of a broken heart and Guy wondered, not for the first time, whether it was kinder to let the dog be where he wanted to be.

'Have you decided what to do about the young man Sarah mentioned?'

'No,' he said rather too sharply.

He was grateful when she didn't press him further on the subject, but he knew it would probably be a good time to take on another apprentice. He gave an audible sigh, and Ellie looked up questioningly from where she was clearing the next table.

An hour later, as Sarah got up to go, Guy also got up and walked over to her.

'Send the lad down to see me next Saturday and I'll speak with him.'

Sarah touched him gently on his arm. 'Thank you, Guy. I think this man needs a helping hand. I know he'll never replace Silas, but if you take him on it will help to ease your burden.'

*

Ryan's mouth dropped in astonishment, when Sarah pulled her horse to a halt in the field where he was scything, to tell him the news.

'Why, thank you, my lady.'

'Just don't let me down, Mr Penrose. I have recommended you highly to Mr Blackthorn.' She flicked the whip on the side of her riding boot and set off at a canter towards the stables.

*

On Monday morning, the staff assembled at the front door, ready to bid the Dowager Countess and Carole farewell as they headed off, back to Carole's château in the South of France. When the car pulled up in front of the manor, having just picked them up from the Dower Lodge, Joe stepped forward to open the car door for them.

Peter and Sarah stepped forward, and Peter embraced his mother warmly and Carole a little more coolly.

'I hope you both have a good journey. Send word when you arrive at the château.'

'Of course, we will. I'm not sure we will be back for Christmas though. The winter in the south of France may suit mother better. She's feeling the cold nowadays - aren't you, Mother?'

'Only on account on the Dower Lodge being a draughty old place,' she grumbled.

'You know you are welcome to live with us in the manor, Mother,' Peter said.

'I know, son, but this is *your* home now. I lived here long enough. I am rather looking forward to rattling around Carole's château.'

'I'm sure you'll enjoy it.'

'Of course, she will, and she'll be a welcome visitor to my home.' Carole kissed her brother warmly and whispered, 'Unlike the one you have in your attic at the moment,' she whispered in Peter's ear. 'If I can give you some advice - get rid of Justin as soon as you can, otherwise he'll settle here permanently and leach you dry.'

'Don't be ridiculous. Justin can stay as long as he wants. He is Sarah's brother and has no need of anything from me. He's a wealthy man in his own right.'

'So he says,' she said darkly.

Peter smiled inwardly, realising his sister was still smarting at Justin's rebuff of her. It took a brave man to put Carole in her place, and she didn't like failing to get what she wanted.

Carole moved to kiss Sarah lightly on the cheek – there had always been a marked coolness between the sister-in-laws, and it felt more so now.

'Have a safe journey,' Sarah said, fighting to keep the elation from her voice. She had had more than enough of Carole's interference in the running of her house and the way she treated her servants.

'Don't you forget what I told you about how to deal with the staff, Sarah,' she said in clear earshot of everyone. 'You are far too lenient with them. They will cheat you and steal from you if you don't treat them more severely. They're not friends, you know?'

Sarah shot her a sharp look. 'I beg to differ, Carole. I am friends with everyone in the household, which makes it a happy home for all.' *Unlike when you held the household purse.* 'My household are loyal and wonderful, and I am very happy with the way my house is run, Carole. Ruby and Joe take the upmost pride in keeping this manor ship-shape.'

'There you go again. You should not be using their Christian names - you will give them airs and graces and they will think they are on your level.'

Sarah laughed incredulously. 'They *are* on my level, as you call it.'

'Oh, I give up!' Carole shook her head. 'Don't say I didn't warn you. Peter, you really need to speak to your wife.'

'And you need to keep a civil tongue in your head,' Peter hissed.

'Children, stop this at once,' the Dowager Countess warned.

'We are not children anymore, Mother,' Peter snapped.

'Then cease acting like children! This is no way to say goodbye.'

'Sorry, Mother,' Peter and Carole muttered in unison.

The Dowager looked at Sarah for *her* apology, but she was too angry to give her that satisfaction, merely nodding instead.

'Well, we'll be off then.' The Dowager led Carole to the car.

'Good riddance,' Sarah said under her breath. Behind her, Joe and Ruby gave a hint of a smile.

Peter watched as the car pulled off up the drive and came back to kiss Sarah.

'Let's hope Carole doesn't visit again too soon,' he whispered, and Sarah's heart went out to her husband for supporting her.

*

Justin was in the kitchen, enjoying a mug of coffee and a slice of cake, when everyone filed back indoors.

'Has she gone?' he asked - his eyes fixed firmly on Ruby.

'Yes,' Ruby answered happily, suddenly feeling very hot under his gaze.

'And with a flea in her ear,' Dorothy grinned and Mary

sniggered.

'Dorothy!' Ruby warned. 'That's enough.'

'Ah, I wish I'd been there then.' Justin raised his mug.

Joe cleared his throat. 'Is there anything else we can get you, Mr Devereux,' he said, trying to steer the conversation away, before anyone said anything else derogatory about the Countess de Auberive.

'No thank you, only that you call me Justin, *please*.' He grinned as he put the last bit of cake in his mouth and drained his cup. 'I will leave you good people to your work. I too have work to do. If I may, I'll see you all at tea-time?' He winked.

*

A few minutes after Justin left, Jim Riley, the leather maker, came into the kitchen to present Betsy with an oversized boot for her to wear. It had a thick sole for walking outdoors and was the ugliest thing she had ever seen, but oh, she was so grateful for it.

Betsy clasped her hands together gleefully. 'At last, I can go outside! I feel like I've been cooped up like a caged lion since I trapped my foot!'

'Talking of which, Betsy,' Joe said brightly, 'Ryan Penrose who rescued you, has got a job interview with the thatcher, Guy Blackthorn, down at Poldhu. Her ladyship organised it for him.'

'Oh, how wonderful, I hope he is successful,' Betsy exclaimed, but as she said it, Juliet emitted a small cry, thus making both Betsy and Joe turn to her questioningly.

'Does the news of Ryan moving away upset you, Juliet?' Joe asked cautiously, unsure if he wanted to know or not.

Juliet blanched. 'Goodness no! I had a twinge of pain that's all,' she lied as she touched her forehead.

For reasons neither of them understood, Joe and Betsy did not believe her.

12

Betsy donned her over-boot and walked around the kitchen – the new leather squeaking as she moved about. It was her half day off, and as the weather was fine and dry, she was determined to get out in the fresh air to see how far the harvesters had progressed. With her hair unpinned from the tight chignon she normally wore, she allowed it to fall down her back in a waterfall of curls - with the exception of the sides, which she'd combed up to tie at the back with a ribbon. Wearing a heavy cotton blue skirt and white blouse, she pulled on her jacket - a garment she later wished she'd left at home when she realised how warm the September sunshine was.

As she stood by the stables surveying the fields that had been harvested, white fluffy clouds scudded across the cobalt blue sky, and wisps of hair streamed around her face in the warm breeze. Taking a deep breath, she marvelled at how good it felt to be outside again. She could see that all but one of the fields had been harvested and that was the wheat field, where she'd caught her foot – it was the biggest field on the estate.

'Where are the harvesters working, Mr Parson?' she asked the estate steward.

'With the barometer set fair, and the harvesters having worked from early dawn till dusk every day, they've been given this afternoon off to rest,' he told her. 'Tomorrow will be a long, hard day for them!'

Betsy knew that all the local children would be given a day off school to help with their last day of harvest, and preparations were well underway in the Bochym kitchen for a harvest picnic at noon tomorrow, followed by a harvest supper at the end of day. A huge pig was being prepared on the spit for the hog roast and there would be music and dancing followed by copious amounts of cider and ale to herald the end of the Bochym harvest

Betsy left Mr Parson to walk down to the stile to the

field where she had had her accident. It was as beautiful as always, though she trembled at the thought of what might lie in the depths of the long swaying wheat. The path peripheral to the field was stark with stubbles of wheat stalks, where a couple of feet had already been scythed ready to allow the horses to drag the threshing machine through the next day. Betsy consciously kept to this path as she set off in the direction of the woods. She was on a mission, hoping to come across Ryan, to thank him for rescuing her. If all the harvesters had been given the afternoon off, there was a good chance she might come across him. She'd heard that he was living rough in the woods, apparently making his home under the tarpaulin of the wood store. It was a place Betsy knew well, as she'd often walked past it on her way down to Poldhu, and even sheltered there on occasions when she'd been caught in a downpour. Having picked her way through the twiggy undergrowth – somewhat difficult to negotiate with her big boot - she was relieved when she stepped onto the smoother ground of the glade where the wood shelter was situated.

The sight before her shocked her to the core, and brought her to a sudden halt. There he was – naked, swilling his body with a pail of water. Having never seen a man without clothes before, Betsy felt momentarily breathless. She watched only for a moment as the water trickled from his hair in rivulets down his back, and then very tentatively started to step back in order to leave, cringing when her foot broke a twig. Ryan stopped his ablutions, but did not look around - instead, he reached for his threadbare towel and wrapped it around his waist.

'If you'll give me a moment, I'll make myself decent,' he said.

Betsy didn't know which way to turn - should she walk quickly away, pretending she'd not been there, or seen anything? But it was too late – before he'd walked into his shelter, he had turned and seen her.

'Will you wait?' he asked looking straight at her.

'Yes,' she answered tremulously. She clasped her hand to her face when she felt a flush rise. *What on earth would she say to him?* He was gone no more than two minutes, before he emerged dressed in dark trousers, a shirt and braces and boots, albeit without the laces done. His blond, wet curls hung about his shoulders, leaching dark patches onto his shirt - which Betsy thought needed a good laundering. Remarkably he showed no embarrassment at being caught in a state of undress, or made any initial comment about it as he beckoned her forward.

'I'm so sorry to intrude,' she said, as she neared him, suddenly aware of the aroma of Pears soap - the type used by Her Ladyship!

'You're not intruding,' he said smiling warmly. 'I'm glad to see you looking so well.'

Betsy nodded shyly. 'I was in rather a state last time I saw you. I came to thank you for your kindness.'

'I was happy to help,' he smiled gently. 'Your foot – it mended well?'

'It's still a little sore, and I can't get my proper boot on my foot yet, but Mr Riley kindly made me this over-boot - though I'm not sure it will grace any fashion magazines!' She turned her foot this way and that. 'At least it gives me the freedom to walk outside at last,' she added brightly.

'I was really worried about you – I understand you suffered a fever shortly after.' His eyes and voice were sympathetic.

'I did, yes – I was a little poorly for a day or so,' she said wondering who had told him.

'I'm really sorry.'

'You have nothing to be sorry about, Mr Penrose.'

He hummed in his throat, and for a moment could not look her in the eye. 'I have *everything* to be sorry about - I set the trap you were caught in, you see.'

'What?' She stepped back horrified.

'I'm so dreadfully sorry, but I cannot let you go on

thinking that I'm some sort of hero – I'm not. But I'm grieved beyond belief that you were caught in it.'

Betsy was quite literally stunned into silence. To think of the pain and discomfort she'd endured, only to find the man who had rescued her had caused it.

'I fear you must hate me now,' he said downcast.

Betsy remained silent while she continued to process what he'd told her.

'It's no excuse, but I was starving, you see. I'd only eaten blackberries and field mushrooms that week. I'm not used to living off the land. I came across the trap in the woods – it looked like it had been abandoned by some poachers, so I brought it back and sharpened it.' He must have seen her wince at this, because he apologised again. 'I could see rabbits in abundance in the wheat field, and I'd tried without success to snare them, so I set the trap. I hadn't seen anyone walking in that field before, so I thought it was safe. I cannot tell you how sorry I am – I'm ashamed of myself.'

Betsy put her hand to her heart, but still could not speak. He had risked everything by telling her this – she could have him prosecuted for it if she so pleased.

'Please, forgive me?'

Betsy nodded. 'I do forgive you, Mr Penrose. I can see how sorry you are, and I thank you for your honesty. Other men would not have been so truthful when they knew how much harm it caused me.'

'I thank you for your forgiveness.' Ryan visibly relaxed. 'I would do anything to right the wrong I've done you.'

'No need. I'll mend. I can also relax now, knowing I can walk through my favourite field without the fear of someone setting another trap.'

'Hand on heart I would never set another trap like that again. I would rather die of starvation next time.'

'Why do you have to forage for your food?'

'I couldn't get work, you see. But I don't have to do it as much at the moment, now I'm working as a harvester –

the pasty at mid-day sustains me.'

Betsy frowned. 'But that's not enough to sustain a hungry man!'

Ryan smiled at her concern. 'I'm managing, don't worry.'

'What did you do before you came here, Mr Penrose - if you don't mind me asking?'

'Let's drop the formalities, shall we? I'm Ryan, and if I may call you by your first name, Betsy I believe?'

Betsy smiled and nodded.

'It's a pretty name.'

'My real name is Elizabeth after my ma, but my pa always called me Betsy, so it stuck – it's a little childish.'

He shook his head. 'It's lovely. As I say, it's a pretty name and it suits you. As to your question - I was working in a boatyard for a couple of years.'

She tipped her head. 'What brought you over here?'

'I,' he hesitated for a moment, 'I fancied being nearer the sea. I thought, hoped, there might be something here at the manor after the harvest. Fortunately, the Countess de Bochym seems to have taken pity on me and has actually arranged for me to see about a job!'

'Yes, we've heard talk up at the manor that you're going to see Guy Blackthorn about some work.'

'Do you know Guy Blackthorn then?'

'I do - my friend, Jessie was married to his brother, Silas.'

'Was?'

'Silas died a couple of weeks back in a shooting incident?'

'Oh, yes, I've heard about that. My goodness - your friend must be devastated.'

'Ah, well, that's a long story. Jessie was estranged from Silas and has moved away to London since. It was *her* letter I was reading when I stepped on the trap – the letter you so kindly brought back for me.'

'What's this Guy Blackthorn fellow like?'

'Guy is a nice man, but by all accounts, he's naturally devastated by what has happened. I should think you will be filling his brother's place in the thatching business. It might be best not to mention my friend Jessie to Guy when you see him. I believe he hasn't taken too kindly to the fact that Jessie left so soon after Silas was killed.'

'Thank you. I'm glad you told me. I might have said something out of turn and scuppered my chances of a job - if he's happy with me.'

'I'm sure he'll be very happy with you,' she said smiling shyly, as she glanced around the encampment. 'Hopefully then you will be able to move somewhere more suitable. The autumn and winter will be on us before we know it. I don't think you'll be very comfortable here then!'

'That is my intention. Forgive me, Betsy, I haven't been able to go shopping so I have nothing to offer you to eat or drink, or indeed somewhere to sit I'm afraid. Oh, wait!' He picked up a dish of blackberries and held it out to her, 'I have these if you care to share them with me.'

'Oh, no, Ryan. You shouldn't be eating blackberries after St Michaelmas day.'

'Why?' he laughed, 'because the devil has taken possession of them?'

'Exactly,' she put her hands on her hips, '*and* he'll have poisoned them!'

'I don't believe in that old wives' tale, and I'm happy to go along with picking them until the 10th October - which is the *old* Michaelmas Day. The only reason I'll give up after that is because the fruit gets bitter, mushy and mouldy. Oh, and I do like to leave fruit for the birds to eat their fill before winter sets in.'

There was a slight pause in the conversation, so Betsy said, 'Well, I think I must go, I've probably taken up too much of your time already.'

'Not at all - It's nice to have some company. Let me walk back with you towards the manor - unless you were going on somewhere else.' He bent down to lace his boots.

'No, I admit, I came purely to see you, to thank you.'

'I'm sorry you saw more than you had bargained for then.' He looked up at her and grinned.

Betsy laughed. 'Oh don't - you'll have me blushing again.'

They walked amiably along the edge of the field – enjoying the earthy richness of exposed soil between the stubble, drying in the sun, filling their senses with a calming balm. Birds flocked down, picking the fallen seed off the wheat field, lifting in unison only to settle again as they walked past.

'This is a rare fine estate. Have you lived here long, Betsy.'

'Yes, ten years - since I was eleven. I came as a scullery maid and worked my way up to senior maid.'

They'd arrived at the stile – the same stile he'd sat her on as he climbed over before picking her up again to carry her to the manor. This time he stepped up and held his hand out for her to join him at the top. He then jumped down and turned to help her over. The last step down was a little high and Betsy hesitated as she changed foot so her good one would take the weight of the jump, but before she knew it, he'd clasped his hands about her waist and lifted her down. He held her for a moment, their faces close together - he didn't say anything, he just smiled brightly.

'Thank you.'

'It's always a pleasure to help a lady. I'll leave you here now. I'm going to walk back to Mullion to do some shopping. Will I see you at the harvest picnic tomorrow?'

'Yes of course.'

'Until then,' he bowed courteously and climbed the stile again.

*

Henry Trencrom stood near his hive with his fists thumped into his sides as he watched the interaction between Betsy and that wastrel who lived in the woods.

One of the bees buzzed in his face and he swatted it angrily. He'd have to nip that romance in the bud – Betsy Tamblin was his.

13

As dawn broke on the last day of the harvest at Bochym Manor, Cook and Mary were extra busy making pasties and bread, cutting cheese, and collecting bottles of pickles from the larder, ready to fill the picnic baskets. The weather was dry and sunny - but with a hint of autumn in the air. The last day of harvest was the most looked forward to and often the busiest and longest of all the harvest days, especially as the last field to cut was always the wheat field which was the largest. The children from the local schools had arrived first thing that morning and could be heard laughing and squealing with delight. They would help to carry the ale and water refreshment to the harvesters and help to stack the wheat sheaves after they'd been reaped. Everyone was in a happy mood that day, even in the kitchen Mrs Blair was humming to herself.

*

Peter had finished his breakfast and was about to leave as Justin walked into the French drawing room.

'Busy day?' Justin asked.

'Yes, the last day of the harvest. I always help out.'

'Sounds fun, can I help?'

Peter grabbed one of Justin's hands to inspect it. 'I'm not sure these soft hands will hold up,' he chortled.

'I'll risk it.' Justin pulled his hand away.

'Meet me down in the field behind the boating lake when you've breakfasted then, though you might rue the day you offered.'

Justin rolled his eyes. 'Will you be down there,' Justin asked Sarah as he kissed her on the cheek.

'I will. The whole household will be there at some stage of the day. We have a picnic at noon and a hog roast this evening with dancing to a local fiddle band.'

'Sounds like fun. I enjoy dancing.'

'By the end of the day, you'll be too tired to dance. Harvesting is hard work!'

'I get the distinct impression that you and Peter think I'm not up to anything other than painting pictures!'

Sarah smiled sweetly. 'Only on account that you've looked a little tired since you came.'

'Well, I shall prove you both wrong,' he said adamantly, taking a bite of toast.

'Good for you,' she cheered. 'Just be careful though - I don't want anything to spoil those beautiful artistic hands of yours.'

*

As noon approached, the maids carried the picnic baskets down to the wheat field. A good part of the crop from the edge of the field had been reaped already and the harvesters were moving inwards in a spiral. The maids stood for a few moments enjoying the sunshine, while the workers gathered the wheat, tied them into sheaves, and stood them up against each other to dry out in the mid-day sun.

The outer parts of the field where the horse and reaper could not get to were being scythed by hand, and one of the workers doing this was, to Betsy's delight, Ryan Penrose. He glanced up when he saw the maids' approach, wiped his brow with his sleeve, and then, if Betsy wasn't mistaken, he seemed to wave directly at her, making her tummy all a flutter. His sleeves were rolled up and the shirt on his back was stained dark with perspiration. Betsy smiled, observing him working, enjoying the way his body moved with the gentle scything motion. He looked to be a good, strong worker who never slacked for a second. When she turned towards Juliet – she too was watching Ryan. Betsy felt a pang of unease that she was not the only one sweet on him.

'Betsy! Juliet! Stop daydreaming, and come and help with the picnic,' Ruby scolded.

'Sorry, Mrs Sanders,' they said in unison.

The sun was hot and the air was filled with the sweet fragrance of newly scythed wheat as they laid their tablecloths down and set the harvest picnic out ready. As the island of wheat got smaller, more and more birds and animals hiding within it would emerge. Every now and then a shout would go up when a rabbit or pheasant emerged from the ever-decreasing island of grain. Mr Oliver the gamekeeper was ever ready with his gun, and because of the stubble left from the reaping, the rabbits and hares found their escape difficult, therefore easy prey. There would be many a tasty pot of game cooking in the vicinity over the next few days. The Earl was a fair landowner and the kill would undoubtedly be shared out to the harvesters.

A whistle was blown at mid-day for the men to lay down their tools and make their way to the picnic. Ryan made a beeline to sit beside Betsy and Juliet, but whereas Betsy's stomach was doing somersaults at his presence, Juliet seemed terribly tense to a point that she turned her back on him and concentrated on serving the other men.

*

While Peter made his way to Sarah, who was sitting under the shade of a parasol at the table and chairs set up for them, Justin chose instead to join the other harvesters - namely the ones settled near Ruby. A keen eye would have seen the body language between Justin and Ruby as he sat beside her, but thankfully everyone was more intent on eating and drinking their fill.

Ruby, despite the frisson of pleasure coursing through her body, was deeply aware that sitting in such close proximity to a man such as Justin Devereux, was not the correct protocol for a woman in her position. She made the effort to sit with her back ramrod straight, as prim and proper as possible, whilst trying to keep the conversation with him as neutral as possible - which was difficult with Justin, because he kept asking her searching questions.

'Do you ever let your hair down and relax, Ruby?' he whispered.

'Shush,' her eyes widened as they darted around to see

if anyone had heard, 'you must not ask me such things,' she hissed.

'I only want to know if you'll dance with me tonight at the harvest supper.'

Ruby tipped her head to observe him and her eyes softened. His blond hair was stuck to his face with perspiration and his cheeks were flushed with exertion. More than anything else she wanted to dance with this man, but in truth, she didn't think he would last the rest of the day reaping, never mind dance with her later.

'You may be too exhausted to dance, after a day in the field,' she teased.

'Oh, not you as well! My sister and brother-in-law think I am too weak in limb to do a hard day's work.'

'Sorry,' she smiled, 'but If you're still standing when the music starts up this evening, yes, I will dance with you - but goodness knows what that will do for my reputation here.'

'Your reputation is safe with me,' he said with a raffish grin.

Ruby raised an eyebrow – she very much doubted that statement, nevertheless, an excitement began to swirl inside her

*

Pasties were devoured by the harvesters, washed down with the cider, ale and water the children were pouring from jugs into their waiting mugs. Bread was torn from loaves, and chunks of cheese and crisp apples newly collected from the orchard that morning completed their meal.

When Ryan had his fill of food and drink, he lay back to rest in the sun.

'You make scything look easy,' Betsy said to him.

He lifted himself up onto his elbows. 'If you get the swing right, it is, to a degree, but its tiring work. After the first full day of harvest the muscles on my arms seemed to swell to twice their size - I could hardly lift them the next day,' he laughed gently.

'I'd love to have a go,' Betsy said brightly.

'Well, I'll show you if you want.'

'Oh, no, Ryan, you need your rest.'

'No really,' he sat up straight, 'come with me up to that edge there, where I was working and I'll show you how to do it, it's really not difficult.'

'I bet she can't do it,' a harvester nearby joked as he puffed on his pipe.

'I say anyone can do it - if they're shown the correct way,' Ryan parried.

There was a ripple of laughter from the other harvesters.

'Come on, Betsy - let's show them what you're made of.' He stood up and held his hand out to her.

Betsy laughed with delight, but hesitated and glanced over at Ruby.

'Mrs Sanders, do you mind if Mr Penrose shows me how to scythe?' She waited a moment, but Ruby seemed not to have heard, so engrossed was she in something Justin was saying to her. Betsy glanced back at Ryan and shrugged. 'I can't go without Mrs Sander's permission.'

'Mrs Sanders?' Ruby looked startled to find Ryan looking down at her. 'Forgive me, but I'd like to show Betsy how to scythe, if that's all right with you?'

Ruby's eyes darted between Ryan and Betsy. 'Oh, um, I don't know…'

'Let her have a go,' Justin whispered to her.

'Very well then,' Ruby said slightly flustered, 'but stay where you can both be seen, and Betsy, don't injure yourself again!'

'Yes, no misbehaving in the long grass,' one of the harvesters joked.

Fortunately, Betsy didn't see the raised eyebrows from the other harvesters when she walked over to where Ryan had been working.

Ryan pulled a stone sharpener from his back pocket,

sharpened the blade of his scythe and then showed Betsy how to hold the scythe. There were hoots and whistles when Ryan stood behind her, his arms slipping down hers to put her hands in the correct position.

'Ignore them, Betsy,' he whispered. 'Right, every swing of the scythe begins with a smooth draw back and to the side - loading energy in your body like a spring.' He showed her how to pull back and Betsy swallowed hard trying to concentrate on the task in hand while enjoying the closeness of his hot body to hers as he showed her the action.

'As the scythe swings back around, it slips behind each stem, effortlessly sliding across through the stems of the wheat?' He guided her with a single, smooth swing of the scythe and almost a five-foot strip of wheat was severed, dropped and left in a neat pile - heads on one end and cut stems on the other. 'There, see, it's easy - now you try it.'

He moved away from her, but loosening his hands on hers pulled her out of the correct position. He stepped back to her for a moment to position her again, and then stepped away as she swung the scythe through the next five foot of wheat. A round of applause came from the harvesters watching, and Betsy stood back to admire her work.

'Well done - you just need to sweep it a bit lower to the ground next time and we'll be recruiting you to help us finish.'

Flushed with elation, Betsy walked back to the others to another round of applause. When she sat back down, Mary, Dorothy and Izzy patted her on the back, Juliet however, could barely hide her consternation, which renewed Betsy's thoughts that Juliet might be sweet on Ryan. From her initial elation, Betsy's euphoria fell, thinking she might have a rival in love. Typical – she'd waited all these years for someone to pique her interest romantically, only to be thwarted by a younger, much prettier maid.

*

Once the picnic had been devoured and the harvesters had gone back to work, the staff returned to the manor to get on with their everyday tasks. Mrs Blair had more pasties to make, while Mary was kneading the dough to make enough bread to feed the army of workers. The gamekeeper and the steward had set up the hog roast in front of the entrance to the parterre garden earlier that morning and the smell of roasting pork permeated the air, teasing everybody's taste buds.

Joe and Thomas had set up trestle tables on the front lawn and Ruby had draped them with white tablecloths. The local school girls settled at the tables to busy themselves making corn dollies to dress the supper tables. Mr Oliver, Mr Hubbard and Lyndon FitzSimmons had collected hay bales from the barn, to act as seats, the residue of which, Mr Hubbard the gardener despaired of - as bits of straw would blow around the manicured lawns and flower borders for days after the supper!

The smell of the hog roast attracted Henry Trencrom from where he'd been idling near his hives.

'What time is this supper then?' he asked Mr Hubbard.

'What's it to you? You're not invited.'

Trencrom scowled. 'Well, I was led to believe everyone was invited.'

'Everyone who helped with the harvest and the setting up of the supper are invited.'

'Well, no one told me to help!' he said indignantly.

'We, who do a proper job on the estate, don't need to be told when help is needed,' Mr Hubbard snapped and then turned on his heel to walk away.

*

An hour before the last sheath of wheat was cut and the Crying of the Neck would be sounded, Betsy and Juliet were busy filling jugs of cider, mead, ale, and barley water from the barrels, ready for the evening. There was a marked reserve between the two women that Betsy needed to get to the bottom of.

'Juliet?'

Seemingly startled at hearing her name, Juliet looked up

'Sorry, I didn't mean to make you jump. I just wondered what you thought of Mr Penrose.'

'What do you mean?'

'You know - do *you* like him?'

'I don't dislike him.'

'It's just that….I really like him,' Betsy said tentatively.

'I think you've made that quite obvious today.'

Betsy felt her cheeks pink. 'I'll not let my feelings go any further for him if they conflict with yours.' Whilst her cheeks burned, Juliet's face paled.

'I..I don't know what you mean,' Juliet said stiffly.

'I don't want us to fall out over him.'

'Betsy, there is really nothing to speak about here,' she sniffed dismissively, picking up a tray full of jugs and walking out of the pantry away from the conversation.

14

At half-past-seven, everyone left the manor to go down to the field to witness the 'Crying of the Neck!'

The hog roast now produced a deeply delicious smell of hot crackling, which wafted temptingly into the fields beyond, making stomachs rumble as everyone gathered around the Earl and the last handful of standing wheat.

There was much anticipation when Peter cut it down, lifted the bunch high above his head and called out, 'I 'ave 'un! I 'ave 'un! I 'ave 'un!'

Everyone cheered and shouted, 'What 'ave 'ee? What 'ave 'ee? What 'ave 'ee?'

'A neck! A neck! A neck!' Peter called.

Again, everyone joined in, 'Hurrah! Hurrah for the neck! Hurrah for the Earl de Bochym!'

The neck of wheat was tossed into the waiting horse drawn wagon, which had been decorated with ribbons and flowers, while everyone gathered their belongings and followed it happily, though a little wearily to where the tables were laid out in front of the manor.

Ryan fell into step with Betsy as they walked back, and then remembered he'd forgotten his jacket! She held back from the others to wait for him, but Trencrom stepped out of the shadows. For a moment, with the fading light, Betsy struggled to see who it was, but when she heard his voice, her skin crawled.

'Why have you not been to see me, Betsy Tamblin?' he said grabbing her by the arm.

Betsy shrieked, but everyone had drifted too far away to hear her.

'Get off me!' she said, through gritted teeth. With a sharp pull, she wrenched her arm away - almost falling backwards.

He grabbed her again. 'I've been waiting for an answered to my proposal.'

Suddenly, Ryan's hand came from nowhere and

clamped it around Trencrom's wrist with such force, that Trencrom winced audibly.

'Leave her be,' Ryan said quietly and Betsy felt Trencrom's grip on her arm loosen.

When Trencrom saw who it was, he pulled his fist back to thump him.

'Oh, no, you don't!' Ryan, being younger and more powerful, shoved Trencrom to the ground and put his foot on his neck. 'I'll give you one warning only. I could not retaliate last time you threw a thump at me, but if you *ever* raise your fist to me again, I swear you'll be on liquids for the rest of your life, because I'll knock every single one of your rotting teeth out of your measly mouth.' He pressed his boot down until Trencrom gagged, before releasing him and walking away with Betsy.

'I'm sorry you saw that, Betsy. I'm not a violent man, but I'll not let another thump from him go unanswered.'

'Don't apologise, I'm thankful to you. He's a horrible man, who's got it into his head that I'll marry him for god's sake!'

'Do you want me to warn him off from bothering you - because I will?'

'No, I don't want you to get into any trouble with anyone on the estate - not now Her Ladyship has put a good word in for you with Guy Blackthorn. Come on - let's forget about him, the music has started.'

*

Trencrom scrambled to his feet, clutching his hand to his neck - the bastard had almost choked him! Despite the warning, he'd bloody well show him one day not to poke his nose into his affairs. He gave a low growl as he watched them walk off together. He'd get a favourable answer out of that wench if it killed him. He needed to wed Betsy and fast, to secure that vacant tied cottage on the estate, and her apathetic feelings towards him would not sway him from his mission. He'd change tack - woo her with flowers - or whatever silly women needed to be wooed with, but he *would* wed her! He picked up his hat which had fallen into the dusty field and brushed it down. His lip curled derisively, one thing was certain, as soon as they were wed, he'd beat any trace of apathy out of her should it rear its ugly head again! He felt a stirring in his groin at the thought of beating her. Just to lift that petticoat and slap the bare skin on her behind until it was raw excited him beyond belief. His tongue flicked in and out of his lips as he rubbed his trousers - by god but he needed to settle things with her sooner rather than later.

*

While a small group of musicians played their merry tunes, Mrs Blair carved slices of juicy pork onto the plates the maids were holding. Within the hour, the fatigue and aching bones of the day were pushed aside and the dancing started.

The first to get up and dance was Lyndon FitzSimmons, sending Mary, Dorothy and Izzy into a frenzy to partner him – all no doubt hoping to change his mind about the girl he intended to marry.

Juliet watched as Ryan asked Betsy to dance, and was relieved when she had to decline because of her foot. *Oh Juliet,* she berated herself for being so possessive of Ryan, but if his attention was diverted elsewhere, what would happen then?

*

Betsy was happy. She'd been sitting with Ryan during supper and he'd been extremely attentive to her. He'd even given her a present - a royal blue ribbon for her hair! They had spoken of things she loved to do, walking and enjoying nature, and Betsy felt she had found a kindred spirit in him – someone who could fill the void left by the departure of her friend Jessie. When the music started, although her foot rendered it impossible to dance with Ryan, she watched happily as he danced with the other maids, aware that all the while, he kept looking back to smile at her.

Betsy knew that Juliet had been watching their interaction most of the evening, and believed her friend did not look too favourably on it. If only Juliet would admit that she was interested in Ryan, then Betsy would of course put a stop to these growing feelings she was having for him – if she could! Having said that, Ryan was not showing any preference to Juliet! One thing for sure, if Juliet didn't declare herself soon, it would be too late, because Betsy was in great danger of falling very much in love with Ryan. Betsy was pondering on this happy thought when she heard Juliet shriek behind her. She turned to see Juliet trying to deflect the advances of one of the harvesters who wanted to dance with her.

'Mr Treen,' Betsy shouted over to Joe who was toe tapping to the music, and alerted him to Juliet's plight. He got up in a shot to go to her aid. Betsy hoped that that his intervention might just show Juliet how much Joe cared for her, and was prepared to defend her, and yes, she knew she was matchmaking for her own sake. If Juliet and Joe could find a way to each other - that would pave the way for Betsy to follow her heart.

*

Every nerve in Juliet's body stood alert as she tried to deflect the unwanted advances of the man trying to make her dance. Panic rose, and her eyes locked with Ryan's who was dancing with Izzy. She saw him stop in the middle of the jig, prepared to come to her aid, but then Joe stepped in to help and Ryan stood down.

Thankfully, Joe had put his hand on the man's arm who was trying, without success, to pull Juliet away from her seat, and when the next man approached to ask her, Joe stood firmly in his way, stating that Juliet was tired and didn't want to dance.

'Are you quite well, Juliet?' Joe asked softly. 'You look rather uncomfortable.'

'I'm well, Mr Treen. I know I'm making a fuss, but I don't dance. I prefer to watch.'

'That's fine, Juliet. If you'll permit me, I'll stay to stop anyone bothering you.'

'Thank you, Mr Treen.' Juliet relaxed, glanced at Ryan, who was still watching her, and they nodded to each other. Unfortunately, a moment later someone called Joe away to deal with a broken trestle table leg, and he had to leave his seat. In a matter of seconds, Juliet's heart began to pound again when another of the harvesters advanced on her, taking umbrage when she shrank away from his hand, and began to beckon her more strongly, eventually grasping her arm. She glanced around for someone to help, but no one was watching. Filled with horror at his touch, she pulled violently away from him, and scrambled towards the open front door to make her escape. Joe must have seen her run, because she could hear him calling her name, but she'd escaped to her bedroom. Slamming the door behind her, she flung herself on the bed and wept pitifully, wondering now if every day, even days as joyous as this, was going to be such a struggle from now on?

*

After a thorough search of the house, Joe stepped out into the kitchen courtyard and looked up at the soft light flickering in Juliet's bedroom. Feeling relief and heavy-hearted in equal measure, he returned to join the harvest supper. He'd harboured the hope that a gathering such as this, with drink, food and dancing would have brought Juliet out of the shell she had disappeared into. His hope was for her to relax enough so they might return to a more friendly footing with each other, but she seemed so highly strung nowadays, no one could get near her. He glanced at Ruby, sitting alone - she seemed to be enjoying the fiddle music, though perhaps a little preoccupied with something – whatever, he decided to ask her to dance.

*

Ruby sat tapping her foot to the fiddle, occasionally glancing around for any sight of Justin, but he was nowhere to be seen. The Earl and Countess were sat at their own table, but Justin's chair remained vacant for the duration of the supper – so much for his wanting to dance with her! Ah well, such is life as she knew it. Dancing with handsome artists was not for dowdy housekeepers! She looked up and smiled when Joe approached her.

'Would you care to dance?'

'Oh, yes, please, Joe,' she took his hand, 'I thought nobody would ever ask me,'

*

Justin had had every intention of dancing with Ruby when he'd wearily climbed the stairs after the harvest. He was sore, and tired of limb, but a hot bath would surely take the strain of the day away. It seemed though that Sarah and Peter had been correct in their assumption - he was not built for a hard day's manual work, because no sooner had he dried himself after his bath, and despite the music and laughter from below his bedroom window, he'd fallen fast asleep atop of the eiderdown.

*

When the supper came to an end, the plates and cutlery were cleared, as were the tablecloths. The crockery was put into the great Belfast sink in the scullery to soak overnight, and the tablecloths were piled up for Izzy to work her magic on removing countless greasy stains from the linen. The tables were left to be moved first thing in the morning – the most important thing was for everyone to go to bed happy after the harvest supper. In truth, out of Ruby, Juliet, Joe and Betsy, only the latter climbed into bed truly happy that night. Ryan had taken Betsy's hand in his and brought it to his lips as he bid her goodnight. The kiss, she hoped, was the start of something a whole lot more. She glanced at Juliet sound asleep, unaware that her friend had cried herself into that state, or why she'd left the party so early. Turning the oil lamp off, she fetched the image of Ryan to the forefront of her mind and whispered happily, 'Goodnight, Ryan.'

*

Ruby lay awake listening to the creaks and groans of a house settling down to sleep - disappointment lay heavy on her heart. Whereas she had dismissed Justin's absence from the harvest supper as nothing more than a silly misplaced romantic notion that a man was actually interested in her, her mind would not stop running through the conversation in the hay field. She couldn't help but feel a little put out that he'd played with her affections and then let her down. She turned on her side, plumped the pillow up, and sighed, *for goodness' sake, Ruby stop acting like a lovesick schoolgirl.*

*

A slow, creeping darkness loomed in Juliet's dream. She curled her hands into a tight fist as the familiar visceral sense of foreboding cloaked her body. Her mouth dried as an empty loneliness engulfed her, dragging her deep into a dark despair. 'No, no,' she tried to scream, but no sound came. Still the horror came towards her – dark, filthy hands, grabbing and tearing her clothes. 'No, get off, get off me,' she screamed as she struggled and pushed herself away from her tormentor.

*

Betsy woke with a start, hearing Juliet cry out, and blinked into the darkness. She fumbled to light the oil lamp, but when she'd touched Juliet to see what was the matter, Juliet screamed, scrambled towards the headboard, curled herself into a ball, and began shaking like a leaf. Her eyes look wild and her mouth open and closed like a fish out of water.

'Juliet, what is it – what's frightened you?' Betsy said, unsure of whether to touch her again or not.

Juliet's eyes scanned the room, making Betsy uneasy.

'What have you seen, Juliet?' she asked tentatively, the hairs on the back of her neck rising at the thought of any ghostly goings on.

Juliet's gaze settled back on Betsy and then she burst into tears.

Climbing onto the bed with her, Betsy gathered her

into her arms.

'Don't cry – it was just a bad dream, that's all. I'm here, you're safe now.'

While Juliet trembled violently in her arms, Betsy wondered if any of the household had heard the scream - but no one came.

When eventually Juliet calmed, she whispered, 'Thank you, Betsy.'

'You're welcome. Do you want me to sleep with you?'

'No, I'll be all right now – as you say it was just a dream.'

'Can you remember it?'

'No!' she answered sharply.

'That's good.' Betsy got off the bed and beckoned Juliet to lie back down. She tucked her in as a mother would do a child. 'Shall we leave the light on?'

'No,' she said more softly, 'I'll be fine now.'

15

Justin woke with a start the morning after the harvest supper when Thomas came in to open his curtains. Shivering, he realised he was still atop of the bed with only a towel draped over his modesty.

He tried to sit up and groaned audibly. 'Oh, god, Thomas, help me up, will you? I feel as though I've been run over by the wheels of a carriage. Every single muscle in my body is protesting.'

Thomas pulled him up off the bed. 'I'll run another hot bath for you, and pop some Epson's Salts in it. That should do the trick!'

'Thank you, I think it might. I take it you all had a good harvest supper? How is your head this morning?'

Thomas winced. 'A little worse for wear - I have to admit.'

'I'll be mindful not to call on your time too much today then.' He winked.

As he soaked his aching body in the hot water, he thought of Ruby and hoped she hadn't been too upset that he'd failed to fulfil his commitment to dance with her. He would have to find a way of apologising to her today.

After a leisurely breakfast, deflecting his brother-in-law's teasing for going to bed early, Justin settled in the front garden to sketch. All traces of the harvest supper had been cleared away from the front of the house – not even a blade of straw from the bales was evident. After sitting for an hour, he felt his neck stiffen. He stood up and stretched languidly in the late morning sunshine, deciding to take a walk around the parterre to ease the strain from his muscles. Crossing the drive towards the garden entrance, he noticed the familiar figure of Ruby walking up the long drive towards the tradesmen's entrance of the manor. He pushed his hands deep into the pockets of his linen jacket and began to walk up the drive to see where she was heading. By the time he reached the junction in the road from Bochym which joined the main Lizard to Helston road, he could see Ruby standing with a couple of other people. He stood back, resting against a wall and watched until a wagon pulled up. Several people got off and Ruby and the others boarded. He waited until the wagon turned off down another road, before he approached one of the passengers who had just alighted from the wagon.

'Good morning,' he said taking his hat off.

The woman nodded curiously

'Could you tell me where the wagon is going next?'

'Cury, Poldhu and then onto Mullion,' she answered with a nod, and then added, 'There'll not be another one until three this afternoon though I'm afraid. It's a good two miles to Poldhu and another to Mullion if you're to walk it.'

'Thank you, good day to you.' He walked quickly back to Bochym and sought out Joe, to ask if there was a mode of transport he could borrow.

'I can have the carriage fetched around for you. We also have a pony trap, or I could get a groom to saddle one of Her Ladyship's horses. It depends how far you want to go.'

'I thought perhaps Poldhu or Mullion, so the pony trap would suffice.'

'Ah, Ruby has taken herself off to Poldhu. That's a shame, you could have perhaps given her a lift – saved her walking up to the wagon,' he added.

'And what's at Poldhu?' he enquired.

Joe smiled. 'It's a beautiful cove – you're in for such a treat if you've never seen it. There is also a lovely tea room down there.'

'Is that where Ruby was heading to?' he asked nonchalantly.

'I doubt it, she asked Mrs Blair to make up a picnic for her. I must say, and I don't think I'm speaking out of term here, but it's good to see her go out for a change – she so often stays in on her day off.'

*

It was indeed rare for Ruby to wander far from Bochym Manor on her days off, but having watched Justin sketching in the garden these past few days, her fingers were itching to pick up a pencil and go out sketching herself. At school, she'd enjoyed drawing - in fact she'd been quite good at all her studies. Her headmaster had even suggested that if she stayed on at school, she would be able to take up the baton of teaching, but then both she and her dearest school friend, Pearl, lost their parents and siblings to diphtheria and influenza within months of each other. They were only twelve at the time and with no immediate family to take them in - they both had to go into service, so that was the end of that.

Ruby sat on the wagon, excited that she was actually doing something for herself for once. She had on her lap a basket in which Mrs Blair had made her a picnic, with enough food to feed an army!

Ruby had also packed a blanket, her old yellowing drawing book and her watercolour pallet - which had dried almost back to the edges of the squares the colours sat in. Perhaps with a little water she could still get some faded colour from them. She'd sharpened her pencil just in case the colours were too old to use. As she neared Poldhu, a bubble of excitement welled within her. She hoped this day out would take her mind off her disappointment, because no matter how hard she tried to make excuses for Justin, she really felt let down by him. She needed to rid this romantic nonsense she'd conjured in her head, act her age and settle back down to what she knew best – being a housekeeper.

*

Justin pulled the pony trap to a halt at Poldhu Cove and shielded his eyes to scan the beach. Despite it being the 2nd of October, there were several people by the sea. Some were paddling, one or two were picnicking and a man holding onto four scruffy little dogs on a lead was walking along the dunes. The tea room looked busy, but Justin could see no sign of Ruby there. He sighed, if she had been there, what would she think of him following her like this? *Why have you followed her, Justin?* He gave a secret smile, *because I rather like her, that's why.* He glanced up towards the impressive building on the left side of the cove and then to the grassy cliffs to the right, and decided that he rather fancied a walk up there. He noted there was a couple of horse stalls in a stable at the entrance of the beach and assumed they would be something to do with the tea room - perhaps he could settle his horse there so he could take a walk.

*

With the fine weather, the tea room was busy, and all the tables on the veranda were full of people enjoying their cream teas.

Ellie Blackthorn was behind the counter filling a tea pot when the doorbell tinkled. She looked up and smiled at the gentleman who stepped inside and removed his battered fedora hat to acknowledge her.

'Hello. Welcome, please take a seat - I'm afraid we only have tables inside today.'

Justin glanced around the pretty blue and white interior – every table had a crisp white tablecloth and a vase of flowers atop. 'Thank you, I wasn't looking for a table at the moment – I need to stable my horse for an hour or so, so I can explore the cliffs hereabouts. Do the stalls belong to the tea room?'

'They do, but you're welcome to use one if they are vacant,' she said putting the teapot on a tray. 'Are you on holiday - I don't believe we've seen you before?'

'Yes, I'm staying with my sister, Sarah Dunstan.'

'Oh goodness!' Ellie's smile widened as she wiped her hands on her teacloth to come and greet him. 'You must be Justin then? Sarah has told me all about you.' She held her hand out to shake his.

'Has she?' he said taking the offered hand.

'Yes, we're the best of friends. I'm Ellie Blackthorn, Sarah might have mentioned me, although she uses my proper name Elise,' she grinned, 'but you can call me Ellie. I was hoping you would come and see us. Are you sure we can't tempt you with tea?'

'Thank you, not at the moment. I'd rather like to stretch my legs a little.'

'May I suggest you take a walk up to Poldhu Head and over to Church Cove then. On a day such as this, you can see for miles and the sea, well, go and take a look for yourself, it's crystal clear today.'

'It sounds delightful. Is it all right to leave the trap by the stalls too?'

'Absolutely, as long as you promise you'll come back and see us soon.'

'I promise.'

When he'd gone, Meg came out from the kitchen with a tray of cream teas and an enquiring look.

'Who was *that*?'

'Sarah's brother, Justin Devereux.'

'Gosh, he's rather easy on the eye, isn't he?'

'Meg,' Ellie raised an eyebrow, 'shame on you for looking at other men, when you're about to marry Tobias.'

'There's no harm in looking,' Meg said, shimmying outside with her tray.

*

Ruby settled down on the soft mossy cliff top, marvelling at the vista before her. The October sky was a sparkling blue, dazzling to look up at, and the low sun glistened across the sea like an explosion of diamonds. Nearer the rocks, the water was so clear you could see the seabed. It always looked so inviting, but although she knew how to swim, she very rarely got the opportunity to do so. Perhaps she would bring her costume next time. Adjusting her straw hat to shade her eyes, she wondered again why she hadn't spent more time out on these cliffs. There was a whole beautiful coast to explore beyond the boundaries of Bochym Manor. Although she'd visited Poldhu a few times, she'd only ever walked over to Church Cove in the next bay. Glancing down at her heeled boots, she would perhaps need something sturdier though, if she was going to go exploring in the future. As the sun beat down, she shed her jacket and rolled the sleeves up on her white blouse. She was thankful she'd put on a lighter skirt today – her black dress would have been far too warm. She didn't possess many nice clothes – she didn't really need them - she only had this outfit and another skirt and blouse, which she wore if she ever went anywhere nice. With that in mind, she donned an apron, so as not to get paint on her clothes. She felt inwardly amused as she readied herself to paint, wondering what Joe and the maids would think of their housekeeper pretending to be an artist on the Cornish cliffs!

*

A warm, rich gamey aroma filled the Bochym kitchen. Mrs Blair was roasting a pheasant for the family and cooking a rabbit stew for the staff. Mary was setting the table ready for dinner when she alerted Mrs Blair to their unwelcome guest.

Mrs Blair folded her arms over her ample bosoms when Henry Trencrom walked into the kitchen. 'And what's your business here?' she said tapping her foot.

'None of yours,' he parried, looking past her - his eyes scanning the kitchen.

'You're in my kitchen - so it is my business!'

He sighed irritably. 'I want to see Betsy. We have arrangements to make.'

'Well, you'll have a long wait - she's gone out for the day.'

'Where too? It's not her day off!'

'Mind your own business.'

'*I'm trying to, woman!*' he snapped. 'When will she be back?'

Mrs Blair shrugged her shoulders.

'Tell her, I'm looking for her, then.'

'I'm sure she'll be thrilled at that prospect.'

'*Just tell her*,' he growled and stomped off.

Mrs Blair gave it a couple of seconds and shouted, 'He's gone now.'

Betsy emerged pale and wan from where she'd been hiding in the scullery, and watched Trencrom retreat across the courtyard. He was beginning to unnerve her now.

'I suggest you speak to Mr Treen about him!' Mrs Blair offered. 'He'll have him stopped from coming here bothering you.'

Betsy nodded as a curl of unease formed in her tummy. 'I think I'll have to.' The last thing she wanted though was for Ryan to hear that Trencrom was bothering her again, especially after hearing Ryan's threat against him last night. She did not want him to get into trouble on her account.

*

Ruby had been relatively easy to find. Justin had only walked half way up the coast road towards Poldhu Head, before he caught a glimpse of her sitting on the cliff. His heart stilled at the sight of her. Even from where he was standing, some sixty yards away, the sun lit her glossy dark hair, burnishing it with a gold red autumnal halo – no woman had ever captivated him, or excited his artistic tendencies like Ruby had.

He shaded his eyes. She appeared to be writing, or perhaps drawing, and it was then he felt the error of his folly in following her. Because now that he had found her, it didn't seem right to intrude - her personal free time must be at a premium. Fortunately, she seemed quite unaware he was watching her, so he carefully back-tracked a few yards, before settling on the grass. If he didn't feel able to join her, then he would allow himself a few moments to drink in the image of her. Those few moments turned into half-an-hour, before he shook his head. *Enough, Justin, leave her be.* He stood and brushed the grass from the seat of his trousers and continued on the coast road towards Poldhu Head.

*

Lost in her creative world, Ruby had managed to capture Mullion Island in her seascape watercolour, but had struggled with the limited colours her paint pallet offered – most of the bright colours having long since been used. She held the painting out and then rested it on her lap when her stomach gave an involuntary groan of hunger. It was then she saw Justin walking along the coast road with his jacket slung casually over his right shoulder. Her breath caught, and despite her resolve not to think of him again, before she could stop herself, she stood up and called out to him.

16

Ruby's heart accelerated as she stood and quickly brushed down her skirt - generally tidying herself.

'Forgive me for interrupting your walk,' she said shyly as he approached.

'Not at all, I was only on my way to Poldhu Head, but now I find I have a much more pleasant vista to enjoy.'

The smile he gave her dazzled her, and a tiny excited noise escaped her throat.

'Ruby,' he said in earnest, 'forgive me for not turning up to the supper last night. I was overcome with a tiredness I have never known before! I took a bath and fell asleep before I could climb between the covers. I swear I was going to fulfil my obligation to dance with you. Now, I feel you will never give me the chance again.'

Warmed, not only by his presence, but his apology, she smiled. 'You're forgiven, and well, you never know, if you're still at Bochym at New Year, we can dance then.'

His eyes lit. 'Well then, that's a good enough reason to stay.'

She raised an eyebrow. 'I'm heartened that we'll have your company for at least another three months, then.'

'And I'm truly heartened that you think that!' He glanced down to her painting book and smiled. 'Do I detect that you and I share a kindred spirit?'

For a moment, Ruby was unsure as to what he was referring too.

He nodded to her painting. 'It seems you too have artistic tendencies I see.'

'Hardly.' She cleared her throat, closing the page on her little painting.

He knelt to inspect her tin of watercolour paints and raised an eyebrow, at the muddy colours left in it. 'You're either a voracious colourist, or you've found this much-used pallet lurking in some dark forgotten attic.'

Ruby laughed. 'It's the latter - It's what I had at school

many years ago. I just felt like getting it out again today.'

'Pray tell - why has it not seen the light of day since your schooldays. What has stopped you from your art?'

She shrugged. 'Life - death!' Justin tipped his head inquisitively, so she added, 'All my family died when I was twelve. All childhood things were swept away, and I had to grow up very quickly because I was put into service by the authorities.'

'Oh, Ruby,' his face fell, 'I'm sorry you suffered such losses.'

'Well, I was lucky - I had my best friend, Pearl with me. She too suffered the same fate when her family were taken by illness at the same time as mine. We started our working lives together.'

He nodded. 'Good friends are hard to come by. Do you still see Pearl?'

'No, Pearl's story ended very badly,' she answered downcast.

'Oh, dear, I see I've evoked a memory that saddens you, and that is the last thing I want to do on a bright, sunny day like today.'

'You're right - it is not a day to tell tragic stories,' she added. 'I may tell you Pearl's story another day, but for now, I'm just about to open my picnic.'

'Then I'll leave you to your luncheon.'

'Oh, no, you're very welcome to stay. Mrs Blair has made far too much for me, please, stay and join me. I'd like some company - unless of course you need to continue with your walk. Please don't feel obliged.'

Their eyes locked. 'I want to be nowhere, but here, with you, Ruby.'

Ruby's heart shifted, something very wonderful was happening between them.

Ruby found Justin such an easy person to be with. They chatted amiably as they shared the picnic whilst watching the turquoise waves roll onto the golden beach below them. Once the picnic was over, he lazed languidly on the grass while she returned to her painting.

'We'll excite comment you know, if anyone sees us together,' she teased. 'It is quite improper for me to be alone with you.'

'Nonsense! We're family - we live in the same house! Do we not?'

Ruby tipped her head. 'That's not the same thing - and you know it.'

'Do you never do anything improper, Ruby?'

She paused, held her brush mid-air and turned to him. 'What sort of question is that to ask a decent woman?'

He propped himself up on his elbows. 'Sorry, let me rephrase. Do you never throw caution to the wind - let your hair down so the breeze can blow through it?'

Ruby regarded him seriously. 'It's hard for me. I have an important position in a fine house as a housekeeper. It would not do for me to run around with the wind blowing in my hair.'

'That's such a pity, that image would make such a beautiful painting,' he smiled, '*you* would make a beautiful painting.'

And I would lose my station in life, if I let that happen, she thought.

'But surely, you're able to do as you please in your free time. You may be the housekeeper at the manor for six days a week, but you are also a beautiful woman, who needs to feel free for a day.' He got up and moved towards her, crouched down and gazed deep into her eyes.

Ruby felt her heart constrict, wondering what was about to happen.

'I wonder - if you took the pins from your hair now, could you redress it later without a mirror?'

'Perhaps,' she breathed.

'Then let your hair down, Ruby,' he pleaded, 'let me see.'

Her heart began to thrum in her chest as she reached to release the clasp which held the majority of her hair. Her curls tumbled onto her shoulders like falling leaves.

Justin sighed appreciatively as his fingers gently teased her curls out. 'You have the most beautiful hair, Ruby.'

'It's just brown,' she answered trembling under his touch.

'No, it is the colour of autumn. Look,' he lifted the cascade of curls to let the sun shine through them, 'It's a kaleidoscope of gold and red.'

Ruby looked down at her hair in his hand hardly daring to breathe.

'May I beg a page from your drawing book - and with your permission, may I sketch you? You are truly a sight to behold!'

*

After the busy previous day, the kitchen at Bochym had returned to its normal routine. It was the hour before teatime and Betsy was pretending to read her book at the kitchen table, whilst keeping one curious eye on Juliet's basket as she set off across the courtyard on her daily egg collecting spree.

'I think I'll get a little fresh air before tea, Mrs Blair,' she said pulling the over-boot over her bandaged foot.

'Well, you mind that foot of yours. You did a lot of walking yesterday – we don't want you injuring yourself again.'

Betsy skirted the drive, which led from the manor to the Dower Lodge, and stopped just before the boating lake to scan the fields and gardens for Juliet. She was determined to find out what she was doing with the food she pilfered from the storeroom every day. She had just about given up searching, when she spotted Juliet emerging from the hay barn, and to her dismay, Ryan followed her out of the building. Betsy felt a sudden prickle of unease. So, they *were* together, and Ryan had played her along like the fool she was! Biting her lip to stop it trembling, she watched miserably as they exchanged a few words before parting company. Fortunately, there was no visible embrace or kiss as lovers would do - perhaps they had made their loving gestures inside the hay barn, she thought sadly. Betsy turned on her heel, and in her haste to avoid being seen, she almost tripped over a fallen branch.

'Are you all right there, Betsy?' Lyndon Fitzsimmons caught her as she stumbled. 'I'm on my way to tea, so let me escort you back to the kitchen.' He held his arm out for her to take, which she did willingly. She wasn't going to pass up on the chance of taking the arm of a handsome man, such as Lyndon's - even though she knew his heart was elsewhere. It was probably going to be the only time she'd get a chance to link arms with a man again!

'Goodness, but there's a chill in the air now, don't you think?' Lyndon said. 'Look, there's a thick sea mist rolling up Poldhu valley now.'

Betsy glanced at the vaporous mist entwining the top branches of the trees flanking the hills towards the coast. She shivered, but it wasn't just the change in weather that had made her feel cold.

*

Henry Trencrom fumed. He'd watched and waited diligently for Betsy to walk down the tradesmen's drive - back from wherever she'd been, but she never appeared. Now, there she was, taking the arm of that hedger fellow! Not only had cook lied to him about Betsy being out, but now there was another man sniffing around his intended. Well, he was not having anyone else queering his pitch. Betsy was his and he was hell bent on satisfaction.

*

At Poldhu, it was Ruby who first aw the bank of mist rolling in from Land's End, because Justin was so engrossed sketching. She'd felt unnerved at first to be so constantly scrutinised, but every exchanged glance between them brought a quiver of something she had never felt before – desire.

'I think our lovely day is to be ruined with a sea mist,'

she said.

'Mmm?' he answered nonchalantly as his pencil scratched at the paper.

'The weather, it's changing - and not for the better. We're going to be engulfed in fog very soon if we don't pack up now.'

Justin followed her gaze. 'Oh! I see!' He quickly folded his sketch, put it in his pocket and scrambled to help Ruby pack her basket.

At first it was a fine mist which curled into the mouth of the cove, but was swiftly followed by a dense bank of fog which quickly obscured the cliff where they'd been sitting.

'Quick, we need to get off this cliff and back onto the road before we lose our footing. By the way - what time is it?' she asked, having given no thought before of how long she'd been here with him.

Justin reached for his pocket watch. 'Half-past-four.'

'Oh no! I'll have missed the wagon to Cury Cross Lanes. It'll take forever to walk home in this fog.'

'Don't upset yourself, Ruby. I have the Bochym pony and trap waiting at the tea room.'

Ruby felt relieved and concerned in equal measure at this news. 'But I can't arrive home with you! What will everyone say?'

'They'll be thankful that I've safely delivered their much-loved housekeeper back through the fog. Now come on.' He picked up her basket and took hold of her hand as they picked their way up the cliff towards the path. Never had Ruby been so relieved to put her feet on the hard ground of the road. She'd thought that once they'd found sound footing, Justin would let go of her hand, but as the fog was so thick - and they could barely see a foot in front of them - he held on tightly as they walked slowly down the road towards the tea room. They were both soaked through and shivering by the time Justin had harnessed the pony to the trap.

'I'm just going to the tea room to see if I can borrow a lantern and a blanket,' he said helping Ruby up onto the trap.

*

Ellie was sweeping the tea room floor when Justin came arrived.

She leant on the broom and said, 'Of course we'll lend you the things you need, but goodness gracious, you can't travel in this weather!'

'I fear we must. I've Mrs Sanders with me. I encountered her on the cliff path, and she must return to the manor this evening, otherwise a search party will be sent!'

They both turned when the doorbell tinkled.

'My goodness, it's like pea soup out there! And there is a pony trap outside the stables,' Guy Blackthorn said as he walked into the tea room

'Hello darling,' Ellie kissed her husband. 'The trap belongs to Bochym – this is Sarah's brother, Justin Devereux.'

'Oh, I see. Guy Blackwell, I'm very pleased to meet you.'

As they shook hands, Ellie said, 'Mr Devereux needs to borrow a couple of lanterns and a blanket to get Mrs Sanders home to the manor.'

Guy raised an eyebrow but Ellie gave a warning look not to read too much into the scenario.

'I'll go and fetch them,' he said, 'but you're going to have a difficult journey back. We can accommodate you both if you need to stay - you'll be very welcome.'

Ellie felt heartened at Guy's offer. He'd been swimming in the doldrums of grief, and his offer gave her a glimpse of the charitable man she knew and loved.

Justin smiled gratefully. 'I thank you for your offer, but Mrs Sanders is keen to get home so the household doesn't fret about her.'

*

With a lantern hung each side of the trap and a warm blanket each, the pony readied itself to take the first tentative steps through the fog.

'Go careful now,' Ellie said pushing a couple of warm pasties into Ruby's basket to eat on the way.

'Thank you. You've both been very kind,' Ruby said.

It was a long, slow, laborious journey home, coupled with periods of high anxiety as other ghostly modes of transport appeared suddenly out of the fog and just as quickly were swallowed up by it again. All noises seemed heightened. Birds flew too low, squawking as they almost flew into them trying to find trees to roost in. The pony lost its footing a couple of times when it veered off the road, and whinnied in protest at having to go on.

Ruby felt chilled in the damp air and tried not to shiver visibly, but then she lost the battle and her body shuddered violently. Justin immediately put both reins in one hand and curled his arm around her waist to pull her closer for warmth.

'We'll put one blanket over our knees and the other around us both. That way we'll stay warmer together.'

This they did, and Ruby felt the instant warmth of his body heat penetrating through her clothes.

'We'll soon be home and dry,' he assured her.

'You never did show me your sketch,' she said, trying not to think of the close proximity of his body to hers.

'I will, one day – I just need it for a while.'

Ruby's heart swelled that he wanted to keep an image of her.

'Now, the smell of those pasties is making my stomach rumble. Please pass one over, will you? We'll have supper on the hoof so to speak.'

Laughing at the flaky crumbs accumulating on the blanket, they both agreed that a pasty had never tasted so good, and that the warming meat, potatoes and swede could stave off any chill they were feeling.

Ruby brushed the crumbs from her mouth and poured

a cup of water from her flask. She took a drink and offered it up to Justin who drank thirstily.

'Everyone is going to be beside themselves wondering where I am. I never normally venture far from the manor.'

'Well, Joe told me you were going to Poldhu, so surely they'll realise that we've both been caught with this weather.'

'Joe told you where I was?' she said pulling away slightly.

Justin pulled her back. 'He said you were heading that way with a picnic.'

'Mr Devereux, if I'm not mistaken, I do believe you were following me!'

He gave her a friendly nudge. 'I do believe I was, Mrs Sanders.'

Ruby stifled a laugh, despite her good reputation being in great peril.

17

When they finally arrived at Bochym - two and a half hours after setting off from Poldhu, Justin dropped Ruby off at the entrance to the kitchen courtyard while he steered the pony trap to the stables.

'Oh, lordy me!' Mrs Blair declared, 'thank goodness you're back safe and sound. We were just about to send a search party out for you. Let me help you off with your damp things. Goodness, look at the state of you. I do believe you look like you've been dragged through a hedge backwards!'

Ruby laughed and patted her hair, realising that she must look quite a fright.

'Mrs Sanders,' Joe said formally, as everyone gathered in the kitchen to see where Ruby had been, 'did you walk home? We were mightily worried when you didn't arrive off the afternoon wagon.'

Realising there was no point in lying, she answered, 'I'm afraid I lost track of time while I was out. Then one minute it was beautifully sunny and the next I couldn't see my hand in front of my face. Fortunately, I came across Mr Devereux at Poldhu with the pony trap. Mr and Mrs Blackthorn lent us lanterns and blankets and offered us accommodation for the night, but I knew we had to get back because you would all be worried.'

'So, is Mr Devereux back now too?' Joe asked looking beyond her.

'Yes, he's taken the pony trap to the stables.'

'I'll go and inform Her Ladyship. She's been fretting about him. Juliet, go and run a hot bath for Mrs Sanders.' Joe turned back to Ruby. 'I suggest you take yourself to bed afterwards so you can recover from your ordeal. I'll send up a supper tray.'

Ruby was heartened at Joe's concern, but in truth, she'd had the best day of her life. 'A warm drink will suffice - I've had plenty to eat today.'

The kitchen door opened and a swirl of fog preceded Justin.

'Ah, I see you're welcoming your precious housekeeper back into the bosom of her family. I hope you find her safe and well. I'll just pop through and tell Sarah and Peter that I'm home.'

'I was just about to do that!' Joe said.

'No matter - I'll do all the explaining.' Justin turned to Ruby. 'I thank you for looking after me on the trip home. I trust you haven't suffered too much by having my company forced upon you.'

'No,' she answered with a smile, 'and I thank you for everything today.'

*

Betsy had been in quiet turmoil since seeing Juliet and Ryan together. It was clear now that Ryan had been falsely playing with her heart, because there was obviously something going on between him and Juliet. She'd retired a little earlier than the others and was reading in bed when Juliet came in.

Juliet frowned when she saw the consternation on Betsy's face, but proceeded to pour some water into the pitcher from the jug.

'You're very quiet, Betsy. I've hardly heard a peep out of you all evening,' she said as she swilled her face.

It was no good - Betsy could keep her counsel no longer. 'Is it serious – between you and Ryan?'

Juliet stopped her ablutions and turned. 'What?'

'You and Ryan! I've asked you before, Juliet, and you've denied it, but I saw you today.' Betsy felt the tears well as she spoke.

'What do you mean you saw me?' There was a tremble in her voice.

'Don't come all innocent with me, Juliet. I thought we were friends and I asked you if you and Ryan were romantically involved.'

Juliet punched her fists into her hips. 'And I told you

we weren't!'

'But you were with him today, I saw you. You've been meeting him while you pretend to go egg hunting. I know you're taking him food from the manor kitchen, and I suspect Her Ladyship's soap – I've smelt it on him.'

Juliet flushed alarmingly. 'I felt sorry for him. He couldn't find work and he's been so kind to you. I've been helping him out, that's all. You won't tell that I've been stealing food and soap, will you?'

'Of course not, but you must stop or you'll be dismissed if you're caught!'

Suitably chastised, Juliet lowered her eyes. 'I will, I promise.'

'So, you're not in love with Ryan then?' she asked tentatively.

'*No, I'm not!*'

Betsy allowed the tears of relief to fall.

Juliet pulled on her nightgown and came to sit on Betsy's bed to offer her a handkerchief. 'But *you* are, aren't you?'

Betsy nodded dabbing her eyes. 'But I get the distinct impression that you're uneasy with that fact - I've seen you watching me with him!'

Juliet pulled a tight smile. 'I just don't want to lose you as a roommate, and I will if you get married.'

'*Married!* I've only just met him!'

Juliet got off the bed and turned down her eiderdown. 'Oh, I have no doubt he'll want to marry you, and sooner rather than later.'

'Really?' Betsy blinked furiously. 'Has he said as such?'

'No, he didn't have to. It's blatantly obvious by the way he looks at you that he's absolutely smitten.'

As Juliet climbed into her own bed, Betsy sniffed back the tears and felt her heart do a happy little dance at the prospect of a brighter future. She looked down at the thick pleat of hair and smiled – maybe she wouldn't be still in this room when the silver threads wove into her brunette curls after all.

*

After lying awake for a good part of the night, thinking of the day he'd spent with Ruby, Justin gave up any hopes of sleep, and was now busy working in the attic before the house woke. He felt energised - thrilled even, at the urge to put brush to canvas. He'd lit several oil lamps and the Valor heater, which had warmed the room a little, and though his fingers were stiff with cold, within a couple of hours of intense work, the image he had in his head was appearing before him. He always marvelled at the process of painting. It was as though the image had always been there - hidden within the tooth of the linen, and with each magical brushstroke he pulled the image out of the stark white canvas. Justin felt truly happy for the first time in a long time. He still had the niggling problem that had brought him home to England, but for now, he had everything he needed in life.

*

It was six the next morning and Dorothy scurried through the kitchens and out to the coal shed to fill her bucket. When she came back in, she kept her head down to make sure she didn't leave coal dust footprints in her wake - otherwise Mrs Blair would scat her, and very nearly bumped into Ruby.

'Watch where you're going Dorothy,' Ruby said side-stepping her.

'Oops sorry, Mrs Sanders, I hope you slept well.'

Ruby smiled. 'I did thank you, Dorothy.' She had indeed had the best night's sleep for a long time. The fresh air and the excitement of Justin's company had worn her out in a nice way. 'Are you nearly done lighting the fires?'

'Yes, Mrs Sanders. I've just Mr Devereux's room to do. He wasn't in his bed when I went in the first time at half-past-four! So, I left his until last. I'm going there now.'

Ruby frowned. 'Has his bed been slept in?'

'I think so. The covers were strewn all over the place. I

think he's up in the attic – I can hear him moving around up there.'

'Off you go then.' Ruby turned to Mrs Blair. 'Has Mr Devereux been down to make himself a drink this morning?'

'Not that I know of.'

'Well, could you please make a pot of coffee for me to take up to him – he must be frozen up there in the attic - there is a real chill in the morning air today.'

At the attic door, Ruby, conscious not to intrude on Justin's private place of work, knocked softly on the door.

'I've left you a warm drink outside the door, Justin,' she said, but as she walked away, she heard the door open.

'Ruby,' he whispered.

She turned and walked back to him.

He smiled warmly. 'Thank you - this is just what I needed.'

She returned his smile and turned to leave.

'Oh, and Ruby?'

'Yes?' she turned back.

He reached up to touch her hair. 'I'm just checking for any loose curls,' he said smiled softly.

Ruby blushed and smiled too.

He bent down to pick up the coffeepot. 'I'll catch up with you later. Thank you again for this, and for yesterday.'

The attic door closed and Ruby stood for a few moments to settle the fluttering in her tummy.

*

The fog lifted with the early morning sun as if it had never happened, but it left in its wake a very autumnal feel to the air.

At Poldhu, Ellie doled out the porridge to her hungry family and broached an idea she'd had to Guy.

'I was thinking - perhaps we should clear everything out of Jess....the cottage. We could perhaps rent it out – maybe even to Ryan Penrose - if he's fit for the job.

'Well, it's a good idea, but perhaps not yet. If I *do* give him a trial, I don't want him ensconced in your cottage, just in case he doesn't come up to standard.'

'Sarah says he's living rough – he'll need somewhere decent to stay.'

'I know. I was thinking that he could lodge with Jake in the same boarding house for now, *if* he is up to the job.'

Ellie secretly pitied Ryan – he would have very big shoes to fill to come up to Silas's standard.

*

At the staff breakfast, Betsy felt more settled in her mind about Ryan since speaking to Juliet, and began to look forward to the next time she would see him – for there would be a next – he'd made that quite clear at the harvest supper. As soon as breakfast was over, Mary started to clear the table, while Betsy prepared to go upstairs with Juliet to make a start on the bedrooms.

'Oh no!' Mary said as she loaded the tray. 'That Mr Trencrom is coming again, Mrs Blair.'

Mrs Blair glanced at Betsy. 'He'll be coming to see you.'

Betsy paled. 'I definitely don't want to see him! The silly man seems to think I'll marry him! I've told him I'm not interested.'

'Mr Treen, you need to speak to him then,' Mrs Blair said sternly. 'There is not a day goes by that he doesn't come bothering our Betsy.'

Betsy looked pleadingly at Joe.

'Off you go to your business, Betsy. I'll deal with him then.'

Betsy grabbed Juliet's sleeve and pulled her out of the room just as Trencrom came in the kitchen door.

*

When Joe opened the door, Trencrom had clearly seen Betsy running out of the kitchen, because he flared his nostrils.

'Betsy Tamblin, I know you're there, you come back here now! We have plans to discuss,' he yelled over Joe's shoulders.

'*Mr Trencrom*,' Joe asserted his authority. 'You will refrain immediately from coming into this kitchen, uninvited and shouting at my staff.'

'But I need to speak to Betsy.'

'Betsy has nothing to say to you - on *any* matter. Now leave, before I have reason to speak to the steward about you.'

Trencrom's face was florid with anger. 'But ...'

'Leave! And understand this, Mr Trencrom. From this day forward, you are not welcome in this kitchen, unless you have an appointment with His Lordship. Have I made myself clear?'

'Well, I...How am I...'

'Good day to you.' Joe closed the door on him before he'd finished speaking.

Everyone who was left in the kitchen clapped with glee.

'Yes, well, on with your work, everybody,' Joe said straightening his cuffs as though he'd been ruffled. He glanced at Mrs Blair who was grinning from ear to ear at Trencrom's banishment. 'If anyone wants me, I'll be in the stables, arranging to have these blankets and lanterns taken back to Poldhu. Her ladyship has a letter she wants delivered down there too,' he said to no one in particular.

18

On Friday morning, Joe was presiding over breakfast in the French drawing room. Only Peter and Justin were eating - Sarah had breakfasted at six before her morning ride, and was now busy with her lady's maid sorting the trunks out for their trip to Trevarno.

As Peter sat down with his plate of devilled kidneys on toast, he turned to address Joe. 'Treen, as we will be away for the weekend, Her Ladyship has asked me to tell you that she would like to give the household staff an extra day off on Sunday to go to the seaside at Poldhu. It's to say thank you for everyone's sterling efforts last weekend.'

'Thank you, my lord.' Joe bowed his head. 'The staff will appreciate the gesture.'

'Her ladyship has arranged for you all to take tea at The Poldhu Tea Rooms at one-o-clock. The trap and the carriage will be at your disposal, but I just ask that you all return before our expected return from Trevarno at six.'

'Of course, my lord, thank you, that is very generous.'

'I'll leave you to convey the news to everyone.' Peter dabbed his mouth with his napkin. 'We plan to leave at eleven this morning. We'll be taking the car, if you could have everything ready by then?'

'Of course, my lord.'

'That sounds rather like fun,' Justin said sipping his coffee. 'I should think I'd rather prefer a day at the sea, than attend a stiff dinner at Trevarno.'

Peter smiled. 'Justin, my dear man, you can go to the sea anytime you want - in fact were you not there on Wednesday? But I think our hosts would be rather put out if you decided to do that instead of visiting them. After all, it's not every day they get to host a dinner for a famous artist.'

Justin nodded resignedly. Being paraded in front of the local gentry was not something he relished. Undoubtedly there would be those individuals who didn't understand how an artist worked, and therefore would spout meaningless questions, such as, "What are you trying to say when you paint?" or "Being an artist must be so easy - I wish I could *just* paint pictures all day." In Italy, none of these utterances would ever leave the lips of his friends, acquaintances and potential clients. They could see his worth, and the amount of time, love and effort that went into creating a painting. They would never look at him as someone who just daubs paint on canvas all day for fun. The Italians too could make their own minds up about what an artist was trying to say in a painting - that was what art was about – to evoke an emotion within oneself to make the painting say whatever they wanted it to say.

Peter must have noted Justin's consternation, because when Justin looked up at him, Peter pulled a wry smile.

'Cheer up, old man, it's only for the weekend and then you'll be free again.'

*

As soon as the breakfast table was cleared away, Joe beckoned the staff together to tell them the good news, to a chorus of excited chatter.

'How lovely, especially as the barometer is set fine, so we should have a nice, sunny, dry day,' Ruby added.

'Are you going with them to Trevarno, Thomas?' Mary asked, clearly hoping that he wasn't - It was no secret that she was a little bit in love with the footman.

'Unfortunately, not, Mary.' Thomas sighed. 'Mr Devereux seems to have no need for a valet. He's up and dressed before I can get to him most mornings – he simply won't ring for me. Lord knows what he's doing up in the attic during those ungodly hours!'

A ghost of a smile passed Ruby's lips.

Mary clasped her hands together joyously. 'So, you'll be coming with us?'

'Yes, I suppose I could do a bit of fishing,' he sighed jadedly. 'There'll be nothing else to do.'

Mary's face fell.

'Will the swimming huts still be in service, Mr Treen?'
Dorothy asked, unable to contain her excitement.

'I believe not. But the cove should be relatively empty
now that it's October, so if you wish to sea bathe, I'm sure
you can find a private part of the beach where you can
change.'

'Don't worry, Dorothy.' Thomas winked. 'I'm more
than happy to hold the towel up for you while you get
changed.'

Dorothy shrieked in mock horror, and Mary looked
even more downcast.

Joe cleared his throat. 'Thank you, Thomas, that won't
be necessary. Perhaps Mrs Sanders, you can sort some sort
of rota so the ladies and gentlemen of our party can bathe
in privacy.'

Ruby smiled and nodded.

'Now, this day off will be extra to what you normally
get, so, if Sunday is your normal half day off, either come
to myself or Mrs Sanders and we'll arrange another day for
you to take.' Joe looked around at the smiling faces and
added, 'As Her Ladyship has arranged for us to take tea in
the tea room, there will be no need to make a picnic, Mrs
Blair - other than the normal cordials and fruit needed for
snacks. Now then, while you're all here, the post has just
come – rather late I'm afraid, due to the postman having a
puncture on his bike!'

Joe began to dole out the bunch of letters he was
holding, but when he handed Juliet a letter, she flinched
from him as though he'd burnt her. Aghast, he retracted
his hand in shock.

'Juliet!' Betsy snapped crossly. 'Whatever is the matter
with you? You're acting like a startled deer.'

'I'm sorry,' Juliet muttered, unable to look at either Joe
or Betsy as she folded the letter into her pocket.

Betsy glanced at Joe – the incident had clearly
unnerved him, but he carried on doling the letters out.

'One for you, Betsy – a London postmark, from Jessie

perhaps?' he said with a slight catch in his voice.

'Thank you, Mr Treen. Gosh if it *is* from Jessie, she must have replied to the letter I sent her by return post, because I only sent it on Monday! Have I time to read it, Mrs Sanders?' Betsy glanced hopefully at Ruby.

'Yes, if you're quick, the family are leaving soon.'

Wednesday 2nd October 1912

My dearest, Betsy, Thank you so much for your lovely letter, but I was shocked to hear that you had suffered such an injury. I hope your foot is mending now, and you don't suffer any long-term effects from it. Hopefully, the person responsible for such a reckless act will soon be caught and publicly horsewhipped.

Betsy bit down on her lip. When she'd written the letter, she had no idea who had set the trap, and now she knew, and was aware of Ryan's heartfelt regret, and the reason he'd set it. She certainly would not want him horsewhipped!

I trust you are well, and that Joe's budding romance is flourishing. I seem to remember he was enjoying the company of the new maid. He deserves to be happy.

Betsy sighed and glanced at Joe and Juliet, both now extremely wary of each other. Romance seemed definitely off the cards now!

The banns for our wedding are being read and we have set the date for Saturday 19th October. I've written to tell Ellie and Meg, but I don't know how the news will be taken in the Blackthorn household. I know Ellie will be happy for me, but as it's only a few short weeks since Silas was killed, I suspect Guy will not look favourably on our haste to marry. But we have to do what is right for us, and being married is an absolute necessity. Although Daniel and I dine out and visit the theatre together, we have to go home to our respective houses, and though it is lovely being at James Blackwell's house, frankly, we just want to be together as soon as possible. God knows, I've waited long enough!

After the terrible year I endured, I can't tell you how happy I am at last. I'm just so sad that you, my good friend, won't be by my side as a bridesmaid again. I hope one day you will be able to make the trip up to London, and I'll show you all the wonderful sights – for they are to behold.

I received a letter from Meg the same day yours came, with word that she and Tobias are to be married on Monday 21ˢᵗ October at 2 p.m. - two days after Daniel and I tie the knot! So, if you happen to be near Cury Church on that day and time, please throw some lucky rice at the couple. I'm so happy that they have found each other relatively late in life. You see, Betsy, you never know when love comes knocking. Having said that, do tell me news of the young man who rescued you. Have you seen him again? You wrote to say you were going to seek him out to thank him.

I will close the letter now. Wish me luck for my wedding day. We are to honeymoon in Italy. Daniel has promised to take me to Venice, Florence and Rome, so I promise to send postcards from everywhere I visit.

Love to you and everyone at Bochym.

Jessie xx

Betsy folded the letter and looked up - her eyes settling on Joe.

'Jessie's getting married to Daniel on the 19ᵗʰ of this month - they're going to Italy for their honeymoon.' Her bottom lip trembled and Joe's face paled at the news. They both felt keenly that this marked the end of what used to be, and confirmed that Jessie's world was so far removed from theirs now. With a myriad of mixed emotions, Betsy stood to leave the room. As she walked along the corridor, she heard footsteps behind her and glanced back to see that Joe had done the same - no doubt heading to his office to digest his own thoughts on Jessie's marriage.

*

The kitchen fell silent, and Juliet felt thankful that Joe and Betsy's reaction to the news of Jessie's forthcoming wedding, followed by their swift departure from the kitchen, had taken the spotlight off the embarrassing incident between herself and Joe.

Everyone looked at Mrs Blair when she sighed, thumped her fists into her ample hips and said, 'Those two, kind, sensitive people are upset at Jessie's news for different reasons. It's time they both found someone to love, so that they too can live the life *they* need to feel fulfilled.' Once she had said her piece, she narrowed her eyes to settle her gaze on Juliet.

Feeling the full force of Mrs Blair's stare, Juliet quickly took her leave from the kitchen. She found Betsy weeping softly in the Earl's bedroom while she was trying to make the bed.

'I thought you'd be happy at your friend's news?' Juliet said, helping to tuck one side of the bed in.

'I am! It's just that I miss her terribly, and to tell you the truth, I *want* what she has, and I don't mean a life in London or a honeymoon in Italy - I just want a husband to settle down with.'

Juliet was silent for a moment.

'I mean,' Betsy continued as she plumped the pillows up, 'doesn't every woman want that?'

'Not every woman, no,' Juliet muttered.

Betsy wiped her eyes furiously. 'I don't believe you, Juliet. I don't know what has got into you nowadays. When you first came here, you enjoyed Joe's kind attention towards you. You gave him hope and we all thought it was a match made in heaven, but then you turned away from him. Can you not see how hurt he is by the strange way you act with him now? And why did you flinch from him like that when he handed you that letter?'

Juliet felt a lump in her throat, but could not answer.

'Joe has been disappointed in love before, Juliet. He loved Jessie once, which is why he also took the news of her upcoming wedding hard today.'

Juliet remained quiet.

'Joe is a handsome man – a good man – the best of men. He doesn't deserve to be so toyed with.'

'I'm not toying with him, Betsy - really I'm not. I thought at first he was just being friendly with me, but when I realised there was more to it, I,' the words caught in her throat, 'I had to put a stop to it.' She lowered her eyes and whispered, 'I just had too.'

'Why?' Betsy snapped.

Juliet began to feel choked by panic. 'Because I cannot let him into my heart, that's why.'

'Well, I think he is already there!' she said crisply, as she placed the cushions on the bed to finish dressing it.

Juliet's lips trembled – no truer word was spoken.

'You need to be straight with Joe - the poor man thinks he's done something terrible to you, and if you continually shrink from his presence, it will make others in the household think the same!'

Juliet's eyes blurred with unshed tears.

'When we go to Poldhu on Sunday, you must take the opportunity of being away from the manor to speak to him, Juliet. Even if you're unable to tell him the real reason you can't be together – and lord knows why you can't - you must let him know that he hasn't done anything wrong to make you so nervous of him. I've known Joe for a long time, and it breaks my heart to see him forever caught up in a tangle of unrequited love. I'll not be friends with you if you do not cease to be cold with him! Understood?'

Juliet nodded sadly.

'Come on then, we have chores to do.'

When Betsy left the room, Juliet stood silently wringing her hands – the last thing in the world she wanted to do was hurt Joe, but there was nothing she could do about it.

*

Betsy walked into Her Ladyship's bedroom with a pile of clean sheets and glanced out of the window in time to see the family leaving for Trevarno. While the Earl and Countess were getting into the car, she saw Mr Devereux look up towards his bedroom window. Betsy followed his gaze, and was sure she could see Mrs Sanders looking back down at him. Without giving it another thought, she began to strip the bed.

*

Ruby felt a real sense of loss as she watched the car drive away and it took several deep breaths to calm the frisson caused by their exchanged glances. With her hand on her heart, she wondered what on earth was happening to her, and indeed, what would happen to her, if she let this madness proceed.

'Ruby.' Joe's voice made her jump. 'Sorry, I didn't mean to startle you. I just thought I'd come and tell you that the family have left now.'

'Oh, right, thank you for letting me know. I thought perhaps with the family away, today would be a good opportunity to take all the rugs outside to beat them.'

'Good idea. I'll get Thomas to help move them all for you - no rest for the wicked, eh?' He must have seen her blanch at the remark, because he tipped his head and asked, 'Are you all right Ruby – you've been a little quiet of late.'

'Oh, I'm fine,' she smiled, 'what about you though, Joe?'

He twisted his mouth. 'Oh, you know.'

She heard the crack of emotion in his voice and nodded.

19

Ryan used some of the money he'd earned at the harvest to buy a new shirt to wear, in readiness to see Guy Blackthorn. His other shirts had a brown hue, due to being laundered in the local stream, and he was not sure he would ever get them to look clean again. He'd washed and shaved carefully, which was not easy without a mirror, and pulled a comb through his thick blond hair. He hoped he'd be successful in his bid for the job, he would need to have steady work, not only to help him find some decent accommodation over the winter, but this last week his mind had moved onto his future, and with whom he wanted to share it with. He'd enjoyed the odd dalliance with a couple of girls in Gweek, though it was just a cuddle and a squeeze - nothing more than that - but he was ready to settle down now, and he knew just the girl he wanted to do that with. So, it was with great trepidation he knocked on the door of Guy Blackthorn's house.

'Good morning,' he said, pulling his hat from his head when Ellie answered the door. 'I'm Ryan Penrose. I was told to come and see Mr Blackthorn about a job.'

'Do come in, my husband is waiting for you.'

Guy stood up and looked him over. 'At least you look strong.'

'Can I offer you a mug of tea?' Ellie smiled.

'Only if you're making one,' he answered politely.

'Have a seat,' Guy said gruffly.

'Can I first offer my condolences for the loss of your brother?'

Both Guy and Ellie took a sharp intake of breath, and Ryan cursed himself that he might just have scuppered his chances by mentioning Silas, but then Guy nodded.

'Thank you, as you can imagine, it's been a trying time.'

Ryan felt his shoulders relax.

'How old are you, Ryan?'

'Twenty, sir.'

The Countess de Bochym tells me you're from Gweek. I too come from Gweek, why do I not know of you, or your family name?'

'My father married a widow in the village, two years ago.'

Guy nodded. 'I see. What work have you done since leaving school?'

'I worked the fields in Manaccan, and latterly in the Gweek and Penryn boatyards, so I'm used to hard work. I'm quick to learn and can turn my hand to most things.'

'Why did you leave the boatyards – were you sacked?'

'No, sir. I didn't get on with my father, so I thought it best to leave the village and chance my arm over this side of the Lizard.'

Again, Guy nodded. 'I have an apprentice – Jake Treen. You may know him, his brother Joe, is the butler at the manor.'

'I don't really know many people at the manor. I've met Betsy, Juliet and Her Ladyship, that's all.'

Guy raised an eyebrow. 'All the ladies, eh?'

'Guy,' Ellie warned, 'no teasing the lad,' she said placing mugs of tea in front of both men.

'If I offered you the job, it would be on a trial basis as an apprentice, and you would be under Jake who is fourteen-years-old and has been with me since Easter. He understands the art of thatching - though he still has a lot to learn, but I can leave him to work unsupervised should I be called away to pitch for another job. Do you think you could work under the authority of a fourteen-year-old?'

'Yes, sir. I'm willing to learn from whoever can take the time to teach me.'

Guy was silent for a few moments and Ryan held his breath, hoping for a favourable answer. It was then that a dog got up from where he lay by the range and walked over to Ryan.

'Hello, boy,' Ryan said tickling the dog behind his ears.

The dog looked up mournfully, sighed and rested his

chin on Ryan's knee.

'What is he, a collie and spaniel cross?'

Guy nodded.

'He feels a bit thin, is he unwell?' Ryan asked.

'This is Blue, my brother's dog, he's pining for him. He hasn't eaten properly since Silas died - we think we'll lose him too. I'm amazed he's come to you though - this is the first time he's taken an interest in anything other than lying by the range.'

'They do take the loss of a master to heart,' Ryan said making a fuss of Blue. 'Is that his bowl over there?'

'Yes.'

'Do you mind if I try and get him to eat a little.'

Guy glanced at Ellie. 'Be our guest.'

Ryan slid onto all fours and snuffled against Blue's neck and Blue responded with a pitiful whine. 'I know boy, I know,' he said softly and crawled towards the dog bowl, and looked into it – it was full of fatty scraps. Blue followed him and whined again. 'Time to eat boy,' he said, as he snuffled again into Blue's neck and because Blue was right over his feeding bowl, he dropped his nose to sniff the food. 'That's a good boy,' Ryan soothed and Blue took his first tentative bite of food. He didn't eat much, but lifted his head as though to wait for praise. Ryan cupped the dog's head with his hands and whispered, 'Who's a good boy.' When he got up to take his seat again, Blue took another mouthful before coming back to sit beside him.

Guy tapped his fingers against his lips thoughtfully. 'I really don't know how you did that, Ryan, but if Blue is endorsing you, then that's good enough for me. Can you start on Monday?'

'Yes, sir.'

'Then you must call me Guy. I understand you're living rough at the moment.'

'Yes, just until I get a little more money together to afford some accommodation.'

'Well, because young Jake's parents live in Penryn, he boards with a lovely lady called Miss Taylor, in Cury - she has a spare room. This is the address - I've already spoken to her and told her if I was happy with you, I'd send you up there today. She will feed you and do your laundry for a fee. As I say, this is a month's trial period, but I've a good feeling that you'll fit in perfectly.'

'Thank you so much for giving me this chance.' Ryan beamed with happiness as he looked down at the address. 'I'll call on Miss Taylor on the way home.' As he got up to leave, Blue followed him to the door, his tail giving the first wag since Silas had died. 'I'll see you soon, boy. Mind you eat all your dinner from now on.' Ryan tickled Blue behind the ears, and before he got to the door, Blue had gone back to his bowl and licked it clean.

*

After introducing himself to Miss Taylor and making friends with her lurcher Nigel, Ryan set off to his shelter to collect his belongings. As soon as everything was bundled up and the shelter tidied, he set off to the manor to leave word with the Countess that he had secured the job she'd put him forward for – he also hoped to see a certain young woman.

*

Betsy kept her fingers crossed all that day in the hope that Ryan was able to secure the job with Guy Blackthorn - though she had no idea when she'd find out!

She was busy filling the oil lamps in the kitchen when Mrs Blair huffed loudly.

'Oh, lordy me! It's that chap who carried you home, Betsy. He smelt to high heaven last time he was in my kitchen – I hope he's cleaned himself up.'

Delighted, Betsy got up so fast she almost upended her chair.

'I'm sure he'll smell sweet today, Mrs Blair, he's been for an interview with Guy Blackthorn!'

Mary also got up from where she was working and

peered through the window. 'He looks like he's carrying something?'

Betsy opened the door with a smile to match Ryan's 'Well?' she asked.

'I've caught your hen! I remember someone telling me she'd escaped, I found her by the hay barn.'

Betsy laughed and took Frances the errant hen from his arms. 'Thank you, but I meant the job – did you get it?'

He grinned and nodded. 'I start on Monday and I've moved into a boarding house today. I thought I'd better come and leave the news for Her Ladyship, as she was good enough to recommend me.'

'Well, the family are away this weekend, but I'll tell Mr Treen and he'll pass the message on when they get back.' Betsy turned to the cook. 'Mr Penrose has some good news to share with us, and he's caught the escapee hen.'

'Excellent news,' Mrs Blair answered, wiping her hands on her tea towel, 'Juliet won't have to go searching for her eggs in the hay barn anymore. Mary, take Frances to the hen coop and make sure it's secure this time.'

'Could Mr Penrose come in for a cup of tea?' Betsy asked Cook hopefully.

Mrs Blair narrowed her eyes suspiciously, and then nodded.

Ryan smiled gratefully to her as he stepped into the warm kitchen and settled at the table. Mrs Blair placed a cup down in front of him, blatantly sniffed him, and when satisfied that he didn't smell, she offered him a slice of cake to go with the tea.

Just as Ryan had taken a generous bite out of the cake, Juliet breezed into the kitchen. She stopped dead in her tracks on seeing him and a small cry escaped her throat.

Everyone stared perplexed at her.

'Mr Penrose has some good news, and something specifically to tell you, Juliet,' Mrs Blair announced.

Juliet's anguished eyes cut from the cook to Ryan, making Ryan quickly swallow his mouthful of cake.

'I've come with good news,' he said urgently. 'I've secured a job with the thatchers at Poldhu. I'm moving to a boarding house in Cury, so I'm not going far.'

Juliet nodded and moistened her lips. 'And the news specifically for me?' she asked tremulously.

'Only that I've caught Frances, the hen,' Ryan said softly, 'I'm told you won't have to go off egg hunting in the hay barn anymore!'

'Oh, I see! Thank you,' she said raggedly.

Betsy watched curiously at this strange exchange – not only was it taking the shine off her initial joy at Ryan's job prospects, but she felt a curl of unease again about their relationship

'If you'll excuse me, I, err, have something I need to attend to,' Juliet said turning on her heel to leave.

'Well! I wonder what all that was about?' Mrs Blair narrowed her eyes at Ryan.

Betsy also turned to him for an explanation, but he just shrugged as though it was a mystery to him too.

'Betsy,' he whispered, 'when can I see you again? I'll only be able to come here at the weekends from now on!'

His words heartened her, and despite her reservations, felt her unease settle. 'I don't know - not tomorrow though, I'm afraid. We're going on an outing to Poldhu.'

'Next Saturday then?' he asked hopefully.

She smiled. 'I shouldn't really,' she glanced at Mrs Blair, who had thankfully returned to her cooking. 'All right, we could meet in the bottom meadow at four-o-clock - unless it's raining of course, I'll not be able to meet you if it is.'

'I shall pray it doesn't rain, then.' He grinned.

Presently, he finished his tea, and so as not to outstay his welcome, he got up to leave. 'Thank you very much, Mrs Blair for the tea and lovely cake.'

She nodded and watched Betsy show him to the door.

'I'll just walk to the end of the courtyard with him,' Betsy said brightly. At the entrance to the stables, they stood and smiled at each other. 'Goodbye, Ryan,' she said shyly, 'Enjoy your first week at work.'

'I will. Thank you.' He wrinkled his nose and set off down the drive to the stile, lifting his hand to wave as he went.

Betsy walked happily back across the courtyard, but a movement at her attic bedroom window made her look up, just in time to see Juliet pull back from sight. When she walked back into the kitchen Mrs Blair was watching her curiously.

'Is he coming back to court you then?'

Betsy felt her face flush and nodded.

'Well, you just make sure he's true to you, afore you lose your heart to him.'

Betsy felt a tingle of anxiety. 'What do you mean?'

Mrs Blair folded her arms. 'You know *exactly* what I mean!'

*

Henry Trencrom burnt with jealous anger as he lent on his ditch shovel watching Penrose bid farewell to his intended. He'd seen him arrive over half an hour ago, and knew damn well what the wastrel was up to. He spat on the ground, disgusted that they allowed a vagrant in the kitchen, when he was denied entrance. Serious action was needed now if he was to stop Penrose from stealing his future.

20

Poldhu Cove was drenched in golden October sunshine when the very excited ensemble arrived from Bochym Manor. Dorothy, Mary and Izzy were the first to jump down from the trap and began to rid themselves of their shoes and stockings. The rest of the group laughed, watching them running down the beach, their skirts hitched, hair and petticoats billowing in the breeze.

Joe helped Betsy carefully down from the carriage – her foot still encased in the over boot, and then he and Thomas supported Mrs Blair as she carefully negotiated the carriage steps. Joe settled Mrs Blair on the dunes on a folded chair under the shade of an umbrella. Betsy sat beside her on a rug to keep her company, while Ruby set off to supervise the girls so that they could swim in privacy.

Once the ladies were settled, Thomas, brandishing a fishing rod he'd borrowed from the gamekeeper, set off towards the rocks. That just left Juliet who had held back from everyone else.

Joe smiled gently at her. 'What about you, Juliet, do you want me to settle you somewhere with a blanket and umbrella?'

'No thank you, Mr Treen. I'd rather like to speak to you, somewhere in private, perhaps.'

'Oh, goodness.' He placed his hand to his heart, 'I can't tell you how much that heartens me, but please, call me Joe when we're alone. I'd like to think we're friends as well as colleagues - more than friends in fact,' he added hopefully.

Seeing his optimism, Juliet's throat thickened with emotion. 'That's what I need to speak to you about,' she said tentatively.

'Oh, I see!' Joe's face fell.

Seeing his countenance rapidly switched from elation to dismay, Juliet began to feel awful, knowing these next few minutes were going to break both their hearts.

He must have noted her disquiet, because he said, 'Come then, Juliet, let's take a walk to the rocks. We'll stay in full view of everyone though, so there is nothing improper about it.'

*

From her vantage point on the dunes, Betsy watched Joe and Juliet walk to the far end of the beach, all the while praying that Juliet was going to do the right thing by Joe.

'What do you think is going on there then?' Mrs Blair nodded at the couple.

'Hopefully, they're settling their differences.'

'It would be certainly beneficial to you if they become romantically entwined,' Mrs Blair said, clicking her knitting needles together.

'Yes, I just wish I knew what was holding her back from opening her heart to him.'

'Or someone!'

Betsy glanced at the cook but remained silent.

'You can't deny it, Betsy, there is something strange going on between that new beau of yours and Juliet – even Mr Treen has noted it. I think she's set her hat at him! Have you asked her?'

It was both a relief and a worry that others had picked up on what she had noticed. 'Yes,' she sighed, 'but she denies any romantic involvement.'

Mrs Blair hummed. 'I rather liked Juliet at first, but I'm not so sure now. I hope she isn't going to break Mr Treen's heart, or I'll be cross with her.'

Betsy shaded her eyes to look at Joe and Juliet on the rocks. *She was very afraid that she might just be doing that right now.*

'Don't be too hard on Juliet, Mrs Blair. Something,' she emphasised the word, 'is bothering her – she has terrible nightmares you know?'

Mrs Blair hummed again and poured a glass of elderflower cordial. 'You like Mr Penrose, don't you?' she said, handing it to Betsy before pouring one herself.

'I do, yes,' she said taking a sip - it smelt like a fragrant summer day.

'Well, if I was you, I'd get him to marry you sharpish.'

Betsy snuffled a laugh and joked. 'Why would Ryan want to marry me? According to Trencrom, I've missed the boat, and as I've clearly been left on the shelf, my only option is to marry that reptile. Ugh!' She shuddered at the thought.

'Phff, what rubbish - you don't want to listen to that horrible man.'

The breeze blew from the sea through the tall marram grasses and Betsy pulled a stray hair away from her face. 'I'm twenty-one, Mrs Blair - I rather think that I have been left on the shelf!'

'Nope, I won't hear another word about it - I think that young man of yours will do the right thing. Think lucky and you'll be lucky, Betsy. You mark my words - you'll be married before the end of the year!'

Betsy cupped her palms over one knee. 'I thought you didn't like Mr Penrose.'

Mrs Blair sniffed dismissively. 'I'm warming to him now that he doesn't smell so awful, and by the sound of it, he has some prospects now. But I'm telling you, act sharp, young lady, before anyone else gets their claws into him.' She narrowed her eyes towards Juliet down on the beach.

Betsy stared out to the glistening sea. There was no doubt about it - there was still a question mark over the relationship between Ryan and Juliet which niggled at the back of her mind. Before she could dare to dream, she needed to know, and to that end she would ask Ryan outright next Saturday.

*

Joe and Juliet had walked as far as the rocks, keeping to the dry sand so as not to spoil their footwear. They sat down, albeit uncomfortably, at the entrance of a small cave.

'Are you going to break my heart then, Juliet?' he asked quietly.

'That's the thing, Mr….Joe - breaking your heart is the last thing I want to do, you've been so kind to me, but….'

He looked at her beautiful heart shaped face so full of angst and his heart plummeted. 'But you're going to anyway?'

'I'm not the woman for you.'

Juliet lifted her eyes to meet his, but he could see they were full of concern. 'Do you think I'm too old for you, is that it? I shall be twenty-eight on Christmas Eve – that's only ten years your senior.'

'No, Joe, it's not that.'

'Is there someone else then?'

'No!' she answered sharply.

He sighed. 'When you first came to us - when I first set eyes on you, I thought there was something special between us. I honestly thought you felt the same, otherwise I would never have presumed to ask you to be more than a friend.'

Juliet drew a breath a little deeper than normal.

'Juliet, please tell me why there's a barrier between us now - when clearly you don't want there to be? Have I done something wrong to make you dislike me?' He reached to put his hand on hers, but she flinched away in revulsion and stood up. A flash of horror clouded Joe's eyes. 'Oh, Juliet, I do beg your pardon. I'll never presume to touch you again. But I can clearly see I *have* done something wrong, haven't I?

Juliet eyes blurred with tears as she wrung her hands. 'No, Joe, it's not you. You've done nothing wrong,' she said as a single tear trickled down her hot cheek.

He climbed down from the rock he was sitting on. 'What is it then? I hate to see you cry, and it grieves me that I can't comfort you.'

She stepped back slightly. 'Please, please don't though.'

He held his hands out. 'I won't, I promise. Goodness -

but I need to ask you, has someone hurt you in the past?' His eyes searched hers for a clue to her distress, but she remained resolutely silent. 'You can talk to me, Juliet, sometimes talking helps.'

She shook her head. 'I can't, I'm sorry - there is nothing to tell. I just, it's just,' her face crumpled, 'I'm afraid I can never return your love.' Juliet knew the ragged breath that followed, spoke volumes.

Joe sighed and dropped his hands. 'I wish I could understand, but let me assure you, I will never touch you again unless *you* reach out to me. My feelings for you run deep - I cannot tamp them down, so be sure in the knowledge that if you change your mind, I'll be waiting.'

Unable to hold back the tears, she dropped her head in her hands to weep openly. 'Please, don't waste your life waiting for me,' she mumbled.

'Juliet, I have no doubt that you've been informed by other members of staff that I have been unlucky in love in the past.'

'Yes,' she sobbed.

'I never thought I'd feel anything for anyone else again, and then you came along.' When she emitted a small strangled cry, he added, 'No, please don't be distressed, Juliet. If we can't be anything else, I ask that we can be just good friends. Can we?' he asked hopefully.

She nodded through her tears.

He smiled sadly at her. 'I'll leave you now to compose yourself. Dry your eyes, sweet girl.' He pushed his hands deep into his pockets and walked away from her.

She turned her head to watch him go and felt her heart shatter at her loss.

*

When Betsy saw Joe and Juliet walking in different directions - Joe towards Ruby and Juliet back up the beach, she got up to walk to join her.

'Well?' she asked hopefully.

Juliet sniffed back the tears. 'I've told Joe that he hasn't

158

done anything wrong, but that I'm not able to return his affections.'

Betsy's heart fell. 'Are you *sure* you can't return them, because I must say, you don't look too happy at the prospect!'

'I'm sure,' she answered miserably. 'Are you still my friend, Betsy?'

'Oh, dear,' Betsy gathered her into her arms, 'of course I am. It was very wrong of me to threaten otherwise. I was upset myself at the time I said it, and really, I just want everyone to be happy. Come on, let me take my boots off and we'll go for a paddle to cheer you up.'

*

Joe walked dejectedly along the waterline which was littered with seaweed and broken shells, to join Ruby who was sitting with her feet in a rock pool gazing out to sea.

Ruby smiled tightly. 'You look like you've lost a crown and found a farthing, have you not settled anything with Juliet? I saw you speaking to her.'

'Alas no, something is holding her back, but she won't say. Has she never said anything to you, Ruby?'

'No, but if she had, I could not divulge it to you, as well you know. Give her time, Joe. It won't be long before she sees what a splendid chap you are.'

'Oh,' he sighed, 'I don't know,' he turned to look out to sea, 'I think you and I are doomed to spend our life in service without the comfort of sharing a bed with a spouse.'

She raised her brow. 'Well, thank you for that unhappy thought.'

He wrinkled his nose. 'Sorry, I'm a little melancholy that's all.'

'What you need is to take off your shoes and socks and put your feet into this rock pool. It's lovely, come on.' She budged up along the rock.

He placed his hand on his heart in feigned shock. 'Mrs Sanders, are you asking me to share your footbath?

Whatever will the others say?' he grinned, pulling off his socks and rolling up his trousers.

'Oh, you never know, it might make a certain someone jealous,' she nodded towards Juliet.

He settled beside Ruby, and followed her gaze to watch Juliet and Betsy holding hands as they splashed in the surf.

'At the moment, it is *I* who is jealous of Betsy – at least she gets to hold Juliet's hand!' he said, fishing a clump of seaweed from the pool to toss aside. He wiggled his toes in the water and sighed. 'I wonder how Mr Devereux is getting on.

Ruby felt herself colour up at the mention of his name.

'He really didn't want to go to Trevarno, you know? I think he'd have preferred to come here with us.'

Ruby smiled inwardly. 'Yes,' she said, 'I think he would.'

*

At Trevarno, Justin was biding his time until he could return to Bochym. Having to leave *everything* at Bochym, to eat, drink and make small-talk with people he did not know, did not sit well with him at the moment. He was not an unsociable man, in fact normally quite the opposite, and could hold his own in any situation, but recently he felt weary of company such as this. Granted, the intimate family dinner on Friday night at Trevarno, had been nice. The Bickford family were lovely people, therefore none of his previous misconceptions of how they would perceive him and the work he undertook had not materialised. The dinner had followed an extensive guided tour around the estate by Matthew Bickford and his father Andrew, but in truth, it was Peter who was more interested in that than he - for obvious reasons. Sarah too had found her time much taken up with Eleanor Bickford and her daughter Mellissa, whom, Justin suspected, he was going to be asked to paint. So, to entertain himself on Saturday morning, he'd escaped the confines of Trevarno and taken the car to Helston to take a look around the ancient town. Returning with several purchases, he set off with his sketchbook to spend the afternoon by the boathouse on the lake. The grounds at Trevarno had been his saviour. He'd wandered around the lush, subtropical garden which fringed the small waterfall feeding the lake, amazed at the abundance of plants on display. The garden hosted an array of succulents, towering palms and giant gunneras, and in between drifts of spires of blue echium, strelitzia stood proud - they really did look like birds of paradise peeping through the greenery.

On Saturday evening the Bickford's hosted a dinner in his honour - inviting all the local gentry. It was good of them, but he really wished they hadn't, and vowed this would be the last time he was going to be paraded around the fine houses in Cornwall. He'd been placed next to Melissa Bickford at dinner, a beautiful, albeit shallow woman, whose only interests were in horses and herself. She seemed to take it for granted that he *was* going to paint her. Fortunately, all was not lost, to his other side he had the company of a gentleman who had been to the Norwich School of Art with Alfred Munnings - one of the Newlyn Artists. This piqued Justin's interest immensely, especially when the gentleman told him about the artist colony down the coast in Lamorna where Munnings and his new wife Florence Carter-Wood now resided. It made Justin think of Lionel, his artist friend in London, who, if he remembered correctly, had a cottage down at Lamorna. Perhaps he'd go up to London to see him, and maybe even take a trip to Lamorna.

It was Sunday now, and as Justin sat in a secluded spot within the confines of the peaceful Italian sunken garden, he thought of the Bochym staff at Poldhu and wished he could be there. He missed Ruby, and wondered if she was missing him as much. He allowed himself a smile, and thought, perhaps she was - after all, hadn't she watched him leave on Friday morning, and given him a small wave? After spending time with the more affluent society, he realised how much he'd missed Ruby's naturalness and her company. Though he'd only spent a short time with her, he felt he'd found a kindred spirit in her and was eager to get back to Bochym.

21

At one-o-clock, the Bochym party assembled at the tea room. Ellie and Meg had pushed two tables together to accommodate everyone, and plates of sandwiches, scones and scrumptious cake stood pride of place in the centre.

Dorothy, Mary and Izzy were first to the table, flushed with the excitement of swimming in the sea, and though they had both changed out of their swimming attire, they were scratching alarmingly at their salty skin. Mrs Blair, Betsy and Juliet were the next to arrive, swiftly followed by Ruby and Joe – only Thomas was missing as the clock struck one.

Although this was a very informal party, everyone had resumed their normal places around the table as they would have done in the Bochym kitchen, with the exception of Mrs Blair and Mary, who never normally ate with the rest of the staff. They took the places normally held for Theo and Lowenna Trevail today. As was protocol, everyone stood when Joe came to the table. As he beckoned them to sit, Joe apologised to Ellie and Meg for the lateness of Thomas, and insisted on them serving tea without him.

It was a couple of minutes past the hour when Thomas came running in, flushed and apologetic, but Joe's eyebrows knitted disapprovingly.

'Did you catch anything, Thomas,' Mary asked fluttering her eyelashes at him.

'Did he eck - he's been watching us swimming,' Dorothy teased.

'I have not!' Thomas blustered, flushing even more as he walked to his place. Everyone around the table laughed, except Juliet. Thomas, spotting this, clamped his hands around Juliet's shoulders and said, 'Cheer up, it might never happen.'

The moment Thomas's hands touched her Juliet felt a sense of dread overwhelm her. 'Get off me,' she shrieked like a banshee, pulling away from him, upsetting her cup and saucer, spilling tea over the clean white tablecloth.

Thomas pulled back in horrified shock and Joe stood up. In a deep authoritative voice he said, '*Thomas*, take your seat immediately.'

'But I was just…'

'*Take your seat.*'

Thomas skulked to his seat and glared at Juliet for making such a fuss, as she gasped and staggered away from the table, seemingly unable to catch her breath. She flayed her arms around in search of something to hold on to, and both Ruby and Betsy rushed to her aid.

'Don't worry, there's no harm done,' Ellie said to her, mopping up the tea as Meg expertly lifted everything off the table, changed the tablecloth and put everything back as though nothing had happened.

Juliet was bent double, open-mouthed and clutching her chest. Her heart was palpitating so much - she honestly thought she was about to die.

'Here,' Ruby grabbed a paper bag from the till counter and scrunched it up at the end, 'breathe in and out into this.'

'A bit of an overreaction, don't you think,' Thomas muttered to Mary who agreed to please him.

'Thomas!' Joe warned, and watched with growing concern at how ill Juliet looked.

'I was only playing,' Thomas said in his defence. 'She's mighty sensitive for a maid, don't you think?'

'Enough,' Joe warned again.

Ruby sat Juliet down at a spare table while she inhaled and exhaled into the paper bag. It took a few minutes, but eventually her breath began to slow and return to normal and the fear she was going to die subsided, but she was appalled that all eyes were on her.

'Better now?' Ruby asked, handing her a clean handkerchief to wipe her tears.

'Yes, thank you, Mrs Sanders,' she trembled.

'Are you ready to come back to the table then?'

'Yes,' she said her breath ragged, but although she'd agreed, returning to the table was the last thing she wanted - though she knew she must.

'Are you all right, Juliet?' Joe asked sympathetically as she settled back down at the table.

Her eyes flickered towards him. 'Yes, thank you, Mr Treen. I'm so sorry everyone.'

'No need to apologise,' Joe said gently.

But she did feel the need to apologise - to deflect any questions of why she had reacted so, and replied, 'But I am sorry. I feel that I have spoilt the party and Thomas, I apologise to you too – you just made me jump and I couldn't catch my breath.'

'Oh, all right, I'm sorry too,' Thomas muttered, albeit reluctantly.

Once everyone had settled again, fresh pots of tea were brought to the table.

'Tuck in then,' Meg said, filling everyone's cup.

Soon the incident was forgotten and happy chatter accompanied the enjoyment of the wonderful tea.

Juliet kept her head low. Her eyes felt grainy and she was shaken to the core by what had just happened to her. She forced a piece of sandwich down her dry throat, all the while trying to quell the sick sensation in her stomach as she fought her unseen demons.

*

During the course of the tea, Betsy reached over to squeeze Juliet's hand for comfort, but she appeared to be elsewhere in her head. Realising that something terrible must have happened to her for her to react so, Betsy glanced at Joe, who looked ashen faced – he too must realise there was some dreadful reason behind Juliet's strange reaction to men. If only she would open up to them – perhaps they could help. Patting Juliet on the hand again to show solidarity, Betsy turned her attention to Ellie and Meg as they darted about, keeping everyone happy and tea cups full. It seemed they were managing quite well without Jessie. She had always envied Jessie her job here at the tea rooms and imagined how wonderful it would be to look out at that beautiful view every single day of your life. She missed Jessie, and missed coming down here every other week to see her on her half day off.

'I hear you're to be married, Meg,' Betsy said when she came to the table again.

'Aye, I am. Married again at my age – who'd have thought it, eh?'

'I hope you and Tobias will be very happy.'

'Thank you – I'm sure we will.'

'With Jessie gone, how will Ellie manage while you're on your honeymoon?'

Meg laughed. 'Honeymoons are for t'youngsters. Tobias and I are a bit long in t'tooth for all that malarkey, but I'm taking a couple of days off while my family are down from Yorkshire. The tea room should be quiet at the end of October, so Ellie will manage, but I must say we all miss Jessie - as I should think you do too.'

'I do,' she sighed. Did you know that she's getting married a couple of days before you?'

'Yes, she sent me a letter. I'm so thrilled those two are going to get their 'happy ever after at last'.'

'So am I.' Betsy smiled, and she was.

*

After having another paddle, the party arrived home at half-past-four – most of them happy, slightly sunburnt and full of sandwiches and cake.

Peter, Sarah and Justin returned from Trevarno at six, by which time all the domestic staff had bathed away the salt from their skin.

The family only required a light supper that evening - having supped well at Trevarno, and by nine-thirty, they'd retired to bed early. The staff, still high on excitement from their day out, sat around the kitchen table chatting, enjoying a biscuit and a cup of hot chocolate for their supper. They all glowed with the sun and fresh air and most declared it was the best day out they'd had for a long time.

*

When Betsy and Juliet retired, Betsy inspected her sun burnt nose in the mirror with dismay. 'Well, I've ruined my English rose complexion,' she joked, but Juliet remained as quiet as she had been all afternoon. 'Are you all right now, Juliet?' Betsy turned to her.

'Yes, thank you,' Juliet said quietly, pulling the covers almost over her head. It seemed that the conversation was over.

Betsy looked down on her friend - she could see her shoulders shaking as though she was crying. 'Are you sure you're all right? Are you sad about what you said to Joe?'

Juliet sniffed. 'Go to sleep, Betsy, please.'

*

Ruby was checking that all the maid's bedroom doors were closed and there were no lights showing under the door. Mary and Dorothy had been told twice that week not to read past eleven. She smiled, by the lack of light under the door - their day by the sea had worn them out. Realising she'd left her book in the housekeeper's room, she descended the back stairs, swiftly and silently but for the gentle chink of the keys she wore around her waist and almost collided with Justin who was coming out of the kitchen.

'Goodness gracious, you startled me there!'

'Oops! I'm sorry, Ruby.'

Ruby looked around to see if anyone else was about.

'Don't worry – there's no one about, I waited until everyone retired, well, I thought everyone had retired – but now I have the delightful company of my favourite member of staff.' He smiled broadly.

She tipped her head, smiled and eyed the roughly made sandwich he was carrying. 'Can I get you anything else?'

'No, I've managed on my own.'

167

'Did they not feed you at Trevarno?'

'They did, and very well I might say, but I'm working through the night in the attic, so I thought I'd gather some sustenance to see me through.' He grinned again. 'Mrs Blair will think she has a larder thief. Could you tell her it was me – I don't want anyone to get into trouble.'

'I will. Shall I make you a hot beverage to go with your - *sandwich?*' Her lip curled.

'Only if you'll share a cup with me.'

Though the corridor was dimly lit, she felt his eyes burning down intently on her and unconsciously smoothed her dress down and looked about her again.

'It's all right, Ruby, as I said, everyone is tucked up in bed.'

She moistened her lips, wanting desperately to spend a little more time with Justin. 'All right, I'll put the kettle on to boil - we'll take it to the housekeeper's room.'

*

Justin put his plate down on her desk and sat down, his legs crossed languidly while he waited. He looked around the room where Ruby spent most of her time – it was devoid of anything personal to her – possibly because it was well used with the maids coming in and out. From their conversation the other day, he felt concerned that she spent too many days confined to this house, especially after seeing a different, freer version of her.

He got up to close the door after her when she brought in the tray. She was about to sit at her chair behind the desk, but he gestured her to sit on his, while he brought her chair and placed it opposite her.

'I could lose my position, you know, being here with you alone.'

'I'd speak up for you and say it was entirely my fault. Sarah knows my unconventional ways. She'll think I've imposed myself on you, which in truth, I have.'

'Believe me, Justin,' Ruby smiled, 'having you here with me is no imposition.'

He crinkled his eyes. 'That's heartening to hear.'

'How was your trip to Trevarno, then?'

'Better than expected. I didn't feel paraded like I normally feel. Andrew and Eleanor Bickford, Matthew's parents, were genuinely interested in my work and asked if I could paint their daughter Mellissa.'

'Will you?'

'I don't know.' He shrugged. 'I'm a little preoccupied at the moment.'

Ruby tipped her head. 'With what?'

He snuffled a laugh, and shook his head. 'How was your day at the beach? I'd have loved to have been there, with *you*.' He saw Ruby's eyes shine at the emphasis.

'It was lovely – I don't often get to sit on the beach,' she said, averting her eyes shyly by blowing on her tea so she could sip it.

'So, is Poldhu the best beach around here?'

'One of them, yes - though it gets very busy.'

'Even now it's winter?'

She laughed gently. 'It's not winter yet. Down here we can expect a good month or more of nice weather before the rain sets in for the winter.'

'Autumn then?'

'It can get busy on nice days, yes.'

He took a drink from his cup and asked casually, 'Which are the quieter beaches then?'

'Polurrian Cove or Church Cove, Gunwalloe.'

'Which do *you* prefer?'

'Church Cove, I think - it has a rather lovely church buried into the cliff.'

'Perhaps next time you have a day off, you might visit Church Cove?' he asked over the rim of his cup. She must have seen the twinkle in his eyes, because she smiled.

'Perhaps I will.'

Justin stood and put his empty cup on the tray. 'I'll let you get to your bed.'

Ruby stood too. 'Don't forget your sandwich,' she

laughed, as she handed him the monstrosity on the plate. He took it, but put it back down again for a moment, cupped her face in his hands and kissed her very tenderly on the lips. 'Until Wednesday, lovely Ruby,' he said, picking up the plate again before leaving the room.

*

Ruby sat down, closed her eyes and traced her fingers across her lips where he'd kissed her. This dalliance with Her Ladyship's brother could only end badly - she knew that. But she was thirty-four-years-old and had never before experienced these powerful feelings! Opening her eyes, she looked around the room where she spent her life, sorting sheets, organising maids and generally making sure everyone in the household was comfortable. Was this to be her lot? Was she never to have anything for herself? Was it so wrong to feel – what - what did she feel? Cherished for once, that's what she felt - and loved - though there had been no mention of love, but if this feeling deep down in her heart was not love for Justin, then she knew not what was. *Oh, Ruby,* she knew her position in the household would be in deep jeopardy if she continued on this path with him, but it was a path she was willing to take after that kiss, and she suspected that after Wednesday – her fate would be sealed.

22

Juliet's nightmares were the last thing she'd thought of, after she had cried for her lost future with Joe. These past few weeks she'd managed to put her past horrors to the back of her mind, but trying to explain to Joe yesterday why they couldn't be together, without telling him the real reason, coupled with Thomas's misguided gesture, her terrors had been brought to the forefront of her mind.

She woke with a start, drenched in perspiration. Her eyes wide-open darted about the room to see if her nightmare was real. Her mouth was dry and sour, but before she could quench her thirst, she knew she must erase the memory, the feeling, and horror of what had woken her. Pouring water into the pitcher, she began to arduously scrub the palms of her hands. Tears streamed down her face when the bristles of the nailbrush and carbolic soap drew blood on her poor work-worn hands. But try as she might, she could not erase that dreadful feeling on her skin, and when a hand joined hers in the water, she whimpered in terror.

'Shush, Juliet it's me, Betsy.' Having stopped Juliet from the act of scrubbing her hands, Betsy quickly lit the oil lamp which revealed Juliet's tragic tear-stained face. 'It's four in the morning, Juliet, what are you doing?'

'Washing my hands,' she answered shakily.

'You're making them bleed, look, they'll be no use to you raw,' she said quietly.

Juliet dropped the soap, letting it plop into the water, and wiped her tears with the sleeve of her nightdress. She allowed Betsy to dry her trembling hands with the towel, but had to call on all her reserves not to pull away when Betsy wrapped her arms tightly around her to comfort her.

'You have my ear if you need to tell me why you were doing this,' Betsy said softly.

Juliet closed her eyes and nodded, and then allowed Betsy to lead her back to bed, but no matter how kind her room-mate was, she knew she could not, would not ever, be able to tell her.

*

Ryan was up and about in the boarding house a good hour before Jake Treen - Guy Blackthorn's other apprentice thatcher. He'd had the best couple of night's sleep he'd had for a long time, in his comfortable horse-hair bed. By the time Miss Taylor had got up to make them a hearty breakfast, Ryan had taken her dog, Nigel for a walk, brought in the wood and lit the fires. He was rewarded with an extra slice of bacon on his plate for his efforts.

Without doubt he felt a curl of apprehension as he and Jake walked down the road towards Poldhu for his first work day. He had no idea if he could do the job he'd been employed to do, but Jake assured him, as long as he was not afraid of heights and was able to keep sure-footed, he'd get along just grand.

*

When Ellie let them into the Blackthorn's kitchen, Blue, Silas's dog, got up from where he laid beside Ellie's dog, Brandy, and rushed towards Ryan, greeting him like he would his master.

'Hello again, boy,' Ryan tickled his ears, 'I hope you've eaten your breakfast today?'

Guy watched with mixed emotions at the dog's change of allegiance. 'He has, actually -he's a changed dog.'

He beckoned Ryan over to the table. After hours of deliberation, Guy had decided to lend Ryan Silas's thatching tools – there was no point in buying in more when these would go to waste now. He unrolled the canvas tool bag on the kitchen table – inside were a legget, side rake, shearing hook, eaves hook, short eaves knife and a whetstone – Guy demonstrated with the latter how to sharpen the tools.

'The best way to teach you is on the job. Watch, listen and learn. It takes approximately five years to become a master thatcher, but you'll feel like you're one long before

172

that. As I told you the other day, Jake here has been with me since Easter, and he can thatch as good as the next person, but there is so much more to learn. Each house is different and can throw up problems that only someone who has thatched for a long time will have come across. The best advice I can give you is - take pride in your work, never cut corners, make sure the finish is top quality and you won't go far wrong. Right, come on - let's see what you're made of.'

'Here you are lads,' Ellie said, handing out pasties wrapped in cloths, 'your dinner. There are some apples and three flasks of water in there to take as well.'

'Thank you, Ellie,' they said in unison. As they all picked up their bags and pasties, Blue wagged his tale as though to come with them.

'Do the dogs come with us?' Ryan asked.

Brandy doesn't. Blue, however, never left Silas's side. He used to climb the ladder and sit on the ridge while he worked,' Guy said, his voice catching.

'Are we to take him then?' Ryan asked.

Guy glanced over to Ellie who nodded.

'As long as you can carry him back down the ladder on your shoulder, Ryan - Blue can climb up, but not down, you see.'

'Well, if you're happy for him to come with us, I'm happy to carry him down the ladder. Come on, boy.' Ryan snapped his fingers and Blue came to heel.

*

When Betsy and Juliet washed and dressed ready to start the day, nothing else was said regarding the previous night. They both went off to do their allocated chores before the household woke, both with their own thoughts about the incident.

Ruby, however, seemed to be in a dream that morning and Betsy had to peek at the rota herself to see what chores everyone had been allocated. At breakfast too, Ruby knocked over the milk jug and seemingly tripped over fresh air as she went to get a cloth to mop up the spill.

'Goodness me, but I'm clumsy today,' Ruby said brightly as she went to refill the jug.

Fortunately, Ruby's mishaps diverted attention from Juliet, who if anyone had noticed, was clearly having trouble holding the spoon in her porridge. Betsy watched with concern as Juliet winced with every mouthful, so after breakfast she sought Izzy out in the laundry and begged a pot of her homemade antiseptic cream. Izzy gave Betsy a pot without asking questions, and when she in turn gave it to Juliet, she just said, 'It's for your hands,' and left it at that, hoping that her friend would find the courage to tell her why she had scrubbed them raw.

*

Joe retreated to his office after breakfast service. The Earl and Countess had gone to Truro for the day, and it seemed Mr Devereux had ensconced himself in the attic and had not slept in his bed all night. He sat back in his chair and steepled his fingers - was it his imagination, or was Ruby in a strange, almost excitable frame of mind. She was certainly at sixes and sevens this morning, before and during breakfast, which was so unlike her. He'd never known her so clumsy and unorganised to start the day's work. Thank goodness Betsy had had her wits about her and organised the other maids with their jobs, because Ruby seemed oblivious to everything going on around her. Perhaps she was sickening for something. If she was no better later today, he'd offer to bring the doctor to her.

If the truth be known, he too was in a contemplative mood. He ran his fingers through his hair until it stood on end, as he thought of Juliet. His hopes had been completely dashed after their strange conversation yesterday. It seemed that even though they'd agreed to be friends, the incident in the tea room had rendered her even more reserved than normal. In fact, she looked totally miserable at breakfast, and could barely look at him - or anyone for that matter. He sighed deeply and almost jumped out of his skin when a knock came at the door.

'Come in,' he said trying to tamp down his ruffled hair.

Betsy put her head around the door. 'I wonder - can I have a word, Mr Treen?'

'Of course, Betsy, please take a seat. Is something amiss?' He wondered if she was going to mention Ruby's strange disposition.

'Forgive me for speaking so boldly, Mr Treen, but I believe Juliet spoke to you yesterday about….well, about how she feels for you.'

Joe inhaled deeply. 'I rather thought our conversation was private.' He tempered his displeasure when he saw Betsy nervously folding her hands on her lap as though to stop herself from wringing them.

'Well, I knew about it, because it was I who insisted that she speak to you.'

'Oh?' Joe raised an eyebrow.

'When I saw her shy away from you the other day - and your obvious dismay when she did, I questioned her, and asked if you'd done or said something to upset her. When she assured me that you'd done nothing to merit her slight, I told her in no uncertain terms that if she didn't explain to you why she reacted so, then I couldn't remain friends with her.'

'Well, that was kind of you, Betsy, but there was really no need.'

'You're a good and kind man, Mr Treen. I know how disappointed you were over Jessie, and I had high-hopes when Juliet came to work here – because you seemed to like each other.'

Joe cleared his throat, unsettled to be having this conversation.

'I want to apologise, for forcing her hand. I thought I was doing the right thing for both of you, by making her address the problem – if there was one, but I fear it didn't help, did it? When she returned from speaking to you, she only reiterated that there could be nothing between you. So, I'm sorry.'

Joe was beginning to feel deeply uncomfortable now. 'Well, apology accepted, Betsy – you were only trying to help. But Juliet made it clear that I was wrong in my assumption that she felt the same way about me as I did for her.' He stood up hoping to terminate the conversation, but Betsy remained seated.

'Well, I don't want to speak out of term, but I think she's fibbing! We could see that she liked you - in fact she told me as much, and, Juliet cried herself to sleep last night - she was so upset at what she'd told you!'

Joe sat back down in his chair.

'That's not all, I woke in the middle of the night to find her stood over the pitcher, crying and scrubbing the palms of her hands so much she made them bleed.'

He frowned. 'Whatever was she doing *that* for?'

Betsy bit her lip. 'She had a nightmare, but I think her terrors are real. I think someone - some man has hurt her in the past. We all saw how she reacted with Thomas yesterday, and she shrinks away from you, but it doesn't happen if I or the other maids touch her. I don't think I'm wrong, Mr Treen, but I think *this* is why she cannot give her heart to you.'

Joe clenched his teeth, angry at the very thought that someone had harmed her. 'If she won't tell us, how do you propose we help her?'

'Well, I've been thinking on that, and perhaps just kindness is the way forward.'

'I'm always kind to her!' he said defensively.

'I know you are, but perhaps if she *does* shrink from you, try not to show it matters, just smile and talk to her as normal as though it never happened. Speak to her of things she is interested in, get to know her, let her begin to trust you – without the added worry that you want more from the relationship. Show her that not all men want to harm her. Join us if we take a walk around the garden in the fresh air. Pick a secret flower for her and leave it where only she will find it, things like that. Let her know she's safe with you. I just think she needs to learn how to trust again.'

'Oh, Betsy, you have a very wise head on those young shoulders, you know.'

Betsy smiled shyly.

'Thank you for taking the time to be bothered about me.'

'I've known you a long time, Mr Treen, I'm glad you've allowed me to speak so candidly to you.'

*

With the harvest finished, and only Mr Devereux in the house - as the Earl and Countess were away in Truro for the day, the staff had a little more time on their hands that Monday. Almost everyone felt buoyant after having a day by the sea yesterday.

Betsy was trying to ease her foot into her normal boots without success, and had to revert back to her ugly over boot in order to take a walk in the sunshine. It was her half day off, but with Ryan starting his job today and her favourite field having been harvested, she thought that instead of walking the fields, she'd sit in the garden and write another letter to Jessie – she had lots to tell her.

She looked up when Dorothy came back from emptying the pig swill bucket, her face screwed up as though the pig smell was still in her nostrils.

'Your face will stay like that if the wind changes,' Mrs Blair berated. 'What's amiss?'

'That horrible Mr Trencrom is out there – he's waiting for you, Betsy.'

'Oh, no!' Betsy felt her heart sink. 'Did he say that?'

'Well, he asked what time your half day starts.'

'Oh, lord. Well, that's settled it. I'm not going out,' she said taking her boots off again, annoyed that he was going to spoil her day off. She slumped down at the table and pulled out a sheet of writing paper from her bag.

A couple of hours later, having finished her letter to Jessie, Betsy was now reading her book at the dining room table when Joe came into the kitchen. They smiled companionably to each other.

'Are you not going out today, Betsy? It's a lovely day!' Joe asked.

Not wanting to make a fuss about Mr Trencrom, but still wishing to go out, she decided to put a suggestion to Joe.

'Well, I was thinking, that because it *is* such a lovely day, and the family are in Truro, why don't we all take our leisure time out in the garden – we could even have our tea early in the orchard - it'll be like a picnic.'

'Oh, that sounds fun,' Dorothy said excitedly, 'but, what would Her Ladyship say?'

Lowenna Trevail, Sarah's lady's maid looked up from her sewing. 'She would no doubt say, "Please feel free to dead-head as you walk past the flower borders".'

'Shall we go then?' Betsy asked. 'We've all got a couple of hours off before tea.'

Joe glanced at Ruby, who had finally snapped out of her reverie and she agreed. 'Very well, then,' he said, 'I'll fetch some blankets and a chair for Mrs Blair to sit on.'

'No, don't bother about me,' Mrs Blair flapped her tea cloth, 'I'll prepare the baskets, but I'd rather put my feet up than wander around in the sun.'

When everyone went off to get ready, Mrs Blair turned to Betsy and tipped her head. 'You should have told Mr Treen about Trencrom hanging about. You can't hide from him forever, you know!' she said.

'I don't want to make a fuss, Mrs Blair.'

'He'll not give up you know – he's too arrogant. Take my advice and have him stopped, because I wouldn't trust that rogue as far as I could throw him!'

23

The members of the Bochym Arts and Crafts Association who occupied the workshops behind the manor, seemed to have had the same idea, and had abandoned their work for the day to picnic down by the lake. They'd taken the gramophone down with them, pushed the boats out and the sound of music and laughter floated on the warm afternoon air.

The domestic staff walked through the avenue of linden trees and settled their blankets in the walled orchard amongst trees heavy with ripe apples, pears and plums.

Mrs Blair had made ham sandwiches for everyone, fluffy warm scones had been wrapped in a cloth, ready to take a spoonful of jam and cream. Theo and Lowenna were sat apart from the others, deep in happy conversation. Ruby wondered, not for the first time, if Lowenna would have some happy news for them soon. The couple had been married for over eight years, but recently Ruby had seen Lowenna dreamily watching the Earl and Countesses' children, whenever Nanny brought them into the kitchen to thank Mrs Blair for their tea. If that was the case, Ruby was happy for them - if not a little envious. At thirty-four she herself was perhaps a little old to still harbour hopes of becoming a mother. In fact, the chance of that ever happening had been zero until….. she turned towards the manor, and in particular the attic windows where Justin was working. Was she reading too much into his attentions of her? Was he sincere? The promise she'd made to meet Justin again on Wednesday at Church Cove was scandalous in the highest degree, but she felt compelled to do it, despite the consequences. A few weeks ago, she would not have believed that anything could have shaken her position and her standing in life.

*

Justin observed Ruby and the others in the garden from the attic window. He smiled - while the cat's away the mice will play. More than anything else he'd have loved to have joined them, but this was their treat and he didn't want to impose.

'Ruby,' he whispered, remembering the kiss he'd stolen so brazenly from her last night. He could still feel the softness of her lips against his. She had not been shocked at the gesture, nor pulled away, which gave him hope to believe that she felt the same way as he. He knew though that she was cautious of him, and he didn't blame her. She would know that in his profession of an artist he'd have had his pick of women – he was after all forty-years-old and a red-blooded man - of course he'd enjoyed a few dalliances, but never had any woman so intrigued him as Ruby had. She was like a rosebud just waiting to open, hidden behind other blousy blooms until someone picked her and allowed her to blossom.

*

The lure of the picnic baskets meant they took tea early that afternoon and now everyone was lazing languidly in the dappled sunlight of the trees.

Betsy sat up and shook the sleep which threatened out of her head.

'I'm going for a walk around the flower borders,' she announced, 'anyone coming with me? Juliet, will you come?' As both women stood and brushed their skirts down, Betsy surreptitiously gestured for Joe to join them.

Juliet appeared to shrink within herself when she realised Joe was following, but he kept a good space between them and spoke mostly to Betsy, until he asked them both what their favourite flower was.

'Roses for me,' Betsy answered, 'I like red ones of course, but yellow roses are my favourite.'

'Ah, now, that is because a yellow rose denotes friendship, joy and happiness – all the traits you possess, Betsy.' Joe smiled warmly.

'Thank you, Mr Treen.' Their conversation earlier seemed to have sealed their friendship.

Juliet looked at Joe with new admiration. 'You know about flowers then, Mr Treen?'

'I do - and their meaning.'

'I know a little too,' she said tentatively. 'My father loved his garden, so too my grandmother. She wrote a little notebook, which I still have, about the language of flowers.

Betsy gave a ghost of a smile, realising Joe and Juliet had found some common ground.

As the threesome walked slowly along the early autumn flower borders, Betsy challenged them to tell her the meaning of every bloom they came across.

'Dahlias depict dignity and elegance,' Juliet was the first to answer when Betsy pointed them out.

'These mean a fanciful nature,' Joe said when Betsy pointed at a beautiful yellow Begonia.

Betsy giggled and whispered, 'That should be Dorothy's flower then.' They moved a little further. 'What about Cyclamen then?' she asked, just as Ruby joined them in their game.

Juliet answered this one, 'Although they are lovely, especially because they brighten a garden during the winter months, they mean resignation or good-bye, so that makes me think sad thoughts.'

'Well don't think of them too often, you've had enough sad thoughts,' Betsy whispered to her.

Joe pointed to the Michaelmas daisies. 'Whereas red roses are associated with love - so too are these pretty little flowers. These are my favourite flowers at this time of year. I also love paperwhite narcissus, which fortunately bloom early here – sometimes before Christmas!'

'You two are so informative, who would have known you know so much about flowers,' Betsy said, thrilled to witness Juliet and Joe sharing their love of something. 'Which is your favourite, Juliet?'

'These,' she said shyly pointing to the alstroemerias, 'I've seen them in the flower arrangements Her Ladyship makes, and they seem to last a lot longer than any other flowers. I don't know the meaning of them though - I'd never seen them before I came here.'

'Ah, the beautiful alstroemerias,' Joe smiled. 'Bochym has them all year due to Mr Hubbard growing them through the winter in the hot house. Their blooms have a meaning of friendship, love, strength and devotion. The meaning derives from the six beautiful petals of the flower.' He touched the delicate flower with his fingers. 'Each petal represents a different characteristic - understanding, humour, patience, empathy, commitment and respect. Their twisted leaves are also a symbol of bonding, stability and overcoming difficulties together.'

Juliet smiled sweetly at Joe. 'You really are an expert on flowers, aren't you Mr Treen?'

'I wouldn't say expert, but I learnt a lot from my father too. He was head gardener at Trelissick before his rheumatism set in.'

'Oh, dear - is he unable to work now?'

'Unfortunately, he had to retire, but because of my job, and my younger brother Jake working as a thatching with Guy Blackthorn, we manage to send enough to keep their household going.'

'Where do they live?' Juliet questioned.

'They've moved to Penryn - where my mother's family came from. I don't see a great deal of them. Jake and I only go once every couple of months when our days off correspond.

Betsy watched as they chatted, they both looked happy and relaxed today – a far cry from their shared sadness yesterday. Suddenly her thoughts were distracted when Henry Trencrom approached.

Joe must have noted Betsy's obvious unease at the unwelcome visitor and stepped forward. 'Yes, Mr Trencrom, what can we do for you? As you see we are having a staff gathering.'

'Not all staff have been invited again I see,' he

grumbled.

'It's for household staff only,' he reiterated.

'It's Betsy I want a word with.'

'I'm rather busy at the moment,' Betsy said shortly.

His lip curled, unable to hide his scorn. 'It'll take no more than a minute of your *precious* time.'

Joe glanced at Betsy. 'Do you want to give him a minute of your time? I'll stay right here.'

She nodded, folded her arms and reluctantly walked towards Trencrom.

'Right, Betsy Tamblin, it's been over a week now since I declared to you. I think you owe me an answer.'

'I owe you nothing of the kind. I told you at the time you made your unwelcome proposal to me, that I wasn't interested.'

'Aye and I know why - you've been flirting with other men, haven't you?'

'I beg your pardon? I've flirted with no one!'

'I've seen you, waving Penrose off, and linking arms with that hedger fellow. You're barking up the wrong tree with that one - his fancy lies elsewhere.'

'I'm barking up no one's tree, thank you very much.' she snapped affronted. 'And for your information Mr Penrose came to leave a message with Her Ladyship, and Mr FitzSimmons took my arm only once, and that was to steady me when I nearly tripped over a branch!'

'Good, because I'll not have anyone queering my pitch - I asked you first and I expect you to honour my request. And think on - fruit goes off you know, if it's left on the branch for too long. You'll not get another offer better than mine.'

'How dare you? Let me tell you once and for all. I would rather die an old maid than take *your* hand in marriage. Your very presence is offensive to me. Good day to you.' As she turned, he grabbed her by the arm.

'Why you little minx, I'll not have my offer thrown in my face like that.'

Joe and Ruby were at Betsy's side in a heartbeat, and Joe clamped his hand over Trencrom's arm.

'Unhand her at once,' he demanded.

'She was being rude.'

'Betsy hasn't a rude bone in her body. Now be off with you, otherwise I'll report you to His Lordship.'

Trencrom released her arm, bared his rotting teeth at Betsy, and then stormed off down the garden.

Ruby took Betsy in her arms protectively. 'Shall Mr Treen report it, Betsy?'

Betsy rubbed her arm where he'd grabbed her. 'I don't know. I *was* rather rude to him!' She looked sheepishly between them.

Joe smiled tightly. 'I suspect you were hard pressed not to be. We'll leave it for now, but if you have any more trouble from him, you must inform me immediately, do you understand?'

'Yes, Mr Treen.'

When the group walked back to Juliet, Betsy noted that she looked more shaken than she did!

'Oh, god, are you all right, Betsy?' Juliet cried reaching out to Betsy's hand.

'Yes, he's just a nasty piece of work, that's all. Mr Treen saw him off, thank goodness. One thing is certain, living here you can always depend on Mr Treen.'

*

When everyone settled down again after the upset, Ruby noticed a figure standing in the front garden – she knew at once it was Justin and stood up to brush her skirt down.

'I think Mr Devereux needs something,' she said to Joe. 'I'll go. I need to pop inside for something. You stay with the maids.' By the time she'd walked through the avenue of linden trees and into the parterre, Justin had walked down to join her.

'Do you need something?' she said smiling brightly.

'Only to spend more time with you, if possible,' his eyes crinkled. They laughed softly together. 'I was watching you all out in the sunshine, so I thought I'd take a walk in the fresh air. I see the Arts and Crafts people are by the lake – I think I'll join them for a while.'

'Kindred spirits?' Ruby asked.

Justin nodded. 'If I cannot be with you, they are the second-best thing. I wish you could come with me though,' he said earnestly.

Ruby glanced down at the bohemian group laughing and listening to the gramophone by the lake. 'Alas,' she sighed, 'I lead a very different life from them.'

'Yes – except perhaps on your days off,' he mused.

'Shush,' her eyes glistened.

'About Wednesday, Ruby....' he started to say, but then stopped as Joe approached them.

'I'm just going to make sure the boilers are lit for hot water in time for the family coming home, Ruby. Is everything all right, Mr Devereux?' he asked.

Justin laughed. 'Will I never get you to call me Justin?'

Joe just gave him a wry smile.

'Everything is fine, thank you, Joe,' Justin answered, 'I'm just about to partake in a glass of champagne by the lake – though my stomach will protest alarmingly later on. Sometimes a little effervescent is needed to put a sparkle in one's life.' His eyes flickered in Ruby's direction, before bidding them both a good afternoon.

'Who needs champagne?' Joe smiled at Ruby. 'When a walk in the garden with three of my favourite members of staff, is all the effervescence I need?'

'I agree, Joe – it's the small pleasures in life that mean a great deal.'

*

With his chance to speak to Ruby about Wednesday thwarted by Joe earlier, Justin managed to catch up with her later that evening. He knew that her early evening routine involved meticulously checking the bedrooms to make sure the maids had turned down the beds while the family enjoyed a pre-dinner drink. So, he made his excuses to Sarah that he needed to fetch a handkerchief, and found Ruby near his bed, her fingers smoothing down the eiderdown.

This time he stayed where he was by the door until she turned.

'Oh!' She blushed profusely at being caught. 'I thought you were downstairs.'

'I came to see who'd been stroking my bed,' he joked.

Clearly abashed, she explained, 'I'm just checking all is well.' She made to walk past him, but he caught her arm gently and she did not resist him, she just lifted her eyes to meet his.

'Will you still meet me on Wednesday?'

She trembled under his touch. 'All being well here, yes,' she whispered.

'At Church Cove?'

She nodded. 'I'll catch the ten-o-clock wagon from Cury Cross Roads.'

His smile widened, he so wanted to kiss her again, instead, he lifted his finger to her face and ever so softly touched her hot pink cheek. 'Until Wednesday then, lovely Ruby,' he murmured.

24

Wednesday morning dawned and Ruby had been up and about, busying herself to make sure all was shipshape in the manor before she started her day off. From the windows she could see that the weather promised a day of bright blue skies and sunshine. A small part of Ruby wanted the day to dawn cloudy and rainy – this would stop her from going to Church Cove and...... and what? Enjoying the day with someone who was good company? She glanced up at the mirror, to tidy her hair, *but it wouldn't just be spending the day with someone who was good company, would it Ruby?* It would be much more than that, because deep down, and certainly after that kiss, she knew that this day would change her life forever. The only thing that could save her from herself was if some incident happened in the manor that meant she could not go. Alas, no such incident had occurred. Ruby put on her hat and coat, picked up her bag and glanced around her bedroom, knowing that the Ruby who returned to this room might be a very different person.

She popped into Joe's office before leaving. 'I'm going out now, unless you need me here for anything.'

'No, Ruby, you're free to go. I must say it's good to see you getting out and about - you look like a different person for doing so. I often thought that you spent too much time with us.'

'Well, I like you all, that's why, and now you're pushing me out of the door.'

'I'm doing nothing of the sort,' he smiled, 'I'm urging you to go and enjoy yourself. Are you going far?'

'I thought perhaps I would take the wagon to Poldhu. Have a walk and a paddle,' she said, hoping that the lie would not show on her face. 'I did so enjoy my day on the beach on Sunday - these fine, sunny days may not last much longer now.'

'Oh, I don't know - there has been talk of an Indian

summer. Has Mrs Blair made you a picnic basket?'

'Yes,' she lifted the basket to show.

'I believe she was making one up for Mr Devereux too,' Joe said.

'Oh!' Ruby felt her voice waver.

'I think he's doing much the same. He's ordered the pony trap for ten and has loaded his easel and paints in the hall ready.'

They both turned when someone knocked.

Justin entered the room. 'Did I just hear my name mentioned?'

'Only on account on me telling Mrs Sanders that you were going out in the trap today,' Joe answered.

He smiled broadly, 'And that's precisely why I'm looming in your doorway - to see if the trap is ready?'

'It's waiting out the front. It seems that you and Mrs Sanders have the same idea.'

'Really?' Justin's eyes glistened.

'Yes, she too is heading for the coast.'

'Well then, perhaps I can give you a lift?'

Ruby baulked at the idea. The plan was for her to take the wagon to Poldhu golf club and walk down the path to Church Cove to meet Justin there. This arrangement now seemed to blow their day out in the open.

'No, thank you,' she declined. 'I'm happy to take the wagon.'

'Don't be daft,' Joe laughed. 'It'll save you the fare. Go with Mr Devereux.'

Justin tipped his head. 'Please, let me give you a lift.'

Ruby glanced between Joe and Justin. 'Very well, thank you.'

Once settled on the trap, and just in case anyone was watching them leave, Ruby sat bolt upright with her basket on her lap, her face frozen and her knees slightly turned away from Justin, who took the reins. She remained like this until they turned off the main Lizard road to make their way towards Cury Churchtown.

'You can relax now, Ruby,' Justin grinned.

'It's all very well you smiling at my discomfort,' she parried. 'I feel so exposed being on this trap.'

He pulled his mouth downwards. 'I'm sorry I make you uncomfortable.'

She turned and allowed herself a smile. 'It's not you, Justin.'

He reached over for her hand and held it tightly. 'I'm glad to hear it.'

His touch made her body quiver. 'It's what people will read into it!'

'All they will see is that I'm giving you a lift.'

She turned to meet his gaze. 'But you're not just giving me a lift, are you?'

'No,' he said squeezing her hand. 'I'm not.'

'What exactly *are* you doing?'

His eyes crinkled. 'I'm spending time with a beautiful woman. What are *you* doing, Ruby?'

'I'm about to spend the day with the most handsome man I've ever had the privilege to meet.'

'Oh, dear – and I thought you were going to spend it with me?'

They both laughed and he leant over and kissed her cheek, making her glance wildly around to see if anyone had seen them.

'All we're doing, Ruby, is living.' He flicked the reins to move the pony along more quickly.

They turned into the lane that cut through the Poldhu golf course down to Church Cove, where the view of the wide, blue, luminescent sea opened up before them, gloriously inviting them down. To the right of the golden sandy beach nestled St Winwaloe's Church and that was where they headed.

'Good, the beach looks deserted,' he said pulling up outside the church gates.

They settled under the shade of the churchyard wall on a couple of blankets Justin had taken from the back of the trap.

Justin turned his tanned face towards the sun. 'What a truly perfect spot for a picnic.'

Ruby watched as he closed his eyes. *Imagining this is what he would look like sleeping.* The scenario that Justin would be the man she perhaps would share a bed with one day, had indeed entered her head a few times.

He opened his eyes and smiled when he found her watching him.

'It's a bit too soon for a picnic, don't you think?'

'A little,' she answered.

'But, not too soon to receive a gift, I hope.' He started to rummage in his large leather satchel. 'This is for the other artist in the family,' he said handing her a parcel wrapped in brown paper.

Ruby looked at it questioningly.

'Well, open it then!' he said excitedly.

Slowly un-wrapping the gift, she found a watercolour book, a tin of new watercolour paints, and a selection of paintbrushes.

'Oh, Justin!' She pressed the gifts to her chest. 'Thank you, so much.'

'I thought your artist equipment was in dire need of updating. So you can paint and enjoy being free with colour now.'

'I will, I will,' her eyes glistened with delight.

'We'll spend the afternoon painting, but there's something I must do first.'

Ruby watched him unlace his shoes and pull off his socks – he had lovely slender feet. He stood up, rolled his trousers up and opened a couple of buttons on his shirt, revealing a light sprinkling of blonde hairs on his chest, slightly darker than the hair on his head. 'I'm going to dip my feet in the sea.' He held his hand out for her. 'And you're coming too, aren't you?'

Ruby hesitated and then nodded. She unlaced her boots, then turning away from him, she pulled her skirts up to undo the ribbons holding her stockings up, but she knew he was watching as she rolled them down her legs. When she turned, he was smiling and still holding his hand out to her.

'I'd tuck your skirt and petticoat into your belt or else you'll get soaked.'

She pulled the material to one side and did just that and then held her hand out tentatively to him. His fingers curled around hers and he brought her hand to his lips to kiss it, before leading her down to the water's edge.

As the surf splashed up their legs, they both gasped at the sudden coldness.

'Are you near the sea in Tuscany?' she asked, her feet sinking into wet sand.

'Not really, but I do take a trip to the coast a couple of times a month. I can tell you - the sea is a darn sight warmer than this.'

'This is the warmest the sea gets here.

'Brrr.'

She laughed. 'I take it you won't be swimming then.'

'Who says I won't? I'm only here to test the water, and…..to kiss my lovely companion. He pulled her towards him to kiss her passionately.

She could hardly catch her breath when he let her go.

'Can you swim?' he asked.

'Yes.'

'Let's go in then.'

'But I didn't bring my swimming costume.'

'You don't need one, there's no one about,' he said with a twinkle in his eyes.

Ruby pulled her hand from his - a curl of anxiety forming in her stomach.

'What is it – what's the matter?'

'Justin, I have no doubt that you've enjoyed the company of many women, who have been as free as you, but I'm not one of those women. Yes, I've let you kiss me, I'm flattered that you want to, but I am not a woman of loose morals.'

He reached for her and pulled her back to him and very gently cupped her face with his hands. 'Ruby, you are most definitely not like any woman I've met before. My interest in you goes way beyond seducing you. I want to love you - I want you to love me.'

'But, but you don't know me at all!'

'I know I love you.'

A small noise escaped her throat. 'So, you *are* trying to seduce me.'

'I swear I'm not. Of course, I want you - I want to feel you in my arms, I want to kiss your slender neck, but I want you to want me first. I want you to come to me and ask for more than a kiss. Most of all, I want you to be free from being the Bochym Manor housekeeper. Free to be able to swim naked and feel the silky softness of the sea as it caresses your skin if you want to. You're a woman first and a housekeeper second.'

'Oh, good grief!' she said, her heart hammering in her chest, 'no one has ever said those things to me before. Why me? Look at you Justin, you're a beautiful man, you could have anyone, but you choose me - a dowdy housekeeper.'

'My darling girl,' his eyes searched deep into hers, 'you are anything but dowdy. Look at you - your hair is the colour of autumn, your eyes sparkle, as blue as the sea, and, I might add, they're the most beautiful eyes I've ever had the pleasure of looking into. Your skin is like porcelain,' he touched her cheek tenderly, 'and under those dark foreboding clothes you wear, you have a heart crying out to be loved. Let me into your heart Ruby – let's fall in love.'

Ruby's breathing deepened. 'And then what? You'll go back to Italy, and my life will be ruined. *I* will be ruined! What if a baby comes? I'm still young enough for that to happen. What will happen to me when you've gone?'

'No, Ruby, you don't understand. If you come to me, if

you return my love, I would not leave you to flounder. We would marry, and return to Italy together to spend the rest of our lives side-by-side.'

Ruby's mouth dropped. 'And you know all this after only kissing me a couple of times?'

'Love comes from the heart, Ruby. My heart told me the moment I set eyes on you when I arrived at Bochym, that *you* were the one I've been looking for. Kissing you confirmed my feelings.'

'Good god! What will Her Ladyship say?'

'It's nothing to do with anyone else. Now, go and get ready to swim – there are towels in my satchel. I promise I'll not look at you until you're in the water.'

As Ruby walked back up the beach to where their picnic baskets lay, she felt breathless at his declaration of love. Taking off her dress, she unlaced her stays and looked around to see Justin walking naked into the water. Her throat gave an involuntary squeak of pleasure – he looked magnificent.

Taking one last look around the beach to make sure no one was about she stepped out of her petticoat and wrapped her towel around her. Her heart was in her throat as to what she was about to do, and for a moment she could not make her legs move. *Go on Ruby, go swim free.* Taking a deep breath, she clutched the towel to her body, grabbed another for Justin and walked to the sea.

Justin stood waist deep, the gentle waves rippling across him. Seeing her approach, he smiled and turned away, to let her shed her towel and step into the sea.

The cold water caught her breath for a moment, but then she plunged in and swam. She laughed - It felt gloriously wicked to feel the cold water caress her body. When she swam level with Justin, he held his arms out to her. This was it - this was where she made the decision that would change her life. Hesitating for only a moment, she reached out to him until their arms entwined, and salty lips met. Turning and laughing together in the waves, their bodies brushed against each other for the first of many occasions to come.

They swam together for five minutes until Ruby started to shiver and Justin sent her out of the sea to get dressed. As she towelled herself dry, she kept glancing back to see if he was watching, but he was the perfect gentlemen and kept his gaze towards the horizon.

'Tell me when you're respectable,' he shouted, 'sooner, rather than later, I'm freezing now!'

She smiled as she pulled her petticoat over her damp skin, and with her modesty covered, she shouted, 'You can come out now.'

He dried and dressed himself quickly, before returning to her, to kiss her passionately.

'I'm ravenous now – and in dire need of whatever delights Mrs Blair has packed us,' he said delving into the first basket.

They settled down companionably after eating their fill. Justin sat with his back against the wall while Ruby lay with her head resting on his thighs.

'So, Ruby, can I take it you might fall in love with me?'

Ruby laughed gently. 'Yes, I think I will.'

His smile widened. 'You've made me such a happy man today. When shall I tell my sister?'

Panic rose in her throat and she sat up. 'Not yet – I think perhaps I would like us to meet in secret for a while longer.'

'You're still unsure of me?'

'A little, yes. I'm thirty-four, Justin - I've never felt like this before. This is all very new to me.'

'All the more reason for us to enjoy life together,' he murmured as he stroked her damp hair.

'Just give me a little more time, please.'

'Of course – I'll wait until you're ready.'

They spent the next few hours companionably – Justin happily sketching Ruby, while she painted her first *colourful* watercolour. Neither wanted the day to end, but end it must. They packed up the pony trap and Justin took her as far as Cury Cross lanes to let her walk alone down the long driveway to the manor, while he partook in glass of beer in The Wheel Inn. Both knew that tongues would wag if they arrived home together again!

Ruby tried without success to sneak in through the laundry exit, but Joe caught sight of her as he was coming out of his office.

'Goodness, Ruby, did you fall in while having your paddle,' he joked.

She pushed him playfully. 'I did not. I've been swimming, if you don't mind.'

'And you look radiant for it, albeit slightly dishevelled, if I might be so bold.'

'Do I?' she said abashed, 'I better go and bathe and tidy myself then.'

As she drew a bath she glanced in the mirror. Her hair was tousled and hanging limp where she'd been unable to pin it back up properly. Horrified that Justin had spent the afternoon with - quoting Mrs Blair, "someone who looked like they'd been dragged through a hedge backwards" - but then a smile lit her face - if he could see her at her worst and still love her, he must be genuine.

Shedding the last of her clothes, she stepped into the hot water to wash the salt from her hair and skin. Once submerged, she closed her eyes to re-live the memory of Justin's skin on hers. Thankfully he'd agreed not to make their relationship public until she was ready, but she trembled at the thought of telling Her Ladyship. How would she explain her betrayal of trust, and that she'd fallen in love with her brother? Oh, but for now she was happy and kicked her feet in delight, splashing water over the side of the bath, unconcerned that she'd have to mop it up later. She was in love, and she was loved!

*

After a wonderful night's sleep, Ruby felt as though she was walking on air the next morning and had to physically stop herself from humming a happy tune.

'Mrs Sanders's day at the beach must have done her the world of good - she's very bright and breezy this morning,'

Joe said to Thomas.

'Unlike Mr Devereux this morning,' Thomas declared. 'I don't know what he was doing yesterday, but he's not left his bed this morning. Something has knocked the stuffing out of him – he's terribly pale and extremely tired.'

Joe frowned. 'Do we need to call a doctor?'

'He says not - he told me he has days like this and it will pass.'

Joe furrowed his brow. 'Does the Countess know he's ill?'

'No, he doesn't want her to know either.'

Joe sighed heavily. 'This is highly irregular.'

'What's highly irregular?' Ruby asked breezing into the kitchen.

'Mr Devereux is ill,' Joe answered.

Ruby felt her world tip on its axis. 'Ill – in what way?' she said fighting to keep the panic from her voice.

'I don't think he is ill as such, he's just very pale and extremely tired,' Thomas reiterated, 'he says he isn't getting up today.'

'I see.' Ruby smoothed down her skirt as she tried to keep her composure. 'I'll tell the maids not to disturb him.'

*

Justin was deeply worried that he could hardly lift a limb this morning. When he'd gone to his bed last night – he'd felt on top of the world, but had woken in the middle of the night to use the bathroom, to find his legs would not hold his weight. He was generally fit, ailed nothing as such - perhaps a stomach ache if he ate or drank anything rich, but this was not the first time it had happened, he'd put the other occasions down to heat exhaustion - the main reason he'd returned to England.

He'd told Thomas not to tell Sarah – she would only fuss, and from previous bouts of malaise, he knew that he would recover after a day's rest in bed. He sighed in frustration, lazing about did not suit him – his fingers were itching to paint.

He shifted uneasily when he heard a gentle knock and Ruby popped her head around the door.

'May I come in?' she said softly.

'Oh, no,' he hid his face in his hands, 'I didn't want you to see me like this!'

She put her hands on her hips. 'What do you mean, like this?'

'Weak like this. Damn it! Please excuse my profanity, but I can't even get up today. I fear you'll not love me if you see my weak side.'

'Are you saying this is a regular occurrence?' She sat on his bed, and placed her cool hand to his brow to check his temperature.

'It's happened a few times – I thought it was the heat in Tuscany that was exhausting me, but the harvest wiped me out and yesterday's swim did the same.'

'So, It could be the heat – it was sunny on both those occasions,' Ruby suggested. 'Does Her Ladyship know you're still abed?'

'No, and don't tell her - I don't want her fretting, it's bad enough that you're fretting for me now.'

'Let me call Dr Martin. He's new to the area and a good doctor – he might find out what is causing your malaise.'

'No,' he said emphatically. 'No country quack doctors, please – I've had my fill of them. I'll be fine tomorrow after a rest.' He softened his eyes, and he reached up to touch her worried face. 'I suppose you won't want to love a man who can't get out of bed for risk of tiring himself out?'

'You suppose wrong.' She brushed her lips against his. 'But if you want me to continue loving you, you have to let me care for you when you're feeling poorly.'

Footsteps walking towards the room halted their conversation, and Ruby stood up to straighten her skirt.

'Justin? Oh!' Sarah's eyes cut between Ruby and her brother. 'Why are you not out of bed?'

'I've a splitting headache, Sarah. Ruby very kindly came to see if I needed anything – she's going to bring me a headache draft.'

Ruby dropped a curtsy. 'I won't be long, Mr Devereux, my lady.'

Sarah waited until Ruby left before turning her attention to Justin. 'Why was I not informed that you were ill?' She laid her hand on his brow just as Ruby had done.

'Because it's just a headache, I'll be fine. I just feel a little under the weather – perhaps I walked too far yesterday,' he said to appease.

*

At Poldhu that morning, Ellie and Guy were discussing Ryan over breakfast.

'He looks promising and is eager to work to earn some money,' Guy said, brushing toast crumbs from his shirt. 'He has a love interest at Bochym, and is looking to the future' he added.

'Oh!' Ellie tipped her head.

'He's sweet on Betsy Tamblin - Jessie's friend.'

Ellie's breath caught - this was the first time Guy had mentioned Jessie without actually spitting her name out – she hoped he'd started to forgive her.

'In fact, he's more than sweet,' he added with a smile, 'he's really smitten. The poor lad is fretting that it might rain on Saturday and he wanted to go and see her.'

'Ah, loves' young dream,' Ellie smiled. 'It's time Betsy found someone, but the barometer states it *is* going to rain on Saturday - so much for our Indian summer.'

The conversation gave Ellie an idea. If Ryan decided to marry Betsy, they would need somewhere to start their married life, and Jessie's cottage would be perfect. She decided to make a start on clearing out the cupboards and drawers that morning, before she opened the tea room.

When Ellie entered Jessie's cottage, the building felt as cold as the grave, something shifted inside her, as a visceral sense of foreboding filled the room. While she emptied the bedroom drawers, a ripple in the atmosphere confirmed that there was definitely a presence in there with her, and it was most probably Silas. There had been a delay in the hanging of Silas's killer, Philip Goldsworthy, and this, she thought, might be the reason for Silas's unrest. Sometimes a spirit could not move on until justice had been served. There was no doubt that Philip had killed Silas. It had been witnessed by Tobias Williams, an ex-policeman, and Philip himself had confessed - even stating that he wished he'd killed the whole of the Blackthorn family! Ellie shivered involuntary at that thought. The delay was due to Philip's parents trying to get his murder conviction overturned. They wanted him moved to a private asylum - claiming the brain tumour he was suffering from at the time diminished his reason. Philip would undoubtedly die of the brain tumour, but, if he did, without justice being served, Silas may never rest in peace. Many would dismiss her theory as nonsense, but Ellie had lived at Bochym as a child, and experienced many such unearthly disturbances. She knew the spirits could not harm, but they were unsettling to some, and this would indeed pose a huge problem in renting the cottage out.

*

Joe felt the whole household to be on edge, which was often the case when one of them was ill. He watched Ruby's mood change with interest - she'd swung from being buoyant earlier on, to plummeting into quiet concern. He wondered then if Ruby held a candle for Mr Devereux – he certainly hoped not. Not that he didn't want Ruby to find someone to love and settled down with - he did, but if there was some attraction between her and Mr Devereux, it would only end in tears. It was a shame for Ruby, she was such a lovely woman, but meeting anyone when you were in service was difficult unless they too were in the same occupation. He laughed to himself, who was he kidding? He and Juliet couldn't work more closely, but forming a relationship seemed unattainable.

That hadn't stopped him from placing a small posy of flowers in her coat pocket before he'd gone down to the cellar to fetch some bottles of wine for that evening's dinner. Little by little, he'd gently try to get Juliet to trust him.

*

It was late morning and the day was glorious. Juliet had finished her morning chores and was itching to go out in the sunshine, so once again offered to collect the eggs. It was whilst collecting her coat and outdoor boots that she found a tiny sprig of alstroemerias, tied with string, peeking out from the pocket of her coat. Puzzled, she picked them up, and then remembered Joe's words, "Each petal of the alstroemerias represents - understanding, humour, patience, empathy, commitment and respect." She glanced over to Joe who was wiping down the wine bottles he'd just brought up from the cellar. Had he left these for her? He must have. She felt a strange, though not unpleasant frisson, as her fingers curled around the posy of flowers. She'd never been given flowers before. Quickly placing them in her basket, she walked into the kitchen.

Joe looked up, smiling and enquired, 'Are you going out?'

'Yes, I'm collecting eggs.'

'Enjoy the fresh air then. I'll tell Mrs Sanders where you've gone.'

Juliet paused for a moment, but when no mention was made of the flowers, she walked to the door, turning before she went through to see if Joe was watching her, but he'd returned to his task. As she walked along the kitchen courtyard, she could not resist fitting the posy into her buttonhole.

Back in the kitchen, Betsy, who was polishing the cutlery, glanced up at Joe and they exchanged the briefest of smiles.

*

Justin had slept for the best part of the day. Ruby had

201

checked on him a couple of times, but had not disturbed him. Whatever was wrong with him - and she knew it wasn't just a headache - it had wiped him out.

'Wake him up and make him eat something,' Mrs Blair insisted, as she handed Ruby a bowl of broth on a tray at teatime.

Placing the tray on his bedside table, Ruby opened the curtains to let in what light remained of the day, and this roused him from his slumber.

'Broth,' Ruby said, 'Mrs Blair insists you eat it.'

She watched in concern at the very great effort it took Justin to pull himself up to a sitting position. He took a long drink of water and nodded thankfully for the tray to be lowered on his lap.

'Justin, you really don't look well,' Ruby said firmly.

He reached for her hand to squeeze. 'I'll be fine tomorrow, I promise.'

She brought a chair close to his bed. 'I'm worried about spending another day with you, if it's going to do this to you.'

'Ruby, don't say that. I cannot wait until you're in my arms again.'

'I can't wait for that day either,' she whispered. As she moved to kiss him, footsteps coming along the corridor made her pull back before her lips touched his.

'Ah, I see you are awake and taking nourishment,' Sarah said breezing into the bedroom.

Ruby stood up and curtsied.

Sarah glanced curiously between Ruby and Justin. 'I see you are keeping my housekeeper from her leisure time.'

'I probably am, but I asked her to stay and talk to me. I'm in dire need of company.'

Sarah nodded. 'Are you feeling any better?'

'A little, Mrs Blair has made me some broth and it's delicious.' He looked at Ruby and smiled.

'I'll tell her you said so, Mr Devereux,' Ruby said.

Sarah smiled at Ruby. 'Thank you, Ruby, I'll keep my

brother company now and I'll bring his tray down when he's finished. I don't want you to miss your tea.'

'Thank you, my lady.' Ruby curtsied and left the room, but was still in earshot when Justin berated Sarah.

'I was rather enjoying my little chat with Ruby,' he said.

'I'm sure you were, but she works very hard and I will not have you eating into her precious time off. It's not fair on her.'

'I'm sure she doesn't mind,' he argued.

'She is too polite to say no to you, Justin - besides it isn't proper for a woman to be sitting by a gentleman's bedside chatting. Think of her reputation - you're not in Tuscany now.'

Justin placed his spoon in the broth and pushed it away – his appetite lost.

'Justin, you're not…?'

'Not what?' he snapped.

'Becoming too friendly with her, are you?'

Ruby stood outside the door and closed her eyes - *please don't tell her yet?*

'Rest assured, Sarah,' he sighed, 'her reputation is not in jeopardy.'

Ruby's eyes snapped opened. *That statement was debatable after yesterday!* She crept silently away to join the others for tea, wondering in reality how long they could keep their secret from Her Ladyship.

*

Ruby was updating her accounts after tea when Sarah knocked on the door of the housekeeper's room.

Ruby stood up as Sarah put her head around the door. 'May I come in?'

'Of course, my lady, please take a seat.'

'Thank you for your care towards my brother today, Ruby.'

'It's best that I manage the situation, rather than one of the younger maids.'

Sarah smiled and nodded as she folded her hands on

her lap. 'My brother is, as you no doubt have realised, a very free and easy character to get along with.'

Ruby swallowed hard.

'He's a fascinating man who enchants everyone with his unusual zest for life.'

'Yes, my lady,' Ruby answered knowing she had to say something. 'He is certainly a breath of fresh air.'

'I don't want him taking advantage of any of my staff.'

Ruby lifted her chin. 'I assure you…'

'And for that reason, I will tend to my brother from now on while he is confined to his bed.'

'Of course, as you wish. Just let me know what you need to take to him,' she answered as professionally as possible.

'Thank you, Ruby.'

Sarah swept out of the room, leaving only a faint whiff of expensive perfume - and Ruby not quite knowing if she'd just received a warning or a reprimand!

26

On Friday, Ryan sat on the roof they were thatching - watching with dismay as a weather front clouded the blue sky. Rain was imminent, which meant his plan to meet Betsy tomorrow would be scuppered. He could hardly call on her at the manor – it wasn't the correct way to go about things. He smiled inwardly, meeting her in secret like they had planned wasn't appropriate either, but how else was he meant to get to know her? He knew he had to devise a way of meeting her on Sunday somehow. He glanced at Jake Treen. He'd been getting along well with Jake who seemed a lot older than his fourteen years. He knew that Jake visited Bochym on Sundays to see his brother Joe, maybe - just maybe - there was a chance that he could accompany him.

*

Ruby was like a cat on a hot tin roof. Though she had many chores to oversee, she could not quell the unsettling feeling about Justin's sudden illness. She had not slept well, and was desperate to go to Justin to see for herself if he'd recovered, but she knew she could not. So, when Thomas informed them that morning that Justin was still unable to get out of bed, her emotions were in turmoil.

Unconsciously placing her hand to her neck, Ruby, asked, 'And he still won't have the doctor sent for?'

'No, Her Ladyship thinks he's just come down with a summer cold,' Joe said noting the concern on her face. 'Her ladyship is probably right, Ruby. These things can knock a body off kilter.'

Ruby did her best to raise a smile, and then the drawing room bell rang for Joe to attend Her Ladyship, so he pulled his jacket straight and went to answer it. He returned a few moments later.

'Her ladyship needs her horse saddling. Thomas, can you inform the stables please. She's going down to Poldhu to see Mrs Blackthorn. I believe Her Ladyship received a letter at breakfast this morning, with the news that the Trevellick's have safely welcomed a baby boy into the world. She's away to see if Mrs Blackthorn has also heard the news.'

Everyone smiled, Sophie and Kit were not only good friends of Sara and Peter Dunstan, but they were also members of the Arts and Crafts Association here, so everyone shared in their joy.

The moment Ruby heard Her Ladyship cantering out of the stables she swiftly swept up the back stairs and along the corridor towards Justin's room. This was her chance to see for herself if indeed Justin just had a late summer cold.

She knocked softly. 'It's me, Justin.'

'Ruby! I thought you'd forsaken this invalid, come to me, come.' He held his hand out and pulled her into an embrace and kissed her passionately on the lips.

'I'm sorry, but Her Ladyship thinks it's improper for me to be in here with you. She's gone out, but I can't stay long - His Lordship is still home. Are you still feeling unwell?' she said constantly looking around, worried about being caught there.

'I'm much better today, lovely Ruby. Don't fret. I will be well again very soon, and if Sarah will not allow you to come to me, then I'll have to urge my weary body to get up out of this bed. Now go, I don't want to cause you any trouble.'

Very boldly she bent down and kissed him with as much fervour as he had kissed her. 'I think it's a bit too late for causing me trouble, don't you?' She laughed as she swept out of the room. She turned at his door to see him blow a kiss to her.

*

Sarah cantered over the dunes at Poldhu towards the tea room and tied her horse on the railings, though for some reason the animal was skittish again.

Ellie met her on the veranda of the tea room and kissed

her warmly.

'Have you heard from Kit and Sophie,' Sarah asked pulling off her gloves.

'I have, yes. Benjamin Christopher Trevellick – such a fine name. I am so happy for them both, but I suspect now Sophie has delivered safely they'll be making plans to set off north,' Ellie said, settling Sarah at an inside table.

'Yes, I believe they are planning to leave on the 11th of November.'

'I'll miss them terribly,' Ellie said poised to take her order.

'As will I, so, I'm planning to hold a dinner with Kit and Sophie on the 2nd of November to give them a send-off. I was hoping that you and Guy would be able to come? There will be just the six of us – sorry seven - I forget that Justin is here sometimes. He keeps himself to himself in the attic – probably creating another masterpiece,' she smiled, 'having said that, he's not been feeling too well recently, and is confined to his bed again, for the second day. '

'Oh dear. Nothing serious?'

'I hope not, but he won't let me call for a doctor. It's perhaps a late summer cold.'

'Well, send him my regards. As for the dinner, I'll ask Guy, but I'm not hopeful. This delay in Philip Goldsworthy's hanging is playing on his mind – he's not good company at the moment. He's struggling to move on until we get some closure.'

Sarah frowned. 'Do you want me to speak to Peter about it? Perhaps he can get Mr Sheldon, our lawyer, onto the case.'

'Any help would be very much appreciated, because I fear that Silas is still with us.'

'Oh?' Sarah's interest was piqued.

'I think his spirit is unsettled. I felt his presence in Jessie's cottage and it was not at all pleasant.'

'Oh, that explains it, Sarah nodded knowingly. 'When I

rode past the cottage this morning, Beau my horse shied away from it.'

'Well, that confirms my fears.'

'Leave it with me, Elise - I'll get Peter to ask Mr Sheldon to look into the delay. All will be well.'

*

Justin was determined to fight his malaise. He would not be parted from Ruby – no matter what Sarah's good intentions were. Once he was up and about, he'd be able to engineer the odd secret meeting with Ruby.

He pushed the covers down and swung his legs over the end of the bed. His head swam and his feet and hands started to tingle as he sat for a moment. There was no doubt about it, he felt as weak as a kitten, but he knew he must get his body moving again. All this talk of bringing a doctor had got him thinking – if there was something wrong – and clearly there was, he *should* see a doctor, though it wouldn't be some country quack coming to bleed him. He felt exhausted enough without having his veins opened. He had never agreed with the practice, and had night terrors as a child having gone through many such procedures when he suffered childhood illnesses. Fortunately, bleeding was fast losing favour nowadays.

After shaving and swilling his face, he got dressed and pulled his chair to the window to get some fresh air. The day was dull, and the garden colours muted. He thought of his studio in the attic, the stairs up to it would be a challenge, but he needed to be with his paints and easel if he couldn't be with the woman he loved.

*

The weather had indeed deteriorated and thatching had been abandoned for the day. The threesome spent the last couple of hours of work in Ellie's warm kitchen, making spurs out of willow to secure the thatch.

Once back at the boarding house, and whilst they were enjoying one of Miss Taylor's delicious suppers, Ryan casually dropped a mention of Bochym into the conversation.

'Do you go up to Bochym every Sunday, Jake?'

Jake made a soft hum in his throat as he chewed a tender piece of rabbit. He swallowed the mouthful and grinned. 'I wouldn't miss one of Mrs Blair's Sunday teatime treats for the world. Her cakes are the best I've ever tasted.'

'Shush, don't let Miss Taylor hear you say that,' Ryan nudged him.

'Come with me, on Sunday. No one will mind, after all wasn't it Her Ladyship who got you the job with us?' Ryan nodded. 'Well then. You've been well and truly welcomed into the Bochym family.'

Ryan's heart lifted. 'Well, if you think they won't mind.'

'I know they won't,' Jake said taking another mouthful.

Ryan finished his meal, barely able to contain his excitement at seeing Betsy again.

*

True to her word, Sarah had explained Guy's predicament to Peter, and Guy was astonished when he opened his door on Saturday morning to Mr Sheldon, who introduced himself as the Earl's lawyer.

'Your good wife mentioned to the Countess de Bochym, yesterday, about the delay in justice being served for the death of your brother, Mr Blackthorn,' he said removing his hat. 'The Earl contacted me first thing this morning, and if you're willing, I will look into the case for you.'

Guy arched an eyebrow at Ellie, who gave him a lop-sided smile. He turned back to Mr Sheldon. 'Thank you. I'd very much appreciate that.'

'Splendid - to tell you the truth Mr Blackthorn, this is something I am eager to get my teeth into. I hate injustice. So do you have some time now, so we can finish this business once and for all?'

'Of course, please take a seat.

*

Betsy felt as dreary as the rain on Saturday - even though she'd known that it was coming. There had been a downpour yesterday afternoon, but the sky had cleared somewhat overnight, which had lifted Betsy's spirits slightly. This morning though, the drifting rain had moved slowly in again, and by the afternoon it came in heavy squalls, as low dank clouds raced across the sky. The ground, hard from such a long period of dry weather, could not yield to the downpour and mud ran in rivers from the fields around the estate.

Betsy pressed her hot face against the bedroom window pane, watching the rain overflowing from the guttering. It was four-o-clock - the time she should have been meeting Ryan. She had no idea now when she would see him again. Her heart lifted on seeing a figure running across the courtyard, only to plummet again when she realised it was Lyndon FitzSimmons coming to bid his goodbyes to everyone.

*

Lyndon stood in the kitchen trying not to drip on Mrs Blair's floor. His work here was done and he was already a little late for his next job on the Tehidy Estate over on the North Coast. He'd promised a certain young lady that he would be back in Gweek at the end of November, and if he didn't get a move on, he'd be late for that too, and he did not want to disappoint his sweetheart. Unlike the disappointment both Mary and Dorothy were feeling at his leaving - they had been convinced they could turn his head and make him forget about his sweetheart in Gweek. He'd been kind and courteous to them both, but had managed to deflect any possible romantic notion they had about him.

'I'll inform His Lordship that you've finished, and ready to go,' Joe said to him.

He shed his wet coat and hung it up. 'Mmm,' he said, inhaling the aroma of the pot of beef stew Cook was stirring. 'That smells delicious. I'm going to miss your cooking, Mrs Blair.'

She quickly ladled some into a dish, covered it in wax paper and secured it with string.

'Here, that'll keep you warm and hearty tonight when you don't have anyone to cook for you,' she said, giving him a smile that might have suggested that she too was a little in love with the handsome hedger.

Joe came back and beckoned Lyndon to follow him to the Earl's study where he was paid handsomely for his work.

'I shall definitely put word out far and wide of your excellent skills. I wish you good luck in the future, and I hope we will see you again very soon.' Peter shook his hand.

'Thank you, my lord, I hope so too.'

He made his way back to the kitchen and Mrs Blair asked, 'Are you sure you won't stay for tea, Lyndon, we're just going to sit down.'

'Thank you, but no, I must go now.' He began to say his last goodbye to everyone. When he came to Dorothy and Mary, he smiled sympathetically as their eyes filled with unshed tears. 'Your time will come, ladies,' he said gently, kissing them both on the cheek. Lyndon noted the look of horror on Juliet's face at the thought of him touching her, never mind kissing her goodbye! Fortunately, he'd become attuned to her reserve over the days he'd been working and eating with them. So, he kept his distance, smiled and bid her goodbye.

'Good luck with that young lady of yours,' Joe said shaking his hand. 'Are you going straight to Gweek now?'

Juliet took a sharp intake of breath behind him, but when Joe turned to look at her, she'd put her hand to her mouth and coughed as though to disguise it.

27

On Sunday, the rain was jumping off the road as Jake and Ryan ran down the drive to Bochym Manor. After fretting all morning that Jake would not venture out in this weather, Ryan was heartened to find that nothing was going to deter Jake either from one of Mrs Blair's teas.

At Bochym, none of the household staff had ventured far that day, after seeing Juliet return from collecting eggs, thoroughly soaked through to the skin. Ruby had ordered her upstairs to get a hot bath so as not to catch a chill. Needless to say, everyone was astonished when the kitchen door opened that afternoon and two people spilled into the room from the rain.

Joe stood up when he saw it was Jake and shook his head. 'What the devil are you doing out in this weather?'

'I'm here to see you, and I've brought my friend and colleague with me.'

As Ryan pulled his hat off, Betsy squeaked with delight. Juliet however, stiffened and paled at the sight of him.

'We're both wearing gum boots and the oilskins which we use when thatching in the rain! So, we're actually not that wet, look.' Jake grinned as they both shed their wet coats - sure enough they were as dry as a bone underneath.

'I do hope you don't mind me coming too,' Ryan said to no one in particular.

Ruby glanced at Betsy's delighted face. 'Not at all, you're very welcome, come, sit down. We're having tea early today and we're going to play games later.'

Betsy glanced at Juliet, who seemed quiet and apprehensive at Ryan's appearance. 'What's the matter, Juliet?' she whispered.

'Nothing,' she answered sharply, her eyes cutting to Ryan.

Betsy noted the unspoken uneasiness between them, and a horrible thought jumped into Betsy's head - had Ryan something to do with Juliet's distrust of men? But then why would Juliet have met him in secret and stolen food for him if she didn't trust him - so she dismissed that thought. One thing for sure though - before Betsy let her heart loose on Ryan, she would question him about their relationship, because she was absolutely sure there was some sort of history there. That conversation would have to wait for another day though – there would be little chance of speaking in private here in the kitchen, so she pushed her concerns to the back of her mind and tried to enjoy his company.

The talk around the table was lively, as Ryan and Jake shared stories of Ryan's first week at work. Betsy noted that Juliet remained resolutely quiet, and that Dorothy was making puppy eyes at Ryan – she'd have to nip *that* in the bud!

'Ryan has taken to thatching like a duck to water,' Jake said. 'Even Silas's dog is back on the roof with him.'

'How does it get up there?' Dorothy asked cupping her hands under her chin whilst looking dreamily at Ryan – Lyndon FitzSimmons, clearly forgotten.

'It follows me up the ladder and sits on the apex while I work, but I have to carry the dog down the ladder on my shoulder. It's bad enough trying to negotiate the ladder rungs, without balancing a heavy dog on my shoulder!'

'Well, it seems you two have hit it off,' Joe glanced between Jake and Ryan.

'Yes, we have,' Jake nodded, 'I don't mean to speak ill of the dead, but I couldn't get on with Silas - he never liked me - I could never do anything right.'

Joe hummed in agreement. 'He *was* a difficult man.'

They played card games for an hour after tea, before it was time for the young men to brave the elements and make their way back to their cosy boarding-house.

When they got up to take their leave, Joe gave his little brother a hug. 'Will we see you next weekend, Jake,' he asked.

'All being well. We're working on Saturday, because

we're taking Monday off. Meg, who works with Ellie Blackthorn in the tea room, is getting married to Tobias Williams that day, and they are having the wedding breakfast in the tea room.'

'Oh! I'm going to go and watch that wedding!' Betsy said, 'Jessie wrote and asked me to go and throw some lucky rice at the couple, because she can't be there.' She glanced over at Joe knowing that the mention of Jessie was hard, but he remained smiling today – perhaps he was getting over Jessie, now his sights were set on gently romancing Juliet with flowers.

Before they put their coats back on, Ryan begged Ruby's permission for a private word with Betsy.

'Very well, but stay in view of us,' Ruby answered.

'Can I see you next Sunday afternoon?' he whispered. 'I'd like to spend a little time *alone* with you.'

'Shush,' she said, feeling a bubble of excitement in her tummy. 'Yes, if the weather is fine, I'll do what I was going to do yesterday, and take a walk down the bottom meadow at four. If not, it will have to be around the tea table here again.'

Ryan frowned. 'I can't really just turn up for tea every Sunday.'

'Of course, you can – you rescued me remember and I'm sure you'll always be as welcome as Jake is now.'

'Betsy, let the young man get off home now the weather has eased a little.'

'Yes, Mrs Sanders. Goodbye, Ryan.' She smiled sweetly at him.

'Goodbye, my lovely Betsy - roll on next weekend.'

*

The weather remained resolutely wet on Monday and Tuesday, and showed no sign of abating, so a trip to the beach on Ruby's day off was completely out of the question. The burning question was - where could she and Justin meet? The attic would have been the perfect place, but Justin kept the door locked and had requested that no one enter, stating that he disliked to be disturbed whilst painting. Ruby put this suggestion to him, when their paths briefly crossed on the landing after breakfast on Tuesday.

'Oh, Ruby,' his face fell at the suggestion, 'I'd rather not if possible. But of course,' he added, brushing his hand gently across hers, 'if we really can't find anywhere else, then of course we *will* use it - I don't want to miss an opportunity of being alone with you.'

'The last thing I want is to disrupt your painting, so leave it with me,' she whispered, 'I'll have another think.'

After much deliberation, Ruby decided that there was only one other place where they could meet in secret. She popped into Joe's office later with a suggestion.

'I might light a fire in the Dower Lodge this week, Joe! Left cold and unaired it will soon turn musty.'

Joe looked up from his work. 'I agree – it's a good idea.'

'I thought that with it being my day off tomorrow, and the day looks like it's going to be wet, I'd light it and spend the day down there. It will give me time to put my feet up and read - I might take a lunch basket down with me. Do you think my lord and lady would mind?'

'I think they'd thank you for it. I understand the Dowager Countess will be away all winter, so it's a good plan, and, it will give you some time away from anyone trying to disturb your day off.'

'I don't mind being disturbed really,' she smiled.

'I know you don't – the Dunstan's are lucky to have you as their housekeeper.'

Ruby's breath caught hearing this - knowing that in this, she was betraying the Dunstan's trust.

'I'll make sure you aren't disturbed, Ruby.'

'Thank you, Joe.' Ruby's relief was palpable. 'I will of course make sure the fire has gone out before I come back here. I also thought that it would be beneficial for me to take a walk down every morning and afternoon to open and close the windows, to try and keep it aired. With the house nestled under the arboretum, I worry about mildew forming.'

'I'm sure one of the maids could run down and do that for you.'

'I'm sure they could, but it gives me a little walk.'

Joe tipped his head. 'Are you finding life in the manor a little constrictive? It's not like you to want to get away from it all.'

'Not at all,' she smiled, 'I think the days out recently have fired my enthusiasm for taking walks and getting some fresh air. I normally hibernate in the colder months, but I think this year I'll force myself out and about.'

'Well, it's certainly put some colour in your cheeks. You seem to have a real spring in your step recently.'

Ruby smiled and retreated quickly from the office, before the blush she felt rising up her neck reached her face.

*

On Wednesday, Ruby sat on the thick-pile Turkish hearth rug, waiting for Justin in the Dower Lodge, feeling as nervous as a kitten. The fire had been lit for almost an hour and though the room felt toasty warm, she shivered with nervous anticipation. The room was furnished in fine, albeit uncomfortable French furniture and rich crimson velvet curtains draped the windows. Priceless antiques stood on highly polished furniture and works of art adorned the walls. She smiled inwardly - just for a few hours she could pretend that all this was hers. Every fibre of her body stood alert, when the front door latch clicked just after eleven, and a rush of adrenalin coursed through her when she heard him turn the key to lock the door.

'Ruby,' his voice was a whisper.

'In here,' she said, unable to make her legs move to stand and greet him.

With a whoosh of cold, damp air preceding him, he stepped into the drawing room and was on his knees beside her in an instant.

Slipping her fingers through his thick blonde hair as she kissed him, she noted the coldness of his ears to her touch. 'You feel chilled,' she said moving her hands to his face.

'Oh, but you feel lovely and warm, Ruby,' he murmured, pulling her into an embrace and held her for a long time. 'Come lay down with me.' He pulled a couple of cushions from the settee to lay their heads upon. Ruby settled her arm across his chest as his fingers pulled at her curls which he'd unpinned, and they lay there in quiet contentment in front of the roaring fire.

*

Sarah swept into the kitchen after luncheon in search of both Mrs Blair and Ruby.

'Do you know where Ruby is, Joe?' Sarah always used their Christian names when Peter wasn't about.

'It's Ruby's day off, my lady.'

'Yes, I know, but if she could spare a few minutes. I thought we could run through the informal dinner party I'm planning for the 2nd of November.'

'I believe she's gone out.'

Sarah glanced out of the window at the pouring rain. 'In this weather?'

'Yes, my lady. If you remember, I informed you that Ruby was to spend the day down at the Dower Lodge. She was going to light a fire to keep it aired.'

'Of course, I forgot, never mind, we can manage without her.'

Mrs Blair checked all the pots she had simmering and left Mary to watch everything while she settled down at the table with her notepad.

Juliet, who was polishing the candlesticks and not wanting to be in the way, made to get up from the table, but Sarah bid her to sit again and stay.

'This will be a farewell dinner for Kit and Sophie Trevellick – they are going away for a while, so I thought it would be nice to have a little get together with them, and

Guy and Elise Blackthorn. Hopefully they will feel able to join us, as almost six weeks will have past then since the death of Mr Blackthorn's brother.'

Juliet listened to Her Ladyship arranging the dinner, feeling an enormous sense of dread creeping upon her. Last time the Trevellick's had come to dinner she'd managed to keep out of their way by feigning a headache. How on earth was she going to manage to keep out of their way again?

*

Justin was so relaxed lying beside Ruby, he very nearly fell asleep.

'I don't believe I've ever felt so settled and at ease with a woman, as I do with you, Ruby. It's like I've known you all my life.'

She reached up and kissed him. 'I feel the same.'

'Are you going to let me love you forever then?'

She smiled brilliantly. 'You know I am.'

'I can't tell you how much that fills my heart with joy. Let me tell Sarah about us, I can't bear all this secrecy. I want us to be openly together.'

'It's too soon, Justin. It's only been a couple of weeks - give me a little more time, and besides, I need time to try and find my replacement.'

He frowned. 'How do you propose to do that in secret?'

'I'll look in the 'Lady' magazine, to see if I can find anyone suitable to take on the role of housekeeper. You said you'd be staying here until the New Year.'

'Yes, I need to go back to Italy in January. I have an exhibition to work on.'

'Then I'll hand in my notice at the end of November. That should give me time to find someone, and we'll tell Her Ladyship then. I need everything in place in case Her Ladyship takes our news badly and she asks me to leave. It simply won't be fair to leave Joe to find my replacement with Christmas approaching.'

'I do think you underestimate how Sarah will react to the news.'

'Justin, I will have betrayed their trust.'

He gently touched her face. 'Sarah *will* understand - you won't have to leave.'

'Well then, if I'm allowed to stay, I will have to work my notice.'

He laughed. 'You can't continue to work once we're engaged.'

'I can, and I will!'

'But, as my fiancée, you'll be part of the family.'

'Justin, I'm their housekeeper. 'People like me don't usually marry people like you. It won't sit easy with *any* of us in the house for me to join the family at their dining table – it will embarrass everyone. Please, let's not quarrel about this.'

Justin sighed resignedly. 'I'm sorry darling, but don't put yourself down. You will hold your own in any society once we're married, which will be at New Year, and then we'll honeymoon in Italy.'

'It all sounds wonderful - I never would have believed that this could happen to me,' she murmured. 'Tell me about where you live.'

'I live in a villa just outside the tiny village of Pedona. It's only an hour's journey by pony trap to the charming town of Lucca, where Giacomo Puccini the Italian composer was born – do you know who I mean?'

Ruby shook her head.

'His renowned works are the operas, La Bohème, Tosca and Madama Butterfly. Puccini's music is beautiful. I'll take you to the opera - though I have no doubt when we visit Lucca, you will hear one of his arias being sung in the Piazza dell'Anfiteatro. You'll love my villa, Ruby.'

She laughed gently. 'I'm sure I will.'

'The villa is red-roofed, with walls the colour of a sunrise, and it dominates the top of a hill. It's not large, but not too small. It's nestled within a wall of tall lush green cypress trees, which shade the rooms and keeps them cool in the height of a Tuscan summer – which can be fierce - I warn you. The terrace overlooks vineyards, where rows of vines, laid out in formation, reach out into the rolling hillsides beyond. It's about a two-and-a-half-hour ride in the pony trap to the coast - though I am seriously considering buying a car now I've been in Peter's. Just think – we can breakfast on the terrace, set off to the coast to dip our toes into the Adriatic Sea and be back in time to open a bottle of wine and dine out as the sun goes down. Then we'll spend the night making love,' he turned and gazed into her eyes, 'I can't wait to make love to you, Ruby.'

'Oh!' She began to tremble.

'No, not yet – don't worry, my love, I have no intention of compromising you before we're married.' He felt her relax back into his arms.

'I do want you to make love to me, Justin – but thank you for waiting.'

'I hope I feel a little stronger by New Year – to be truthful I couldn't make love to you now if I tried - I seem to have lost a lot of my strength since the harvest. I think I must have caught a virus or something that's sapping my energy.'

Ruby sat up and took a long look at him. 'You do look rather pale, I must say. I wish you'd let me call on Dr Martin – he could give you a tonic to build you up.'

'You're the only tonic I need, Ruby. Now,' he sat up with her, 'did you manage to get a luncheon basket from Mrs Blair? I dare not ask for one again. I didn't want the kitchen staff to wonder where I was going with it in the rain.'

Ruby smiled as she pulled the cloth off her basket. 'We have a flask of tea, a ham sandwich, cheese and pickles and an apple - oh, and a piece of tiffin!'

'A feast then! I'll go fetch some cups. Where is the kitchen?'

'Through that door and down the corridor.'

As he got up, he staggered slightly, and had to sit for a moment with his head in his hands.

'My love?' Ruby stopped picking things from the basket and knelt before him.

He shook the dizziness from his head and kissed the frown that had appeared on her brow. 'I'm fine. I got up too quickly, that's all.' He smiled, but he wasn't fine, he knew he wasn't, but he didn't want to worry Ruby.

28

It was Saturday and as Betsy went about her chores, she had mixed emotions about the day. Sad, because today was her best friend, Jessie's wedding to Daniel Chandler and she could not be there with her, but equally happy that Jessie had at last found someone she loved and wanted to spend the rest of her life with.

As she made the beds, she wondered if marriage was ever going to happen to her. Would Ryan be the one she would spend her life with, or would she spoil her chances of happiness when she put her doubts to him about his relationship with Juliet? Whatever the outcome - she simply had to know. She glanced out of the window at the pouring rain – though if this weather didn't improve, her chance of asking him tomorrow would be scuppered again.

*

The Bochym staff had gathered together for their mid-day meal and when they'd finished their pudding, Betsy glanced at the clock. In ten minutes, somewhere in London, Jessie would exchange marriage vows with Daniel Chandler and her new life would begin. Betsy planned to excuse herself for a few minutes, because she was unsure as to whether marking the time Jessie was to be married was going to make her cry or not. She was just about to get up and excuse herself when Sarah walked into the kitchen, sending everyone into a whirl as they stood and bowed or curtseyed.

'Forgive me for disturbing your meal, but I wonder, could Joe and Betsy be so kind as to join me in the drawing room just before one-o-clock?'

'Of course, my lady,' they said in unison. They looked at each other in puzzlement, and Betsy felt a pang of sadness that she wouldn't now be able to think of her friend as she became Mrs Daniel Chandler.

The Jacobean drawing room was one of the cosiest rooms in the manor. The rich walnut wall panelling gave the room warmth, three sumptuous red sofas flanked the grand fireplace, and Sarah's grand piano sat by the large mullion window. When Joe and Betsy filed in as requested, Sarah beckoned them towards an occasional table which held three small glasses of sherry.

'I know it's early in the day, but I've gathered you here to celebrate our mutual friend, Jessie, on her marriage today. Betsy, I know you would have loved to be there with her, and I'm sorry that you aren't.'

Betsy felt herself tear up.

'Joe, I know also that Jessie was always a very special friend to you.'

Joe nodded, with a resigned smile.

'I, well, I got to know Jessie properly when she accompanied me to London almost a year ago. Not a lot of people knew that we took a trip there together - and I won't divulge the reason for going, but those few days we spent together sealed our friendship. We shopped, went to a concert and dined together, and Jessie fitted into London life as though she was born to it. I know her life with Daniel will be filled with love and joy. So, let us raise our glasses. 'To Jessie and Daniel – Mr and Mrs Daniel Chandler, may their future together be long and happy.'

They all raised their glass in chorus.

'Thank you very much, my lady,' Joe said with heartfelt gratitude.

The door opened and Justin walked in. 'Hello, are we having a celebration?'

'We are.' Sarah smiled and kissed Justin on the cheek. 'We are toasting the good health of Jessie, a former maid, who has married a fine orchestral musician today.'

'Splendid. So, dreams do come true for those in service! I always believed that class has no barriers.' Justin poured himself a tiny amount of sherry and raised his glass. 'I toast everyone in service - may you all find love and happiness – no matter who you choose.'

Joe and Betsy beamed a smile when Sarah raised her

glass in agreement.

'Well,' she smiled and they all chinked glasses, 'as long as you don't all leave me en-masse if you do.'

*

By the time Betsy went to bed on Saturday there had been a marked improvement in the weather, so she kept her fingers crossed that Sunday would be dry enough for her to meet with Ryan. Thankfully, her wish came true. Sunday dawned bright and breezy, with small white clouds scudding across the pale blue sky. At a quarter-to-four, Betsy managed to pull on her ordinary boots for the first time since injuring her foot, and was out of the manor in a shot. The watery sun was shining, but there was a waft of decay in the air – a sure sign autumn was taking its hold. She ran down the shorn wheat field towards the far stile, and when she saw he was waiting there, her heart did a happy little dance.

*

Trencrom stood by his hives, his hand clamped to his mouth in dismay - all his bees were lying at the base of the hive. The bowls of sugar syrup he'd left for them to feed from, were filled with rain water – he hadn't given the hives a moment's thought during this week of torrential rain. He quickly lifted the lid and pulled out the frames – but the hive's inhabitants were all dead. His eyes darted around in panic – how on earth was he going to hide this from the Earl? He'd not be able to arrange for a swarm to replenish the hive until late spring next year! He worried his bottom lip with his teeth for a moment - if anyone found out that he'd let this happen, his plans for a tied cottage would be scuppered, unless… He smiled inwardly, if he could wed Betsy quickly and get himself established in a cottage before anyone found out about the hives, the Earl would surely not evict them - especially as Betsy was well thought of. It was then he spotted Betsy walking down towards the meadow. He narrowed his eyes – it was time to put into place the plan he'd been hatching to *make* her marry him. He dropped the frame back in the hive and walked towards a large oak tree at the edge of the meadow from here he could see she was heading towards someone sitting on the far stile. Though the figure was a way off, it looked very much like Penrose! He gritted his teeth - filled with rage.

'Why you little minx, so, you think you're going to do me out of a tied cottage, do you?' He glanced at his watch - four-o-clock. She'd have to return for tea at five, so he'd wait. It was time she was taught a lesson she would never forget.

*

Ryan jumped down to greet her, but they did not kiss on the lips when they met – their relationship had not reached that stage, instead he lifted her hand to his lips to kiss, which made her smile.

'The grass is a bit damp to sit on, so we'll sit up here on the stile,' he suggested, 'I've put my coat down for us.' He stepped up and held his hand out to help her up.

They sat down, and for a few moments, neither spoke, then they both started to speak together and laughed in unison.

'You first,' Betsy said.

'I was just going to enquire about your health.' He grinned.

Betsy giggled. 'I'm very well, thank you, and yourself?'

'In rude health,' he grinned back and she laughed again – the ice was well and truly broken.

'Your turn now,' he said.

Betsy dropped her chin. *Did she really want to spoil the day now they had managed to meet?* He must have seen her consternation because he frowned and touched her chin lightly with his finger.

'What is it, Betsy?'

'It's about Juliet.'

'What about Juliet?'

She noted the urgency in his voice and how serious his

face had become. 'Do you know her well?'

He pulled his top lip over his teeth. 'Why do you ask?'

'*Do you?*'

'I know her family, yes.'

'It's just that…. she seems uneasy in your presence. Granted, she seems uneasy with most men, but you particularly seem to unsettle her.'

'Really - I was not aware of that!'

Betsy raised an eyebrow. 'You must be - everyone else has noticed.'

'Well, if she is, I can see no reason for her uneasiness with me. In fact, she's been very kind to me, as you know, because she told me you'd found out that she was bringing me food when I was in need.'

Betsy tried to decipher if he was still holding something back from her, she was sure he was, and balled her hands into fists. 'Ryan, I have to ask - have you ever had a relationship with her?'

'No, Betsy - absolutely not!' He shifted uneasily. 'Has she said something about me?'

She shook her head. 'It's just that when I started to feel,' she bit down on her lip, 'when I started to feel - close to you, and then saw that she was helping you - I asked her much the same question.'

'And?'

'She denied it.'

'Well, there's your answer. Think nothing more of it.'

'All right,' she said meekly, still feeling a little uneasy, 'I'm sorry I had to ask, it's just that, well, I like you, Ryan - a lot, but I don't want to step on anyone's toes.'

'I like you too, Betsy - *a lot*.' He picked up her hand and kissed it again. 'I can assure you - nobody's toes are being trampled on.'

'I just needed to be sure, you understand?'

He smiled broadly. 'Well, be sure of this, I am well and truly yours, and yours only, my lovely Betsy.'

Betsy rested her head on Ryan's shoulder

companionably and looked out at the trees which had begun to turn - shedding leaves thick and fast.

'I do hate to see the summer end,' she sighed heavily and she felt him kiss the top of her head.

'It has to end, to let the earth regenerate, Betsy, but look at autumn - look how beautiful the colours are when the world turns red, and golden.'

'But the cold will set in soon and I do like the warmth of the sunshine. There is no better smell than a field of crops baking in the hot sun - or the sound of birds nesting and twittering. Summer is a sublime time.'

He put his hand in hers. 'And as sure as eggs is eggs, it will come again next year! For now, you must enjoy the wind as it whips up the leaves, and enjoy the robins in the garden - their breasts turning deep red as they feast on the hedgerows full of hips. It's a time to wrap up in warm clothes, hats and scarves, and a time to snuggle together around a roaring fire.'

She turned, smiled and gazed into his eyes. 'You make it sound wonderful. I could learn to enjoy the autumn and winter months snuggled around a fireside.'

'Now then, young Betsy.'

A voice came from behind which made them jump apart. They both turned to see Mr Oliver the gamekeeper walking up to the stile.

'Oh, no!' Betsy whispered. 'I'm in trouble now!'

Mr Oliver must have heard, because he laughed gently and said, 'I'm not here to cause trouble, Betsy, and I'll not say anything, but it's not right for you to be alone with a young man without an escort.'

'I just happened upon him while I was walking, and we were just speaking about the onset of autumn.'

Mr Oliver raised a dubious eyebrow. 'Well perhaps it's time for me to escort you home. I'm sure Mr Penrose has somewhere he needs to be.'

'He's actually coming to tea, Mr Oliver.'

'Is he now?' He grinned. 'Then I'll chaperone you both

up to the manor.'

*

As the threesome made their way across the meadow, Henry Trencrom pulled back into the undergrowth - his nose twitching in annoyance.

'You may have foiled me this time, missy, he hissed, 'but I will get that cottage, one way or another.' He shoved his hands deep in his pockets and made his way back to his hives to clear up the dead bees.

29

It was Monday the 21st October. The day was sunny with a hint of autumnal chill –perfect weather for the marriage of Meg and Tobias from Poldhu. Betsy had finished her chores for the day and dressed in her Sunday best, was almost ready to go out. Today she would kill two birds with one stone – so to speak. In her hand she held a posy of flowers from the garden, given by kind permission of Her Ladyship. These she would put on Jessie's baby's grave. Betsy had promised her that she'd look after Cordelia's grave as the baby would have been her godchild if she'd lived. Betsy had another mission that day - in her pocket was a handful of rice to throw over the newlyweds, which had been another request from Jessie. With good fortune, Thomas was taking the pony trap out to Mullion, so Betsy had gratefully accepted a lift to Cury Churchyard, but she had something to do before she set out. With the weather being so wet lately, Joe hadn't been able to gather any flowers for Juliet. So, she carefully teased a sprig of flowers out of her posy, to give to him. She wanted to do all she could to help Joe in his quest to woo Juliet.

*

Not having been officially invited, Betsy sneaked into the church and found a pew at the back to watch the ceremony. Amongst the guests, and there were only a few - which made the service more intimate, Betsy saw Ellie with their children, and Tobias, whom Betsy had always believed to be a bit of an old curmudgeon, nervously waiting in the front pew in his best suit. When the organist started to play the bridle chorus, everyone stood and tuned to watch Guy escort Meg up the aisle. Meg was dressed in a navy coat over a pale blue cotton dress, and walked towards her intended with a smile as broad as Poldhu Cove.

After the ceremony, which had been so lovely it had made Betsy cry, she'd positioned herself by the church gates, ready to throw rice when Ryan approached her.

'Are you all right, Betsy?' he asked. 'Have you been crying?'

'Yes,' she sniffed, 'only on account that I'm happy for the couple to have found love so late in life. Perhaps I should take hope that it is never too late, and it might just happen to me one day.'

'It *will* happen to you, lovely Betsy, and perhaps sooner than you think!' He winked, surreptitiously slipping his hand into Betsy's.

Astonished by what he'd said, coupled with the shock of his hand in hers, she almost dropped the rice and nearly missed the happy couple as they passed through the church gates. When she finally threw the rice, it barely hit them and before Betsy could question Ryan on his startling statement, Ellie had approached them.

'Meg and Tobias would like you both to join them at the tea room for their wedding breakfast. We'll give you a lift on the wagon if you want.'

'Thank you, we'd love to, wouldn't we Betsy?' Ryan grinned.

*

The wedding breakfast was a jolly affair. Meg's two sons and her daughter, along with their families, had travelled down from Yorkshire for the wedding, and nicer people you could not meet. They made up for Tobias's family, who could not attend, because both his sons were in the merchant navy.

Ellie smiled as she watched Ryan and Betsy sitting in the corner, quietly enjoying each other's company. She knew Betsy missed Jessie – she missed her too, and was glad that Betsy had found someone to help bridge that loss.

'I think you were right, Guy, we have a budding romance there.'

Guy looked around and nodded. 'I hope it doesn't distract him from his work.'

'You know it won't. You've said yourself that he's a good worker and a quick learner. Have you decided whether to keep him on or not?'

'I think I decided the day Silas's dog took to him. In a strange way I feel that now the dog is back on the roof – so too is Silas. Does that sound mad?'

'You are asking me, if I think you're mad thinking Silas may still be with you? You should know by now my beliefs about what happens to people who have passed on.' She smiled. 'I can safely say, Silas will never leave you – he'll always be in your heart.'

'That's nice to know. Maybe I do believe a little more now.'

Ellie touched his sleeve companionably. She just hoped Mr Sheldon would be able to bring about some justice soon, so that Silas could pass through to the next life, because he was still very much evident in Jessie's cottage. She'd never been afraid of spirits, but his presence, whenever she entered the cottage, was quite unnerving.

'Are you going to wait the full month before you tell Ryan he can stay?'

'No, but only on account that I'm worried he'll get a job elsewhere if he thinks this one might not pan out.'

'I insist that you go and tell him now then.'

*

Ryan looked up from talking to Betsy and smiled when Guy approached.

'Ryan, you know I said I was going to give you a month's trial?'

Ryan felt his heart sink - *had he not come up to the job?*

Guy laughed when he saw his consternation. 'Cheer up - I've decided to give you a permanent job. I don't think I could have chosen a better man than you to do it. You've proved your weight in gold. Welcome to our family of thatchers.'

Ryan stood up and shook Guy's hand vigorously. 'Thank you, Guy, you don't know what this means to me.'

'Oh, I think I have a good idea,' Guy winked, glancing at Betsy,

*

Juliet had taken a walk around the garden before tea. She'd smiled and waved at Mrs Sanders who was walking up from the Dower Lodge. Mrs Sanders had recently started to go down to the house each morning and afternoon to air the lodge. Juliet had offered to do it for her - it would have been a nice excuse to take a walk a couple of times a day. Mrs Sanders had thanked her, but insisted she was happy to do the job herself. Juliet wandered around the flower borders, taking in the aroma of the flowers which had survived being battered by the recent rain. She nodded to Mr Hubbard who was busy doing his best to tidy everywhere. It was only when she saw that dreadful Mr Trencrom skulking around his beehives did she quickly turn tail. Wary of most men, Trencrom in particular truly gave her the creeps.

There was still a while before tea, so Juliet picked up the book she was reading which she'd left on the mantelpiece - Howards End, a novel by E. M. Forster. When she opened the book, she found some flowers pressed into the flysheet and her breath caught at their newly pressed beauty. Glancing up to see if anyone else had seen it, she realised everyone was busy occupying themselves. Allowing herself a ghost of a smile, she put the flowers back into the book and began to read.

*

The wedding party were still celebrating when Betsy glanced at the clock - It was half-past-three.

'I'd better go, Ryan. Ruby normally likes us to be back by teatime unless we've told her otherwise, and it's a good hours walk back. '

'I'll walk you home, then.'

They thanked Meg and Tobias for the invite, said their goodbyes to everyone else, and stepped out of the tea room. The sun that had shone most of the day had disappeared behind the great bank of clouds which was lowering by the minute.

'I think it's going to rain again, Ryan, perhaps you'd better not walk me all the way home, otherwise you'll get caught in it on the way back.'

'Don't worry - I haven't shrunk yet in the rain. I want to walk you home. It's not often I get a chance to be alone with you for any great length of time.' He bumped against her arm softly and it wasn't an accident.

Betsy smiled shyly. 'We shouldn't really be alone together.'

'I doubt we'll see anyone on the way home to make a protest.'

The air began to grow chilly and by the time they passed Cury churchyard, thunderous clouds were rolling in from the west.

Betsy grimaced. 'I think we're going to get a thorough soaking before we get to the manor!'

Low thunder began as they entered the woods, so they quickened their pace until a blinding flash of lightening almost stopped them in their tracks. Betsy shrieked when another crack of thunder broke almost overhead. It hurt her foot to run over the uneven ground in the woods, and she limped slightly. Another thunderclap stopped them and they both looked up as a bolt of lightning cracked its way to earth just in front of them. Betsy grasped Ryan's hand for protection as the rain poured from the heavens.

'Here, over here.' He yanked her arm and pulled her towards the wood shelter he had once lived in. 'The tarpaulin is watertight and will give us some shelter.'

Being in the woods was not the safest place to be in a thunder storm, but Ryan assured her he'd be ready to pull her away from any danger should the familiar crack of a branch sound above them!

They were both drenched through to the skin, so Ryan pulled Betsy into his arms and wrapped the sides of his coat around her to keep her warm.

'It'll pass soon,' he said gently kissing the top of her head.

She wrapped her arms around his strong body, feeling his muscles ripple under her touch, and turned her damp face to his. He looked down at her and gently pushed her wet hair from her face. She felt his breathing change from that of exertion from the run to something more fervent. Damp lips found each other and they kissed ardently. Feeling his arms tightening around her body she yielded to his embrace.

'Oh god, Betsy, I need to marry you quickly, I can't not be with you - it's driving me crazy.'

Betsy squeaked with delight as he stood back and knelt down on one knee before her.

'I know we haven't known each other long, but I knew I was going to fall in love with you the day you came here to see me. I think you felt the same, yes?'

'I did, yes,' she laughed brightly.

'I also know that what I'm about to say will throw your world in disarray, but…' a flash of lightning and crack of thunder drowned his words and they both flinched. He pulled her down to where he knelt as the thunder rumbled away. 'Will you be my wife?'

Betsy could hardly believe this was happening. She'd waited such a long time for someone to come along and fall in love with her, and now it was happening.

'What's the matter,' Ryan frowned, 'don't you want to be my wife?'

'Of course, I do,' she cupped his troubled face in her hands, 'I'd love to be your wife, Ryan. It's just - well I can't believe this is happening. You've just made me the happiest woman on earth.'

'I suspect you'll have to leave service, though,' he said cautiously.

'Yes, I will, and though I like working at the manor, I should be more than happy to give it up for you.'

'I'll take great care of you, I promise, and now Guy has

offered me a permanent job, It means I have a regular good wage coming in, so I can support us both.'

Betsy clasped her hands together. 'When shall we marry?'

'If you can get away next Saturday afternoon, I'll make arrangements for us to go and see the vicar to see if we can get the banns read. I'll send word about what time the vicar can see us. He pushed her wet hair back from her face, gazed into her eyes, and kissed her very tenderly on the lips. 'I am going to love being your husband.'

The rain had ceased and the thunder was rolling away up towards the north coast.

'You're absolutely soaked, Ryan. You need to go home and change.'

'I said I'd walk you home.'

'Walk me to the lower stile of the wheat field then and I'll make my own way home from there.'

He reluctantly agreed, and when they parted, he kissed her again.

The rain was dripping off the leaves in the hedgerows and the birds were twittering and fluttering their wings to try and dry them. Betsy was humming a happy tune to herself as she walked dreamily through the field. At last, it had happened - someone had walked into her life and fallen in love with her. Wrapping her arms about herself, she squeezed her eyes shut momentarily, savouring the feeling of Ryan's lips on hers. Lost in her reverie, she became suddenly aware she was no longer alone. She opened her eyes and every fibre in her body stood alert when she realised Henry Trencrom had stepped out in front of her!

30

Betsy stepped back when she saw Trencrom, but he grabbed her by the arm, pinching her skin with his fingernails.

'Let me go,' she squealed.

He tightened his grip, baring his teeth threateningly. 'I've seen you, gallivanting about the countryside with that vagrant.' He yanked her arm and brought her up close to his face. 'I asked you first, so I claim you as mine.'

She tugged away violently. 'Let go of me this instant.'

'Oh, no, missy you're going nowhere. I'm going to make sure no one else will want you after I've finished. You're mine, and I'm going to make it so. You've trifled with my affections long enough.'

Betsy felt her body clench and tremble as he unbuttoned the fly of his trousers. In wide-eyed horror she pulled violently back from him, and screamed at the top of her voice.

'Shut up!'

He slapped her hard across the face sending her skidding into the muddy ground. Momentarily shocked and stunned, she came to her senses tasting blood and soil in her mouth. She spat out several times and rolled over, baulking at the sight of Trencrom looming over her, half naked and exposed. She screamed in terror, but was silenced when he threw his weight upon her - winding her.

'Shut up you stupid bitch,' he hissed, clamping his filthy hand over her mouth. 'It'll be over in a minute, and then you'll be mine and damn well begging me to marry you.'

Hot tears blurred her vision. He reeked of stale sweat and the smell of his hot revolting breath turned her stomach, but the fight within in her prevailed. She squealed and struggled, thumping him desperately in an attempt to unseat him, but his hand covering her mouth, muffling her squeals - pressing her head deeper into the dirt - almost suffocating her. With his knee on her thigh to stop her moving, his hand shot up her skirt, fingernails scratching the insides of her thighs as he tore at her underwear. She felt the pressure on her mouth ease slightly as he readied himself to do the filthy deed, so she bit down on his hand, ripping at his flesh, until his blood mingled in her mouth with hers.

'Ouch! You little bitch!'

As soon as he whipped his hand away, she screamed again but his time he thumped her in the stomach to silence her - a blow so powerful Betsy felt the air expel from her lungs. Black fog clouded her vision - stars danced before her eyes, and she feared her strength and will to fight weaken. His hand made its way up her skirts again, producing a sudden visceral sense of creeping flesh which covered her body with goose pimples as his fingers found the soft flesh in-between her thighs. She shuddered as vomit began to rise in her throat at his touch. *Fight Betsy, you must fight!* She dug her heels into the muddy ground, desperate to find some purchase in an effort to move backwards from his fingers. Suddenly his hand stopped probing, and the weight of his body left her. Ryan's voice was somewhere close by and Betsy drew a trembling breath, curled herself into a ball and wept bitterly.

*

Ryan yanked Trencrom to his feet - red mist clouding his vision as his anger became all consuming. 'You filthy sod,' he yelled, he administered a punch so hard he felt Trencrom's teeth shatter on his knuckles. The punch sent Trencrom flaying backwards, but Ryan grabbed him by the collar and thumped him again and again, until Trencrom's head lolled stupefied. He threw him on the ground and watched with pleasure as the blood trickled from Trencrom's mouth and nose. Disgusted at the sight of him, writhing half naked in front of him, Ryan kicked him hard in the groin. 'You filthy, filthy bastard,' he repeated.

'Hey! Hey!' Gerald Oliver the gamekeeper came running over the field with his shotgun over his shoulder.

Cradling his painful fist, Ryan stood panting, swaying with adrenalin, as he watched Trencrom vomit blood and rotten teeth into the mud.

'What the hell is going on here?' Mr Oliver demanded.

'He's attacked Betsy - *I've* dealt with him!' Ryan said evenly, turning towards Betsy who was in a dreadful state of distress. Her dress was covered in wet straw and mud, and her hair, always so neatly brushed, splayed out around her in wild untidy tendrils. Moving to her side, he noted she was holding herself between her thighs where fragments of white clothing hung down in tattered shreds. *Oh, god, am I too late?* 'Betsy?' he whispered gently, 'has he hurt you?'

Betsy's mouth moved, but no words came.

Ryan looked up at the gamekeeper in desperation. 'I heard her scream - I'd only left her a couple of minutes ago,' he said tremulously.

'Aye, I heard her scream too,' the gamekeeper answered gravely, glancing between Betsy and Trencrom, who was crawling around, spitting fragments of teeth and blood. He prodded him with the butt of his gun. 'What have you got to say for yourself?'

Trencrom lifted his head and pointed a trembling finger at Ryan. 'That bastard attacked me, Mr Oliver, when all I was doing was courting my woman.'

Betsy omitted a pitiful cry. 'It's all right, Betsy, it's all over,' Ryan said gently stroking her hair.

Trencrom snarled and scrambled to his feet to charge at Ryan. 'Get your bloody hands off her, Penrose - she belongs to me now.'

Betsy curled into a tight ball, as Ryan scrambled to his feet ready to defend her, fortunately Mr Oliver cocked his shotgun and the noise stopped Trencrom in his tracks.

'Get out of my sight, Trencrom,' the gamekeeper ordered.

'You belong to me now, Betsy Tamblin - remember that,' Trencrom snarled, 'and I'm bringing charges against you, Penrose. You aint heard the last of this.'

'Move! Now!' Mr Oliver pointed the shotgun at Trencrom.

As he staggered off across the field, Ryan pulled Betsy into his arms rocking her like a baby. 'It's over now. Let's see if you can get up.'

Once she was standing, Mr Oliver asked her gently, 'Can you walk, Betsy?'

She nodded tremulously.

'Mr Penrose, if you can see Betsy safely to the house, please. I need to go and see the estate steward.'

*

Grateful for Ryan's strong arms around her, Betsy's legs felt like jelly and were trembling alarmingly as he walked her to the kitchen door.

'Oh, lordy me!' Mrs Blair flapped her tea cloth. 'Every time you come in here with Betsy, she's in a terrible state. What on earth has happened this time?'

'Trencrom attacked her!'

Mrs Blair's hand shot to her mouth. 'Sit her down, quickly. Mr Treen, Mrs Sanders,' she yelled, 'come quick!'

Juliet, who had been sitting at the table, stood up letting the book she was reading tumble to the floor, but instead of rushing to Betsy's aid, she staggered backwards into the corner of the room in horrified silence.

Joe was the first in the kitchen on hearing the shouting. 'Whatever is the matter, Mrs Blair?'

'Oh, Mr Treen,' she wailed, 'wicked Trencrom has attacked our Betsy! I knew it would happen - I knew it – I could see he was a wrong un.'

Seeing Betsy's dishevelled state, Joe turned quickly to Juliet. 'Go and find Mrs Sanders, quickly,' he ordered, but Juliet stayed frozen to the spot. He frowned. 'Juliet, did you hear me?' he snapped, but still, she did not move.

'I'm here, what is it, what's happened?' Ruby ran into the kitchen. 'Oh, my poor girl, whatever has happened?' She threw her arms around her Betsy.

'Trencrom,' she said, her chin wobbling, her mouth white with shock. 'He, he,' she choked on the words as her eyes filled with great fat tears.

'Come with me, Betsy, you're safely home now,' she said leading her to the housekeeper's room for some privacy.

Joe turned to Ryan accusingly. 'And where were *you* when this happened?'

'I'd walked Betsy home from the Williams's wedding at Poldhu, but we got a thorough soaking in that thunderstorm. So, once we reached the lower stile of the wheat meadow, Betsy insisted that I go back home to get dry,' his voice caught. 'I'd not gone two hundred yards back when I heard her screaming.' He felt his face crumpled and it took all his resolve to not cry. 'By the time I'd got to her she was fighting him off. The bastard had his trousers open and was tearing at her underclothes.'

Joe was shocked at Ryan's language in front of the ladies, but did not berate him, for the name fitted Trencrom's character for what he had done to poor Betsy.

'Oh, god, Joe,' Ryan raked his fingers through his wet hair, 'I don't know what he's done to her.'

'Best to leave her to Ruby,' Joe patted Ryan on the arm, 'she'll do what is best. Where's Trencrom now?'

'Mr Oliver sent him away.' Just as he spoke, Mr Oliver walked in the kitchen with Mr Pearson the estate steward.

'We need a word with His Lordship, Mr Treen,' Mr Oliver said gravely.

'Of course, I'll tell him you're here.'

'How is the lass, is she hurt badly?' Mr Oliver asked Ryan.

'I don't know. She's gone off with Ruby.'

'You perhaps need to come with us to see His Lordship, and explain exactly what you saw and did then.'

*

Betsy was wrapped in a blanket, but nothing could stop her trembling. She sat, albeit uncomfortably on the chair in

Ruby's office. The inside and back of her thighs stung where Trencrom had scratched her skin trying to rip away her underwear. The very thought of his hands on her, made her shudder.

Ruby knelt at her feet and held her hands. 'Betsy,' she asked gently, 'did he violate you?'

Betsy lifted her tear-stained face, her mouth turned downwards, but she could not speak for a moment.

'Are you still a maiden?'

Her chin wobbled. 'I think so – he touched me though,' she shuddered, 'he touched me where he shouldn't,' she whispered. Great hot tears began to trickle down her face and Ruby handed her a freshly laundered handkerchief.

'Oh, Mrs Sanders,' she sobbed raggedly, 'he said,' she hiccupped, 'he said, "I'm going to make sure no one else will want you after I've had you." She squeezed her eyes tight shut to blot out the memory. 'He'd seen me with Ryan, you see.' She wiped the handkerchief across her eyes. 'Oh god, Mrs Sanders!' She reached out to Ruby, needing someone to hold her and Ruby took her in her arms and held her tight.

'It's all right, Betsy, it's all right.'

'It's not all right,' she sobbed in her arms, 'Ryan won't want me now, and he'd just proposed to me - not fifteen minutes earlier!'

'I'm sure he will.' Ruby patted her gently on the back. 'This is not your fault.'

'But I'm soiled, now that horrible man has had his hands on me,' she cried.

'No, Betsy!' she said emphatically. '*You are not!*'

'I hate Trencrom,' she said through bared teeth, 'I *hate* him. I kept telling him I wasn't interested in him. Why wouldn't he take no for an answer?' She shifted uncomfortably and winced when she spoke.

'Are you in pain?' Ruby asked gently.

She nodded. 'He slapped me across the face - I think

he's dislodged a tooth – because it aches terribly. He punched me in the tummy, and that feels tender too, and he did this…' She gathered her skirts up to reveal great long scratch marks running the length of her thighs. 'They sting terribly.' She shuddered. 'I feel so dirty.'

'My poor girl,' Ruby said hugging her again.

A knock came at the door and Betsy pushed her skirt and petticoats down, as Mrs Blair popped her head around the door. 'I've brought Betsy a cup of sweet tea.'

Betsy took the cup with her shaking hands and thanked her. 'Is Ryan still here,' she asked hopefully.

'No, he spoke to His Lordship and now he's gone home - he was soaked through to the skin.'

'Did - did he say anything?'

Mrs Blair shook her head. 'I think he was quite shocked by everything.'

'Oh!' Betsy's lip trembled as tears trickled down her face.

'Mrs Blair, can you ask Juliet to run a hot bath please.'

'Of course, Mrs Sanders,' she said gravely.

Ten minutes later, as Ruby was escorting Betsy up the stairs to the bathroom, Joe called out to her. 'His Lordship would like a word when you've a moment.' Ruby turned and nodded. 'He wants to know Betsy's side of the story,' he whispered.

Well, when she'd finished speaking to him, His Lordship would be left in no doubt at all who was to blame for what had happened - she would make sure of that.

*

Twenty minutes later, after speaking to Ruby, Peter had heard all the evidence he needed. He set off with Mr Oliver and Mr Pearson towards the fields where Trencrom was digging ditches.

Trencrom looked up as they approached and lifted his chin defiantly.

'I'm glad you're here, my lord,' he said stepping forward to meet them, 'I want to make a formal complaint about that bloody vagrant Penrose who was living on your land until recently – he's been trespassing and ….'

Feeling his bile rise, Peter snapped, 'Be *quiet,* man.'

Trencrom's mouth dropped for a moment, then began to speak again, 'I was just about to say, he's been sniffing around my intended, like a dog after a bitch on heat. Bloody decked me, he did, when I claimed back what was rightfully mine – Mr Oliver will vouch he hit me, won't you? He knocked my teeth out, look,' he bared his bloody gums, 'and probably broke my nose! I need you to bring charges against him.'

'*I said be quiet!*' Peter dropped his voice to a low hiss.

Trencrom was dumb-struck at the cool ferocity in the Earl's voice, and looked anxiously at the men standing before him.

'I want you off my land now!' Peter snapped.

'What?' Trencrom laughed incredulously. 'Well, I - I don't know what the maid has told you, but we're courting, we were playing, that's all.'

Peter seethed with contempt. 'You have attempted to rape one of my maids.'

'Rubbish - we have an understanding - I'm allowed to touch her.'

'You are not allowed to touch her! It is my understanding that she loathes the very *sight* of you - *as do I*. You have attempted to violate an innocent young woman, and for that reason you are dismissed, without a reference!'

'Phaa! I doubt she's as innocent as she makes out. She's probably been rolling in the hay with Penrose. He's turned her damn head - well I'm not letting him have her. I'll make sure he goes to prison for attacking me.'

'*You* are the one who should go to prison, Trencrom! Now, if you don't hold a civil tongue in your head and get off my land this instant, I shall bring the constable, and charges of attempted rape *will* be brought against you. And, I warn you, if you *ever* come anywhere near Betsy or

Mr Penrose again, I will personally make sure you go to prison for a very long time. Do I make myself clear?'

Trencrom could not speak for shaking with anger.

'Mr Oliver, Mr Pearson, escort this *person* off my land and *out* of my sight.'

31

While Betsy took a bath and had been given orders to go straight to bed afterwards, Ruby addressed everyone around the tea table about the situation.

'As you'll all be wondering how poor Betsy is - I can tell you that the attack was very frightening for her, and she's sustained some cuts and bruises, by the sound of it she put up a valiant fight. Thankfully Ryan arrived in time, before…. anything deeply untoward happened.'

There was a collective sigh of relief, all grateful that Betsy would not have to bear the stigma of being ruined.

Joe stood up and added, 'I'm sure I don't need to state this, but what has happened to Betsy today must go no further, understand? It's wrong, I know, but if word gets out, Betsy's good name will be tarnished - and none of us want that!'

Everyone nodded in agreement.

'What about Ryan Penrose - what if he says anything?' Thomas asked.

'He won't!' Juliet said adamantly, as soon as the words came out, her breath hitched.

Everyone looked at her in surprise - not least Joe, whose gaze sharpened. 'How can you be so sure of him, Juliet?' he asked cautiously.

Juliet took a deep breath as she formulated an answer. 'I'm sure, only on account of Ryan being romantically interested in Betsy. I don't think he'd do or say anything to bring her good name into disrepute.'

'I don't think he would either,' Ruby said, touching Joe on his sleeve to assure him. 'I think we can all see he's a good man.'

'I'll send Betsy a tray of supper up, shall I?' Mrs Blair asked.

Ruby smiled. 'Thank you, Mrs Blair, but she says she's not at all hungry.'

'Juliet can take some cocoa up to her later then.'

'Where's Trencrom now Mr Treen?' Thomas said, unable to stem his anger a moment longer.

'Rest assured, Thomas, Trencrom has been removed from the estate on His Lordship's orders - and good riddance to him I say.'

'Here, here,' everyone joined in.

*

The mood in the house had become very sombre – even the family dinner was a solemn affair.

Sarah had been up to see Betsy with a posy of flowers to cheer her, which Betsy tearfully thanked her for.

'I don't understand why you're not going to fetch charges against Trencrom,' Justin challenged Peter.

'Because it will tarnish that poor girl's reputation irrevocably, if it comes to court – even if it wasn't her fault – the fact that she was attacked by him is enough to ruin her.'

Justin frowned. 'The injustice makes me so angry!'

'It makes us all angry, Justin,' Peter glanced at Sarah, whose countenance had remained sickly pale since learning what had happened. 'But Trencrom has been warned, and no further action will be taken, unless he breaks the rules I set out. I left him in no doubt that I would make sure he would be put away for a very long time if he did. And if by doing that, and Betsy's reputation *is* tarnished, I'll do everything in my power to settle her somewhere away from here where no one knows her – it's the least I can do after she was attacked on my land.'

Sarah put her cutlery down – her appetite lost. The thought of poor Betsy being sent away because of Trencrom, *made her* very angry indeed.

*

Juliet's head had been in turmoil since Ryan had brought Betsy home. She could not settle – she'd broken a glass, spilt water over Her Ladyship's eiderdown, and almost tripped and fallen down the stairs. She'd been so clumsy, even Ruby had been in two minds whether to allow her to take a cup of cocoa up to Betsy for fear of her spilling it everywhere. In the end she'd allowed her to as long as she carried it on a tray.

Juliet put the cocoa down on the bedside table and looked down at Betsy who was curled up, crying softly. Juliet found herself struggling to find the words to ease Betsy's sorrow – what had happened today had frightened and angered her too. So, she sat on her bed and pushed Betsy's hair gently from her face.

'Can I do anything?' she asked.

Betsy shook her head tearfully. 'That odious man has ruined everything!' Juliet nodded, and folded her hands on her lap. 'You'll be heartened to know, His Lordship had Trencrom marched off the estate as soon as he found out.'

'The damage is done though, isn't it?' Betsy dabbed her eyes.

'Yes.' Juliet sighed sadly.

'Ryan proposed to me this afternoon – we were going to be married!' the words caught in her throat.

'Oh, Betsy, I'm so sorry for you, truly I am, but… I don't suppose you want another man to touch you now - not after what Trencrom did to you?'

Betsy furrowed her brow and pulled herself up to a sitting position. 'Of course, I do! I love Ryan,' she sniffed. 'I love him,' she said again more quietly.

'But…but surely, this has put you off men for life? They're all brutes!' she said darkly.

'No, they're not!' Betsy said incredulously, 'what a strange thing to say! People like Trencrom are brutes, yes, but men like that are few and far between. I'm certainly not going to let that horrible man put me off men – otherwise he'll have won, won't he? I will *not* be a victim!' Her face flushed indignantly.

Juliet's mouth formed an O, taken aback at her statement.

Betsy's chin trembled. 'Having said that though, I suspect Ryan will not want me now that he knows someone else has touched me. Oh, god,' She buried her head in her hands, 'just when I began to dream of being a wife, the dream is over - it's all over!' She pushed herself down under the sheets, her cocoa forgotten, and cried angry tears.

Juliet stood up from Betsy's bed to ready herself for bed. When she crawled beneath the sheets, she wished that she shared Betsy's brave determination - instead she was left to fight her own demons which the events of the day had thrown up for her.

*

Joe was sharing a glass of sherry with Ruby in his office at the end of the day.

'Have they all gone to bed?' Ruby asked.

'I think so. Mr Devereux was going to work in the attic for a couple of hours, but to be truthful - he looks like he needs an early night more than anyone. I think he's burning the candle at both ends at the moment – the man looks worn out.'

Ruby silently agreed with him. Since spending Wednesday with Justin, she'd managed to see him each day, albeit briefly at the Dower Lodge, while she opened and closed the windows to air the place. Justin knew where the spare key was hiding so he was often waiting for her. Every single day she'd watched a slow decline in his health, and often found him out of breath just from the short walk down from the manor. She'd pleaded with him again to call Dr Martin, but he was emphatic that no 'country quack' as he called him, would touch him. It had been a great relief to her when he'd called into the housekeeping room on Saturday evening and told her he was going up to London on Tuesday with Sarah and Peter, to visit, amongst other people, the Dunstan's private physician.

'I have no doubt he'll give me the tonic you think I need - but without the bloodletting,' he'd mused.

Her conflicting heart rose and plummeted at him going.

'We'll be back on Saturday,' he'd said holding her hands in earnest. 'I wish you were coming with me.'

'I wish I was too,' she'd sighed.' I've never been to London.'

He'd clasped her face in his hands. 'Life is going to be so different for you, for us, very soon.'

Ruby! Ruby!' Joe pulled her from her reverie. 'You were miles away then.'

'Sorry,' she smiled apologetically. 'It's been a long day, Joe.'

'Yes,' he sat back and relaxed, 'and one I hope we never have to live through again.'

'Poor, Betsy! That nice young man, Ryan proposed to her today as well.'

'Oh goodness,' Joe breathed, 'are we going to lose one of our best maids then?'

Ruby shrugged. 'Betsy thinks he'll not want her now.'

Joe tipped his head and smiled. 'Oh, I think he will!'

'I hope you're right, Joe, though she'll be a great loss to the manor.'

'Mmm. What on earth are we going to do without her? Betsy knows how to run this place, almost as well as you do. I don't know - these young girls falling in love and not giving a thought as to how the household is going to run,' he joked, 'thank goodness we'll never have to lose you!'

Ruby's breath caught. 'Do you think I'm not worthy of love?' she teased.

'Goodness no, I don't think that at all! But please, Ruby, don't leave - I can't run this place without you *and* Betsy.'

'So,' she arched an eyebrow, 'I'm to become an old maid to please you - so that this household runs like clockwork.'

Joe pulled a tight smile. 'I think I am digging myself into a great big hole here, aren't I?'

'Yes, I think you are,' she laughed. 'Don't worry, Joe. If I fall in love and marry, I promise it'll be someone from this household.' She regretted saying it immediately and flushed furiously.

'Goodness, don't tell me you've got your sights set on Thomas, have you?'

'Now, that would be telling,' she teased.

*

Despite her ordeal, Betsy was up bright and early as always but with a heavy heart. When she looked in the mirror she shrieked, horrified to find she sported a large bruise that ran from under her left eye, down her cheek and along her jaw. Her eyes were red and puffy from crying, but fortunately, when she ran her tongue along the tooth she had feared she would lose, it felt a little more stable - though it still ached a bit.

Dressing in the grey uniform and white apron she believed she'd be very soon swapping for a wedding dress, she sighed resignedly. Being Ryan's bride was all just a pipe dream now, especially after Mrs Blair said, "Ryan has gone home - I think he was quite shocked by everything."

When she entered the housekeeper's room, to look at the rotas, Ruby took her into her arms and hugged her as a big sister would.

'You have my ear if you need it, Betsy.'

'Thank you, Mrs Sanders, but I'm all right,' she said sadly and set off to her early morning chores.

*

The manor was bustling that morning. Peter, Sarah and Justin had breakfasted early to catch the morning train to London.

After checking that Her Ladyship was downstairs, Ruby chanced a quick meeting with Justin in his bedroom a few moments after his luggage – all one bag of it - had been taken down to the car by Thomas. Their encounter was brief and urgent, and for a few moments after he left her, Ruby's lips felt bruised from the passion. As she watched them drive away, the manor fell silent and a great emptiness settled on her heart.

*

Ryan had been very quiet all day at work – his mind filled with the horrors of what had happened yesterday. He'd been so happy yesterday, but this - this dreadful event clouded everything now. He realised he must have looked downright miserable, because Guy had asked him twice if he was sure he was happy to have a permanent job with them.

'I am, Guy. I'm very grateful - truly I am.'

'Well, do you want to tell your face that,' Guy teased, as he pushed a willow spur into the thatch.

Ryan laughed. 'I have a headache that's all – perhaps I had too much to drink yesterday,' he said to pacify - there was no way he could divulge what had happened to Betsy to anyone. He grabbed the next armful of reed to settle on the roof, and as much as he loved this job, all he wanted was for the end of the day to come.

*

With the family away, everyone was more relaxed, though they all had plenty of jobs to do. Both Ruby and Joe ran a tight ship, and the family absent meant certain dirty jobs could be done without causing too much upheaval. Most of the maids had been busy in the French dining room all day, atop of ladders, dusting the intricate ornate plaster coving around the ceiling. With the family away, they were all excused from wearing their dusty aprons and caps when they sat down at teatime.

The talk was lively around the table, though Betsy was notably and understandably quiet, unable to dredge up any enthusiasm today for anything. It seemed a continual battle to fight the onset of tears which pricked behind her eyelids with alarming regularity whenever she thought of what she'd lost.

'Betsy.'

Betsy lifted her head. 'Yes, Mr Treen?'

'I think you have a visitor.' He nodded to the figure walking across the kitchen courtyard.

251

Betsy turned and her stomach flipped when she saw Ryan, but the serious look on his face made her heart implode - he was clearly coming to tell her the bad news that he could not now marry her.

32

Betsy opened the door tentatively, to be met with the face she loved smiling sympathetically back at her.

'Can I come in?'

She stepped back to allow him entry into the kitchen, but Ryan looked beyond her towards Joe and Ruby. 'May I have a private word with Betsy outside, please?'

'You may,' Joe granted.

Beckoning her into the courtyard, he turned and gazed down at her – his eyes pained and bloodshot.

'Oh, Betsy, my love, I didn't sleep last night, and couldn't settle all day at work for worrying about you. Are you all right? Look at your poor face.' He lifted his hand to gently touch her bruised cheek.

His gentle manner made her hope that he still loved her. 'I'm, I'm fine, Ryan, he didn't manage to,' she lowered her eyes, 'he touched me - I'll not lie to you, but,' she waivered, 'thankfully you came in time to stop him doing anything else.'

He reached for her hands and squeezed them tightly. 'Oh, thank god for that!'

'So,' she tipped her head apprehensively, '*are we all right,* Ryan?'

'Of course, we are, my lovely Betsy.' He gathered her into his arms and held her close. 'Please don't ever doubt my love for you.'

His jacket smelt of old leather and thatching reed, and she savoured the warmth of his arms around her. 'I feared that you would not love me anymore, because he had touched me,' she murmured.

'And I was so afraid that dreadful man would put you off men for life.'

Betsy turned her face to his. 'Strangely enough, Juliet came to the same conclusion.'

'Well, it does happen sometime.'

'So… you still want to marry me?' her voice quivered

with uncertainty.

'Yes, of course, I do.' He kissed the top of her head. 'Do you still want to go and see the vicar on Saturday to set the date like we planned?'

'Yes please,' she said blinking back the tears.

'Don't cry, my love.' He wiped her tears with his thumb. 'All will be well.'

Joe must have seen their embrace, because he came to the door and cleared his throat. 'I think perhaps you both need to come inside now.'

'Could Ryan stay for tea, Mr Treen?' she asked.

'Yes, if he wants to.'

'Thank you, I will. I've missed supper at Miss Taylor's, so tea and cake would be very much appreciated.'

As they settled down at the table, the horrors and sadness of the last twenty-four-hours melted away and Betsy glowed with happiness.

'Whatever you've said to Betsy, Ryan, it has cheered her up no end,' Thomas said, lifting his cup.

Ryan glanced at Betsy. 'Shall we share our news?'

She nodded happily.

'I've asked Betsy to marry me, and she's said yes.'

A whoop of joy erupted and there were hugs and congratulations all round, though Betsy couldn't fail to notice Juliet's consternation.

Ryan leaned in to Joe and whispered, 'What has been done about Trencrom? Have the police been called for?'

'He's been dismissed and warned not to come near either of you again or he'll be prosecuted.'

'Is that all?' Ryan looked dismayed. 'So, he's just going to get away with it?'

'I know it's a bitter pill to swallow, but if the police become involved, Betsy would have to testify, and though it seems unjust, it would tarnish her reputation irrevocably. I don't think any of us want that, do we?'

'No, we don't.' Ryan glanced at Betsy – her happiness shining from within. 'Is she all right, really?'

'I think so. She's shaken up, obviously, but we're taking good care of her for you.'

'Thank you, Joe.'

When the tea was over and Betsy bade farewell to Ryan, she came back to help Juliet clear the table. 'Are you not happy for me?' she whispered to her.

'I am, yes of course, I am, it's just, well…. I'm envious of your happiness - and please don't say anything about Joe,' she frowned, 'I know he likes me and I like him too, but it's terribly complicated.'

'I wish I could do something to help you!'

Juliet's eyes blurred with unshed tears. 'No one can.'

Betsy glanced up to see Joe standing at the kitchen door. He pulled his mouth into a tight line, before taking himself off to his office.

*

When the tea table had been cleared, Ruby beckoned Betsy into the housekeeper's room.

'So, all is well between you and Ryan?'

'Yes,' Betsy smiled and then winced at the shooting pain in her tooth.

'I can see your tooth is bothering you. Do you need us to call for Dr Martin to remove it - I understand the good doctor has extracted a few teeth, since he's heard the horror stories of that butcher dentist in Helston.'

Betsy shook her head violently. 'I'll wait a bit - hopefully it'll settle.'

'So, we are to lose you, Betsy?'

'I'm afraid so, but I can't give in my notice until we have a date for the wedding. We're hoping that the vicar will be able to fit us in, as soon as all the banns have been read.'

'Goodness, that soon! Well, let's assume the vicar *can* fit you in, and I'll take your notice from today. It should normally be four weeks, but I'm sure we can bend the rules a little for want of a few days.'

Betsy clasped her hands together. 'Thank you so much.'

'Have you thought about where you'll live?'

'Not yet – we have lots to sort out.'

'I'm very happy for you, but naturally we will all be very sad to lose you.'

Betsy pressed her lips tightly together. 'I'll be sad to go – I've grown up here, but I can't really stay, can I?'

'No, not really, unless, Ryan comes to work on the estate.'

Betsy shook her head. 'He's happy working as a thatcher, and has a permanent job with them now.'

'Then you must make a new life together away from us.'

'Oh, Mrs Sanders,' her face broke into a broad smile, 'I never thought this would happen to me.'

Ruby joy was infectious. 'Your happy news just shows that dreams can come true, Betsy.'

'Yes, they can,' she replied softly. 'I can't wait until next Saturday to get things sorted with the vicar.'

'Roll on Saturday then.' Ruby smiled, for she too could not wait for Saturday because Justin would be coming home then.

*

When Ryan arrived at the Blackthorn's kitchen the next morning, and relayed his news to them, Ellie pulled him into a hug.

'That's such good news, I'm so happy for you both!'

When she let him go, Guy shook his hand and joked. 'Is that what was wrong with you all day yesterday? Were you worried she'd say no?'

Ryan hummed in his throat. 'Something like that yes.'

Ellie put her hands on her hips. 'You shouldn't have worried. Betsy knows a good thing when she sees it, and without doubt, she'll make you a fine wife. We said as much when we saw you together at the wedding on Monday. You seemed to be very well matched.'

'Thank you - sometimes you just know when someone is right for you!'

'You certainly do.' Guy reached out for Ellie's hand.

Jake, who was standing in the kitchen, folded his arms and grimaced.

Guy laughed at him. 'You may well pull that face, Jake Treen, but it'll happen to you one day too.'

Jake shot him a dubious look.

'Betsy will have to leave the manor though, and we'll have to find somewhere to live. I'm wondering about asking Miss Taylor to accommodate us.'

Guy slapped him on the back, 'You've a few weeks to go before the wedding – so let's see what turns up, eh?' He winked at Ellie, as he ushered them out of the kitchen to go to work.

*

At supper time in the Blackthorn's kitchen, Guy scraped his plate clean and sat back full and satisfied.

'I've been thinking about Ryan's news, Ellie. Perhaps now is a good time to consider renting the cottage out to him and Betsy. He's earning a good wage - he can afford it. You could even take Betsy on at the tea room, if she wanted, and of course if Ryan is happy about her going out to work after they're married.'

'I've been thinking much the same. Meg really doesn't want to work full time – she was only filling in after Je....'

Guy tipped his head. 'You can mention her name you know – I won't fly off the handle.'

Ellie tipped her head cautiously. 'Have you forgiven her then?'

'No, and I don't think I will. It cut too deep when she took off with Daniel Chandler so soon after Silas's death – god knows, he wasn't even cold in his grave!'

Ellie shifted uncomfortably, thinking, he's maybe cold now in his grave, but he's certainly not resting in peace. She'd been back in Jessie's cottage only that morning, and his spirit was very much present.

She handed him the mail which had come late today.

'That postman really needs to get a new tyre for his

bicycle – this was the second time in a few weeks that he'd had a puncture and been late delivering,' she said, as she watched him sort through the letters.

'Is there anything from the Bochym lawyer - I thought we would have heard something by now?'

'Not yet, I just wish they would hang Goldsworthy – I need some justice for Silas.'

So do I, Ellie mused. *Otherwise, Silas will forever haunt that cottage and they would never be able to rent it out!*

*

By providence, the very next day, Guy received an early visit from Mr Sheldon the Earl's lawyer.

'I'm here to tell you, the evidence shows that Philip Goldsworthy, although suffering from a tumour to the brain at the time of the killing, was in sound mind and acted with intent. Therefore, he will hang at Exeter jail, tomorrow morning at eight-thirty.'

Guy nodded gravely. 'Would they let me go and watch him hang?'

'Guy!' Ellie said aghast, dropping the pan she was washing with a clatter.

Mr Sheldon shook his head. 'No, Mr Blackthorn - no one is allowed to witness executions now.'

'Damn it! I wanted to see him strung high to be sure he was out of our lives forever.'

Ellie was truly shocked – she'd never heard Guy speak like this before – he'd always been such a gentle soul. She felt compelled to reach out and put a comforting hand on his arm to calm him.

'Rest assured, Mr Blackthorn – I'll send a telegram informing you when the deed has been done.'

*

Guy had not slept. With the hanging of Goldsworthy playing on his mind, he knew the events of the day would distract him, and working on a roof, you needed to have your wits about you. He decided then to give Jake and Ryan an unexpected day off.

When the clock chimed ten-past-eight, the kitchen fell silent after the children had set off to school.

Ellie put a gentle hand on Guy's shoulders. 'Shall we take a walk down the beach to get some fresh air?'

Guy sighed and patted her hand.

It was a raw day - the chill wind blowing in from the sea, cut like a knife, so they were glad they had wrapped up warmly. It was twenty-past-eight when they crossed the dunes, but Ellie had something she needed to do in Jessie's cottage before the bottom of the hour.

'I'll just need to make a quick detour to open the windows in the cottage, to air the place first, if you don't mind?' she announced.

He followed her through the door, but stopped short on entering the room. 'Christ, but it feels as cold as the grave in here!'

'I think an airing might help,' she said, as she pushed the sash windows up, but Guy had turned heel and gone back outside. 'You'll soon be free, Silas,' she whispered, and felt the room quiver with a rippling energy that gave her a brief unpleasant sensation of being underwater. She shuddered and quickly ran to the door to join Guy outside.

Linking her arm in his, they walked slowly down to the sea. Clumps of black glistening seaweed lay strewn along the tide line, and they watched as gulls swooped and picked at the small crustaceans hidden within it.

Guy's fingers reached into his waistcoat pocket, retrieved his watch and studied it for a moment – it was twenty-eight-minutes-past-eight. Those last two minutes seemed like an age to tick away, but at half-past-eight prompt, hundreds of rooks roosting in the pine trees at the far end of the cove suddenly lifted in a noisy, hawking cloud. Startled, Guy and Ellie looked up as the birds moved and gyrated in a huge black murmuration over the flat grey water, before settling back in the trees. Philip Goldsworthy was dead.

Guy's eyes blurred and Ellie curled her fingers around

his hand.

'Are you all right?' she asked gently.

He could not speak – but gazed out to sea where he and Philip had swum together as young men. They'd been unlikely friends since childhood - Philip, the privileged son of a mill owner, wanting and expecting everything he desired. He the son of a thatcher, expecting nothing, but what he had earned. Class held no barriers between them - only love tore them apart and made them bitter enemies with devastating consequences. Now the deed had been done, justice had been served. Philip had been denied his last privilege – life. It turned out to be a hollow victory for Guy.

33

With the unexpected day off, and instead of waiting until Saturday to see the vicar, Ryan took himself off to Cury Church to see if he could bring the appointment forward for later that day.

Betsy clasped her hands in delight when he arrived at the Bochym Kitchen door at three to tell her that the vicar could see them that afternoon if she could get away.

Betsy turned expectantly to Ruby. 'May I have permission to leave the estate?'

'Yes, of course you can go, and bring Ryan back for tea – we can celebrate your wedding date then.'

Ruby smiled as they ran across the courtyard. She too was in a buoyant mood – the prospect of Justin returning the next day filled her heart with joy. To keep up appearances, Ruby had continued to make her trip down to the Dower Lodge twice a day to open the windows. Last Wednesday, she'd taken a picnic basket down, along with her paints, and spent the day painting the view of the arboretum from the Dower Lodge's dining room window. There was no doubt about it - her perspective was improving, and she was rather pleased with her finished painting, but she longed to get her hands on an easel and large canvas. Justin had promised she would have her own studio in Tuscany and she simply could not wait for that.

*

Ryan and Betsy returned to the manor just before teatime, flushed with excitement, and a date for their wedding - Saturday the 16th of November!

Mrs Blair had made a selection of sandwiches along with a splendid Victoria cake especially for the occasion. As the family were still away, Joe brought the sherry in and poured everyone a tot to raise a toast to their upcoming nuptials.

When Joe put his glass down, he sighed and exchanged a glance with Juliet. He had an uneasy feeling that despite the flowers he was still leaving her and the gentler approach he had to dealing with her wariness, he feared there would never be an occasion for them to celebrate an event such as this.

Juliet must have read his face, because she whispered, 'I'm sorry Joe.'

He nodded resignedly - she could not be sorrier than he was.

*

It was Saturday and though the train bringing the family back home from London was not due until five that afternoon, the manor was a hive of activity. All the fires had been lit, the beds aired, flowers were brought in from the hot-house and the furniture and silverware shone like new pins. The staff took their tea slightly earlier to enable them to be at the door to greet the car when it arrived.

'His Lordship isn't going to be too pleased when I tell him what Mr Hubbard told me earlier today,' Joe said gravely.

Ruby looked up. 'What was that, Mr Treen?'

'He's checked the Manuka hives and all the bees are dead! Apparently Trencrom...,' he stopped when he saw Betsy shudder at the mention of his name, 'begging your pardon, Betsy, but it appears the scoundrel took all the honey from the hives and left the bees to starve to death.'

'Shocking!' Mrs Blair banged the teapot on the table. 'That man needs stringing up!'

Everyone around the table glanced at each other but nobody disagreed.

*

Ruby could hardly contain her excitement as the family's car came up the drive and Thomas stepped forward to open the door for them. Sarah was the first to take his hand and alight, swiftly followed by Peter. Ruby's skin tingled at the first glimpse of Justin in five long days, but when he emerged, she noted it was not without Thomas's help. Her breath hitched - Justin looked crumpled, tired

262

and extremely unsteady on his feet as though he was inebriated. She watched anxiously as he held onto the car door for a few moments, before gathering himself to make his way to the front door. When he passed Ruby, he shot a stricken look in her direction, and a sense of dread hit the pit of her stomach. She moved involuntarily - the urge to step forward and wrap her loving arms around her man was intense, but she pulled back before anyone noticed.

'If we could have some light refreshments in the drawing room in fifteen minutes that would be appreciated, Mr Treen' Sarah asked.

'Certainly, my lady.'

Justin put his hand to his brow. 'Sarah, would you mind awfully if I just go straight to my room - I need to lie down.'

'Of course not, it's been a very tiring journey. I'll arrange to have a tray sent up to you.'

'No, don't bother, thank you. I need nothing except rest.'

Once everyone had made their way upstairs to change out of their travelling clothes, Joe turned anxiously to Ruby. 'Mr Devereux does not look at all well in my opinion.'

'No,' she answered tremulously, 'he doesn't!'

*

Just before the dinner gong rang at eight that evening, Thomas came into the kitchen to collect the dinner platters.

'Mr Devereux will not be joining them for dinner tonight, Mrs Blair. Her ladyship asks if a tray could be made up for him.'

'Very well, let me take a plate of dinner off those platters then before you take them through to the dining room.'

Desperately anxious to know what the doctor had said to Justin, and with His Lord and Her Ladyship safely ensconced in the dining room, Ruby offered to take the tray up to Justin.

She knocked softly and opened the door. 'Justin.'

'Ruby, is that you?' His voice sounded raspy, having just woken.

'Yes, my love.' She put the tray down, sat beside him on the bed and curled her hand over his. 'I'm sorry to disturb you, but I've been so worried about you.'

'Ah, Ruby, this is indeed a sorry state you find me in, but rest assured, I'm just tired from the journey. I've perhaps burnt myself out with London life.'

Lacing her fingers in his, she tipped her head. 'What did the doctor say?'

'He says I'm run down and gave me a tonic,' his eyes twinkled, 'and he took some bloods. He'll write to me next week with the results.' He put his hand up to Ruby's stricken face. 'Don't fret, my love - all will be well.'

'Well, we must build you up, so you must eat what Mrs Blair has sent up.'

'Yes, nurse.' He grinned as he pulled himself up with great effort to accept the tray on his lap.

'I must go – you know I should not be alone with you in your bedroom, and they'll wonder downstairs what is taking me so long.'

'A kiss first, for the weary traveller.'

They brushed lips, lightly at first and then again with more passion.

He touched her face tenderly. 'I've missed you so much.'

'And I've missed you too, my love.' She kissed him one last time and wished him good night. 'Thomas will come and take your tray later.'

'Goodnight, sweet Ruby, I love you.'

'I love you too,' she whispered. As she closed the door she blew him a kiss, unaware that Betsy was in the corridor, albeit stood in the shadows out of sight.

*

So as not to embarrass Ruby, Betsy pushed herself deeper

into the shadowy recess of the alcove until the housekeeper had swept past by. She smiled at what she'd seen and heard. It heartened her to know that Ruby was experiencing the same throws of love as she. One thing for sure, her secret was safe with her. A romance between staff and family would certainly be frowned upon.

*

When on Monday morning Ryan told Ellie and Guy that a wedding date had been set, Ellie made the decision to speak to them both later that day regarding the renting of Jessie's cottage. She'd checked the cottage late on Friday afternoon and to her infinite relief could find no evidence of any unearthly disturbances – Silas had thankfully passed through to the next world.

Speaking to Betsy first, or perhaps Sarah, was a priority though. As soon as the children set off to school, Ellie caught the wagon to Cury Cross Lanes and walked down to Bochym Manor. It was a sunny, breezy day, and the chill had gone from the air. Ellie knew exactly where Sarah would be on such a day and headed straight to the flower borders. There she found her with the gardener, clearing the debris of battered flowers left in the wake of the recent thunder storm.

'Elise, how lovely!' Sarah pulled off her gardening gloves and kissed Ellie warmly on the cheek. 'To what do I owe this pleasure?'

'I'd like to speak to you about Betsy if I may.'

'Ah, our bride-to-be! I'm so happy for her, but we will be sad to lose her, as lose her we must. With Ryan based down at Poldhu, I should think they will settle somewhere in Mullion after their marriage. It would be difficult for her to continue her work here, because her husband and the home where they settle will take priority.'

'Well, that's what I want to speak to you and Betsy about actually.'

'I'm intrigued! Come let's take some refreshment indoors and you can enlighten me.' She turned to the gardener, 'I shall be back to help shortly, Mr Hubbard.'

'Thank you, my lady.' He doffed his hat.

*

Betsy quickly patted her hair and straightened her cap after being summoned to the drawing room to see Ellie Blackthorn and Her Ladyship. She walked into the cosy room with wide-eyed curiosity and curtsied.

'Hello, Betsy. Do come and sit down.' Sarah gestured to the sofa opposite.

Astonished at the invite to sit, Betsy perched tentatively on the edge of the seat.

'Elise has a proposition to make to you.'

Betsy's eyes rested on Ellie who was smiling broadly.

'I'd like to offer you and Ryan Jessie's cottage to start your married life in.'

The shock of the offer sent a frisson of excitement through her. 'Really?' *She'd always loved that cottage and was already sewing cushions in her head to make the place homely.*

Ellie laughed. 'Yes really. Do you think Ryan will be happy with that arrangement?'

'Oh yes, yes I'm sure he will,' she smiled. 'Thank you, Ellie.'

'I'll speak to Ryan this afternoon then and tell him you agree, if he does.'

She clasped her hands to her chest. 'Ellie, I'm so happy, I could cry.'

'Good, but there's something else I wanted to ask?'

Betsy waited with bated breath.

'I need someone to work in the tea room to fill Jessie's job. Meg has just been a temporary replacement, but I want someone I know and trust, and I've known you a long time, Betsy. You'd be perfect for the job - *if* Ryan agrees.'

'Oh, gosh! All my dreams are coming true at once. Yes, I'd love to work with you, Ellie. When you speak to Ryan later today, will you ask him if I can work there as well?'

'Rest assured, I will.'

'Do you think Ryan will allow it?' Sarah asked cautiously.

Betsy tapped her lips thoughtfully. 'I hope so, my lady, though he was fierce about wanting a job to provide for me. Oh,' she clasped her hands, 'I do hope so though.'

'I'll fight your corner for the working woman, don't worry,' Ellie mused. 'Now, I understand that Mrs Sanders has allowed your notice to be worked out by Friday 15th October?'

'Yes, she has.'

'Well, Sarah has agreed to release you on Thursday the 14th. That should give you a little more time to settle yourself into the cottage and get ready for the wedding, and if you're in agreement, you can be married from Poldhu.'

'Yes, I'd love to do that.' Betsy looked between them – her eyes shining with happy tears. 'Thank you, Ellie, thank you, my lady. I never believed I could feel this happy.'

'You're very welcome, Betsy. I'll ask Ryan to call in at the manor this evening after I've spoken to him, so you won't have long to wait to start making your plans. If all is well, come down to Poldhu next Monday on your half day off and have a look around the cottage and tea room.'

*

Joe was clearing away the tea tray after seeing Ellie Blackthorn out of the door when he caught a glimpse of Justin walking slowly down the front path. He smiled - at last he must be feeling better to be up and about. A spot of fresh air would do him the power of good, he thought as he watched him turn down the drive towards the arboretum. He thought nothing more, until he walked back into the kitchen, where Ruby was humming happily to herself as she put on her hat and coat. He watched as she set off across the kitchen courtyard with a clear spring in her step, and a curl of unease stirred in his stomach.

34

When Thomas told her at breakfast on Monday that Justin had managed to get up that morning, Ruby knew he'd be waiting for her at the Dower Lodge when she went to open the windows at eleven.

Justin did not look at all well, but Ruby didn't want to bring attention to it – she was just so happy that he was up and about and in her arms.

He covered her face with soft kisses. 'Ruby, can we get away from the manor on your day off.'

'Of course, where do you want to go?'

'Anywhere, but here! Sarah is mollycoddling me, bless her, but I don't want to be treated like an invalid – I'm just a little tired that's all! The tonic the doctor in London has given me should start to make me feel better soon.' He cupped her face in his hands. 'I so want to sit on a beach with you and draw you.'

Ruby laughed gently. 'Draw me again?'

'I want to draw you every day – capture each and every nuance of your lovely face. I'm an artist – it's what I do!' He shrugged and kissed her tenderly on the lips.

'When will you show me your drawings?'

'One day soon, but for now I need them with me.' His lips curled into gentle smile. 'I need to look at you when I can't be with you.'

Nestling in his loving arms, Ruby marvelled at the warmth of his body radiating through her clothes. She breathed in the fresh citrus oil he used after shaving, and knew her clothes and hair would pick up his scent - reminding her for the rest of the day about these few precious moments in his arms.

'I must go, Justin, or I'll be missed,' she said, reluctantly pulling away.

'I don't want you to go, I want to be with you always – *I want to marry you, woman!*' he grumbled, pulling her back to kiss her again.

'And we *will* be together. As I say, I'll have to find my replacement and I'll need to replace Betsy now she is going off to get married!'

'God, but this wait is driving me mad!' He raked his fingers through his hair.

'Take yourself off to the sea for some fresh air. It'll do you good. Go and have a look at Polurrian Cove on the other side of Poldhu and decide whether you want to take me there on my day off.' Her eyes twinkled. Knowing she must get back to the manor before anyone came looking for her - she stole one last kiss. She began to move away, though she held his hand until she could hold it no longer. 'Goodbye my love,' she said. He blew her a kiss, but she saw his shoulders slump at her leaving.

*

Betsy kept the news about her cottage and job under wraps for the rest of the morning, though it was clear to all she was brimming with joy.

'I don't know how you're going to get through the next few weeks, Betsy,' Thomas teased, as they all sat at the dinner table. 'You look fit to burst with happiness.'

Betsy laughed.

'What are you going to wear?' Mary asked.

'I don't know – my Sunday best dress I suppose.' She felt a little deflated at the thought.

'Don't you want a wedding dress then?' Dorothy chipped in.

'Of course, I want one – but where does a lowly maid such as I get the money for a wedding gown?'

'You could make one! Perhaps Izzy has an old sheet that's past its best you could use?' Dorothy looked over to Izzy who nodded that she had.

'I can darn a sock, make a cushion cover and sew a button on a shirt, but that's just about it for my needlework skills – besides, I don't think a holey sheet is quite what I had in mind,' she answered rather gloomily.

'You'll look radiant whatever you wear, Betsy,' Ruby

assured her.

After the mid-day meal was cleared away, Joe asked Betsy what she was doing for her day off.

'I'll go to see if Mr Hubbard will give me a small posy of flowers from the hothouse to put on Jessie's baby's grave, and then take a walk down to the church.'

'Have a lovely day then – it looks like it'll stay fine.'

Mr Hubbard had duly supplied her with a posy of flowers, including some astromania which she pulled out of the posy to give to Joe for Juliet.

'Thank you, Betsy,' he sighed forlornly, 'but I'm not sure this way of wooing Juliet is working.'

'Oh, I don't know - I've seen her smiling at the flowers you've left her. She knows they're from you and they always go in a jar by her bed. Don't give up hope.'

It was not without a degree of anxiety that Betsy walked down the wheat field that day, though she'd been assured Trencrom had been warned never to approach her again, otherwise he'd find himself in jail. It heartened her to see Mr Oliver walking the adjoining fields with his gun, and this eased her anxiety somewhat. There was a noted spring in her step as she walked along the lane towards Cury Church– this is where she would become Mrs Ryan Penrose. Her thoughts were of the letter she'd write to Jessie later that day – though she knew her friend would be in Italy until well after her own wedding. Still, she was bursting to share her news!

After placing her posy of flowers on the grave, she had just started to tidy the grass around it when she felt a shiver run down her back - and it wasn't because she was surrounded by the dead. Pulling herself to her feet, she glanced around the peaceful graveyard, but despite seeing nothing but trees and gravestones, the hairs on the back of her neck began to rise. Unnerved now, she made a conscious decision to walk home via the main road.

*

Henry Trencrom narrowed his eyes when he realised the

change of direction Betsy was taking to go home. He knew she'd visit the graveyard today – she often did on her half day off – he'd just never had the time to follow her before. But now the little minx had had him dismissed, he was out for revenge. His disappointment was intense though– the road she was taking was a busy one, but... he scratched the stubble on his chin, if he stayed back out of sight until she cut through to Cury Cross Roads - which she'd have to do - that would give him the opportunity he needed. He licked his lips at the thought of dragging her into a field. He had a hood with him, and once it was over her head, if he kept quiet, she'd never know who had de-flowered her. He wasn't daft – he'd already arranged for an alibi should the finger of blame be pointed at him. An equally disreputable friend of his, had, for the princely sum of five pounds, promised to vouch for him being in Helston all day. It was money well spent. If he couldn't have her as his bride, he would make damn sure no one would want her after he'd finished with her.

*

Betsy was starting to regret taking the long way home. Her boots still pinched the scars where her foot had been caught in the rabbit trap, and she began to limp as she approached the cut-through road to Cury Cross Roads. She'd not gone twenty-yards when she heard something behind her.

*

The thatcher's arrived back at Poldhu as the clock struck three. They'd finished work early that day after completing a roof at Cadgwith. After making them all a cup of tea, Ellie asked Ryan to walk over to Jessie's cottage with her. Once through the door she explained her offer of the cottage and a job for Betsy. She watched as Ryan silently wandered around the rooms of the tiny cottage, running his hand over the well-worn, albeit sparse furniture. Try as she might she could not read his face.

'And you've spoken to Betsy?' he asked tentatively.

'I have and she liked the idea, but I told her I'd put the offers to you this afternoon. I think she's rather eager to hear your thoughts on it.'

Ryan nodded, but said nothing at first as he took a last look around the cottage.

'The cottage is wonderful, thank you, Ellie. I'll go and see Betsy now, and if I may, I'll speak to you in the morning regarding the job offer.'

'Very well.' Ellie's heart sank – she'd rather hoped that he would have embraced a more modern way of life for his wife. Still, it was his decision, but, oh, she so wanted Betsy to join her in the tea room – she could think of no one better to take Jessie's place.

*

It was gone four when Ryan arrived breathless at the Bochym kitchen door to be greeted by Cook and Ruby.

'Is Betsy around, may I see her?'

'She's not, no,' Ruby answered. 'She went to Cury Church at about a quarter past two to put some flowers on Jessie's baby's grave. I'm surprised you didn't see her on the path up through the fields. Did you come that way?'

'Yes, I cut across the fields to Chypons Road.'

Ruby tipped her head. 'I don't know where she could be then!'

Ryan raked his hands through his hair. 'I might walk back to meet her – I probably passed her while she was still in the churchyard.'

'Most probably - she'll definitely be on her way home now – she's never late for tea at five.'

It took Ryan a good forty minutes to walk to the church and back to the manor after his unfruitful search.

Everyone was sitting down to tea when he arrived and Ruby looked up and smiled. 'Ah, here they are now - you very nearly missed tea. Oh, are you alone?'

'Yes, is she not back?' Ryan asked fearfully – the attack from a week ago springing to mind.

Joe and Ruby both stood up - clearly having much the

same thoughts.

Ryan's eyes widened with panic. 'Oh, god, where is she? It'll be dark soon!'

'Give me a moment,' Joe said, 'I'll go and see His Lordship to see if we can borrow a couple of horses – I'll ride out with you to find her.'

*

Ten minutes later, Ryan, Joe and Mr Oliver, were mounted on horseback. They were just setting out a plan to split up to find Betsy when Justin drove the pony-trap into the stables yard with Betsy by his side.

'Betsy!' Ryan dismounted and ran to the trap to help her down, pulling her into a great big bear hug. 'You're safe – oh, thank god you're safe,' he said kissing the top of her head.

'Apologies everyone,' Justin said climbing down from the trap, 'Betsy coming home at this late hour, is entirely my fault. Come, let's go inside and I'll explain.'

Betsy was overwhelmed at the fuss that was made of her return, and was quickly sat down and tea and cake were thrust in front of her.

'I had the pleasure of coming across Betsy on the main road on my way home from Poldhu and offered her a lift. We had not gone fifty-yards when one of the irons came away from the wheel. Betsy very kindly came with myself and the pony trap to the wheelwrights to have it mended. As I was feeling a little unwell, she very kindly stayed with me until the wheel had been fixed.' As soon as he spoke the last sentence, he saw the worry flash in Ruby's eyes.

'Are you quite well now?' Ruby asked tentatively.

'I am, thanks to Betsy.' He turned and smiled when he saw Ryan with his arm protectively around her.

'Joe, do you think you can come with me to Peter's study?' Justin asked casually.

'Of course.'

*

Peter and Joe listened with dismay as Justin relayed what

he'd seen and the action he'd taken.

'And it was definitely Trencrom?'

'Most definitely! I was on my way home when I saw him skulk in the gate of a field, and then not twenty-yards up the lane, I spotted Betsy walking home. I insisted she climb aboard to ride home with me - though bless her, she was reluctant to ride in the Bochym trap – thinking it improper of her. When the damn wheel broke, she came with me to the Wheelwrights, but then wanted to walk home from there! As you know it's only a stone throw to the manor from the Wheelwrights, but I knew Trencrom was out there somewhere, and I could not let her walk away alone. So, I feigned illness to make her stay with me. Unfortunately, I seem to have averted one catastrophe, only to have caused a lot of concern back here.'

'Well, thank you for your quick thinking, Justin,' Peter said, and Joe nodded in approval. 'It is clear now that I need to take serious action about that man. I just don't know how to do it without involving Betsy. The poor girl is getting married – the last thing she needs is her reputation tarnishing. Leave it with me. Treen, keep her close to the house until I have dealt with Trencrom.'

'Yes, my lord.'

*

On leaving the Earl's office, Joe went straight to the housekeeper's room in search of Ruby. She frowned when she saw the serious look on his face.

'Ruby,' he said sitting down without invitation, 'did Betsy say why she walked back along the main road?'

Ruby nodded. 'She thought she was being watched in the churchyard. I think, although she doesn't show it, she's still shaken about what happened with Trencrom, so she felt the safest route home was on the main road. What was said in His Lordship's study – is Justin all right?' she asked anxiously.

'He is yes,' and proceeded to tell her what he had just learned.

35

As long as Ryan and Betsy stayed in full view of everyone, Ruby had granted them a private corner in the kitchen dining room to speak to each other.

'So,' Ryan held Betsy's hands in his, 'have you seen the cottage Ellie is offering?'

'Yes, I've been in it many times – it belonged to my friend Jessie.'

'And you like it?'

'Like it? I love it!'

'Then we'll make our home there. Now,' he said seriously, 'about the job offer?'

'Yes,' she said tentatively.

'Is it not my job as a husband to provide for his wife?'

Betsy nodded, but could not help but feel just a tad deflated.

He gave a wry smile. 'Do you want to work in the tea room?'

She smiled and nodded. 'But it's up to you.'

'No Betsy, it's up to *you*. I want you to be happy in our new life together, and if it means you working too, then I am happy for you to do that.'

A wide smile split her face as she flung her arms around him and kissed him on the lips. 'Oh, thank you, Ryan.'

'Now, now!' Mrs Blair flapped her tea towel at them. 'No hanky-panky until the wedding night.'

*

The atmosphere was tense in the gamekeeper's lodge the next morning as Peter Dunstan sat with Gerald Oliver discussing the incident yesterday with Trencrom.

Peter folded his arms. 'I need him out of the county. Do you have any ideas how we can do that?'

'Bringing charges against him is still out of the question then, my lord?'

'I'm afraid it is – Betsy is about to be married and the

last thing she wants is a tarnished reputation.'

Gerald drummed his fingers on the table. 'It makes my blood boil that he's getting away with this scot-free.'

Peter raised an eyebrow. 'I think we all agree on that!'

'From what you've told me, my lord, he seems to have taken no heed of your warning about him coming anywhere near Betsy.

'Exactly, and he only lives up the road at The Wheel Inn.'

'Yes, much to the consternation of Jim the landlord there,' Gerald answered dryly, 'Jim knows Trencrom has been dismissed, though not why, and is hoping to evict him as soon as he can't pay the rent.'

Peter rubbed his chin thoughtfully. 'I can't wait that long - he is far too close for comfort.'

Gerald tapped his lips as an idea came to him. 'I think you should go and speak to a friend of mine – an ex-policeman. No,' he held his hand up when the Earl was about to protest, 'he's a good man and knows a lot of people. If anyone can help you, he can!

*

Meg Williams's mouth dropped when she answered the door to the Earl de Bochym that evening. She was used to speaking to Sarah, the Countess, but rarely had an occasion to meet with the Earl.

'Good evening, Mrs Williams - could I possibly speak with your husband?'

'Of course, my lord,' she said breathlessly. 'Come in.'

Tobias folded the newspaper he was reading and stood up when he saw who his visitor was.

'Can I get you some tea, my lord?' Meg said, mentally selecting which of her best crockery to use.

'No, thank you. Mrs Williams.' He turned to Tobias. 'Mr Williams, do you still have connections with the police – I believe you were in the force some time ago?'

'I do, my lord.'

'I have a problem of a delicate nature that I need help

with.'

Tobias nodded and glanced at Meg, who graciously backed out of the room so they could speak in private.

'I didn't want to go to the police direct - I wanted to ask you first. Is there any way I can have an undesirable moved out of the county, and is there any way we can force him to stay there.'

'It depends on what he's done.'

Peter proceeded to tell him about the attack on Betsy, on the proviso it was to be kept an absolute secret, for obvious reasons.'

Tobias ran his hands through his white hair.

'Oh, the poor lass! Betsy is such a lovely girl, and so looking forward to her wedding and new job here. I understand why you don't want this made public. You say, Betsy thought she was being watched in the churchyard yesterday?'

'Yes, it's somewhere she goes most Monday's. She's not actually aware that he was following her yesterday – we don't want to alarm her, but if it hadn't been for my brother-in-law giving her a lift, I shudder to think what would have happened to her. We are keeping her close to the manor for the moment. I cannot allow him to pursue her like this.'

Tobias nodded gravely. 'We need to catch him and put him away, rather than just have him removed, especially if he has an inclination to harm women. I think perhaps we need to set a trap.'

'I do not want to put Betsy at any risk.'

'I understand, my lord. Now, I know you didn't want to involve the police, but we're more discreet than you think. I'm sure there is something we can do without involving Betsy. Let me speak to the sergeant in Mullion about it. I can tell you though - there is nothing that gets a policeman's goat, more than someone getting away with a crime. I'll come and see you tomorrow morning with a plan.'

'Thank you, Mr Williams.'

*

Everyone looked up in curiosity when Tobias Williams, the beach hut man from Poldhu, came to the back door the next morning to see His Lordship. Everyone except Joe that is - because he ushered him straight through to the Earl's study. Tobias was there for three-quarters of an hour, before departing through the front door, leaving everyone none the wiser for his visit.

*

For the next couple of days, every time Betsy ventured out of the manor to collect eggs or feed the pigs, Joe dropped what he was doing and followed her. She didn't notice at first, but then turned back one day having realised she forgotten her handkerchief, and saw Joe quickly stepping into one of the outhouses.

She frowned. 'Are you all right, Mr Treen?' she asked popping her head around the door to the outhouse.

'Perfectly,' he answered, straightening his jacket.

Betsy shrugged and went to collect a handkerchief from her bedside drawer, but as she picked up the pigswill bucket, she caught sight of Joe again pulling back into the shadows of the woodshed.

*

With a farewell dinner party planned for the Trevellick's that weekend - there was a great deal to do that week in the manor. Sophie, Kit and their two children were to stay over on Saturday night, so the guestroom had to be prepared, cots and spare beds were to be erected in the nursery bedrooms and silverware was to have a special polish. With so much work, Ruby's day off was very much in question - much to the concern of both her and Justin.

'Of course, you must take your day off,' Sarah urged when Ruby reluctantly offered to forgo the day. 'It's not like last time. We only have four guests for dinner and only two of them and their children staying. And of course, this time we have Betsy, now her foot has mended. Speaking of which, we need to find Betsy's replacement – though it will be difficult to find another maid as conscientious as her.'

'I agree, but I'll do my best. I've placed an advertisement in the West Britain.'

'Excellent. Have a good day off. Are you going anywhere nice?'

'I haven't decided yet,' she said, trying to rein her excitement in.

*

On Wednesday morning, Ruby packed her watercolours in her basket, along with the picnic lunch and a towel – though she was unsure as to whether they would brave the water today with it being almost November. Their plan was for Ruby to walk as far as Cury Cross Lanes where Justin would pick her up in the pony trap.

When Joe bade her goodbye that morning, Ruby was unaware that he could have, but had purposely not asked Justin to give her a lift in the pony trap this time, even though he knew they were probably heading in the same direction. She was also unaware that Joe was seriously concerned that he had, albeit unintentionally, thrown them together the last time they had gone out, and was deeply worried about the dire consequences his actions might bring.

*

After walking over to Polurrian Cove on Monday, Justin decided that the cove was inaccessible to the pony trap, so they made their decision to go to Church Cove again.

The cove basked in the late October sunshine as Justin steered the pony trap down the rutted lane to the beach. The sea was calm and the sky devoid of any clouds to block the sun and chill the day. After unpacking their things by the church wall, they walked hand-in-hand down to the water's edge. The sea glittered golden starbursts as they looked out to the horizon, both quiet in their happy companionship. Oystercatchers ran back and forth with the tide, picking at whatever morsels it gave up. They walked the length of the beach, and when they turned to walk back, they braved the water for a paddle, but the cold surf made them both jump back laughing - a swim was definitely off the agenda.

Ruby was secretly pleased they weren't going to swim – she was concerned that the exertion in the cold water would put Justin back in bed for the next few days. He did, however, seem a little stronger today – though he was still very pale.

When they returned and settled beside the church wall, Justin turned his face to the sun. 'I can hardly wait until we speak with Sarah. I very much need you to be my wife and to get back to the warmth of a Tuscan winter – my bones do not care for draughty England.'

Ruby smiled as she laid the picnic out on the blanket. 'Well, I've circled one or two candidates in 'The Lady' as my replacement, but I obviously can't interview anyone until the end of next month.'

He took her hand and brought it to his lips.

'I hope that tonic the doctor gave me starts to work soon, I need something to give me some strength - otherwise our wedding night will be a huge disappointment for you.'

Ruby reached up and burrowed her fingers in his thick blonde hair. 'If we can only hold each other all night I will be the happiest bride.'

'But I want to give you so much more.' He gathered her into his arms and held her as though he feared he would lose her.

The shadows by the church wall grew long and chilly after their picnic, so they moved further up the beach where the sun still warmed the sand between their toes. Ruby took out her paints and pad and began to paint St Winwaloe's Church, while Justin quietly sketched her again. After about an hour, she put down her paints and smiled at him.

'Can I look?' he asked.

She passed it over to him and he inspected it carefully and with great admiration.

'This is very good, Ruby – you have a real raw talent. When we get to Italy, I'll introduce you to some people I know – you could sell your work.'

'Oh no!' Ruby began to fidget, picking imaginary fluff off her clothing. 'I'm not *that* good.'

'Yes, you are, and don't be so coy.' He brushed his lips on hers and glanced at the church she'd just painted. 'Have you ever been in the church?'

'No - if we ever go to a service, it's to Cury Church.'

'Let's go and explore then.'

As they walked the path to the church door, a rather sinister looking statue greeted them.

'I see you have met our Breton saint,' a voice behind startled them, and they turned to address the vicar who smiled cordially. 'This is St Winwaloe, who is said to have founded the first church on this site. The church you see now was built in the 15th and 16th centuries, but originated in the 13th century. It was heavily restored after storm damage in 1869. The church is locally referred to as 'The Church of the Storms' and is the only one in Cornwall actually located on a beach.' He tipped his head. 'Tell me, are you local?'

'From Italy,' Justin said squeezing Ruby's hand.

'Then you'll have seen many beautiful churches. Come - take a look around my simple church.'

When they emerged back out into the bright sunlight, Justin pulled Ruby into an embrace. 'What a lovely place - I think we should marry here. After all it's where you fell in love with me.'

Ruby smiled. 'I think I fell in love with you the first day I saw you.'

'But still, you make me wait to marry you! I've a good mind to make arrangements to go back to Italy next week, whisk you away with me and marry you in Italy!'

'No, don't you dare!' She slapped him playfully – though in truth, if that were to happen, she wouldn't have to face the music when their relationship became public.

36

It was Thursday morning when Betsy realised Joe was actually following her. She saw him hide behind the copper beech tree as she took a walk in the gardens before tea. Keeping her counsel, she walked nonchalantly back to the manor and sat at the kitchen dining table waiting for Joe to return - which he did, a couple of minutes later.

Joe smiled cordially at Betsy and addressed Ruby, 'I'll be in my office *if* you need me.'

Betsy narrowed her eyes when Joe surreptitiously glanced between Ruby and herself - something very strange was afoot. She waited until Ruby went back to the housekeeper's room and then followed her.

Ruby turned and smiled. 'Do you need something, Betsy?'

'Yes,' she said, clearing her throat. 'I'd rather like to know why I'm being followed. Do you think I'm going to steal something before I leave?'

Ruby blanched. 'Good gracious, no!'

'Then why?'

Ruby bit down on her lip. 'Close the door, Betsy and sit down. Now, you weren't meant to know this, but Trencrom has been following you.'

Betsy baulked. 'Pardon?'

'We think he's going to do you some harm.'

'How... how do you know?' she asked feeling her heart race.

'When Mr Devereux picked you up on Monday afternoon, Trencrom was following you. That's why he wouldn't let you walk home from the Wheelwrights. He feigned illness so that you would stay with him, but it was to keep you safe.'

Betsy's mouth dropped. 'You know, I thought someone was watching me when I was in the churchyard. That's why I walked that way home. Oh no, does that mean I can never go out alone now?'

'Not at the moment, that's why Mr Treen is following you.'

Betsy's lip curled into a smile. 'He would never make a sleuth – I spotted him every day! But I'm thankful. But where does that leave me?'

'There are plans afoot for the police to remove Trencrom from the county – I'm not sure how, but you must not say a word to anyone. I wasn't meant to tell you all this - His Lordship didn't want to frighten you. Let Mr Treen continue to follow you and keep you safe. It's probably best to stay close to the manor until Trencrom is caught though.'

Betsy shoulders drooped - she'd been looking forward to going down to Poldhu to see her new cottage on Monday. *Perhaps, if the police were watching Trencrom, and if she took the wagon, surely, she'd be safe and able to still go!*

'When he *is* caught, may I speak with Mr Devereux to thank him for his care and kindness?'

'Yes, I'll arrange that for you.'

*

A drinks party preceded dinner on Saturday night to give the Bochym Arts and Craft Association members a chance to wish Kit and Sophie Trevellick farewell.

Juliet could see no way out of being present at this function, unlike last time when the Trevellick's were here and she'd feigned a headache. She and Betsy were working alongside Thomas, handing out canapés, all the while Juliet was studiously avoiding going anywhere near the Trevellick's. If anyone beckoned her over near where they stood, she kept her head lowered so as not to make eye contact. She managed to keep a low profile for the first fifteen minutes of the get-together, until Ellie Blackthorn stopped Betsy from working and took her around the room, introducing her to everyone as her soon-to-be new tea room assistant. This left the lion's share of the work to Thomas and herself, giving her nowhere to hide.

Twice she thought Kit had spotted her when she

chanced a look at him, and once he'd even locked eyes with her, but Juliet thought if she ignored him, he'd think he was mistaken. She'd never been more relieved when the drinks party finished at seven-thirty. This meant Juliet could escape from view and hide in the kitchens away from any unwanted questions.

*

Justin felt slightly out of place at dinner – the other guests were old friends of Peter and Sarah's, and more than anything else, Justin would have liked Ruby at his side at the dinner table. It didn't seem right that she was somewhere busy working in the background, making sure the guests were comfortable during their visit, when in a few weeks she would be his wife and would sit by his side for every meal

*

While Joe presided over dinner with Thomas, he watched Justin curiously. If he wasn't mistaken, Justin wore the same lost expression Ruby had been wearing earlier that evening. Should he say something to Ruby? Warn her? But then looking at them both, it was probably too late for counsel. One thing was sure - this household was going to be in turmoil when their love affair came to light. What with that, and Betsy leaving in a few weeks, he felt all at sea as to what to do.

'Treen, Treen!'

His lordships voice cut through his thoughts.

'Are you quite well, Treen? You seem not to be yourself,' he said.

'I do beg your pardon, my lord. A momentary lapse of concentration I believe.'

Peter smiled and nodded. 'I think perhaps we will all go through to the drawing room for drinks now.' As they all got up, Peter patted Joe on the sleeve. 'We'll manage on our own for the rest of the night - I'll let you finish up here.'

'Thank you, my lord, and I do apologise again.'

'Think nothing of it, Treen. I know you have been working extra hard doing a sterling job keeping Betsy safe,' he whispered.

Joe nodded - he just wished he could have kept Ruby safe from her inevitable downfall. He had nothing against Justin Devereux – he was a nice chap, but Joe couldn't be sure that his intentions towards Ruby were honourable. Even if they were - they were from a completely different class – it just wouldn't work! Damn the gentry! Yes, he served them well and was happy to do just that, but it was the fact that they seemed to feel they could exploit - le droit de seigneur - the right of the master to use the servants, as and when they wanted! Having thought that, Ruby seemed quite enamoured with Justin, but soon he would go back to Italy and Ruby would lose her position. What then?

*

Joe sat in his office and waited - he would not go to bed until everyone was settled in their own bedchambers, though the dinner guests seemed to be in no hurry to go to them. On hearing footsteps on the stairs at around eleven, he came out of his office to find that Justin had been the first to leave the party.

'Do you need anything before you retire?' he asked him.

Justin shook his head, bade him goodnight and started to climb the stairs again, but no sooner had Joe closed his office door, the footsteps came back downstairs and he heard a soft knock on the housekeeper's door down the corridor. Joe opened his door again just in time to see Justin enter the housekeeper's room. He sighed – there really was nothing he could do now.

*

Delighted, Ruby was in his arms the moment he'd closed her door.

'I was just on my way to bed when I wondered if you were still here - and here you are! He beamed. 'Oh, but

I've missed you all evening, Ruby,' he said covering her face with kisses.

'Shhh, I think Joe is still up.'

'He is! I've just said goodnight to him.'

'Oh, my, goodness! What if he's seen you coming in here?'

'I'll say I just came for a blanket, that's all!'

Ruby pulled away from him and opened the cupboard door, selected a blanket and placed it in his hands. 'Go, go now!' She ushered him to the door.

He smiled at the blanket. 'This is all very déjà vu.' He stole another kiss.

'Yes, and I think the last time you asked me for a blanket you didn't really need one, did you?' she teased.

'Perhaps I didn't.' His lips curled into a smile. 'Goodnight, my lovely Ruby.'

'Goodnight, Justin,' she whispered.

*

The chat had been lively around the dining room table, but all that evening there had been 'an elephant in the room' so to speak. This had been the first social occasion Guy had attended since losing Silas, and he was still clearly grieving.

It was Kit who brought the subject up. Things like this needed to be spoken about – the more you bottled things up the worse things got in his opinion.

'I should think it was a relief to get some closure on that dreadful event, Guy,' Kit asked.

Everyone turned to Guy - waiting for his response.

Eventually he nodded. 'Yes, thanks to Peter's lawyer, we have at last had some closure of what happened. It was just dragging on and on – dragging us down – dragging me down,' he said, his voice almost inaudible.

'We're so grateful to you for sending Mr Sheldon to us, Peter.' Ellie interjected.

Peter raised his glass. 'You are very welcome. I was happy to help.'

'I should think Silas's soul will rest in peace now, justice has been done,' Sarah said, raising an eyebrow to Ellie.

Guy laughed gently at them. 'Well, I think we've disproved your theory that ghosts hang around if justice isn't done. Because knowing Silas, he'd have made his presence known and played holy havoc if that was the case!' He drained his glass.

Sarah and Ellie exchanged knowing glances, but said nothing else.

'You know though, I do feel that Silas is still with me on the roof,' he said thoughtfully.

'I think Silas will always be with you in your heart, Guy,' Sarah answered.

The mood of the room had turned melancholic, so to lift the conversation, Ellie turned to Kit and Sophie. 'Are you coming down to Poldhu before you go home tomorrow?'

Sophie, who had never liked Silas, but would never have wished him any harm, was glad of the change of subject, 'Oh yes, Kit will not venture north without sampling one last cream tea.'

Guy guffawed. 'You sound like it's going to be your last supper.'

'Don't mock, Guy. I simply don't know how I'll get through the next year without one,' Kit declared.

'You'll have to make do with pikelets in Yorkshire,' Ellie answered. 'Meg tells me they are like flat crumpets or thick pancakes.'

Kit sighed. 'Can you eat them with cream and jam?'

'I'm sure any Yorkshire tea room of worth will make you just that.'

'They'd better.'

'When do you leave?' Peter asked.

'We go a week on Monday - but before that, we really *are* having a last supper at the Williams's farm and they've invited us all,' Sophie answered and turned to Sarah and Peter, 'Lydia and Eric Williams have extended the invitation to you too.'

'Thank you, but alas, we are dining with the Bickfords at Trevarno next weekend, so we will say our last goodbyes to you in the morning.'

'Speaking of which, if we don't retire soon, it will be morning already,' Guy said. 'Thank goodness our children are staying at Meg and Tobias's tonight - we won't have to sneak around trying not to wake them when we get in, which is no mean feat after several glasses of your fine port, Peter!'

*

After breakfast the next morning there was a flurry of activity and emotional farewells before the manor fell back into its normal routine.

Justin joined the staff for tea later that afternoon. His presence at the tea table no longer put them all on their best behaviour - they were used to him now and would chat to him as one of their own. Although Ruby relished Justin being there, she was terrified that her face would give away her true feelings for him.

Being Sunday, they were joined as usual by Jake and Ryan. Ruby watched the way Ryan looked at Betsy – he could not keep his adoring eyes off her as they planned their wedding. For a moment she dropped her guard and smiled at their happiness, knowing she too would be planning her own wedding soon. When she glanced at Justin, it was as though he knew what she was thinking, because his eyes twinkled back at her. She didn't notice that Joe was watching them - or that he swallowed hard as though unable to stomach what was to come.

*

It was Monday afternoon and though it was a little chilly, Trencrom was sweating from the exertion of his walk. The weather was thankfully fine so he knew the game was on. He rubbed his hands gleefully - there was only one place he needed to be – Cury churchyard. How he thanked Betsy's predictability and her unstinting, reliable care of that bastard child's grave. He patted his pocket – he had his hood and a scarf to gag her with, and licked his lips at the prospect of the prize that would very soon be his. This time no one was going to snatch it from him! He felt a stirring in his groin, he was going to enjoy every single moment of de-flowering Betsy Tamblin. He knew he had to take a different tack today because it was clear she had sensed someone watching her last week, otherwise she would not have taken the main road home. Hopefully, if he kept well out of the way, she'd walk back home down the country lane this time and then he would have her.

He crept into the churchyard, keeping well out of sight. There was no one about but for one lone figure kneeling over that damn baby's gravestone. Perhaps she should say a little prayer for herself, he mused, although God would not help her this afternoon. He glanced around - the place was completely deserted, perhaps he needn't wait for her to walk home today. This was too good an opportunity to waste and he began to unbutton his flies.

*

Joe came out of his study and looked around the kitchen. He frowned when he found Juliet alone.

'Where's Betsy, Juliet.'

She looked up from her polishing. 'Isn't it her half day off?'

'Well, normally it is, but I asked Ruby if it could be changed,' he said, trying to keep the panic from his voice.

Juliet looked puzzled at his concern, but his face softened and asked, 'Do you know where she's gone?'

'To the churchyard, I should think. Does she not go every Monday? And I'm absolutely sure I heard her telling Ryan that she was going to Poldhu to look at her cottage on her next day off.'

'Oh, my, god!' Joe whispered and felt the blood drain from his face as he shot off to find Ruby.

37

Trencrom's breath quickened – Betsy was dressed in a hooded cloak, which meant she wouldn't see him advancing on her. Hearing an unusual bird call, he frowned and glanced up at the trees - he'd never heard the likes before. Shrugging when he saw nothing unusual, he began to salivate as he readied the scarf to gag her, and glanced around again - there was still no one about. If he grabbed her from behind, he could drag her over to the far side of the churchyard where the long grass grew. His tongue flicked furiously in excitement as he surged forward and pinioned her to the ground. He assumed the shock of the attack must have rendered her speechless, because though she struggled, she made no sound – not even a muffle when he pulled the gag tight across her mouth. Covering her head with the hood, he pushed her down into the mound of earth in front of the gravestone. The way she bucked and struggled added to his excitement, but by the strength of the fight she was putting up, dragging her over to the long grass was going to prove problematic. Deciding instead to take her here and now, he straddled her thighs and released himself from his trousers.

*

Joe burst into the housekeeping room without knocking, but Ruby wasn't there. He climbed the stairs two at a time, searching the bedrooms – bizarrely praying that he wouldn't catch Ruby and Justin in a compromising position somewhere. In the end he shouted Ruby's name.

Ruby came out of one of the bathrooms, shocked at Joe's anxious state 'Whatever is it, Joe?'

'We should have told Betsy that Trencrom was following her! Did you not change her day off like I asked you to?' Before she could answer, he said, 'Oh, god Ruby, I think she's gone to the churchyard – she'll have walked right into his trap!'

'Joe, be calm!' She put her hand on his arm to pacify

him and pushed the bathroom door open. There, atop of the stepladder hanging a pair of curtains stood Betsy safe and sound.

*

The first Trencrom knew something was amiss, was when the figure underneath him began to growl like an angry dog, and as he lifted her skirts, he revealed two very hairy legs. The next thing he knew, an arm hooked around his neck, almost choking him and he was yanked from where he sat. He fell back onto the damp grass, his limbs flaying and his private parts clearly on show. As he tried to right himself, he looked fearfully up at the three policemen standing over him scowling – it was then Trencrom's bowels turn to liquid.

The policeman pretending to be Betsy pulled off the gag and grabbed Trencrom by his jacket lapels to drag him to his feet, grimacing at the smell of his fear.

The sergeant stepped forward and sneered, 'You filthy little man! You're under arrest for indecent exposure to a police officer and intent to cause grievous bodily harm.' He turned to his colleagues. 'Take this pathetic little worm out of my sight,' he ordered.

The two other officers grabbed Trencrom, but before they could cuff him, Trencrom's flight or fight reflex set in. *Nobody was going to put him in jail!* He broke free, and for one wonderful moment believed he'd gained his liberty. He ran like the wind, twisting to see if he was being followed, and so didn't see the vicar who had just stepped out of the vestry door to see what was going on. There was a sickening crunch of skulls as Trencrom ran straight into him and they both hit the ground with a heavy thud. Winded, Trencrom scrambled to his feet, but was rugby tackled to the ground by one of the policemen and hit on the head with a truncheon.

'Thank you, vicar,' the sergeant said, helping him to his feet, as Trencrom was dragged off to the police wagon hidden down the back lane.

'You're welcome,' the vicar said tremulously, holding his handkerchief to his bloody nose with one hand, while brushing the dirt off his cassock with the other!

*

On Tuesday morning, Joe was presiding over breakfast service when Thomas brought in the silver platter of letters - two for Peter, three for Sarah, and one for Justin.

Peter looked up as Justin took his. 'More invites from people wanting to show you off to their friends,' he teased.

'I sincerely hope not!' Justin grimaced as he pushed his breakfast plate away to open his letter.

'Ah, splendid news,' Peter declared as he read the note from Tobias Williams.

Sarah smiled and waited to hear.

'It's a note from Mr Williams to tell me they've arrested Trencrom on a charge of indecent exposure, and assault with intent to cause grievous bodily harm.'

'Gracious me,' Sarah held her hand to her chest, 'and to think we employed that dreadful man!'

'Exactly! Treen please could you inform Betsy that she no longer needs to worry about Trencrom.'

'I will, my lord.' Joe beamed.

Peter laughed heartily. 'It seems he was caught in a police honey trap – the irony of it! To be a beekeeper and get caught in a honey trap, eh? Though I should use the term beekeeper very loosely - after what he did to those poor bees!'

Sarah hummed in agreement, but was startled when Justin stood up abruptly.

'Excuse me.' He left the room, leaving the letter he was reading on the table.

A moment later the front door open and closed and Sarah craned her neck to look out of the window to see where Justin was going without his coat. He stopped at the front gate, and when he buried his face in his hands, Sarah knew something was seriously wrong and picked up his letter.

Harley Street, London
Dear Mr Devereux,
Further to your visit to my practice and consequent blood tests on the 23rd October 1912. It is with great regret that I must tell you that the blood tests have come back with extremely unfavourable results. You are suffering from a condition called pernicious anaemia. As to your prognosis, I regret to tell you that there is no cure, and there is little we can do for you, as it is in an advanced stage. May I suggest that you do not delay in putting your affairs in order? If you wish to discuss this further, please telephone me on London 495
Yours sincerely
Mr Webb MD

Sarah gasped and dropped the letter from her trembling fingers.

'What is it, Sarah?'

'Oh, Peter!' She turned her tear-filled eyes to him. 'It's from Harley Street. Justin is dying!' She pushed her chair out to stand before Joe could pull it away, and rushed out of the dining room.

Joe and Peter watched from the window as Sarah ran to her brother and gathered him up in her arms.

'Please convey the news to the household, Treen, and tell them Mr Devereux and Her Ladyship must not be disturbed,' he said gravely.

'Yes, my lord.'

*

Ruby was putting her hat on to go down to the Dower Lodge when Joe knocked on the housekeeper's room door.

'Come in,' she said happily, smiling when she saw who it was.

'Oh, Ruby,' he breathed.

Ruby tipped her head quizzically – he looked as white as a sheet. 'Whatever is the matter?'

He closed the door behind him quickly and Ruby

surmised he was about to tell her something he wanted to keep secret from the other members of staff.

'I think you need to know that something grave has happened in the household today.'

'Oh, no!' Ruby stopped pinning her hat on. 'Is someone ill?'

Joe nodded. 'Very ill by the sound of it - Her Ladyship has taken to her room and Lowenna is with her now.'

'My goodness, what's happened? Is it the Earl or the Dowager Countess?'

'No, Ruby,' he said tremulously, 'it's Justin.'

Suddenly struck by a deeply unpleasant visceral feeling running through her veins, Ruby stammered, 'What…what do you mean?'

'Justin received a letter this morning from London. It seems he saw a specialist up there and his findings were not favourable.'

Ruby stared at Joe, and the silence seemed to fill the room.

'He's dying, Ruby.'

Suddenly feeling very light-headed, a strange ringing sound filled her ears and before she could reach out to Joe she'd crumpled to the floor. Joe had his arms around her and though she had not quite fainted, she felt completely disorientated and incapable of moving. When eventually she gathered her senses, she lifted her stricken face. 'Where is Justin now?'

'I believe he took himself off for a breath of air,' he said helping her onto the chair.

A myriad of emotions ran through her head. She needed to find him - he would need her. 'I'm sorry Joe, it's,' she waved her hand to try and explain her reaction, 'it's just the shock,' but as she said it, tears rolled down her face.

Joe knelt at her feet and handed her his clean handkerchief. 'Perhaps, you too need to get some fresh air.' He squeezed her hand. 'I'll cover for you, take your time. I need to convey the news to the rest of the staff. Betsy will run everything here.'

Ruby's eyes blurred again - she knew then that Joe knew about them. 'Thank you, Joe,' she said shakily.

*

Ruby ran blindly through the arboretum, tears streaming down her face, hoping she would not meet anyone on her desperate journey. Bursting breathlessly into the Dower Lodge, she found him standing by the unlit fire - his face ashen. All she was aware of was her desperate rasping breath as she walked the few paces towards him.

'Tell me - tell me what I've just heard is untrue?' she whispered fearfully.

Justin's mouth moved, but no words came forth.

A fierce ragged cry rose from her throat as she clamped her hands around his arms. 'It must be untrue,' she shook him, 'it must be!'

He gathered her into his arms and finally finding his voice, he answered tearfully, 'Unfortunately not, my love.'

'No, Justin - Is it certain – can you not get a second opinion?'

'It's quite certain,' his voice wavered.

Her tears flowing unchecked drenched his shirt as she clung desperately to him. Feeling his body shake with emotion in her arms, she lifted her face to his and kissed his quivering lips.

'I'm so sorry, Ruby, I can't be brave for you,' he said wiping his tears on his shirt sleeve. 'I'm devastated.' He hung onto her, so as not to let this thing - this terrible condition - tear him away from her. 'Ruby, I need to lie down. This news has utterly exhausted me.'

'Of course, my love, do you want to go back to the house?'

'No, I want to be here - with you. Will you come and lie down with me and hold me? I need to feel you close to me. I can't get through this without you.'

Through blurred eyes, she let him lead her to one of

the bedrooms, where they climbed under the satin eiderdown to ward off the chill of the room. As he gathered her into his strong arms, she wondered - how could this man - so strong and alive, with blood flowing freely in his veins and a heartbeat so strong – how could he be dying?

'When I got the news, you were all I wanted, Ruby. Just to be with you so we could hold each other.' His body trembled as he spoke.

'I'm here now, my love.'

'I wanted so much for us. I had such plans for our life in Tuscany,' his voice cracked, 'all those dreams have turned to dust now.'

'I know, my love, I know,' she whispered, as tears trickled down her cheeks.

'I dare not take you to Italy now, because I may not have long, and I can't leave you in a foreign land on your own – it would not be fair on you.'

'Do you know how long?' she asked tremulously.

'I don't know,' his voice wavered, 'I've been told to put my affairs in order as soon as possible, so, that must mean I only have weeks rather than months.'

'Oh, Justin,' she kissed his stricken face tenderly, 'I'm so sorry for you.'

'*I'm* sorry for us, Ruby.' He kissed her hands. 'I'll make sure you're well cared for, Ruby.'

She had no idea what he meant by that, but smiled tremulously and tightened her hold on him.

38

There was an air of melancholia throughout the house, and none more so when the staff sat down for their mid-day meal. No one had an appetite for Mrs Blair's beef and potato pot, and this time the cook did not reprimand anyone for not eating. The news had shocked and saddened everyone. To them, Justin felt like one of their own.

'Why is good news always squashed by bad news?' Betsy bemoaned.

'I don't think that's always the case, Betsy, Joe said flatly.

'Well, it is in this case! I could have danced a happy little jig when you told me horrible Mr Trencrom had been arrested, and then,' she sniffed back a tear, 'we receive this dreadful news about Mr Devereux.'

Everyone agreed, and turned when they heard Ruby's footsteps coming across the kitchen courtyard.

When she entered the kitchen, Joe noted that her face was pale and wan and she'd evidently been crying.

'I'm sorry I've been so long,' she said to no one in particular.

'Don't worry, Mrs Sanders, we've all managed. I do hope the walk in the fresh air cleared your headache?' Joe said, covering for her.

'Thank you, Mr Treen, it helped a little, but....' Ruby's lips began to tremble.

'Perhaps you should go and lie down for a while,' he said, seeing her eyes fill with tears. 'Betsy and Juliet will manage, won't you?'

They both nodded readily.

'Thank you, I think I will,' she said pulling off her hat.

When Ruby had gone upstairs Juliet exclaimed, 'Gosh, Mrs Sanders didn't look at all well, did she?'

Joe stood up and answered firmly, 'She'll be fine. We'll all look after her, as we always look after each other.' He was unaware that he wasn't the only one who knew what was really wrong with Ruby - Betsy knew too.

*

Justin kept his normal Wednesday assignation with Ruby – this time, spending it in the Dower Lodge. The hours they'd spent apart since learning the news had been purgatory for them both, so the moment they met, they fell into an urgent embrace.

Pulling the cushions onto the rug in front of the fire, they laid in thoughtful silence for a while, until Justin said, 'I wish....'

Ruby glanced up at him. 'What do you wish, my love?'

He sighed deeply. 'I wish I could have fallen asleep with you in my arms at night and woken up next to you the next morning.'

Ruby stroked his clean-shaven face. 'I wish that too.'

He propped himself up on his elbow. 'Ruby, would you come away with me for a couple of days?'

She laughed gently. 'Yes, I would in a heartbeat, but how and where to?'

'I have a friend – an artist friend, Lionel - I went to school with. I met up with him in London last week. He has a cottage in Lamorna, which he offered to me should I want to visit the artist colony that was set up there last century. I've already sent a note to his housekeeper to get it ready for me this weekend - I just need you to say you'll come with me.'

She frowned. 'I'm not sure I can get away at such short notice.'

'Do you not take holidays?'

Ruby laughed and shook her head.

'What? Never!'

She shrugged. 'Where would I go? Everyone I know is here at the manor.'

'Perhaps it's time you took some time off, then. Sarah and Peter are going away to Trevarno this weekend. It would be an ideal opportunity for us to spend some time together.' He tipped his head. 'It might be the last chance to be alone together.'

Could I take the time off? She thought. *Of course, I can - especially while Betsy was still with us. The place will not fall down just because I'm not there.*

Justin took her reticence as concern, and whispered, 'I'm not planning on seducing you, Ruby - I'm not sure I have the stamina - and besides, the last thing I want is to leave you with a baby to bring up all on your own. I just want to hold you all night long.'

Her eyes crinkled, and she kissed him softly on the lips. 'It's what I want too,' she murmured and then they both froze when they heard someone trying the front door.

Ruby got up to look out of the window. 'It's Her Ladyship,' she whispered. 'You must go.'

Justin sighed resignedly as he got up.

'I'm so sorry, Justin.'

He held his hand up. 'It's all right - I'll leave by the back door.'

Ruby quickly tidied the cushions before answering the door.

'I do beg your pardon for keeping you waiting, my lady. I was in the bathroom.'

Sarah lifted her distraught face to meet with Ruby's gaze. 'I'm sorry to disturb you, Ruby, but I saw the smoke from the chimney on my walk and thought I would investigate. Then I remembered that you were keeping the place aired and warm.'

'Yes, my lady, and it gives me the opportunity to be somewhere private on my day off.'

'Oh, yes of course, it's your day off. I'm so sorry to bother you…' her voice cracked with emotion, 'I'm sorry, it's just that - I am trying to stay strong for Justin, but I can't - I just can't.'

When soft tears tumbled down Sarah's face, Ruby pushed all correct protocol aside to gather her into her arms and allow Sarah to cry on her shoulder.

When finally, Sarah recovered her composure, and pulled away to dab her eyes, she reached out to Ruby's stricken face. 'Justin has touched us all in the short time he has been with us, hasn't he?'

Ruby nodded unhappily. *Sarah would never know how much that was true.* 'Let me make you some tea, my lady.'

No, thank you,' she waved a hand.' I seem to do nothing but drink sweet tea at the moment. Forgive me for losing control, Ruby.'

'There's nothing to forgive, my lady. I'm always here should you need a shoulder to cry on.'

'Thank you. What would I do without you?' She squeezed her hand. 'I shall leave you now to your peace and solitude,' she said, turning away before more tears fell.'

As soon as Sarah had left, Justin returned to the Dower Lodge and was back in Ruby's arms. This interruption of their precious few hours together decided them once and for all that they must go away together.

*

Justin joined Sarah and Peter that evening for pre-dinner drinks, though he sat down and declined anything alcoholic offered by Joe.

'Peter and I have been thinking, Justin,' Sarah started, 'In light of your news, we're going to cancel our trip to Trevarno at the weekend.'

'Please don't cancel it on my account.'

'But we can't leave you, Justin – we'll be gone two nights!' Sarah folded her hands on her lap nervously.

'I'm not a child, Sarah, and I know you mean well, but I don't need mollycoddling. I won't be here anyway. I'm leaving in the morning - I'm taking a cottage for the weekend in Lamorna. I always planned to visit the artist colony there and I would very much like to meet the acclaimed artist, Laura Knight. So, while I feel well enough, I'm going to do as much as I can.'

Sarah reached over and cupped her hand over his. 'Well, if you are absolutely sure?'

'I am, and you must go for your weekend away - we must all live and enjoy life while we can.'

*

Ruby sat quietly in Joe's office later that evening after putting in her request for leave. He looked at her face - it was etched and drawn with worry, but even though she probably suspected that he was aware of her relationship with Justin, nothing was mentioned.

'So, you want to take *this* weekend off?'

'Yes, please. The Earl and Countess are away at Trevarno this weekend, so it would be convenient for me to go then. I need a break, and since very soon we'll lose Betsy, I'm not sure I can leave the house again until Juliet is trained up enough to take on my duties in my absence.'

Joe nodded. 'Are you - going anywhere nice?'

Ruby lifted her eyes to Joe's - her silence spoke volumes.

'Of course, you can take the time off,' he said, knowing full well that Justin would be away for the weekend too - he'd ordered the car to take him to Lamorna the next day.

'May I leave first thing Friday morning, as soon as the Earl and Countess leave for Trevarno?'

'Of course – will you need to be taken anywhere - the station?'

She smiled gently. 'Yes please - to the station.'

'I'll arrange that for you, then.'

Ruby's lip trembled. 'Thank you, Joe. You're a good friend.'

*

Before the car came to take Justin away, he met Ruby in the Dower Lodge, to finalise their plans.

'I'll be waiting for you at Penzance station tomorrow - will you be all right travelling alone from Helston?'

'Yes, of course. Joe has arranged for the pony trap to take me to the station.'

Justin cupped her face in his hands and kissed her tenderly. 'Tomorrow night there will be no parting for us.

302

Are you sure you want this?'

'Oh, yes - more than anything,' she said breathlessly, though not without some apprehension.

'Until tomorrow then, my love.'

*

On Friday morning, Ruby caught the Helston to Redruth train where she then boarded the London to Penzance train. It was a short journey and Ruby gasped in awe when St Michael's Mount came into view. The rocky island sitting in the shimmering bay and crowned by a medieval castle and church, seemed almost magical. As the train pulled into its final destination, she checked her reflection in the window to make sure she was neat and tidy, and wondered if she would recognise this woman in the reflection when she boarded the train to go home in two days' time!

Collecting her overnight bag, she walked excitedly out into the pale November sunshine - shielding her eyes to search for Justin.

'Hello, my darling girl,' Justin whispered, as he appeared by her side, and kissed her openly in front of everyone.

He took her bag and put it on the pony trap he'd hired, and though the bag was not heavy, she could see he found the weight a challenge – he seemed to be getting weaker by the day.

'Let me escort you to our weekend home,' he smiled, curling his hand around hers to help her up.

*

The cottage, which was warm, and as clean as a new pin, nestled in a forest of trees which meandered down to Lamorna Cove. Though most of the trees were leafless, they were interspersed with evergreens which still made the valley feel lush and earthy. Justin had bought some groceries while he'd been in Penzance, though he had every intention of eating at the local inn -The Lamorna Wink. It was where everyone who lived in this artist community, gathered to talk art, to sing, argue and laugh. It was just the tonic he needed - especially now he had the special company of his lovely Ruby. He opened a bottle of red wine and measured a small amount in two glasses.

'A little early perhaps, but this is a special occasion,' he grinned.

They chinked glasses, both savouring the soft mellow taste of plum and blackcurrant as it burst on the palate.

'It's lovely,' she said shyly.

'It is, and it is with great regret that I am only able to drink a small amount of it, otherwise my stomach will protest, and we don't want anything to spoil our weekend, do we? Come, sit down. I bought you some things to wear when I was in London – I hope you don't think that was too forward of me for doing so. It's just that I so wanted you to have something beautiful to wear – something to make you sparkle like the jewel you are. I was going to give you them to wear when we announced our engagement, I hope they'll fit you.' He handed her three parcels wrapped in tissue paper. 'I hope you like them.'

Ruby's hand caressed the beautifully wrapped parcels on her lap. 'All for me?'

He nodded and smiled.

Carefully unwrapping the first parcel she lifted out a soft white lace blouse, trimmed at the neck and cuffs with thin blue silk ribbon. 'Justin, it's so beautiful, thank you,' she said holding it to her body. The next parcel contained a pale blue herringbone wool skirt and peplum jacket, trimmed at the collar and waistband with dark blue velvet. Ruby rubbed the soft fine material between her finger and thumb and marvelled at the feel of it.

'Do you like it?' Justin asked.

'Oh yes, I do, I really do, thank you.'

The final parcel contained two scarves - a soft silk embroidered scarf that complemented her new outfit perfectly, and a blue and turquoise velvet one which would lift any of the dark dresses she normally wore.

'Oh!' she gasped, 'they're beautiful.' She lifted each one to her cheek to feel the softness against her skin.

Justin touched the silk one. 'You can wear this simply as a scarf, or around your hair. Whichever you decide you'll look lovely in it. Here, let me show you.' He unpinned her hair to let her curls tumble down her back. Fitting the scarf beneath her hair, he brought it up, twisted it on top of her head, and then back down to fasten at the nape of her neck. He pulled the ends forward with a flourish. 'There, take a look.' He led her to the mirror over the fireplace.

Ruby's breath caught in her throat, she looked so different.

Justin smiled. 'Do you like it?'

'I look…..I look so….' her voice was almost inaudible.

'You look beautiful, and it's not just because of some scarf you're wearing! It's because you're the most beautiful woman I know, and I love you with every fibre of my being.' He wrapped his arms around her waist. 'I'm not able to give you all I wanted to give you now, but I'm glad you like your presents.' He took her hands and led her back to sit by the fire where he knelt at her feet. 'I have something else for you.' He opened the tiny velvet box he'd produced from his pocket, to reveal a ruby and diamond ring. 'I also bought this in London - I think now is the perfect time to give it to you.'

Ruby clasped her hand to her heart. 'Oh, Justin, it's,' her voice cracked with emotion, 'it's beautiful.'

'No tears this weekend, Ruby.' He wiped the stray tear running down her cheek with his thumb. 'Only joy, please.' He slipped the ring on her finger. 'Come, let us eat. I have a table booked for luncheon at the Lamorna Wink to celebrate our engagement.'

'I might take my lovely silk scarf off for now – I feel a little overdressed for luncheon, but this one, I *shall* wear.' She draped the velvet one around her neck and admired herself in the mirror.

The Lamorna Wink was quiet at lunch time, so after their meal they walked down to Lamorna Cove to watch the waves from the harbour. On their return, Justin stoked the fire and they spent a cosy afternoon beside it, laid in each other's arms. They were both very aware that they could no longer plan for their future together so, instead they lay in quiet companionship, enjoying every single precious moment together.

39

Ruby dressed in her new outfit to go to dinner and Justin helped her to tie the scarf around her hair, securing it with pins so it did not slip. She had no need for makeup, her cheeks had pinked and her eyes sparkled when she glanced at the woman who looked back at her in the bedroom mirror.

'You look wonderful, Ruby,' he said admiring her appreciatively. 'The artists residing here are a glorious eclectic bunch of people who live life and party to the full – but you my darling girl,' he kissed her, 'will shine brighter than anyone else in that room.'

*

Twenty-five miles from Lamorna, in Gweek, a hearty supper was being laid on by Eric and Lydia Williams, to bid bon voyage to their good friends Kit and Sophie Trevellick. The ladies of the group, Lydia, Sophie, Ellie and the Williams's lodger Lizzy, were putting the finishing touches to the supper, while Eric, Kit, Guy and the Williams's son, Charlie, enjoyed a farewell drink in The Black Swan with their usual drinking buddies.

Amelia Pascoe, the village stalwart and midwife, was tucked away in the snug, having her regular gill of ale. She too was joining them for supper that evening, and had been put in charge of making sure the men left on time for it. So, as the clock struck seven, Amelia opened the door to the main bar to beckon them out.

'Come on lads, supper will be ready now.'

They drained their drinks and Kit said, 'Oh, Amelia, I meant to tell you. I'm absolutely sure I saw young Juliet Gwyn working at Bochym last week - I wondered where she'd gone too these last four months. I must say she looked very well, albeit a little shy.'

Amelia sucked her breath in and placed her finger to her lips to quieten him.

'What?' Kit frowned.

'No one is meant to know where she is,' she hissed.

'Oh, sorry.' He tipped his head. 'Why?'

'It's best that it's kept secret – please don't ask more,' she whispered. A moment later, she heard an angry grunt, and someone stormed out of the inn door slamming it behind them. Amelia's eyes swept over the room. 'Who was that who just left in a hurry?' she asked in alarm.

Kit shrugged. 'It was probably a disgruntled fisherman I suspect. The tide is almost up now and the fishing boat's bell has just rung to call them all to the boat. Why?'

Amelia drew a deep breath. 'No matter,' she said praying that Kit's comments had not been overheard by a certain fisherman.

*

The artists gathered in the Lamorna Wink that evening were a lively, noisy lot and Ruby was immediately welcomed into the group. There was fiddle music playing, and occasionally people would get up to dance to it. Justin introduced her to Stanhope Forbes and his wife Elizabeth - whose art school particularly appealed to women seeking art tuition. Justin had met with them the previous evening and they were rather interested in meeting Ruby, after Justin had spoken so highly of her emerging talent. Ruby also met Joey Carter Wood and his sister Florence - a rather beautiful, albeit introverted woman, who had acquired the very strange and unflattering nickname *Blote*. Florence, Ruby learned, was married, and by the look of it, not particularly happily, to the rather brash, but she was told, excellent artist Alfred Munnings, or AJ as he preferred to go by. AJ kept the group entertained by reciting poetry from heart. Ruby particularly liked Laura Knight who, along with her husband Harold, had moved to Newlyn in 1907 to become part of the Newlyn School. Laura Knight was an extrovert, smoking cheroots and playing the piano with great skill, clearly loving being part of a social circle, and in many respects, the total opposite of her husband, who was very quiet. All in all, they were a lovely bunch of people and Ruby revelled as she immersed herself in their world.

'Who is that gentleman over there, Justin,' Ruby asked, observing a fine-looking gentleman in a tweed jacket who had kept himself to himself all evening whilst still being part of the group.

'That is Gilbert Evans, I met him last evening. He's not an artist, but a land agent - he's also an army officer who formerly served in the Boer War.'

'He watches Florence a great deal!'

'Yes, I've noticed.'

'Perhaps they are secret lovers like us,' she whispered.

'Perhaps they are.' He smiled and kissed her.

*

As they walked back to the cottage hand in hand that evening, the mist was rolling in from the sea. Ruby felt the butterflies which had fluttered in her tummy all evening, intensify and her knees had started to tremble. It was not from the cold!

Justin must have detected her apprehension because he pulled her close and kissed her. 'I love you, Ruby – you're safe in my arms.'

'I know I am.'

Once they'd locked the door, they took turns to use the privy, which thankfully was indoors. Ruby waited for him to come back into the room, warming her hands on the embers of the fire. When he returned with an oil lamp, he reached for her hand, and although the stairs were steep and narrow, he held her hand as she followed him to the bedroom.

Placing his lamp on his bedside table, he pulled her into his arms, and in the pale flickering light he held her for a few moments.

'I want you, Ruby - don't think I don't, but I know we cannot, and I don't think my failing body will let me love you as I want anyway. But I so want to hold you, to look at you and cherish you, may I?'

Ruby nodded, and trembled as he slowly slipped her new jacket from her shoulders. Very carefully he unbuttoned her blouse and kissed the pale, soft skin on her shoulders, gently moving his lips into the hollow of her throat. While Justin pulled his shirt over his head, Ruby undid her stays and skirt. She'd seen him bare-chested when they'd swum together, and had felt his skin on hers, but then their flesh had been cold with the water. This time when she reached her fingers out to touch him, his skin felt warm and firm and was still tanned from his life in the Tuscan sun. He quickly shed his other clothes, all the while never taking his eyes off hers. Standing naked before her, he kissed her gently on the lips as he untied the ribbon on her chemise. Very slowly he slipped his fingers under the material to ease it down her body until the garment pooled at her feet. Now, for the first time they both looked at each other's bodies, admiring them lovingly in the flickering light. Very gently, almost in unison, they reached out to tenderly trace the contours of each other's body.

'You are beautiful, Ruby,' he whispered.

'So are you,' she answered, trying not to think that she was going to lose this wonderful man so soon after finding him.

'No tears this weekend, Ruby,' he reminded her when he saw the glisten in her eyes. He led her to the bed and sat her down to untie the ribbons on her stockings. Slowly and carefully, he rolled them down her slender legs, kissing each knee as it presented itself. She shivered in anticipation, as she lay down. He laid beside her pulling the crisp cotton sheets over their nakedness and then slipped his arm around her shoulders, and pulled her closer with a long, satisfied sigh.

Ruby had never experienced a more wonderful feeling than lying in his loving arms. A moment later she felt her cheek dampen, but the tears were not hers. She did not remind him of their no tears policy - she simply reached up to brush them away from his cheeks, before she settled back into the crook of his arm.

As they slept, the creeping mist had turned to rain – it was as though the sky was weeping for them, and what could have been.

*

The pale, grey dawn broke and Ruby stirred. She must have turned on her side in the night, because now Justin was snuggled against her back - his gentle breathing soft against her neck. Her wakefulness must have disturbed him, because his breathing changed and then she felt a tender kiss on her shoulder.

'Good morning, lovely Ruby,' he whispered into her hair.

'Good morning,' she answered sleepily, snuggling closer to him. Her skin tingled with the delight of feeling his warm body so close to hers. How she must savour this moment - for there would only be one more time when she would wake up this close to him again.

'Can I introduce you to the decadence of breakfast in bed? I don't suppose you do that ever, do you?'

Ruby laughed. 'No, never, breakfast in bed would certainly be a first.'

'Then I'll serve it to you while you languish in comfort.'

When he moved from her side, she felt the loss keenly. 'Hurry back,' she said watching his naked bottom disappear under the tail of the shirt he'd just pulled over his head.

He turned and winked when he saw her watching him and then set off downstairs.

She heard Justin stoking the downstairs fire into life, and as the kettle began to boil, a warm smell of toasted bread wafted up the stairs making Ruby's stomach rumble. A few minutes later, he returned triumphantly with a tray holding two mugs of tea and two plates of hot buttered toast.

'Your breakfast, my lady, I hope you slept well,' he

mimicked the servants morning greeting as he placed the tea on her bedside table and a plate of toast on her lap. He kissed her. 'Thank you for allowing me this time to be with you.'

Ruby smiled, but had to swallow down the lump that had formed in her throat as she returned his kiss.

*

The staff at Bochym were also enjoying a very leisurely breakfast that morning with the family away - although, there was a great deal to do after breakfast. The most exciting thing though, was a postcard that had arrived that morning from Jessie, and everyone poured over the picture of Venice and read and re-read what she had written.

To Betsy and all at Bochym.

After a beautiful wedding in London, Daniel and I are now in Italy on honeymoon! We have visited Venice and Florence, and plan to see Pisa, Sienna and Rome. I wish you all could see these beautiful sights. Life is wonderful and we are very happy, but I do miss you all. Best wishes. Jessie and Daniel.

Betsy glanced at Joe who smiled resignedly.

'Where are you and Ryan going on honeymoon then?' Thomas grinned.

'Poldhu Cove,' Betsy said with a firm nod, 'and it will be just as wonderful,' she added.

'It certainly will, Betsy,' Joe agreed.

Dorothy gazed at the picture of Venice and sighed. 'I don't think I'll ever have a honeymoon!' she moaned.

'I thought much the same, Dorothy, but now look at me! Your time will come.'

'Yes, but hopefully not just yet,' Joe interjected, 'Losing you, Betsy is going to be hard enough, without losing another maid.'

Betsy got up from the table - she'd had her orders from Ruby to brush down the curtains in all the rooms to shoo out the large house spiders that had crept in. Being afraid of spiders, Dorothy was not looking forward to the task, and neither was Betsy, for she knew Dorothy would emit a deafening scream every time one scurried over the floor after being disturbed. That's why this task was always done when the family were away. Thankfully, Juliet was not afraid of them, and would always pick the spider up in her cupped hands to put them outside, rather than let Dorothy bash them with her broom. The poor thing would meet its end either way, but Juliet felt it was a more humane way of ridding the house of them.

As she worked, Betsy could hardly contain her excitement. This time next week she would be getting ready for her wedding. She would miss everyone at Bochym of course, but she would have a new husband to care for, a house and spiders of her own, and a new exciting job awaiting her at the tea room!

Tomorrow was the last reading of their wedding banns at Cury church. Ryan had attended the first two readings and Mr Treen very kindly had given her permission to go and listen to the final time. She had to pinch herself, every now and then, that this was all happening to her.

*

At Lamorna, the weather had brightened by late morning. So, wrapped up warmly, Justin and Ruby took a walk along the cliffs. There was no doubt about it, Justin was struggling to catch his breath, but when Ruby urged him to stop and return to the harbour, he seemed more determined to walk on. They finally settled on a rocky outcrop and looked out to the chilly waves. With the cloud cover, the sea was grey and they both agreed that it looked not at all inviting.

It seemed they were not alone in their stroll across the cliffs - they looked down and noted another couple walking hand in hand on the lower cliff path – it was Florence Munnings and Gilbert Evans.

'Well, I think that answers our question as to whether they are lovers or not,' Justin mused.

'They seem not to be particularly hiding their affair. AJ could walk along here any minute and catch them,' Ruby pointed out

'Mmm, I wish *we* didn't have to hide our love when we get back home.'

Ruby's face contorted. 'I know.'

'We could still marry you know - I believe with my dire condition a special licence could be obtained. You would have a real position in life as the sister-in-law to the Earl and Countess de Bochym.'

Ruby took his hands in hers. 'I would be so out of place without you by my side though, and when the time comes, and I do lose you, my Bochym family backstairs will be my comfort. We have been together a long time - it's all I know. '

'But I want you to have so much more, Ruby, you have such potential as an artist.'

'If all I am ever granted in life are these special moments with you, then I should be very content with my lot. Let's not talk about life afterwards. You are here with me now, alive, with blood pumping through your veins. I can gaze into your handsome face whenever I need to, and enjoy your delicious kisses – that's all I need in life at the moment.'

40

After their morning walk, Ruby and Justin took luncheon in The Lamorna Wink and met with Henry Knight, who invited them to look around his studio at Oakhill - not far from their own cottage. They spent a rather splendid afternoon in the company of Harold and his wife Laura, and were invited to dinner there. Later the studio seemed to become an open house, as everyone they'd met in the pub previous night started to arrive with bottles of wine. Soon the place buzzed with talk and laughter. The gramophone was wound up and played continuously whilst people danced on the rush matting that covered the stone floor.

When Gilbert Evans arrived, Ruby and Justin watched Florence's reaction, but she made no indication that there was anything between them, perhaps because her husband A J was here too.

'How long are you staying?' Gilbert asked after making his way over to them.

'We leave tomorrow afternoon, unfortunately.'

'Do you have your own transport?'

'No, we'll walk up and catch the Penzance wagon to the station – we're catching the three-o-clock train to Helston.'

'Gosh, no need to bother with all that. I have business in Helston tomorrow afternoon. I'll drive you there. I'm taking A J with me, but you're welcome to the back seat of my car.'

'Well, that's very kind of you.' Justin smiled. 'Thank you. We'll take you up on that offer.'

'I've never been in a car before,' Ruby whispered.

'Don't worry,' he squeezed her hand, 'I'll look after you.'

*

That night in bed, neither wanted to go to sleep, knowing that when the morning came their nights together would be over. They lay entwined in each other's arms, as close as they could be, without making love, finally falling asleep sometime after the clock chimed two.

*

Betsy was up bright and early on Sunday morning to make sure everything was spick and span in the manor ready for the return of the family and Ruby - from wherever she had gone to. She'd asked Joe where Ruby was, but Joe had been quite evasive and answered that he did not know. Betsy surmised he was telling a fib, because no one went anywhere without first telling someone senior in the house where they were going. It had not gone unnoticed by Betsy that Ruby was away the same weekend as Justin, and if her instinct was correct, and they *were* somewhere together, she wished them well. God knows, there would be sad times ahead for them.

At ten-o-clock she ran upstairs to put on her very best Sunday dress to go to church to listen to the banns being read. As she buttoned up her coat, she knew she must remember to keep it buttoned up, for this was the dress she would be married in next week and she didn't want Ryan to see it.

*

With it being Ruby and Justin's final morning at Lamorna, they breakfasted in bed and stayed there decadently until ten. They took one last walk out on the cliffs, holding hands and coming together to kiss and embrace every now and then. After luncheon, they packed up their things and stood with their arms wrapped around each other while they waited for Gilbert and AJ to pick them up.

'We'll still have Wednesdays together, Ruby, won't we?'

'Yes, though this week my time with you will be shortened. We're planning a farewell tea for Betsy.'

'Am I invited?' he asked with a twinkle in his eye.

'Of course, you're one of us.'

'I wish I was! If I wasn't Sarah's brother, being together would be so much easier for us.'

*

Having never been in a motor car before, and with A J insisting on taking the wheel, it was a hair-raising drive up to Helston for Ruby. He drove, like he lived, with gay abandon! Thankfully AJ got out in Helston and Gilbert jumped in the driver's seat and took them on to Bochym at a much more sedate speed. They held each other's hands tightly throughout the journey, knowing that each mile took them away from their blissful weekend and back to reality.

As they approached the main drive, Ruby had requested that she be dropped off at the Dower Lodge, on pretence that she had some business to do there. She knew she could not arrive back with Justin, and if she'd caught the wagon from Helston Station to Cury Cross Lanes as planned, she would not have arrived home for another hour. It was decided that she would sit it out in the Dower Lodge until the time was right for her to go home. The car came to a halt and Gilbert jumped out of the driver's seat. Ruby released Justin's hand - the parting from him now became painfully real.

'I'll help your fiancé out of the car, Justin, while you jump in the front seat with me, otherwise I'll be mistaken for your chauffeur at the manor.' He grinned.

Gilbert opened the door for Ruby and as he took her hand to help her out, he admired the ruby and diamond ring on her finger. 'Have you set a date for your wedding?' he asked,

'Not yet,' she replied glancing at Justin.

'Well, don't wait too long, you two are so obviously meant to be together.' He kissed her hand and bid her farewell.

'Thank you, Gilbert, for your kindness and friendship,' Ruby said softly.

'It's been a pleasure. I do hope we'll meet again. You'll always be welcome at Lamorna.'

She watched the car continue on up the drive, knowing

that she would probably never get a chance to meet all the wonderful people at Lamorna again.

Bending down to retrieve the hidden key, she unlocked the Dower Lodge door and felt the chill of the house engulf her. Pulling an eiderdown from one of the beds, she curled up in front of the unlit fire - she had never felt more alone.

*

Justin went straight up to the attic on his return and started to paint. He needed to take his mind off the parting with Ruby. What cruel twist of fate was it that brought this wonderful woman into his life? To find the one person he'd been searching for all these years, to begin to dream of a future with her, only to have all hopes dashed by a death sentence! Damn it! The situation was madness - he had but a finite time on this earth now and they *should* be together. He had to put the paintbrush down for a moment for chance of ruining the painting he was working on. He began to stalk the room like a caged lion, until he stopped and looked out across the fine gardens, to where the Dower Lodge nestled amongst the arboretum. Poor Ruby, she was hiding down there, so as to safeguard her position in this household. When he had put it to her that they could marry by special licence, he could see she was in a terrible quandary. He did not doubt her love, or the desire to marry him, but she was right, as lovely as his sister, Sarah was, and he was sure she would welcome Ruby into the family - Ruby *would* find it difficult to live here without him. He leant his weary forehead against the cold windowpane. If he couldn't give her all he wanted while he was alive, he would certainly make sure she would want for nothing after his death. He moved to his desk and set about writing his will.

*

After spending a cold and lonely hour in the Dower Lodge, Ruby began to walk up the drive to the manor. It was fortunate that it was teatime when she arrived back, for if anyone had seen her approaching the manor from the wrong direction, there might have been questions asked.

*

When Joe saw Ruby walking across the kitchen courtyard and enter the Manor by the back door instead of the kitchen door, he got up from the table. This prompted everyone to rise, as was protocol, but he quickly gestured them to sit again and went out to meet Ruby in the corridor. She lifted her eyes to his and he searched her face, not actually knowing what he was looking for. Perhaps to see if she looked different in any way after her weekend away, but there was nothing visibly different about her, apart from an evident sadness in her face. 'Everything all right?' he asked gently, but she just nodded and took herself off to take a long hot bath.

*

Sarah and Peter arrived home shortly after seven that evening and though Justin had been in the attic since his return from Lamorna, he joined them for dinner at eight. They all retired to their beds just before ten, leaving Joe to close the manor up for the night. When Joe saw the light under the door of the housekeeper's room, he grabbed a half bottle of claret that had been left over from the dinner and a couple of glasses and knocked softly on her door.

Ruby looked up at him expectantly – perhaps he was not the visitor she was hoping for, but never mind, he smiled and held the bottle aloft.

'Care to indulge in a glass of fine claret?'

'Thank you, Joe,' she gestured for him to sit.

'I thought you'd gone to bed too,' he said pouring the ruby liquid into the best crystal glasses. 'You are still technically on holiday.'

'I know, but I'm interviewing three women for Betsy's job in the morning, so I'm just preparing for it.'

'You'll be hard pushed to get someone good enough to fill Betsy's shoes!'

319

'I agree, but find her we must.'

'It's a horrible feeling, losing someone who has been a large part of our lives, isn't it?' he said taking a sip of his claret - suddenly realising what he'd said. He looked up at Ruby to see her eyes fill with tears, making the blue in them intensify. She did not brush them away when they fell - she just sat silently as they trickled down her cheeks.

'I'm so sorry, Ruby,' he said handing a clean laundered handkerchief to her.

Ruby closed her eyes and nodded. Leaving her glass half full she slowly got up. 'I'm sorry, Joe, I need to go to bed.'

*

In her stark bedroom, alone in her bed, Ruby felt a great sadness swell in her throat. *This is the price you must pay for falling in love.* She wrapped her arms around herself, and silently wept into her pillow.

*

Ruby was up and about early, as normal, that Monday, although nothing would be normal ever again. She glanced in the mirror, alarmed at the puffiness of the skin around her eyes. She dabbed them with a little cold cream, knowing she would shed a river of tears when the inevitable happened, and then, how on earth would her poor fragile heart cope? She patted the ruby and diamond ring Justin had given her, which was tied on a ribbon around her neck and tucked in her blouse, she was terrified of losing it, but needed it to be as close to her body as possible. One day she'd go to Helston and buy a silver chain to thread through it. She would wear it always. But for now, she would not venture far from the manor. If Justin took a turn for the worse, she wanted to be here - though it broke her heart to know that, as a mere housekeeper, she would not be allowed to sit by his side when the end came. There was indeed a growing temptation to throw caution to the wind and run to his side, and to hell with her position here, for there was nothing clearer – she'd not be able to hide her deep sorrow at his passing. Her eyes filled with tears again and the cold cream was washed away.

*

Two young women and one slightly more mature one were sitting in the kitchen dining room waiting to be interviewed for Betsy's job. One, a rather flirty miss, who Mrs Blair saw hitch her skirt up to show her ankles off to Thomas. That earned her a black mark from Cook! The other, a smartly turned-out young woman, looked just the ticket to replace Betsy – the other lady however, looked wise and knowledgeable, and would have fitted perfectly into the housekeeper's role should Mrs Sanders be looking for one – which of course she wasn't!

Juliet and Betsy were working at the kitchen table and had made their own minds up about whom Ruby should engage – definitely the smartly turned out one.

When Joe walked into the kitchen the more mature lady gasped audibly and stood up. 'Why, if it isn't Joe Treen,' she declared.

'Molly Johnson!' Joe exclaimed, 'I haven't seen you since we left Feock School. How are you?' he said hugging her warmly.

'I'm well thank you, and you? You look well. My, what a handsome man you've grown into. You were fourteen when last I saw you.'

Juliet's heart shifted at this warm exchange and the other two hopeful candidates started to look worried that the maid's place was going to be taken before they had a chance to be interviewed.

'What brings you all this way?'

'I live in Helston now, but I'm in need of work. I was widowed last year, so I thought I would try my luck in one of the big houses on the Lizard.'

'I'm so sorry to hear about your loss, Molly.'

She nodded, but said nothing more about her husband.

Well, good luck. I'll tell Mrs Sanders you're *all* here

now,' Joe said happily.

Juliet turned her stricken face to Betsy who just raised her eyebrow.

'If I were you, I'd snap Joe up before Molly decides he'd make a good second husband,' Betsy joked, only adding to Juliet's dismay.

*

The flighty maid was the first to be interviewed, but though Mrs Blair had sought Ruby out to warn her of her character before the interview, it didn't take long for Ruby to get the measure of her and agree with Mrs Blair. The second maid, Lucy Hocking, Ruby found to be a very pleasant, eager girl, who seemed genuinely excited at the prospect of perhaps joining the team at Bochym. Ruby finished the interview with a promise that she would let her know tomorrow if she was successful. The third, more mature lady, who, Joe informed her, had gone to school with him, would ironically have been perfect, should there still be a need to engage a new housekeeper. It was a shame – she'd have like to help her, but she was really too qualified to take over Betsy's role. During the interview, Molly had explained that she'd held the role of housekeeper in a large mansion near Truro, but had left to marry the local butcher. She'd whispered that it had been a grave error of judgment on her part. The marriage had been an unhappy one, and when he'd been run over and killed by the wheels of his own delivery cart, she admitted that she had not shed a single tear for him.

'Take my advice, Mrs Sanders, don't ever get married - it's not all it's cracked up to be! Stay as a housekeeper, I say.'

Ruby swallowed and nodded politely, and then put the question to her, that if Molly was offered the job here as a senior maid, would she continue to search for a position more suited to her experience? To Molly's credit, she answered truthfully, that this would be a transient job until she secured another housekeeping roll. Reluctantly, Ruby knew that she would have to disregard Molly for that reason, but made a note to herself to keep her ear to the ground should anything come up hereabouts that would suit her.

After the candidates had left the premises, Ruby explained to Joe why she could not employ Molly, and though he was disappointed for her, he understood. So, it was decided that the fifteen-year-old local girl Lucy Hocking, would be engaged to join the team at Bochym as a scullery maid. Ruby had decided to make Juliet up to senior maid, but of course nothing could be said to anyone in the household until the letter to Lucy had been delivered and a favourable acceptance had been given. For this reason, Juliet was to spend a very worrying twenty-four-hours wondering if Joe was going to switch allegiance to Molly should she be employed, and if he did, she knew she would only have herself to blame.

41

When Betsy sat down for the mid-day meal on Monday, she was like a cat on a hot tin roof - so excited was she at the prospect of looking over her new cottage with Ellie later. As soon as the meal was over and she'd helped clear the table, she was off like a shot, down the fields in the direction of Poldhu.

*

Ellie opened the door of Jessie's old cottage and stood back to let Betsy go in first. She rested against the door jam, watching Betsy walk around gently touching every stick of furniture as though she was saying hello to everything.

'I'll lend you anything you need until you get your own linen and crockery together.'

'Thank you so much, Ellie, I'd appreciate that. Her ladyship has offered me the curtains from one of the bathrooms – they're silk, would you believe?' She laughed, joyously. 'Imagine *me* with silk curtains!'

Ellie smiled - Betsy's joy was infectious. 'Are you all ready for the wedding on Saturday?'

'I think so now. I can't thank you enough - Ryan tells me you've very kindly offered to make the buffet for our wedding breakfast.'

'It's a wedding present to you both. I'm closing the tea room for the day, so we can set the buffet out in there. Do you know who will be coming from the manor?'

'All of the domestic staff, so six of them, oh no seven - we have a new maid, Lucy - I don't want to leave her out.'

'And have you decided on what you're wearing on the day?'

'Yes,' she sighed, 'I'll wear my best Sunday dress. Juliet and I tried to fashion something out of an old sheet, but in the end, it just looked like an old sheet!'

'Well then,' Ellie ushered Betsy to the bedroom, 'take a look in the wardrobe.'

Betsy's eyes rounded when she pulled out a dress of fine white linen edged with exquisite lace. 'Oh, my, goodness, it's the wedding dress you made for Jessie!'

'It is, and I found it in her wardrobe after she left us. I'm sure she wouldn't mind if her special friend wore it on *her* special day. You might want to air it outside for a while – it'll smell a little musty.'

Betsy sniffed and agreed, then held the dress to her body, smiling at her reflection in the tarnished mirror. 'It's beautiful. Thank you for everything.'

'You're very welcome. The look of joy on your face is all the thanks I need. Now, I'll leave you to acquaint yourself with the cottage. I tidied it a couple of weeks ago, but you might want to spruce it up a little more before you move in on Thursday. I've lit the range this morning, so you have hot water. The bucket and cloths are under the sink.' So eager to get started, Betsy had begun to undo her coat before Ellie had finished speaking. 'I'll pop over with some tea and cake when Ryan gets home with Guy at four, so you can enjoy your first teatime in your new home.'

*

By the time Ryan and Ellie arrived with tea and cake, the cottage shone like a new pin. The windows had been cleaned inside and out, the floors and table had been scrubbed, and the fire had been raked of old ashes and set ready to put a match to it. The evening was drawing in, and Betsy had lit the oil lamps giving the whole room a rosy, warm comforting glow.

Ryan laced his fingers in Betsy's. 'My goodness, you've made us a home.'

Ellie smiled at them and put the tray down. 'I'll leave you to your tea – don't let them know at the manor I left you without a chaperone,' she winked.

They sat opposite each other at the table – a little shy at first at being alone in the room together, until Ryan reached out for her hand.

'We're going to be so contented here. I swear I'll not

give you a moment of unhappiness, I promise.'

She squeezed his hand. 'Oh, Ryan, I'm so happy I could cry!'

'If the truth were known,' he said, leaning over to kiss her, 'I could cry too.'

*

Apart from a quick trip to Helston to buy a wedding present for Betsy, Justin had spent a great deal of time in the attic since returning from Lamorna – much to Sarah's dismay. She so wanted to spend as much time as possible with her darling brother, before this dreadful affliction swept him away for ever, but whatever he was working on held his attention. She was dreadfully worried - he seemed to have got notably weaker since his visit to Lamorna and feared the end was coming a lot sooner than they hoped. Thankfully, he had not yet called for a lawyer to put his affairs in order. He'd explained that when he thought it necessary, he would have him called for, but for the moment he didn't want to think of the inevitable end. One other thing troubling Sarah was his villa and studio in Tuscany. She and Peter had secretly discussed the awful prospect of having to go over to Italy afterwards to clear it out. The thought of sifting through Justin's life, seemed such a terribly sad and personal thing to do, but as his sister, it would be her job to do it. Their father had washed his hands of Justin many years ago, when he would not conform and take on the management of their estate in Devon. That was another thing she fretted over. Should she tell her parents what was happening? Surely her mother had the right to know her only son was dying! Perhaps the rift could be healed before it was too late.

*

Justin managed to snatch a few secret moments with Ruby each day at the lodge. Today being Wednesday, he looked forward to spending a little longer with her, and had diligently worked through the night to do so. When he entered the lodge the look of shock on Ruby's face told him how haggard he must look.

'Are you working too hard in that attic?' she said, kissing the lines on his face as though to take the worry of illness from him.

'I'm fine Ruby, just tired.'

'How tired?'

'Not tired enough to close my eyes forever yet, my darling. I just need to finish something I'm working on, but it will wait today, because I can't waste a single precious moment with you when it's presented to me. Now, if you don't mind crumpling your dress, I'd rather like to lay by the fireside with you for a while.'

*

Betsy clasped her hands to her face in surprise when she walked into the kitchen later that day for tea, and found everyone, even the Earl and Countess and Mr Devereux waiting for her! Ruby had also invited the new maid, Lucy Hocking, to help her settle in and get to know everyone before she started work with them the next day. Needless to say, Juliet couldn't have been more relieved at the choice of maid.

The kitchen table groaned with food, and an array of wedding presents were waiting for Betsy to un-wrap. Joe had been instructed to bring champagne from the cellar, and when he popped the bottle and doled it out to everyone, Peter lifted his glass to propose a toast.

'Let's raise a glass to Betsy. I hope you and Ryan will be blessed with a long and very happy marriage. I know the manor will miss you greatly - Mrs Sanders will especially, and I thank you for all the good work you have done for us.'

Glasses were raised. 'To Betsy!'

'Now, we have a few things to set you up in your new life,' Sarah said gesturing to the parcels.

With fumbling fingers, Betsy un-wrapped the one nearest to her first, to find a lovely floral tea set from all her colleagues. 'Oh, thank you so much,' she beamed happily, 'I'll make you all tea when you come to see me.'

The next one was so big it almost covered the end of the kitchen table.

'This one is from us, Betsy,' Sarah said with a gentle smile.

Betsy un-wrapped layers of tissue, to reveal a set of Egyptian cotton bed linen and towels and ran her hands over the quality of the linen. 'Goodness,' she gasped, 'thank you so much, my lord - my lady. We'll sleep like royalty.'

The last parcel was a long cylinder shape.

'This one is from me,' Justin said, holding tightly on to the back of the chair.

'Gosh, thank you,' she gushed in delight, as she pulled out a brightly coloured, soft wool hearth rug.

'It's for spending nights by the fireside with your husband.' He winked.

Betsy blushed and looked around at everyone she knew and loved. 'Thank you everyone,' she said feeling herself tear up.

'Now, then, no tears, eat, everyone, eat,' Mrs Blair instructed, turning away to hide a stray tear from her own eyes.

*

On Thursday morning, Betsy packed all her belongings and piled them in the kitchen with her wedding presents. The pony trap had been arranged to take her down to Poldhu and her new life there, but before she left, Ruby called her into the housekeeper's room.

'I just wanted to say thank you for being such a wonderful colleague, Betsy - this house will not be the same without you.'

Betsy's eyes blurred. 'Thank you, Mrs Sanders - you made this a special place for me to work.'

'I have a little something for you.' Ruby handed her a package wrapped in tissue. It was a pair of silk and cotton stockings, and blue ribbon ties. Ruby had purchased them for her own wedding day, but as that was not going to happen now, she could think of no one better to have them.

'They are lovely, thank you, Mrs Sanders.'

'You're very welcome, Betsy. As your wedding dress is borrowed from Jessie, this is something new and blue to wear on the day. What have you got that is old?'

'Everything else I own,' Betsy joked, but then added, 'I have a small paste broach which belonged to my mother – I'll wear that on the day.'

Ruby reached out to hold her hand. 'I wish you all the luck in the world and for your future life,' she said with a slight catch in her voice.

'Gosh, I'll be an emotional wreck before I get to Poldhu.' Betsy wiped a stray tear.

'Go and say goodbye to everyone then.'

When Betsy came out of the housekeeper's room, Mrs Blair gave her an enormous hug.

'Now you take heed of all I taught you in the kitchen. Keep your man's belly full of good food and you won't go far wrong,' she said sniffing back a sob.

After a very tearful goodbye to everyone else, and a heartfelt hug with Juliet, Betsy and her things were loaded onto the trap, and she was waved off to her new life.

*

The weather had taken a turn for the worse on Friday morning. The wind howled through the arboretum, whipping the fallen leaves into pyramid piles on the drive to the Dower Lodge. Ruby battled through the buffeting wind to get to the lodge - nothing was going to keep her from Justin's arms.

He was waiting, as always, and tried without success to get up from the sofa where he'd slumped. Ruby thought he looked thoroughly exhausted.

'Are you all right, my love?' - He was clearly not.

'I could hardly breathe when I got here, I couldn't get my breath with this wind, it made my chest feel as though

I had a tight belt around it.'

'You should not have ventured out in this weather.'

He cupped his hands to her worried face. 'I'll always come out to see you – until I can no longer. I think though, you may have to support me on the way back.'

'Of course, I will.'

'If anyone sees us, I'll say you found me floundering on the drive.'

'All these secrets and lies,' she murmured. 'All we wanted was to be together.'

'Now, now, no sad faces to spoil our precious time together,' he said lifting her chin. He kissed her passionately, but when he pulled away, he was clearly struggling for breath.

'Justin, you're not well, and I need to get back to the house soon, I've left the new maid with Juliet, but I fear you're in no fit state to go anywhere yet!'

He stroked her furrowed brow. 'Give me ten minutes in your arms and I'll be fit and able to walk back. Juliet will manage, and Sarah and Peter have gone to Truro for the day, so you should not fret about getting back yet.'

Ruby curled up with him on the settee under an eiderdown and they held on to each other, both wondering how many more days they could meet like this.

*

By the afternoon the wind had strengthened and everyone hoped this stormy weather front would clear in time for Betsy's wedding the next day.

It was three-o-clock - a quiet time before tea at Bochym. Luncheon was over, and Mrs Blair had prepped the dinner and was now with Mary in the pickling room selecting a relish to accompany the lamb that evening. Ruby was settling the new maid into her duties, Dorothy was in her bedroom reading, Thomas had set off for a blustery walk into Mullion and Joe was in his office. Juliet was alone at the kitchen table with only the ticking of the clock for company. She was mending a tear in her best dress, ready to wear at Betsy's wedding the next day. The wind was howling around the manor, and she didn't hear the horse and cart pull up, or if she did, she didn't take a great deal of notice - so intricate was the mend of the tear. It was only when she heard the stomp of heavy boots on the cobbles on the kitchen courtyard that her blood ran suddenly cold. She'd know those footsteps anywhere. Almost in slow motion, she turned in horror, as the kitchen door opened and the chill of the air preceded the uninvited and extremely unwelcome guest.

42

Mrs Blair emerged from the pickle store with a large jar of redcurrant preserve and tutted impatiently – the dress Juliet had been working on was lying on the floor along with her scattered sewing box. She stood for a moment, looked around, called her name, but there was no sign of her.

A moment later Ruby came into the kitchen and found Mrs Blair picking up the scattered buttons from the sewing box.

'Is Juliet about, Mrs Blair?'

'She was here mending this dress when I went through to the larder, but I've just found everything scattered on the floor and the back door wide open! I've told everyone to keep the door closed, to keep that mangy cat out – you know the one that has taken up residence in the wood store.'

Ruby bent down to help retrieve the buttons. 'How strange, Juliet is always so meticulously tidy, she must have had to go somewhere in quite a hurry. If she comes back in the next five minutes, send her through to me, would you?'

*

The footsteps, as Juliet had feared, belonged to her hateful step-father Ronald. Before she had a chance to escape or call out for help, he'd grabbed her by the arm, stifled her squeals with his filthy hand, and had her out of the kitchen door, and bundled onto the cart before anyone knew she'd gone. To her credit, she'd put up a good fight, frantically thumping and kicking him – even biting his hand, which had earned her a sharp, stinging slap across her face. Shocked, and sick with anxiety as to what was happening to her, when the cart pulled away at speed, Juliet looked back at the life she was leaving behind, terribly fearful that no one had witnessed her abduction.

'I can't just leave,' she pleaded, 'I'm employed here!'

'Shut up! Or there'll be hell to pay once I get you home - where you belong.'

Filled with a sense of dread at the hell she was heading back to, her mind began to work furiously. Fixing her eyes on the wheel of the wagon, she visualised the only way out. If she could just inch herself away from her captor, she'd throw herself at the wheel and end her life here and now. Death would be a far better option than what was to come.

Nervously biding her time, she waited until they reached the main road and as soon as they began to gain more speed, she leapt from her seat in an attempt to end her life. Ronald was quick - he caught her by the skirt of her dress, leaving her dangling precariously close to the wheel. Despite the mud and small rocks peppering her face, she just needed to inch a little closer and then it would all be over. The material of her maid's dress tore under his grasp, and she was tantalisingly close to death, but he yanked her back onto the seat, slapped her hard about the head and pulled the horse to a halt. Whilst holding onto her arm, he dragged a coil of rope from the back of the wagon, tied it around her waist and then around his. He pulled the rope so tight she could hardly breathe - never mind move. The stink of sweat and fish on his body in such close contact turned her stomach and brought to life the dreadful night terrors she'd been afflicted with all these months. With hollow despair, Juliet knew now that there was no waking up from this nightmare.

*

An hour later and still no sign of Juliet, Ruby made an extensive search of the house for her, surmising that she must have gone out. She was puzzled and a little cross that she'd gone out without first notifying someone as to where she was going.

When the staff tea bell rang at five, Joe came out of his office with his brother Jake who'd arrived an hour previously, having an unexpected afternoon off from thatching due to the high wind.

'How is Ryan – does he have pre wedding nerves?' Joe asked Jake, as they walked down the corridor towards the kitchen.

'If he has, he's not showing any. He can't wait to marry Betsy. He's definitely gone all soppy on her.' He grimaced.

Joe laughed. 'It'll be the same for you one day, little brother.'

Jake gave him a doubtful look.

'Mr Treen,' Ruby said formally, 'we can't seem to find Juliet. She's nowhere on the premises. Did she tell you she was going out?'

'No,' he looked out of the window – the wind was howling, 'but where could Juliet have gone in this weather?' Joe asked.

'I don't know. I did wonder if she'd gone down to see Betsy about the wedding – Mrs Blair said she seemed to have left in a rush! Jake, did you see Juliet on your walk up here? I would think perhaps your paths would have crossed.'

'No, and I came the normal path through the woods, and fields,' he answered as he put his coat on. 'But if she's gone to Poldhu to see Betsy, she'll be disappointed. I got a lift up to Cury Church with Betsy and Ellie earlier. Tobias was taking them to Helston for some ribbons.'

Mrs Blair put down a fresh pot of tea. 'She'll be back for tea - I've never known Juliet miss a meal. Are you not staying, young Jake, there's enough for everyone?'

'No, thank you, Mrs Blair, I need to get back home. Miss Taylor will have made our supper. If I see Juliet on the way, I'll tell her to hurry home.'

*

In Gweek, Rosemary Gwyn, as she was still known, before she had had the great misfortune to meet and marry her second husband Ronnie, was nursing yet another black eye. The swelling over the eye impaired her vision somewhat, making gutting and salting the fish Ronnie had brought home that afternoon problematic.

Ronnie's homecomings were a constant source of fear and dread for her – the terror normally intensifying later in the evening after he'd drunk his fill in The Black Swan. Slight in build, the abuse, both verbal and physical took its toll on her frail body, but today, the violence had started the moment he'd arrived home.

He'd been away fishing since last Friday night, and arrived a few hours ago, after sailing up the Helford on the afternoon tide. He'd burst through the front door, dumped the fish at her feet and before doing or saying anything else, had punched Rosemary hard in the face. The blow sent her reeling, and for a moment rendered her almost senseless, but she'd heard him kicking the furniture and ranting about secrets being kept from him! She'd no idea what he meant, and was glad when he'd left her in peace to go - god knows where – probably The Black Swan.

With butter on her bruises, Rosemary sharpened her fish knife, wiped her weeping swollen eye with her sleeve, and prepared for a long day's work gutting and salting fish. It was times like this that her thoughts turned to the loss of her dear, departed husband, Ted. He'd been a kind, loving man who had been taken too soon. Rosemary had struggled for almost ten years to make ends meet for herself and her daughter, Juliet, after he had died. She'd taken on menial jobs, cleaning, laundry and sewing, and also worked on Gweek quay, gutting fish. That was where she met Ronnie. He too was a widower, and had moved to Gweek from further down the river to work the fishing boats out of the harbour. He was not a tall man, but stocky with a thick neck and a cheeky charm - which she'd stupidly fallen for. He married her quickly and brought with him a kind, quiet, hardworking son. The money they brought in had been welcome, but Ronnie's charm quickly tarnished. Very soon, his insatiable sexual appetite took its toll on her - he was rough and often hurt her quite badly.

Her pleading with him to *let her heal*, fell on deaf ears and any resistance to his demands was met with violence. Rosemary became terribly fearful when her daughter Juliet began to wear a strained and haunted look – she knew then that Ronnie had started to take an unhealthy interest in her. Ronnie's son, bless him, did his best to protect and shield Juliet from his father's advances. He'd even threatened to kill him if he touched her, prompting Ronnie to throw his son out of the house to fend for himself. Without an ally, Rosemary could no longer keep her daughter safe, so there was only one course of action, and that was to get her away from this house. Though Ronnie was livid and his violence towards her had intensified when he found Juliet had slipped the net, Rosemary thanked the lord that Juliet was safe from his clutches.

It was this thought in her head when the door burst open, and Ronnie dragged Juliet into the small, dank cottage. With an almighty push, he shoved Juliet into the room, sending her sprawling across the floor to crash into the settle.

Rosemary's blood ran cold. Dropping her fish knife, she wiped her hands down her apron and ran to Juliet, wrapping her arms around her trembling daughter.

'Don't you *ever* try to leave again,' Ronnie loomed over them, snarling, 'or I'll do your mother such a mischief for bringing up such a wilful child.'

Huddled together on the floor, they watched in terrified silence as Ronnie grabbed his hammer and nails from the kitchen cupboard. He pounded two nails into each of the window frames to stop them from being opened.

'That'll stop you running off again.' He held the hammer aloft, glowering menacingly over the two women. 'You both thought you were so clever - thought you'd get away with it, didn't you? He laughed sardonically. 'Thankfully that jumped up nobody, Kit Trevellick, had been hobnobbing with his posh friends at Bochym, and I overheard him tell that old hag, Amelia Pascoe, that he'd seen you there!'

Juliet whimpered pitifully and Rosemary tightened her grip on her.

'I'll administer your punishment later.' He prodded Juliet, and then blatantly ran his finger down over her breast.

Feeling Juliet shudder in revulsion, Rosemary pulled her daughter away from her husband's touch. 'Leave her be,' she said bravely, 'It's enough she's home.'

'Hold your tongue, woman.' He raised his fist, and both women flinched. 'She had no right leaving this house or taking a job without my knowledge. I *need* her here.' He ran his eyes salaciously over Juliet's body, curling his lips back over his teeth, no doubt enjoying some unsavoury thought running through his filthy mind.

*

Ronnie left, locking the door behind him, and Juliet broke down in tears.

'Did you know he was coming for me, Ma?' she sobbed.

'No, love, he just came home this afternoon in a terrible rage, shouting about me keeping secrets from him.'

'Did Amelia not tell you that Kit had given the game away?'

'She must not have known that Ronnie had overheard, or she would have.'

'Oh, god, Ma,' she wept, 'I tried my best to keep out of Kit and Sophie's way when they came to Bochym, but they must have seen me.'

'Don't fret so, Juliet, and don't blame the Trevellick's – they're good people. They weren't to know you were there in secret.'

Juliet wrapped her arms around herself and whimpered, 'I'm frightened, Ma. He took me by force from the manor.'

'Perhaps someone from the manor will come and help

then.' She stroked her daughter's stricken face.

Juliet lifted her eyes to her mother. 'Nobody saw it happen.'

'Well, they'll know you've gone, that's for sure! Have you…. have you confided in anyone at the manor about…?'

'God, no!' She flushed furiously. 'I was too ashamed!'

'Oh, my poor darling, you have nothing to be ashamed about. He's the shameful one in this house!'

Juliet drew a deep trembling breath.

'Shush now, by the lovely letters you sent me via Amelia, it sounds like you made a lot of friends there. Surely someone will come and help, and of course you told me Ryan was over there as well. He's a good lad - he'll definitely come looking for you!'

'No, he won't!' she wailed and dropped her head into her hands. 'He'll be getting ready for his wedding tomorrow.'

'Oh, I see!'

Juliet heard the disappointment in her mother's voice – knowing she'd always had high hopes that Ryan would wed her daughter and keep her safe.

'Still,' her ma added, 'he'll come - he always looked out for you.'

'Even if he does - what then?' She threw her arms in the air. 'I'll not be able to go back to my job at Bochym – Ronnie will just come and get me again.'

'Granted, you'll maybe not be able to go there, no, but we'll find somewhere else safe for you again, I promise.'

Her heart imploded - she didn't want to be anywhere else other than Bochym. *Oh, why didn't I tell people my fears? Everyone would have kept an eye on me – protected me – Joe would have protected me. Oh Joe!*

Rosemary's comforting arm did her best to stem the awful tremble in her body. 'Try not to worry. We will get you away again one way or another, I promise. We did it before and we'll do it again.'

'But it'll be too late then, Ma! You heard Ronnie - you know what he'll do to me!' She started to cry, her shoulders heaving. 'Oh, god, I just want to die.'

Rosemary grabbed her shoulders and shook her. 'Juliet, please don't say such things - promise you won't do anything silly?'

Juliet nodded sadly.

'Good, now,' she said heaving herself to her feet, 'I'm sorry but I'll have to try and finish gutting and salting this fish before he gets back home, or I'll be catching another of his fists.'

'Why do you stay with him, Ma?'

She gave a large shuddering breath. 'He's threatened to kill me if I leave.'

*

Ryan was giving his new suit a quick brush down ready for the morning when Jake arrived back from Bochym.

He grinned at him. 'Is all well at the manor - did you see Juliet?'

'You shouldn't be asking about other women if you're getting married in the morning,' Jake joked. 'But funnily enough, no, Juliet appears to have gone missing.

'*Missing!*' Ryan dropped the brush he was holding.

'Yes, Mrs Blair said she left her sewing scattered on the floor and just disappeared. She didn't come home for tea, and she didn't say where she was going - they thought she'd gone down to Poldhu, but.....' Before Jake could finish the sentence, Ryan had grabbed his coat and was out of the door. 'Where are you going?' Jake shouted, following him out into the night, but Ryan had no time for talking and disappeared into the darkness.

*

Fifteen minutes later, Ryan burst into the Bochym kitchen, red-faced, sweating profusely and breathless with anxiety.

'Is she here? Is Juliet back yet?' he asked Mrs Blair who looked up at him in shock.

Joe heard the commotion from the corridor and was in

the kitchen in an instant. 'Ryan? What is it, what's happened?'

'I understand Juliet is missing!'

'Yes, we were just discussing going out to see if she's met with an accident somewhere,' and then added, tentatively, 'though I'm not sure what it is to *you!* I mean, you're getting married to Betsy in the morning.'

'Oh, god, Joe,' Ryan's eyes blazed fear, 'I think Juliet is in grave danger.'

Joe paled. 'Why? What do you know?' he said, as Ruby and Thomas came in to see what the commotion was.

'I know where she is for one thing, and I know who's got her.' He quickly explained who he really was, and his relationship with Juliet, and the mortal fear Juliet had of her father-in-law because of his salacious behaviour.

Visibly disturbed and angered at this news, Joe knew he must do something.

'I've got to go - I've got to help her,' Ryan said and turned on his heel to set off back across the kitchen courtyard.

'Wait, Ryan - I'm coming with you.' Joe yelled. 'We'll take the pony trap.'

43

Ronnie was downing his third glass of beer in the Black Swan with his equally unsavoury drinking pal, George Blewett the blacksmith. Though Ronnie was sweaty and dirty from his fishing trip - his hair wild and unkempt, and he hadn't shaved for seven days, he was feeling very pleased with himself.

'What are you smirking about?' Blewett asked.

Ronnie's lip curled and his eyes gleamed as he wiped his mouth with the back of his hand. 'I've just brought the daughter back, that's what!'

'Have you now?' Blewett raised an eyebrow. 'Where's she been hiding?'

'She was skulking away at Bochym Manor. I overheard Kit Trevellick tell that Pascoe woman that he'd seen her when he attended one of his *many* farewell parties there. I was bloody livid though - we were just about to set off on the fishing trip. I didn't even have time to thump the wife for keeping secrets from me, because we were sailing on the high tide. I gave her what for this morning though, before I went to fetch the daughter. That'll bloody teach her to keep secrets from me!'

Blewett laughed heartily and they ordered another glass of ale.

'It's another mouth to feed though!' Blewett stated.

'Aye, but she'll damn well earn her keep.' He winked.

Blewett, understanding his meaning chinked his glass on Ronnie's. 'You lucky bugger!'

At quarter-to-six Ronnie slammed his glass on the bar and gave George a wide smile. 'I'm off to collect my reward now for all my hard work these past few hours.'

Blewett too drained his glass.

*

Amelia Pascoe had just taken tea with her friends Eric and Lydia Williams and was making her way home along the riverbank. She stopped dead in her tracks when George

Blewett and Ronnie Penrose - two of the most unsavoury characters in the village, spilled out of The Black Swan. Amelia could hold her own verbally against these two if she needed to, but she'd rather just let them make their drunken way to their respective houses. Fortunately, Blewett had no wife at home to molest, but her heart caught for Ronnie's downtrodden wife, Rosemary. Only this afternoon she'd seen her with yet another bruised eye. There was little anyone could do when it was domestic violence. Only very rarely did anyone intervene in the marital fights - it only made matters worse for the wife. It angered Amelia beyond belief – she hated bullies and these two fell into that category. As she waiting for George Blewett to walk to his blacksmiths shop and Ronnie to make his way to his cottage a few doors down from her own, she spotted Constable Treen on one of his early evening walks round the village. She knew now it was safe to continue on her way home.

*

Inside the cottage, and needing to take her mind off her terrifying dilemma, Juliet was helping Rosemary with the last of the fish, when she heard the key in the lock. The two women stopped what they were doing and glanced uneasily at each other, both flinching when the door burst open and Ronnie's drunken frame blundered through.

The light from the meagre oil lamp glimmered in Ronnie's small piggy eyes, as they cut from his wife to Juliet - his prize.

'Get from behind that table, you little bitch,' he said unfastening his belt, I'm gonna teach you not to run away.'

Juliet backed herself towards the far end of the room, fearful of the thrashing - she frantically looked around for something to fend him off with.

'Leave her be, Ronnie,' Rosemary said boldly stepping in front of him.

Shooting a derisory glance at his wife, he gave a low, deep, throaty growl and knocked her sideways with the swipe of his arm.

Juliet's mouth dried, realising that he was unfastening his trousers - a thrashing most definitely wasn't what was on his mind! She screamed, as he lurched towards her, knocking everything out of his way. Grabbing her by the arms, he threw her to the floor and pinned her down. Drooling stinking saliva over her face, he hissed, 'I'm going to enjoy every moment of this.'

Turning to avoid his breath, she squirmed violently and screamed again, until bile rose in her throat and began to choke her.

'Shut it!' He rested his arm against her throat to quieten her as he tore at her clothing.

*

Amelia had just opened her front door when she heard the terrifying screams coming from inside Rosemary's cottage - she felt the hairs on the back of her neck rise.

*

Though hardly able to breathe, the voice inside her urged. *Fight, Juliet, fight him. Do what Betsy did with Trencrom, fight!* Sinking her nails into his face she struggled frantically, until she managed to shift his arm from her neck. Gasping, she emitted a hoarse cry, cleared her throat and screamed again in his ear. A powerful blow hit the side of her head making her ears ring alarmingly, but she was determined to fight. Rosemary stood over them, pulling and screaming at Ronnie to stop, but Ronnie turned and silenced her with another thump which sent her reeling backwards towards the kitchen table scattering the bowl of fish guts across the floor where she landed.

*

George Blewett sat in his outside privy, grinning at the screams and commotion coming from Ronnie's cottage across the way. Thinking it might be good sport to go watch his friend through the window as he had his way with his wayward stepdaughter - he forced his bowels to evacuate faster.

343

*

Hearing her ma weeping desperately fired Juliet up to fight her way out of this, she would not allow him to abuse her without putting up a serious defence. Taking a large intake of breath, she screamed deafeningly in his ear, and then with one enormous effort, she brought a well-aimed knee up into his nether regions. His eyes bugged as he gagged in pain and his grip on her loosened enough for her to push him aside. Scrambling to her feet, she ran towards the open door, but slipped on the scattered fish guts and slithered against to where her ma had fallen.

'You little bitch, let me at you,' Ronnie growled as he lumbered towards them.

Juliet and her ma exchanged a fearful glance, and then keeping Juliet behind her with a protective arm, Rosemary turned towards Ronnie - her knife, still held fast in her hand.

Juliet screamed in terror, and Amelia Pascoe appeared at the open front door, a fraction of a second before Ronnie lost his footing on the fish guts and fell straight onto Rosemary's knife.

Ronnie's face distorted, and Rosemary screamed in agony, as she unlaced her blood-stained fingers from the shaft of the knife. As Ronnie fell backwards clutching his heart, Rosemary bent double, grasping her ribs.

'I can't breathe,' Rosemary cried. 'Oh god, I can't breathe - I think my ribs are broken!' She turned her distraught face to Amelia who had rushed to her aid.

A moment later, Ryan and Joe burst into the room - stopping dead at the scene before them.

'Joe!' Juliet cried out - her arms outstretched to him.

He was at her side in a heartbeat, wrapping his comforting arms protectively around her. 'Juliet, my poor love - whatever has happened to you?'

'Oh, Joe,' she clung tightly to him, sobbing into his arms, 'I was so frightened, but I'm all right, now.'

Ryan took a moment to assess the situation, then knelt

and pulled the knife from his father's heart at the very moment George Blewett arrived at the doorway.

George's eyes bugged when he saw his dead friend on the floor, with Ryan Penrose knelt beside his estranged father, holding the knife that had killed him.

Constable Treen arrived breathless in the cottage seconds later, having heard the commotion from across the green.

'Arrest that bastard,' Blewett pointed at Ryan, 'he's murdered Ronnie.'

Constable Treen's trained eye took in the scene before him, felt for a pulse on Ronnie's neck, and then settled his gaze accusingly on Ryan, who shook his head.

'It was me, Constable,' Rosemary rasped. 'I did it - but it wasn't murder. He ran into my fish knife!' She gasped and doubled up in pain.

'It's true, I saw it happen,' Amelia interjected.

George Blewett growled derisively – clearly having none of it.

'Right,' Constable Treen stood up, 'I want everyone to stay here, except you, Amelia - I need you to fetch Dr Eddy. I need to send a telegram to Helston, because we've a murder on our hands here and the sergeant needs to come down from town.'

'It wasn't murder!' Rosemary cried desperately and then fainted with the pain.

Amelia furiously patted Rosemary's cheek to bring her round. 'We need an ambulance too,' she said, 'I think Rosemary's rib has broken and collapsed her lung.'

'Nobody is to leave this village,' Constable Treen warned, 'I know you all,' he glanced at Joe, 'except you, I don't know you, so don't leave this house.'

'Juliet, come and look after your ma for a few minutes,' Amelia beckoned.

Reluctantly, Juliet pulled herself from Joe's protective arms, to cradle her ma.

Rosemary's eyes fluttered open and turned her stricken

face to her daughter. 'Oh god, you saw it didn't you, Juliet? He ran into my knife. I didn't mean to kill him, he ran into it,' she wept.

'Shhh, don't tire yourself, Ma. It'll be all right,' Juliet soothed.

'What a bloody cock and bull story that is,' George Blewett growled. 'I don't believe it for a moment.' Blewett moved towards Ryan. 'It's as plain as anything that *you* killed him,' he said jabbing his finger at Ryan. 'You've *never* liked him – *never* got on with him, did you? I saw you, oh, yes, I saw you. *You* were the one with the knife in your murderous hand, and I'll swear I'll see you swing for this.'

Juliet watched in horror, as Blewett lurched forward to grab Ryan, but Joe was at Ryan's side in an instant - together they shoved Blewett towards the front door.

'Hey, keep your murderous hands off me,' Blewett snarled.

'Get out, now!' Ryan warned, and Blewett turned tail and left.

The room fell suddenly silent, but for Rosemary's rasping breaths. Everyone looked at each other in anguish, knowing this was going to be a terribly long night.

*

Ruby stood in the kitchen watching the clock tick the minutes away, and still Joe had not returned with Juliet. It was seven-forty-five - dinner would have to be served in fifteen minutes. She and Thomas had set the dining table, but without Joe to preside over dinner, this caused a dilemma.

'Thomas, go to the drawing room and ask Her Ladyship if she could spare me a moment would you, please?'

Ruby waited nervously in the corridor for Sarah to come out to her.

She curtseyed. 'If I may have a word, my lady?'

Sarah seeing the concern on her face, dropped the formality and said softly, 'Certainly, Ruby, what is it?'

'It's Mr Treen, my lady. He set off late this afternoon with Mr Penrose in great haste to Gweek. It appears that Juliet was…. well, she was abducted, not to put to finer point on it. This afternoon she was taken from the kitchen, we think, against her will, by her stepfather.'

'Goodness! Why was I not informed?'

'We all hoped that Joe and Juliet would be back before now and we wouldn't have to bother you with it. By all accounts, Juliet had been hiding from her stepfather and had not told him where she was working, but he must have found out somehow and come to claim her.'

'Well, there really isn't much we can do if he's her kin and claims her back.'

'The thing is…. we all knew she was fearful of someone – some man, but we didn't know who. It appears it was him.'

Sarah furrowed her brow. 'How have you learnt of this?'

'Ryan Penrose told us. He came as soon as he found out Juliet was missing – apparently, he's Juliet's stepbrother. That's why he came to live close by Bochym - to keep an eye on her and save her from the clutches of her hateful stepfather. It seems Ronnie Penrose is a deeply unsavoury character.'

Sarah tipped her head. 'I wasn't aware Ryan Penrose ever claimed a relation to Juliet!?'

'He didn't, my lady - not until today.'

'Oh, I see! So, Mr Treen and Ryan Penrose they have gone to sort things out with Mr Penrose senior?'

'Yes, my lady, but they've been gone nearly two hours now, and if they don't come back soon, Thomas and I will have to preside over dinner this evening - if that's all right with you.'

'Of course, I'll speak to His Lordship and tell him what has occurred, but I wonder what is keeping them?'

*

Betsy was in a happy mood. She'd spent the day helping

out in the tea room kitchen, and had made her first batch of scones - which Ellie praised her for. She'd also made a large Victoria sandwich cake, and cooked a joint of ham ready to be made into sandwiches for the wedding breakfast the next day. After they closed, she joined Ellie, Guy and their children for supper and felt very welcome into her new Poldhu family. Guy had very kindly walked her home across the dunes, and she now lay happily in her own bedroom where her beautiful wedding dress hung behind the bedroom door. She stretched languidly - this time tomorrow, Ryan would be beside her in this bed. The thought of her wedding night made her shiver in anticipation. She was nervous, but oh so eager to start her married life. With one last look around the bedroom, she turned off the oil lamp and settled down to a restful sleep.

*

Whereas Betsy enjoyed a blissful night's sleep, Ruby's night had been filled with sheer anguish. What with Joe and Juliet failing to come back home at all last evening, and Justin taking himself off to bed, feeling none too well, before even the dessert had been served, Ruby had been in turmoil.

Utmost in her mind that morning was of course Justin, but she had no other way of finding out if he was all right other than grilling Thomas.

'He got up, and went up to the attic, but he didn't look well at all. I reckon he isn't long for this world,' Thomas grimaced.

'Yes, thank you, Thomas. I don't think we need that sort of gloomy prediction,' she spoke more sharply than she meant to. 'Now, with Joe, I mean Mr Treen still not home, *you'll* have to preside over breakfast.'

Thomas nodded.

*

Peter had joined Sarah on her morning ride, so they were relatively late walking in for breakfast at ten-o-clock. They were both florid-faced from their bracing ride and glanced

348

questioningly at Thomas.

'Treen?'

'No, my lord. He hasn't come back yet.'

'Where the devil is he then?' Peter said helping himself to breakfast.

They'd been sat for half an hour, after breakfast, reading the newspaper and chatting about the day when Ruby opened the door to the French Drawing room and gestured for Thomas to quickly come to her.

'What is it, Thomas?' Sarah asked when he returned.

'A telephone call, my lady for His Lordship, it's Mr Treen, apparently, he's been arrested along with Ryan Penrose - on a charge of murder!'

44

Juliet had been distraught when Ryan and Joe had been bundled off to Helston Police Station the previous evening, but her priority was her mother, who had been gasping for breath by the time the ambulance arrived. Dr Eddy diagnosed a broken rib which had very likely punctured her lung - she would need an emergency operation and had sent Rosemary straight to the Royal Cornwall Infirmary in Truro. Juliet had been hysterical when she had not been allowed to go with her ma, to a point that when the ambulance drove off, she ran after it until she collapsed weeping in the road. Flanked by Dr Eddy and Amelia Pascoe, she was put to bed in Amelia's cottage, where the doctor administered a draft to make her sleep. He had promised that he would contact the hospital first thing in the morning for an update on Rosemary's condition.

*

For the first time in a long time, Juliet had slept a dreamless sleep. When she woke, she knew not where she was, but was astonished to find the clock in the unfamiliar room read ten-thirty! Had she slept for over ten hours? Suddenly the horrors of yesterday jumped into her head.

'Ma!' she cried. Had she survived the night? And were Ryan and Joe still in jail? She must find out. Pushing the covers back, she stumbled across the room, desperately searching for her clothes, still woozy from the sleeping draft.

Amelia must have heard her moving about, because she was upstairs and by her side in a heartbeat.

'Amelia, what's happened with Ma?'

'It's all right, Juliet. Dr Eddy received a telegram this morning from the hospital. Your ma is recovering from an operation - she's stable, but still very ill.'

Juliet's face crumpled. 'I must go to her?'

'Dr Eddy says no, not yet. When she is well enough,

she'll be brought to Helston Hospital – you'll see her then.'

'And Ryan and Joe, what about them? Ryan was meant to be getting married to my friend Betsy today!'

'Oh, dear!' Amelia put her hand to her heart. 'I'm afraid Constable Treen said they're still detained at Helston. I don't believe there will be a wedding today.'

'Poor Betsy – she must be distraught. Damn Ronnie Penrose – that brute has a lot to answer for – he's ruined so many lives now.' Juliet slumped on the bed and baring her teeth, hissed, 'I'm glad he's dead, Amelia – I hated him!'

'Aye, I don't think he'll be missed by many people. But take heart Juliet, you can look to a brighter future now you're free of him.'

'Am I?' she said flatly, 'I can't forget though.'

'No, but you must not let it define you. This is your chance to step away from what happened. That nice man, Joe, came to your rescue yesterday – perhaps he can help you overcome this.'

Juliet's eyes blurred. 'He's been so kind to me, Amelia – so kind.'

'Well then,' Amelia reached out to hug her, 'you must let him help you.'

'I can't,' she shook her head. 'He'll despise me if he knew.'

'You'll never know unless you tell him. He must think a lot about you to come all this way for you. I think you *should* tell him.'

Juliet closed her eyes, but it was too horrid to think about at the moment.

'Get dressed, Juliet and come and have some breakfast. I'm afraid your dress was in a terrible state – I'm not sure it'll mend, so you'll have to wear one of mine for now. I'm going over to your ma's cottage later. Constable Treen said we can clean the mess now - do you want to come and help? '

Juliet nodded. The least she could do was to get the

cottage spick and span for when Ma came home.

*

Betsy stood before the mirror in her beautiful wedding gown, unable to believe this day had finally arrived. Bochym Manor had delivered her a bouquet of flowers early that morning and Ellie was just pinning the veil to her hair. This was it - *she* was getting married at last!

'Are you ready for your big day?' Ellie cupped her hands around Betsy's arms.

'I'm ready,' she smiled nervously.

The day was bright and breezy when Betsy stepped out of the cottage to make her way across the dunes to a wagon streaming with white ribbons. As Guy helped her aboard, she laughed as the wind caught her veil and had to grab it to stop it from being whipped from her head.

*

Jake, dressed in his Sunday best, began to pace the room of the boarding house nervously glancing at the clock ticking the minutes away. It was ten-fifty. Even if Ryan turned up now - there would barely be enough time to get ready and set off to Cury Church. Miss Taylor had gone out shopping that morning - not wanting to be in to pass the time of day with Ryan when he finally dragged himself home. It was an understatement to say, she'd been none too pleased with Ryan for missing supper last evening, and then spending all night out. She'd had a face like thunder when she doled Jake's breakfast out that morning.

'I must admit, I did not expect such behaviour from him,' she denounced. 'I can only assume he's been up to no good with someone to spend the night away. I pity that poor bride of his. It's to be hoped he mends his ways once he's married!'

While Jake paced the room he wondered if perhaps he should have gone down to Poldhu first thing this morning to tell Guy that Ryan had been missing all night, but he didn't want to get him into trouble with Guy. He glanced at Ryan's wedding suit, still hanging behind the door and decided to wait a while longer. Perhaps Jake had got the time wrong, perhaps the wedding was at half-past- eleven and not at eleven - though he was sure Ryan had said the latter.

*

The journey to the church took ten minutes, and because Cury church bells were pealing, people were stood outside their cottages hoping for a glimpse of the bride-to-be. Betsy smiled and waved, acknowledging the calls of *'good luck'* and *'all the best for the future.'*

It was going to be a small gathering that day. Guy, Ellie and their children, their youngest, Sophie, was dressed in a pretty floral dress and bubbling with excitement at being a bridesmaid. Agnes their eldest, and very much the tomboy, had turned her nose up at the frippery of a dress, but Zack - ever a sweet and thoughtful boy had offered to carry the basket of petals to scatter before the bride as she walked up the aisle. Tobias, Meg and Jake - in the capacity as best man - would be the only other guests at the church. Her friends and colleagues from Bochym were to join them for a wedding breakfast at the tea room at mid-day.

When they pulled up at the church gates a few minutes early, Guy jumped down and gave his hand to Betsy, but just as she was straightening her dress, the vicar came rushing down the path - his cassock and robe flowing freely in the wind.

'If I may have a word, Mr Blackthorn,' he said averting his eyes from the waiting bride.

Betsy glanced nervously at Ellie as high words were exchanged. A moment later Meg and Tobias appeared from within the church and began to walk solemnly down the path towards the gate. Betsy knew then that something was amiss. A moment later, Guy walked back to where Ellie and Betsy were standing, and cleared his throat.

'Ryan isn't here yet, Betsy,' he said gravely.

'Have I got the wrong time?' she said feeling suddenly

light-headed.

'No, Betsy.'

'Has he....has he said he's not coming?' she asked shakily.

'The vicar has had no word from him, and Jake isn't here either.'

The well-wishers at the church gates began to murmur and Betsy lowered her eyes to look at her bouquet. 'What are we to do?' she mumbled.

The vicar says you can come into the vestry to wait, perhaps Ryan has been waylaid, but he does have another wedding at eleven-forty-five!'

Betsy turned to Ellie for direction.

I think we should wait a while, just to see.' She smiled, closing her hand over Betsy's for comfort.

*

At Bochym everyone waited with bated-breath while His Lordship phoned Helston Police Station to find out what was going on. His next phone call was a lengthy one to Mr Sheldon, his lawyer.

'If there has been a murder, as stated, what on earth has happened to poor Juliet?' Mrs Blair asked Ruby as she poured out sweet tea to everyone around the table.

Ruby shuddered. 'It doesn't bear thinking about.'

'I don't suppose we'll be going to the wedding breakfast at Poldhu now,' Thomas bemoaned.

'Oh, my, lord! Poor, Betsy!' Ruby stood up. 'She won't know what's happened!'

They all glanced at the clock as it struck eleven.

'Well, she'll know he's jilted her by now,' Thomas quipped, to which he received a scowl from Ruby.

'He has not jilted her!' Ruby snapped.

'I reckon Betsy will think he has!' Thomas muttered under his breath.

Ruby looked at Mrs Blair. 'As soon as His Lordship tells us what is happening, I'll need to go down to Poldhu to see Betsy. Oh, that poor girl, I shudder to think what she's going through.' Ruby glanced anxiously at the new maid, without Juliet here she would have to rely on Mary and Dorothy to do the housework.

Seeing her consternation, Mrs Blair said, 'Of course you must go to the poor lass. Don't worry about things here, luncheon is already prepared, so Mary can help Lucy and Dorothy. I'll keep an eye on things.'

'Thank you, Mrs Blair, I'll go and speak to Her Ladyship and tell her what I'm planning to do.'

*

At Cury Church those next fifteen minutes, sitting within the cold stone walls of the vestry, all studiously avoiding each other's glances, was the most excruciating time Betsy could ever remember. She was actually relieved when the vicar stood up and made his apologies that he must make himself and the church ready for his next wedding.

Betsy, flanked by Guy and Ellie, walked down the church path and through the smattering of people waiting outside the church gates to wish the bride and groom luck. Many were ready to throw rice, but quickly emptied their fists of the grain when they saw there was no groom with her. Betsy climbed back aboard the wagon and very stoically sat upright. She looked at no one and said nothing - she just stared at the road in front of her.

They were just about to set off, when Jake came running and shouting towards them. Guy got down from the wagon to meet him, but Betsy dared not look around. For a brief second, she hoped that her nightmare was over and Ryan had arrived, but then she felt her heart implode when she heard Jake's breathless words, "He ran off last night and didn't come back. I've been waiting for him at the boarding house." The audible gasps from the church gate crowd almost finished Betsy.

*

As soon as the wagon arrived back at Poldhu, Betsy muffled a swift thank you and goodbye, before running across the dunes to her cottage in a froth of lace and white linen.

'I'd better go to her, Guy,' Ellie said solemnly.

He nodded. 'There had better be a good excuse for Ryan not showing up today, because I'm telling you, Ellie, if he's jilted that poor young woman, he can say goodbye to his job.'

'I agree, but I doubt he's jilted her. I think something else must have happened.'

*

Betsy pulled off her veil and placed it on the kitchen table as she looked around the cottage ready to welcome the newly married couple. Flowers were everywhere, the fire in the grate glowing with embers to warm the chill November day, and the bed - the bed was freshly made and flowers lay on both pillows.

A myriad of emotions circled her head – shock, worry, disappointment, hurt – oh yes, it hurt. It was as though a heavy weight was crushing her heart. The happiest day of her life had crumbled into the very worst in an instant, and she knew not why. There were no jitters visible when she saw him last, no faltering or silent moments between them. He'd cupped her face in his hands and kissed her with all the passion of a man who loved her unequivocally. His very last words to her yesterday morning were, "In twenty-four hours, you will make me the happiest of men."

She turned when Ellie knocked and came in.

'Can I do anything?' she said gently. 'Can I help you off with your dress?'

Betsy nodded silently and turned her back to her so Ellie's nimble fingers could undo the many buttons.

'Are you thinking the same thing, Ellie? That it was bad luck for me to wear this dress - after all, it never brought Jessie any luck, did it? And is this cottage cursed? Is it never to be a happy home?'

'No, Betsy, I don't think the dress nor the cottage bears any bad luck - Guy and I were very happy here.' With the buttons undone she pulled Betsy around to face her.

'Betsy, I have only known Ryan a few weeks and I believe him to be a genuine person. Something major must have happened for him not to show up. I just hope he hasn't had an accident, but I'm sure we'll find out very soon. But for what it's worth, I don't believe he has a bad bone in his body. Now, can I make you a drink or something?'

Betsy shook her head. 'I might just lie down for a while, if that's all right?'

'Whatever you need to do is fine by me. Come and see me if you need to talk.'

Betsy reached out for Ellie's hand. 'Thank you. Jessie always said you were a lovely person and a good friend.' Her eyes filled with tears as she thought of Jessie - how she wished she were here too.

*

At Helston jail, Ryan was in utter despair. Not only because he was locked up in this cold, damp cell on a charge of murder, but more importantly, for what he'd done to Betsy, on this, their wedding day. There had been a glimmer of hope early that morning that he'd be able to get a message to her - having been told they could call someone. Ryan and Joe decided between them, that when the call was allowed, Joe would phone Bochym, hoping that some kind soul there would go down to Poldhu to tell Betsy. Unfortunately, the call had not been allowed until ten-thirty that morning – had it been too late for anyone to stop Betsy going to church? Ryan watched the hand on his pocket watch move to eleven, and dropped his head in his hands. How would he ever make this up to her, and how on earth could he explain why it was so necessary to go to Juliet's aid? She would never trust him again for blatantly lying about his relationship with Juliet, but even now, now that he'd ruined things between them, he could still never tell her why he'd lied and kept secrets from her - for the secrets were not his to tell. Damn these secrets and lies, damn them to all eternity.

45

Betsy stood at the water's edge staring blankly out at the cold grey horizon. The car which had brought Ruby from Bochym to explain what had happened to Ryan, was now heading back up Poldhu Hill towards the manor. It was strange - Betsy had no idea which of the many emotions going around her head was the strongest at first. Shock of course, that Ryan had been arrested for murder! Anxious as to whether he'd be hanged for it – though in truth, she was so angry with him she could string him up herself! Disappointed that he'd chosen to go to Juliet's aid, instead of turning up for his own wedding! This selfish emotion she berated herself for, and tried to rid all thoughts of it. Of course, Ryan would always help a woman in distress - had he not saved her from Trencrom's salacious hands? It was the kind of man he was - she just churlishly wished it hadn't been at the expense of her wedding day. The shame at being let down at the altar so spectacularly, would never leave her, and the hurt that he'd lied to her, over and over, about not knowing Juliet. It was the hurt, above all others, that kept coming to the forefront. To think she would have married him today when he'd so blatantly lied and kept secrets from her.

*

Ellie and Meg had just finished wrapping sandwiches in baking parchment – some they could save - others would have to do for tea. They stood on the veranda and watched the forlorn figure of Betsy down by the sea.

'Goodness me, whatever next is going to happen,' Meg declared, 'I thought we'd been through everything with Jessie, but this with poor Betsy, takes the biscuit.'

*

It was noon when Joe was let out of the cell. But when Ryan tried to follow, he was unceremoniously pushed back in, making Joe spin around in alarm when he heard the jailer lock Ryan in again.

'What about Ryan? Is he getting out?' The jailer shook his head and pushed Joe up the stairs away from the cells. He was led to the desk, where he was met by Mr Sheldon, the de Bochym's lawyer. 'Am I free?' Joe asked shaking his hand.

'You've made bail,' Mr Sheldon said gravely.

Though tired, hungry and dirty from spending a night in a cell with the drunks of Helston, Joe was prepared to fight for Ryan's liberty.

'But what about Ryan?'

'I'm sorry, Joe. His lordship put surety up for you both, but Ryan was refused bail because he's on a charge of murder - you were down as his accessory.'

'That's absurd - neither of us is guilty of any such thing. It was a terrible accident. The deceased ran into Rosemary's knife!'

'I'm afraid there is a witness who says otherwise. He claims that Ryan came with the intent of killing Ronnie Penrose.' He ushered Joe out of the police station. 'I'm sorry there is nothing I can do at the moment. Come, His Lordship is expecting you.'

'No, wait, can you take me to Gweek first? I need to see if Juliet is all right, and I've left the Bochym pony trap there – I took it without permission. Oh, goodness, whatever will my lord and lady think of me?'

'I believe they think a great deal of you, Joe, otherwise I would not be here.'

*

When Mr Sheldon pulled up in Gweek, Juliet and Amelia ran out to greet them.

'Where's Ryan - is he not here?' Juliet looked frantically between the men.

'I'm afraid not,' Mr Sheldon answered darkly.

'But why is he not free like you, Joe?' she asked searchingly.

Joe's broken sigh spoke volumes. 'I'm afraid it's the nature of the charge against him. He's been charged with murder and I,' he raised his brow, 'an accessory. Mr Sheldon here has secured my bail, but Ryan must stay in jail until we appear in court on Friday.'

'No!' Juliet wailed - a sudden intensity in her eyes. 'Ryan didn't kill him – it was an accident. Ronnie slipped and fell onto Ma's gutting knife. He fell against it so hard the handle of the knife broke her rib and punctured her lung!' Her eyes narrowed as she looked towards the blacksmiths. 'This is because of what George Blewett said, isn't it?'

'I believe so,' Mr Sheldon answered.

'Well, he's lying – he's a liar! He wasn't even there when it happened! He's just saying that because Ronnie was his drinking friend. It was just a terrible accident. Oh, Amelia, what are we to do?' she fell into Amelia's arms sobbing.

'Shhh now - the truth will come out.' Amelia patted her gently and glanced at Mr Sheldon. 'Are you dealing with this case then?'

'I don't know yet - I shall have to see what His Lordship says.'

'Because if you are, I'll testify and tell them exactly what happened. Besides Rosemary, only Juliet and I witnessed it!'

Mr Sheldon nodded. 'I'll bear that in mind.'

'Juliet,' Joe's gaze was soft and so was his voice, 'If you're feeling up to it will you come back home to the manor? I think we'll have been sorely missed by now.'

Juliet lifted her tear-stained face to Amelia for guidance.

'I think you should go. You have a job to do. All will be well, I promise you. We'll let you know how your ma is faring, or if there is any change.'

Joe gave Amelia a grateful look. 'Could someone tell me where the Bochym pony and trap is?'

'I'll take you to them,' Amelia said. 'Eric Williams took them to his dairy farm for safekeeping.'

Joe smiled gently at Juliet. 'Do you want to go back

with Mr Sheldon?'

'No, I'd rather like to ride back with you, Joe, if I may?' she smiled tentatively, noting those few words had lifted the weight of the world Joe was carrying on his shoulders.

*

Arriving at the manor, after a quiet, but companionable journey back, they were welcomed with relief and plenty of hugs. Joe was immediately summonsed to Peter's study to join Mr Sheldon there, while Ruby sent Juliet to bed to rest, following her with a cup of hot chocolate.

'I've called for Dr Martin,' Ruby said, 'but I'm told he's away today in Truro. He'll come and see you tomorrow, if that's all right?'

'Thank you. Dr Eddy - my doctor in Gweek, tended my scratches and bruises, so all is well.'

Ruby smiled gently, and was just about to ask her what had happened when she heard a strange commotion out on the attic landing. When she went to investigate, she almost collided with Thomas running towards the stairs.

'Where's Joe, Ruby?' Thomas said forgoing all formality.

'With His Lordship in the study, why?'

'Mr Devereux has collapsed on the landing.

*

After Justin had been put to bed, Sarah sat in vigil with him for the rest of the day. As each hour ticked by, Thomas told Ruby that Justin's health was deteriorating. She was utterly distraught that she could do nothing, or be by his side. That night she could not sleep - endlessly walking the corridors - waiting for the inevitable dreadful news, but all she could glean from Thomas and Joe was that Sarah was with him and Justin was sleeping peacefully. Exhausted from lack of sleep, it took all Ruby's resolve to not break down when Thomas told them the next morning that Justin had refused breakfast and could hardly lift his head from the pillow.

*

Sarah was dishevelled and fatigued, having refused to leave her brother's side all that night. When morning came and after Justin had refused breakfast, he fell back into a deep sleep, so she too rested her head on her arms on the bed and dropped off for a few minutes. She woke, hearing Justin murmuring the same thing over and over. Lifting her head, her eyes widened – suddenly alert to what he was saying.

Justin stirred and opened his eyes.

'You've been talking in your sleep,' Sarah whispered.

'Oh!' He took a deep tremulous breath and closed his eyes. 'I think we need to call for the lawyer now, please?'

*

When Joe informed Ruby that Mr Sheldon had been called for to put Justin's affairs in order, Ruby rushed blindly to the housekeeper's room and wept openly. This could only mean one thing – he didn't have long to live now. Fearful that someone would find her in such a state, Ruby tried to gather herself. She wiped her eyes and straightened her dress, but the tears came again and she wept into her hands. With Lucy being new and Juliet confined to her bedroom after her ordeal, Ruby knew she had to eventually emerge from this room to carry on with the manor's normal duties. She had never missed Betsy more. If she'd have been here, she'd have taken the burden of work from her.

*

Betsy had also spent a sleepless night at Poldhu, but though the hour ticked past nine that morning, she had not yet risen. Instead, she lay in the bed she should have shared with her new husband - staring blankly at the ceiling. The flowers which had adorned each pillow were now limp in a vase by the bed, and Betsy pondered, as she had all night, on her future at Poldhu. This cottage was to be her marital home. Even with the wage she'd get from working in the tea room - it would not cover the rent.

It was a quarter-to-ten when she eventually dragged

herself from her bed. Poking the fire to life, she toasted a slice of bread. It tasted bland and unappetising and she dropped the remnants of the toast on her plate just as a soft knock came to the door.

Ellie stepped in, and without saying anything, pulled Betsy into a hug.

'Did you sleep?'

'No,' Betsy said wearily.

'I've just left the tea room for a moment to come and tell you that Jake's just been to see us. Joe was released on bail yesterday, and is home with Juliet, but Ryan must stay in jail until the trial.'

Betsy's eyes flickered resentfully at the mention of Juliet, but then compassion prevailed and she asked, 'Is Juliet all right?'

'She's beaten up a little and has been put to bed. Unfortunately, Jake also told us that Justin Devereux is very ill and not expected to live. He says the household is in a real quandary.'

'Oh, dear!' Betsy immediately thought of Ruby and suspected she would be terribly upset at this news. 'They'll be short-handed at the manor then,' she said tentatively.

'I think they might be, yes,' Ellie said softly. 'Would you like to go up there to help? It might be better than sitting here all alone.'

Despite the shame of being left at the altar, Betsy knew she'd have to face everyone sooner or later, so she nodded.

'I'll get Guy to take you up there, then.'

*

When Mr Sheldon arrived, Sarah left them to their business to take a walk into the garden. Conscious that Justin would never feel the sun on his face, see the flowers in bloom or the copper beech tree rich and resplendent again, she wrapped her arms around herself and closed her eyes. Of all these beautiful things, she knew there was only one image Justin truly wanted to see.

*

Betsy need not have felt any unease because her arrival at Bochym, offering help, was met with relief coupled with warm hugs - especially from Ruby.

'I thought you might need me here, and perhaps *you* need to be somewhere else,' she whispered to Ruby.

Ruby's eyes filled with tears at Betsy's perception. 'Thank you, Betsy,' her lip trembled, 'I can't be where I want to be, but you being here is a great weight off my mind.'

*

While Ruby gratefully watched Betsy take control of all that needed to be done, she met with Joe coming down the stairs and he beckoned her into his office.

'Mr Devereux has put his affairs in order,' he said solemnly, 'Thomas and I were sent for, to witness the will.'

'Oh, Joe!' Ruby felt her world implode as she crumpled into his arms.

'I know, Ruby,' he soothed, 'I know about you and Justin – you've worn your love for him on your sleeve.'

'Does everyone know?' she hiccupped a sob, 'I think Betsy does, she's just come back to help with the chores.'

'Well, if anyone else knows, they've said nothing to me.'

'I want to be with Justin, Joe. He wanted me to be by his side when the end came, but he knew I couldn't be there, it would expose our relationship and seal my fate in this household. Oh, god, Joe, I don't care - I want to be with him, I know I've done a terrible thing and conducted myself in a way unsuitable for my position as a housekeeper, but I love him – I love him so much,' she wept. 'I know that when Justin dies, I will not be able to hold on to my grief. Our secret will be laid bare and I'll have to leave, so I might as well just go to him.'

A knock came on the door and Ruby lifted her tear-filled eyes to find Sarah standing there.

There was a marked silence for a few moments before Sarah spoke.

'Ruby…. my brother,' her voice faltered, causing Ruby

to emit a desperate cry, 'I think my brother needs you.'

Unable to comprehend at first what Sarah had said, so convinced was she that Justin had already passed, she lowered her eyes and answered softly. 'Yes, my lady. I'll go to him now.'

'Leave your keys with me please,' Sarah asked.

'Of course.' Ruby unhooked the bunch of keys from her belt and ran out of the office and up the stairs - a journey she'd made so many times as a housekeeper. But she was the housekeeper no more, and she didn't care, she had something more important to do. It was time to hold Justin's hand and help him on *his* final journey.

*

On seeing Ruby enter the room, Justin held out his arms in welcome relief.

'Ruby, Ruby, come to me.'

She was at his bedside in a heartbeat and he kissed her openly, despite Mr Sheldon still being in the room.

'I'm sorry, my darling, apparently, I spoke your name in my sleep. I know I've compromised your position here, but I'm so happy that you're here with me. I can't do this alone - I need you by my side.'

'It's all right, my love. I'm where I want to be.' She kissed him tenderly, pushing his hair from his brow.

'I've made sure that you'll be well looked after when I've gone. Mr Sheldon has very kindly sorted everything out for me.' He gestured to the lawyer as he closed his briefcase.

'And rest assured, Mr Devereux, I shall make sure everything is done. I have business with His Lordship now, so I'll bid you.... farewell.' He bowed.

As soon as they were alone, Justin whispered, 'Hold me, Ruby'

Ruby sat on the bed and circled her arms around him.

'No, really hold me – lay next to me, here.' He patted the bed. Kicking off her shoes, she crawled onto the satin eiderdown to lie next to him. He held her close and kissed her hair. 'At least I'll get one more chance to go to sleep with you in my arms,' he whispered.

'Oh, Justin, my love.' Her body began to tremble.

Running his fingers softly down her face, he said softly, 'I want you to know that the villa in Tuscany, the paintings, everything I own is yours, my darling. Sarah has no need of any of it. Mr Sheldon will liaise with my agent in Italy, to sell the remaining paintings there, and also with my bank. All monies will be transferred to you. I'm a rich man, Ruby – you'll never want for anything.'

'*I want you*,' Ruby wept brokenheartedly.

'I know, I know, my love, I want you too,' he said wiping away his own tears, 'but live on for me. Let the artist within you come alive. Everything will be yours for the taking. I know you love your family here, but you'll have a chance to fly - to live a different life. Open your wings and fly for me. Go to Lamorna, talk to Stanhope Forbes, enrol in their art school and be who you really are! Promise me you will - so I can die a happy man.'

His words - the strength of his arms around her, and the enormity of what was to come, overwhelmed her and she could not find her voice.

'Promise me,' he said tensing his hold.

'I will, I promise,' she said tremulously, and he relaxed back with an enormous sigh.

46

Sarah crumpled into the chair in Joe's office and sat there for a good few seconds. Joe noted that her blond hair had lost its sheen and her beautiful face was etched with grief. Eventually she lifted her tired eyes and looked at Joe.

'Can I get you anything, my lady?' he said softly.

She sighed. 'Yes, please,' she lifted the bunch of keys she'd taken from Ruby, 'can you tell me which key is for the attic where Justin has been working?'

*

As Sarah climbed the stairs wearily, she met Mr Sheldon coming down.

'Are all my brother's affairs settled?'

'Yes, my lady, everything is in order. I'm wanted now in His Lordship's study.'

'Thank you,' she said walking slowly past him. At the attic door, Sarah put the key in the lock with shaking hands. An artist herself, she was familiar with the smell of oil paints, turpentine and linseed oil, and as traumatised as she was with what was happening with Justin, the smell stimulated her own creative juices. The daybed was in disarray with crumpled blankets and pillows, and a large canvas sat on an easel in the middle of the room. It was facing away from her, but she had surmised before looking at it, what she would find. Tentatively stepping through the debris of paint and cloths, the painting revealed itself - Sarah closed her eyes and sighed.

*

In his study, Peter gestured for Mr Sheldon to take a seat, and though it was early in the day - a glass of whisky was proffered.

'Terrible business this,' Peter muttered.

'Yes, my lord, and Mr Devereux still so relatively young.'

Peter nodded. 'We can do nothing to help Justin, but there is something we can do to help some other people.'

'My lord?'

'This murder case against Treen and Penrose is concerning me deeply. From what I understand, it was an accident involving young Juliet's mother and her husband, and neither Treen nor Penrose had any involvement in it.'

'Yes, my lord, that too is my understanding of it.'

'Treen tells me there is a rogue witness - someone who was not there when it happened, but is testifying that he was, and that he saw Penrose kill his father.'

'Yes, my lord.'

'Neither you nor I like injustice.'

Mr Sheldon raised his glass. 'We do not, my lord.'

'Then can you build a case for their defence?'

'For all of them, my lord?'

Peter nodded. 'By all accounts Penrose and Juliet's mother cannot afford a lawyer - I can.'

'Then I would be happy to, my lord.'

'Excellent.' He sighed heavily. 'If you go and see Treen, he will fill you in on everything he knows. We must have this case quashed.'

'Very well, my lord.'

*

Sarah stood for a long time staring at the image before her. She was fighting with every single emotion, as Justin's words rang through her head. "I only paint beautiful things I love." Eventually, she locked the door again and slowly descended the attic stairs to stand unobserved at Justin's bedroom door. Ruby had shed her shoes and was scandalously laid on the bed alongside Justin - her black dress spread dark across the golden eiderdown. Sarah's gaze fell on Justin's arm around her, holding her tightly – the fingers on his other hand had laced with Ruby's. Sarah's eyes blurred as she retreated to her own bedroom to quietly process all she had seen – for now she was no long needed at his deathbed.

*

It was a long and very hard decision, but when Sarah went

downstairs, she made a very important phone call, before taking a walk around the gardens. The borders had recovered slightly from the storm, and were wearing their late warm, autumn colours. The Michaelmas daisies and autumn glory sedums stood proud in the November sun, but she gleaned no joy from them, nor could they settle her fragile heart. If Justin was about to die, she needed to be back in that room with him, whether Ruby was there or not.

She knocked quietly and entered the bedroom, Justin smiled weakly, but Ruby was fast asleep, nestled into his neck.

'Like you, I don't think Ruby has slept all night,' he whispered.

Sarah took the seat by the bed and he reached for her hand and pulled his mouth into a tight line.

In hushed tones so as not to wake Ruby, Sarah asked, 'How long has *this* been going on?'

'A while.'

Sarah raised her eyebrow. 'Have you been conducting an affair in the attic?'

He looked at her puzzled. 'The attic, no, why?'

'I've been in there, Justin, I've seen it.'

'Oh!' He looked down at Ruby sleeping in his arms.

'I must ask, is it because she is beautiful or because you love her?'

'Both.'

'So, this is not some flight of fancy?'

'Absolutely not – I love her. The painting was going to be a gift for Ruby, on our wedding day. I'd hoped to marry her in the New Year.' He squeezed Sarah's hand. 'Will you make sure she gets it when I've gone?'

Sarah closed her eyes to the inevitable and nodded.

'Sarah, you have to know, I've arranged with Mr Sheldon for Ruby to inherit everything of mine when I'm gone – I know you will not mind – you have all this.'

'Oh, Justin, if this,' she glanced at Ruby, 'relationship

was so important to you, why did you keep it secret?'

He licked his dry lips. 'You know why! We are both well aware that social lines have been crossed by us falling in love. We were going to tell you at the end of the month though. Ruby is very loyal to you. She's been searching for a replacement housekeeper, so you wouldn't be left without one - in case you asked her to leave.'

Sarah blanched. 'I hope you are jesting with that last comment?'

He raised his eyebrows. 'Then, I take it you'll do the right thing and keep her on when I'm gone - until she decides what she wants to do.'

'Oh, Justin, surely you know the answer to that, but might *you* have left her in a compromising position - with a baby?'

'No!' he spoke adamantly and Ruby stirred in his arms but settled again. 'We're not married, therefore have not been intimate like that – I do have some scruples.' He gave her a weak grin.

'I'm sorry - this has all been quite a shock. How do you feel?'

'Exhausted.'

'Shall I stay?'

'Yes please.'

Sarah looked down at Ruby. 'I'm so sorry for you both.'

*

As Joe had been ensconced in his office with Mr Sheldon for the last hour, it was Thomas who showed Dr Martin in and led him upstairs to check on Juliet.

Dr Martin was a very perceptive doctor. He understood how traumatised a woman could be after being subjected to an attack such as this, so his bedside manner was gentle with her and he smiled kindly as he pulled a chair up to sit beside her.

'Hello, Juliet, would you permit me to examine you?'

Juliet nodded nervously and braced herself.

'Do you want Mrs Sanders to be here with you?'

'She can't come, Mr Devereux is very ill and she's needed at his bedside.'

Dr Martin furrowed his brow. 'Mr Devereux?'

'Her ladyship's brother. He's dying I'm afraid - and he's such a lovely man. We are all so dreadfully sorry for him.'

As the doctor pressed his fingers gently on Juliet's jaw and cheek bones to see if all was intact, he said, 'Do you know what is wrong with Mr Devereux?'

'He saw a doctor in London who told him he had Per, Pin, Pern,' she shook her head, 'some sort of anaemia.'

'Pernicious anaemia?'

'Yes.' She nodded.

Dr Martin was quiet for a while as he carried on with his examination. 'Well, thankfully you're all still in one piece.' He closed his medical bag. 'I'm sorry you've been through this terrible ordeal, Juliet. Do you have anyone you can speak to about it?

She shrugged. 'I don't know - perhaps.'

'It's just that you may suffer some post trauma for a while, and it's best to talk about these things. If you find you need to speak about it, but can't find the right person to listen, let me know – I'm a good listener.'

'Thank you, doctor,' her eyes watered, but she sniffed the tears back, 'May I go back to work now?'

'Yes, perhaps that would be the best way to recover.'

He chatted for another few minutes with her, and as he came back down the stairs, Joe was just coming back through the corridor from letting Mr Sheldon out.

Joe gave a welcoming smile to the doctor. 'How is Juliet?'

'She'll be fine. She wants to get up and come back to work, so that's a good sign. She's been through quite an ordeal, but I think the fact that her assailant is dead is helping her cope with things. Just keep an eye on her, call me if she looks like she's struggling.'

'I will thank you.'

Dr Martin shifted uncomfortably, before he asked, 'I understand Her Ladyship's brother is very ill.'

'Yes,' Joe nodded sadly, 'We don't think he'll live much longer.'

'Is he being attended to by a doctor?'

'No, Ruby and Her Ladyship are with him.'

'Forgive me - I know I'm not the family's doctor, but do you think Mr Devereux will see me. I may be able to give him some pain relief.'

Joe furrowed his brow. 'I'll ask, but he has an inordinate dislike for country practitioners – I understand he was subjected to several bouts of bloodletting when he was young man.'

'I can understand that.' Dr Martin grimaced, following Joe back up the stairs.

*

Sarah left Justin's side to answer the knock on the door, and when she saw who it was, she stepped out to speak to Dr Martin, closing the door behind her.

'Forgive me, my lady, but I just wondered if I could do anything to help to ease your brother's passing?'

'Thank you, Dr Martin, but Mr Webb in Harley Street said there is little we can do to ease the end of his life. He is not in any pain – he is just slipping away.'

'Is he unconscious?'

'No, he is quite lucid at the moment.'

'Please, my lady - if I may just see him.'

Biting down on her lip for a moment, she nodded and opened the door to let him into the room.

Ruby had woken on hearing voices and when she saw Sarah and the doctor enter, she quickly moved from the bed to the waiting chair, much to Justin's dismay.

'This is Dr Martin, Justin,' Sarah announced.

Justin narrowed his eyes. 'Don't even think of bleeding me, I'm weak enough,' he warned, reaching over for Ruby's hand.

Dr Martin smiled. 'I have no intention of doing

anything so barbaric. I just want to ask you some questions - perhaps examine you?'

Justin looked to Ruby for advice and she nodded.

Dr Martin cleared his throat and said, 'Some questions may be a little personal - perhaps the ladies would like to leave the room for a moment.'

Justin shook his head. 'I'd like them to stay, please.'

'Very well, I understand you've been diagnosed with pernicious anaemia.'

'I have, unfortunately.'

'How long have you been unwell for?'

'I've not been unwell as such, just tired since July.'

'And it's got progressively worse?'

Justin nodded. 'I'm becoming more and more exhausted yes.'

'Any tingling of the extremities.'

'Occasionally, but I stand for long periods and paint, so I put it down to that.'

Dr Martin pulled Justin's lower eye lids down. 'Have you had any stomach pains?'

Justin furrowed his brow. 'Yes.'

'Does any particular food make it worse?'

'Everything rich does.'

'Are your stools dark in colour?'

Justin's cheeks pinked as he nodded. 'They were.'

'Were?'

'Before I left Italy.'

'Very dark?'

'Yes, for a while. Things have improved since I stopped drinking claret.'

'Mr Devereux, I know I said I didn't want your blood, but would you agree to me taking a blood sample.'

'What is the point? I've had all the tests in Harley Street!'

'I would just like to check something, if I may.'

'Let him, Justin,' Ruby squeezed his hand. 'You've nothing to lose.'

'Very well,' he sighed and offered up his arm. 'You seem very determined for a country doctor.'

'I graduated in London from the Royal College of Surgeons of England,' he said as he took two vials of blood.

Justin raised an eyebrow. 'In your opinion, how long do you think I have then, doctor?'

'This blood test will tell us. I'll be back this afternoon. Are you in any pain? Can I give you something before I go?'

'No.' Justin glanced between Ruby and Sarah. 'I have everything I need now.'

47

Betsy organised everything that had to be done in the manor, carefully explaining exactly how things should be done correctly to the new maid Lucy. They conducted their work in silence, in respect of the ongoing situation upstairs, and when it was time for a break that afternoon, Betsy was shocked to find Juliet had come downstairs.

Mrs Blair eyed Betsy and Juliet curiously– realising there were clearly unsaid words between them.

'Why don't you two go into the housekeeper's room for a few minutes – I'm sure you have a few things you need to discuss. Mrs Sander's won't mind.'

*

There was an uncomfortable silence as they sat opposite each other in the housekeeper's room. In the end it was Juliet who broke it.

'Betsy, I am so terribly sorry that what happened to me ruined your wedding day.'

Betsy nodded. 'I'm sorry for what happened to you too – it must have been terrifying, but,' Betsy's face set hard, 'it's the lies I can't forgive. You both lied to me when I asked if you knew each other. Can you imagine how I felt when I heard he'd left me at the altar to rescue *you,* his stepsister? It didn't make sense – to all intents and purpose, you told me he had no connection to you!'

'We had to keep it a secret, to keep me safe from my stepfather!'

'How would lying to *me* keep you safe, I don't understand?'

'We didn't lie - we just didn't tell the truth - to anyone.'

'Stop splitting hairs - It's the same thing!'

Juliet dropped her head. 'Ryan has always looked after me, and tried to shield me from my hateful stepfather. With his help and that of Ma and her friend Amelia Pascoe, they got me away from home and *him.* They helped me to find this job, and I reverted back to my late father's name of Gwyn, in order to hide my real identity. Ryan told Ma to spin a yarn to my stepfather that I had gone off with him 'up country'. We hoped, in vain, that Ma would not be punished then for letting me run away,' she lowered her eyes. 'Once Ryan knew I was to be settled here and safe, he took work over in Penryn, but before he went, he told me that he would keep his ear to the ground and would be here in a heartbeat if he thought I was in danger of being found. I had no idea Ryan was living close by, keeping a watch on me, until he brought you home after you'd hurt your foot. So, when I saw him – I was filled with such a dread, knowing that if Ryan was here, that meant my stepfather was looking for me.'

Betsy tipped her head. 'So, what was it that brought Ryan here?'

'Ryan kept in touch with Amelia to make sure I was all right. It was she who told him that my stepfather didn't believe that I'd have gone too far away from my ma, and that he was hell bent on finding me, leaving no stone unturned. So, Ryan left his job in Penryn and came here to keep an eye on me.' She paused for a moment and shook her head. 'When he started to court you, I was in such a continual state of flux every time he turned up - I never knew if he was coming to see you, or coming to warn me that I was in danger, you see.'

Betsy sat back in her chair. 'Well, that explains why you were so uncomfortable whenever he came to the kitchen! But nevertheless, Ryan could have told me you were related – he should have trusted me – I was about to become his wife for goodness' sake!'

'Please don't blame Ryan - we dare not tell anyone of our kinship. Questions about our family might have been asked, and word might have found its way back to Ronnie, my stepfather, that we were both over here.'

Betsy sighed in exasperation. 'I would not have said anything!'

'But you would have questioned Ryan as to why I was

so terrified of my stepfather, and he would not have been able to answer you.'

'Why not?

'Because,.' she faltered, 'because of the nature of my terror. Ryan solemnly promised me he would never tell a soul about it.'

Betsy folded her arms. 'Was your stepfather violent then?'

'He was to my poor mother, yes.'

'But, not to you?'

Juliet paused for a moment, unsure how to answer, and then shook her head.

Betsy leant forward. 'So, will *you* tell *me* why you were so terrified of him?'

Juliet blanched. 'I can't say, please don't ask me. I just can't.'

Betsy threw her hands in the air. 'The happiest day of my life was ruined, but still you will not tell me why my future husband deemed it so necessary to leave me at the altar to save you from…. well, from what? A hateful stepfather?'

'I'm so sorry, Betsy,' Juliet started to cry.

'Oh no, I'm sorry.' Betsy softened and pulled Juliet into a hug. 'I'm still upset about things, but it's all right, you don't have to tell me if you don't want.'

Juliet wiped her tears. 'All these secrets were in vain though. I had no idea Bochym Manor had such connections with Gweek, what with Lyndon FitzSimmons coming here and telling us he had a sweetheart there, and the Trevellick's being regular guests, I was in such a state that someone was going to recognise me and tell my stepfather they'd seen me.' Her shoulders slumped wearily. 'In the end it *was* Kit Trevellick who gave the game away. He wasn't to know that I was hiding of course, but when he returned to Gweek and mentioned that he'd seen me here, apparently my stepfather overheard. And the rest, they say, is history.

'Gosh! Your reticence towards Lyndon, and if I remember correctly, you took to your bed when Kit and Sophie Trevellick came to dinner, all makes sense now. Oh, Juliet,' she squeezed her hand, 'we all knew you were fearful of someone, If only we'd known who, we could have protected you! Secrets always come out you know?'

'I know that now.'

'One good thing came out of this holy mess, though!'

'Did it?'

Betsy grinned. 'It just shows how much Joe thinks of you to come to your rescue like he did.'

Juliet clasped her hand to her face. 'Yes, but look at the consequences of him coming. He and Ryan are facing prison, maybe even death in Ryan's case, because that flipping false witness, George Blewett, says Ryan was coming to kill my stepfather! And I know Ryan will not disclose the real reason he came for me – because he promised to keep it a secret always.'

'Well then, maybe it's time for *you* to tell your secret. As I've always told you - you have my ear if you need to speak to someone.'

'Thank you, Betsy - I don't deserve you as a friend.

'Don't be daft, of course you do.'

*

True to his word, Dr Martin was back at the manor later that afternoon. When Joe let him in, he rather rudely, in Joe's opinion, rushed past him, and made his way swiftly up the stairs towards Justin's bedroom.

'I need to take you to hospital now,' he said when he entered the room.

Justin started. 'No! I really don't want to go to hospital,' he grabbed Ruby and Sarah's hand. 'I want to die here in my own bed with the people I love around me.'

'I have no intention of letting you die anywhere, be it here, or in hospital, Mr Devereux. You are dangerously anaemic, but it is *not*, as diagnosed, pernicious.'

'Pardon?' everyone said in unison.

'I believe you have a slowly haemorrhaging stomach ulcer - you need treatment and a blood transfusion, immediately.'

Justin looked aghast. 'But, but the doctor in Harley Street......'

'The symptoms are very similar to pernicious anaemia, but I would have run several more tests to be sure before giving a diagnosis such as he did.'

Justin struggled to hoist himself up on his elbows. 'So, I'm not going to die?'

'Hopefully not - *If* you come with me now.'

Justin clutched Ruby's hand - a flash of hope passing between them.

'Time is of the essence, Mr Devereux, you are very weak.' Dr Martin looked at Ruby and Sarah. 'Please get him ready to be moved as quickly as possible. I have an ambulance arriving shortly.'

'Can I go with him?' Ruby asked not wanting to let go of his hand.

'I think it is best that he goes alone, but I promise you, I have every hope that I shall return him back home to you soon.'

*

Sarah, Peter, Ruby and Joe watched anxiously as Justin was carried into the waiting ambulance, though their attention was diverted when a car came up the drive at speed.

'It's Mother and Father,' Sarah cried, as Charles and Patricia Devereux emerged from the car.

'Are we too late?' Charles Devereux shouted, as he rounded the back of the ambulance.

Justin's mouth dropped in astonishment, when he saw his estranged father.

'Oh, my boy,' Charles said climbing into the back of the ambulance. 'Forgive me for my stupidity.' He grabbed Justin's hand.

Justin was dumbstruck, but before he could find his voice, Dr Martin pulled his father aside.

'I'm sorry, but my patient needs to go to hospital - you must let us take him.'

'But I need to speak to my son — I need to tell him things, before it is too late.'

'Father,' Sarah said gently pulling at his arm, 'Dr Martin thinks he can save Justin - let the ambulance take him.'

Watching the ambulance set off, Charles Devereux raked his hand through his tidy hair.

'Mr Devereux,' Dr Martin said, 'There is something you *can* do.'

'What is it? I'll do anything - just tell me?' he said abruptly.

'Justin needs an emergency blood transfusion. Someone in the hospital — even I'll do it, if need be, will donate the blood, but as his father, your blood might give him a better chance of recovering.'

'You mean,' he furrowed his brow, 'to take my blood and give it to my boy?'

'Yes. Will you do it?'

'Well, of course! What are we waiting for?' he barked.

Dr Martin gave a nod of his head and said calmly. 'Then if you can follow me to the hospital, now!'

This sent Sarah's mother into a fluster and ran after Dr Martin. 'This donating of blood - will it hurt my husband? Might he die if you take all his blood?'

'Rest assured - we only take a small amount, Mrs Devereux. Your husband and son will be fine, I promise you.'

Patricia Devereux was ashen faced as she watched the cars drive away.

'I think all will be well, Mother,' Sarah said putting her arm around her to walk her indoors.

'I'm glad you called us, Sarah darling. We have wanted to stop this silly feud for such a long time, but didn't know how to approach it.'

'Well, hopefully, if Justin pulls through, you'll get your chance now.'

Before the Devereux's car had left, Thomas had collected their bags and was now looking at Ruby for directions as to where to put the unexpected guests.

'Which room shall I put Her Ladyship's parents in, Mrs Sanders,' he asked.

'The Tweed room is ready, I'll arrange for someone to make the bed up,' Ruby said, and then paused, realising that she may not now have authority as the housekeeper to make that call. She glanced tentatively towards Sarah, who nodded that the Tweed room would be satisfactory.

'Please excuse me.' Peter kissed his wife and his mother-in-law. 'I must return to my study - I have some important business to attend to, but I'll let you all know when we receive any news from the hospital.'

As they followed him indoors, Patricia Devereux glanced at Ruby, clearly noting her crumpled dress and hair astray from lying on the bed.

'Who is *that*?' she whispered to Sarah as she stepped past her. 'She looks as though she's slept in that dress!'

Sarah glanced at Ruby, who looked utterly distraught at parting from Justin.

'This is Mrs Sanders - she's been - looking after Justin. She put her hand to her mother's back. 'Mother, if you would like to follow Thomas, he will show you your room so you can freshen up - I'll come and see you shortly. Ruby, if you could come with me, please.'

*

Ruby stood awkwardly in the Jacobean drawing room while Sarah pulled the cord for Joe. *This was it* she thought - *she was going to be escorted off the premises. Perhaps she would be able to stay with Betsy for the time being.*

'Yes, my lady?' Joe asked, passing a swift glance at Ruby.

'Could you bring us some tea, please?'

'Certainly, my lady,' he said backing out of the room.

'Sit down, please, Ruby.'

'My lady, I'm so sorry. I have not conducted myself as a

woman should in my position, and I understand if you need me to leave.'

Sarah folded her hands on her lap. 'You think I am going to dismiss you?'

Ruby fell silent.

'I admit, Ruby, it was a shock – I had no idea. While you were sleeping up there, Justin told me that it has been going on for a while. How long exactly?'

Ruby moistened her lips. 'Almost as soon as he arrived, my lady.'

Sarah took a large intake of breath. 'Goodness, where on earth did you manage to meet with each other so secretly? No, wait,' she said putting up her hand, 'you don't have to tell me - it is none of my business. Justin tells me he wanted to marry you.'

'Yes,' Ruby put her hand on her heart, 'we love each other very much.'

'I can see that, Ruby and I'm sorry that you have not been able to be open about this. Justin is my brother – all I want in life is for him to find someone to love and be happy with.'

Ruby laughed gently. 'Yes, but not someone like me I suspect. I'm not from your class, and deeply aware that I'm not good enough to join this family. I'm your housekeeper, my lady. This sort of thing doesn't happen normally.'

'But it has!'

'Yes, it has!' Ruby answered firmly.

Joe came in with the tea tray and shot another furtive glance at Ruby. Once he'd left, Sarah got up and poured two cups of tea. She handed one to Ruby and then sat beside her.

'If Justin pulls through this, Ruby, and you do marry, you will be my sister-in-law!'

'Yes,' she answered awkwardly.

Sarah reached out and put her hand on Ruby's. 'I honestly cannot think of anyone more kind or perfect to marry my brother, than you.'

'Oh!' Ruby's eyes blurred with tears. 'Thank you, my lady.'

'I think we should be on first name terms always now though, don't you?' She squeezed Ruby's hand.

48

It was to be a long, agonising wait for news from the hospital, but sister-in-law-to-be or not, Ruby had gone about her normal housekeeping business - she had a house to run - and was grateful for it. After informing Joe that Her Ladyship had accepted her relationship with Justin graciously, she threw herself into her work to stop herself from worrying.

*

Betsy was invited to have tea in the kitchen that evening. Ruby had asked Mrs Blair to make a special cake for Betsy, as a thank you for stepping in when she was sorely needed. Although Betsy had slipped perfectly back into her work at the manor, everyone was very conscious not to mention the wedding or Ryan while they ate, and at times the conversation was stilted. It was such a relief when Theo and Lowenna Trevail decided to share their happy news that they were to become parents around Easter time.

After everyone congratulated them, Betsy asked, 'Will Her Ladyship need a new lady's maid then, Lowenna?'

'No, Her Ladyship told me that if I want to carry on, the baby can stay in the nursery all day with their children and be looked after by Nanny.'

'With this, and the news that Justin could be on the mend, it's good news all round.' Joe said, raising his cup of tea.

'Yes, and just think, if the doctor hadn't come to see Juliet today, Justin might have died,' Ruby said unable to stop her eyes welling.

Juliet sighed. 'Well at least something positive came out of my ordeal.' She lowered her eyes and took a bite of cake.

'Let's hope we have some more good news later this week, Mr Treen. When this silly murder case is cleared up,' Mrs Blair said, topping up everyone's cup.

'Hear, hear to that,' everyone agreed.

Ruby squeezed Betsy's hand. 'You have been an absolute godsend today - you can stay here tonight, if you want. We can make a bed up for you in Juliet and Lucy's room.'

'Thank you, but if I could have a lift, I think I'd rather like to go back to the cottage tonight.'

'I'll arrange for someone to take you home in the pony trap then,' Joe answered.

Betsy smiled gratefully – conscious that she did not think of her cottage as home. In fact, she wasn't sure of her thoughts about it. At the moment it was just a roof over her head. It was to have been her marital home, but with the pending court case, and her unsure feelings about Ryan – it may not be her cottage for long.

*

In Helston jail, Ryan too was thinking about the cottage he should be sharing with Betsy as he sat alone in his cell. He'd had a visit today from Mr Sheldon and given his statement as to what had happened. Mr Sheldon had very kindly taken the two letters he'd written for Betsy and Guy to post for him. His meeting with Mr Sheldon had given him hope that he might, just might, get out of this situation alive, but if he did, would he still have a job and more importantly would Betsy ever forgive him?

*

It was almost eight-thirty before Charles Devereux and Dr Martin returned. The family left their evening meal unfinished, gathering together in the drawing room, eager to hear the news. Ruby was impatiently pacing the corridor outside the drawing room when Joe came out to her.

'Her ladyship requests that you join them, Ruby.'

Ruby brushed her hands down her newly ironed dress and patted her hair tidy before entering the room. She bobbed a curtsey to everyone, but Mr Devereux shot a strange questioning look to Sarah.

'Mrs Sanders has been looking after Justin,' Sarah answered his unasked question, 'I think she should be party to what the doctor has to say.'

Charles Devereux set his eyebrows low and observed Ruby disdainfully - clearly not agreeing to her presence there.

'I'm not going to lie, Justin is not out of danger yet,' Dr Martin said, 'and as with any patient receiving a blood transfusion, it's best to keep them under observation until we know if their body has accepted the donation.'

'Oh, goodness,' Patricia clasped her hands to her face, 'so my boy isn't out of the woods yet?'

'I'm afraid not yet, but we're hoping that because Mr Devereux senior donated the blood, Justin's body has a good chance of accepting it!'

Sarah and Patricia gave Charles a quick burst of applause.

Charles cleared his throat. 'Well, I couldn't let them pump some *commoner's* blood into my son, could I?'

Dr Martin's eyes clouded momentarily. 'I can assure you, Mr Devereux *everyone's* blood - no matter what class, has the exact same precious life-giving properties. Your son may well need some more at some stage, so we may have to use another donor. I myself would be willing if need be!'

Charles grunted dismissively. 'If he needs some more, I insist that I am called for. You will take it from me and no one else, do you understand?'

Dr Martin merely nodded.

'Oh, Charles, don't be ridiculous, you'll have none left in your veins,' Patricia muttered.

'Do not fret, Patricia, I was reliably informed by one of the proper doctors at the hospital, that because I am fit for my age, I will make up any blood loss in forty-eight-hours. So, my son will get *my* blood!'

Ruby glanced at Dr Martin - who looked too weary to argue.

Dr Martin turned to Ruby. 'He will need rest and building up, and I'll make up a prescription of stomach medicine for him when he's allowed home. He must also be on a strict bland diet for at least six weeks while his stomach heals, but I'll write down a list of what he can and cannot eat. I'm sure he'll get all the love and care he needs.' He smiled knowingly.

Ruby nodded through blurred eyes. 'When might he come home, Dr Martin?' she asked boldly.

'For goodness' sake, woman.' Charles huffed. 'Have you got cloth ears? The doctor has already told you - he'll be home when they know his body had accepted my blood!'

Having been put firmly back in her place, Ruby prickled at the rebuff.

'Father!' Sarah scolded, 'please don't speak to Mrs Sanders like that - she has lovingly looked after Justin while he's been ill.'

'Well, let her *lovingly* look after the other members of this family. Go and get some dinner organised for me, woman - I'm starving,' he flicked his hand to dismiss Ruby.

Ruby glanced at Sarah who smiled apologetically. 'Mrs Sanders, I shall come and see you in a moment,' she said softly. 'I'll ring for Treen to organise dinner for my father.'

Ruby nodded and turned to Dr Martin. 'Thank you so much, for intervening and for everything you've done for Justin today doctor.'

'I'm glad I could help.'

She heard Charles tut loudly as she left the room and just as she was closing the door, she heard him say, 'I've always said this, Sarah - you are too soft on these people. Familiarity with servants' only breeds contempt.'

Ruby stood in the corridor and stamped her foot angrily just as Joe arrived to answer the bell. He gave her a curious look and she shook her head angrily and stamped her foot again. 'Oh, that man!' she grumbled.

*

As soon as her father's dinner had been brought, Sarah

sought Ruby out. As always, she was busy keeping the accounts up-to-date.

By habit Ruby got up and bobbed a curtsy when she knocked and entered.

'Please, Ruby, there is no need for that now - you will soon be one of the family.'

Ruby raised an eyebrow.

'Yes, I understand your scepticism - my father can be rather pompous at times and I apologise for him.'

'You don't have to apologise. He has no idea who I am. Though I think I'll have a mountain to climb if I'm to be accepted by him.'

Sarah nodded. 'My father is a stickler for tradition, but do not fear, Justin will always do what he wants to do, and he has never sought our father's approval for anything.' She broke into a wide smile. 'Thank goodness for Dr Martin though - to think this morning we thought we would lose Justin.'

'I know!' Ruby looked skywards.

'Come - let me give you a hug to make up for my father being obnoxious.' Sarah beckoned her into a warm embrace. 'I truly believe that Justin is going to be fine, and we'll soon have him back here with us.'

'Can I ask - does His Lordship know about my relationship with Justin?'

'He does and Peter is very happy for you both. Though like myself, he bemoans the fact that we are going to lose you when you go to Italy.

'Well, I do have the most wonderful woman in mind to take my place – you know I wouldn't leave you with anyone less than perfect.'

'She will have to be someone very special to fill your shoes,' she answered, hugging her again.

*

When the family had retired, Joe and Ruby shared a glass of wine while she told him all that happened that day.

He reached out and put his hand over hers. 'I'm so

relieved, Ruby. We should have both known Sarah's character, and trusted her to accept the situation between you and Justin. I must say though, I'll miss you terribly when you do leave for Italy with him. But my, what a different life you'll lead.'

Ruby traced her finger thoughtfully over the rim of the glass. 'I hardly dare think about it. We're not out of the woods yet. I've heard these blood transfusions can go wrong. I'll not settle until Justin is back here with us – alive and well. We were on the brink of losing him earlier today. I don't think my poor fragile heart could take another setback!'

'All will be well, Ruby, I'm sure of it.' He patted her hand.

'But what about you, Joe, with this dreadful murder case hanging over you and Ryan.'

'Well, I gave a statement to Mr Sheldon earlier. He was going to see Ryan and Mrs Pascoe to get their version of what happened. Unfortunately, Juliet's mother is too ill to give a statement, but if she recovers enough to swear that her husband fell on her knife, we have a good chance of getting this case quashed.'

'Well, let's hope so. Is there a date for your court appearance?'

'This Friday - justice is swift these days.' He gave a tight smile. 'So, what did Her Ladyship's mother say about you and Justin?'

'Her ladyship and I have decided not to tell the Devereux's yet. We think it will be best to wait until Justin has recovered so that we can tell them together.' She took a sip of wine and savoured its mellow fruitiness. 'I don't relish telling Mr Devereux though, he was extremely unpleasant to me earlier, and I don't think Justin got on with him very well before he went to Italy to live.'

'Well, he may mellow. Something like this normally heals family differences. As I say, all will be well.'

49

After a night of broken sleep, Betsy woke to a bright, sunny, albeit cold day. Glancing around the room and having spent all her life sharing a bedroom, she keenly felt the loss of another person in the room. Turning to look at the side of the bed Ryan should have occupied - she was still fighting with the conflicting thoughts about him. She hated to think of him alone in that jail cell, but had not yet forgiven him for keeping secrets from her. Yes, she understood a little more of why Juliet and Ryan had been so secretive about their relationship, but really, what on earth could be so secret between them that he'd been unable to divulge to his wife to be!

After washing and dressing she brought the fire back to life and made a bowl of porridge, but only ate half of it. Missing the chatter at breakfast in the Bochym kitchen, she had never felt lonelier. With much on her mind and too much time on her hands, she wished the tea room was open today to occupy her hours, but it was closed on Mondays. Slowly drumming her fingers on the table, she eyed the wedding presents piled up on the bed in the spare room - waiting for Ryan to see them before she unpacked properly. With no wedding, it felt wrong to hold onto them. Would she have to give everything back? If Ryan was found not guilty of killing Ronnie Penrose, *would she want him back* – could she trust him to not lie to her anymore? Clamping her hands to her head, she feared she would go mad here, alone with these thoughts. Her day at Bochym yesterday, although awkward at times, had at least kept her mind off things. Normally when she had some spare time she would write to Jessie, but being a jilted bride was not something she wanted to write and tell her about. Oh, how she wished Jessie was still here, but she was far away in Italy. This thought heartened Betsy a little - Jessie's bad luck ran out in the end, maybe hers would too.

The watery November sun was streaming through her

windows. She'd only cleaned them a few days ago, but now they were smeared and salt-laden. All the sparkle had gone out of everything it seemed.

Deciding that it was no good being cooped up here brooding and she'd feel better outside, she'd do what Jessie would have done when life became unbearable – she'd walk down to the sea. Despite it being November, she shed her boots and stockings to walk barefoot, having learned the hard way that wet sand was not good for leather boots - she was still trying to get the white salt lines off them from her walk last week! It was a breezy day and Betsy was glad she'd put on a coat to keep out the chill. The sea was ruffled, sunlight winked periodically through the racing clouds as seagulls drifted and cried above her. Closing her eyes, she took a breath of salty air and felt her troubles ease - understanding now why Jessie had always taken this path to the sea to settle her troubled mind. After walking to the far end of the beach, she turned to walk back along the waterline, where scraps of seaweed, intermingled with coils of rope and broken shells, laced the water's edge. It was then she saw Ellie, standing on the rocks - her skirt and petticoat tucked up into her belt to keep them dry. As she walked nearer, Ellie waved and made her way tentatively across the slippery rocks towards her.

Betsy noted Ellie's feet and ankles were red with the cold water, but she wore a rosy glow on her cheeks and smiled warmly at her as she neared.

'Hello, I'm collecting sea glass, look!' She rummaged in her pocket to produce three pieces of coloured glass. 'I used to do it all the time before the children were born, but I slipped in twice and very nearly drowned, so Guy doesn't like me doing it any more. It's just that it's such a lovely day, and with the beach being deserted now, there's a better chance of finding some - and I did!' She beamed. 'How are you, Betsy?'

Betsy nodded. 'I'm all right.'

'Is all well at Bochym? You were a little late home yesterday evening.'

'Yes, I had my tea there.'

'I suspect they were glad of your help. How is poor Justin? I want to go up to offer my support, but I don't want to intrude. It must be awful for the family – I am so sorry for that lovely man.'

'Well, actually, I have some good news on that matter!'

'Oh?'

'Dr Martin thinks he can save him!'

'Really!' Ellie's eyes widened. 'Oh, do come and have a cup of tea with me, and tell me all about it. I need to put my stockings on - my feet feel like they're going to fall off they're so cold.'

When Betsy stepped into Ellie's warm kitchen, Blue, Silas's dog lifted his head, hopeful that it was Ryan walking back into the kitchen. When he saw that it wasn't, he whined and rested his head on his paws.

Ellie gestured Betsy to take a seat at the table and shook her head at the dog as she put the kettle on the range.

'Poor Blue, he's pining all over again. He won't eat - he just lays there whining pitifully. I think he misses Ryan as much as we all do, poor dog. Ryan gave him a new lease of life. I honestly don't think he understands why his masters keep abandoning him.'

Over a cup of tea and a slice of hevva cake, Betsy told Ellie everything that had happened up at the manor, and although Ellie was heartened to hear that Justin may well recover, she gasped in disbelief on learning the false witness was none other than *George Blewett!*

'I know of him,' Ellie breathed. 'He's a nasty piece of work. He tried to grab me many years ago when I was living in Gweek. I was watching the harvest dance and he tried to make me dance with him. I was terrified - he wouldn't take no for an answer. Fortunately, someone intervened and rescued me,' she shuddered. 'I learned later that he was a deeply unpleasant man – someone not to be trusted. Rest assured though, I don't believe anyone, court or otherwise, will hear his lies. Ryan *will* be found not guilty.

Ellie tipped her head at Betsy's forlorn face. 'Is something else bothering you?'

She nodded. 'I just wondered, what's going to happen to me? I feel a little displaced at the moment.'

She reached over to put her hand on Betsy's. 'What on earth do you mean?'

'About the cottage – I'm not sure I can afford it all on my own. It was all bundled into the package of my job and marriage to Ryan.'

'Oh, Betsy, Ryan will be back with you by the end of the week of that, I'm sure. We can get the wedding arranged again very soon.'

Betsy looked away.

'What's the matter?'

'I'm not sure I still want to marry him now.' *There, she'd said it out loud.* 'So, the cottage and the job you offered me, was on the proviso I married Ryan.'

'Do you not love him anymore?'

'Of course, I do!' Her eyes watered involuntarily. 'I just can't trust him to tell me the truth.'

'But wasn't he trying to save Juliet from something by keeping things secret?'

'Yes, but I was about to become his wife, and now I find that I don't really know the man.'

'Betsy,' Ellie squeezed Betsy's hand, 'none of us really knows someone until they marry them. Ryan thought he was doing the best thing – I'm sure there was no malice in him keeping things a secret. You wouldn't have wanted Juliet harmed, would you?'

'Of course not!' She wiped the tears away with the back of her hand.

'Well then, you must try to see his reason for doing so. Don't let this chance of happiness slip away. I'm sure Ryan will never keep another secret from you. Now, until he gets back, there will be no rent to pay on the cottage, and if you'd like, you can start at the tea room tomorrow. You look like you need something to take your mind off things. Think long and hard about Ryan, Betsy. Don't spend your life unhappy like Jessie did– she wouldn't want that, and I believe she would give you the same advice.'

'Now, I'm going to Helston shopping, you're very welcome to come with me, perhaps you could see if they'll let you visit Ryan in jail?' Betsy's face blanched, so she added, 'or maybe you should take the wagon back up to Bochym. It will be good for you to have some company.'

'I think you're right - I will go to Bochym.'

As they got up from the table - a knock came on the door.

'Second delivery, Ellie,' the postman said, 'there's one here for Betsy Tamblin - it has your address on it.'

'Thank you, this is Betsy,' Ellie gestured. 'Betsy is living in Jessie's cottage.'

'Ah, I see.' The postman nodded and smiled a greeting and then left.

'I should think this is from Ryan.' Ellie handed it over.

Betsy took it cautiously.

'Are you going to open it?'

'Perhaps later,' she said, not knowing if she wanted to read it or not.

*

It was ten-thirty and Ruby was inspecting the bedrooms and supervising Lucy in the art of bed-making when she glanced out of the window just in time to see Charles Devereux's car speed away in a cloud of dust. She frowned, wondering where on earth he was going at such speed. Her attention was diverted when Lowenna breezed into Her Ladyship's bedroom.

'Goodness me, that was all a bit of a panic!' she exclaimed.

'Are you referring to Mr Charles driving away?'

'Yes, Her Ladyship and her mother have gone too, they've rushed off to the hospital – I do hope all is well with Mr Justin.'

'Pardon?' Ruby felt suddenly faint and had to grab the dressing table. 'Why, was there a phone call from the hospital?'

'No, Thomas said Dr Martin rang, and the next I knew everyone was calling for me to fetch their coats and hats.'

Ruby felt a deep sense of dread forming in the pit of her stomach. *If something was wrong, why had Sarah not come for her?*

'Excuse me,' Ruby said, leaving Lucy to carry on the best she could. She fled downstairs and burst into Joe's office. 'Joe,' she cried when she couldn't find him there. 'Joe, where are you?'

'Ruby, I'm here, whatever is the matter?' he said emerging from the cellar.

'Why have the family gone to hospital?'

Joe's face paled. 'I wasn't aware they'd gone anywhere. I've been down in the cellar these last thirty minutes doing a stock count.'

Ruby's face was ashen. 'Lowenna said there was a phone call from Dr Martin and then everyone left in a hurry in the Devereux's car. Oh goodness me, what's happened?'

Joe grabbed her by the arms to calm her. 'Come on, let's find out.'

Thomas looked up startled from polishing a pair of boots when Joe and Ruby burst into the kitchen.

'Thomas, where have the family gone, and why wasn't I informed?' Joe scolded.

Thomas coloured slightly. 'They've all gone off to the hospital – they left so fast I didn't have time to inform you.'

'Why have they gone?' Ruby cried.

Thomas shrugged – something to do with Mr Justin I think.'

Ruby gave a strangled cry and grabbed Joe's hand. 'Oh, God, Joe - what's happened?'

Thomas's eyes widened as Joe and Ruby clasped hands, and he glanced at Juliet to see if she knew what was going on with them - but she looked just as mystified.

'Calm yourself, Ruby, we'll find out. Go and get your coat, we'll go up to the hospital. Thomas, can you ask for either the carriage or the pony trap to be brought.'

Clearly puzzled as to what was going on with Ruby and Joe, he answered, 'I don't think I can, Mr Treen. The farrier has just arrived - one of the carriage horses has thrown a shoe, and Mrs Blair has gone to Mullion in the pony trap.'

'Damn,' Joe raked his hand through his oiled hair, 'and His Lordship has taken the car to Truro today. I'm so sorry Ruby,' he said, trying without success to calm her, 'we'll just have to wait and see.'

Unable to hold the tears back any longer, Ruby crumpled into a chair and wept openly for Justin, as Thomas and Juliet looked on in astonishment.

*

Ruby spent the most agonising hour waiting for the family to get back. The rest of the staff watched in confusion as she paced up and down watching and listening for the car to return. They were all worried about Justin for sure, but of course none of them, other than Joe, knew why Ruby was in such a high state of agitation.

When they finally heard the car pull up outside, Ruby did away with all protocol and pushed past both Thomas and Joe to meet it.

Mr and Mrs Devereux looked aghast at the distraught appearance of the housekeeper running towards them.

'Sarah! What's happened to Justin?' she cried, trying to look past Mr Devereux who was blocking her way.

'Control yourself, woman, how dare you address my daughter by her Christian name?'

'It's all right, Father,' Sarah's voice came from behind

him.

'It's not all right to have her hollering and shouting like a fishwife.'

'I *said* it's all right, Father,' Sarah said firmly as she moved him to one side and pulled Ruby towards her. 'I'm so sorry, Ruby - Father was in such a rush, I didn't have time to call for you.'

'But is he all right? Please, tell me.'

'He's fine, Ruby, look.' She stepped aside to let her see Justin standing unsteadily by the car smiling at her.

'Justin!' She fled into his arms almost knocking him over. 'Oh, my love, you're alive! I thought the worst had happened – everyone left for the hospital in such a hurry.'

'I'm sorry, Ruby. It's my fault. I was laying in the hospital bed, being tended on by kindly enough nurses, but all I wanted was for you to be by my side.' He wrapped his arms around her and kissed her tenderly on the lips. 'So, I got up and told the hospital that I was going home. I believe Dr Martin was called for, and consequently Sarah and my parents came to my aid.' He gave a wry smile. 'I think I caused a little bit of a rumpus.'

'Are you all right though?' Ruby asked gently patting his arms.

'I'll live.' He winked.

Mr Devereux stepped forwards. 'What the *devil* is going on here, Justin?' he demanded.

'This beautiful lady is my fiancé, Father, and I wanted to be with her.' Justin took Ruby's arm and began to walk up the path to the door.

'What?' Charles blustered, 'now just a moment.'

But Justin ignored him and turned to Ruby. 'I might have to go back to bed for a while, my love. I'm still very weak.'

'It's all ready for you.' She leant her head against him and smiled broadly as they walked past Thomas, standing open-mouthed at the door.

50

While Ruby helped Justin back to his bedroom, high voices could be heard from the Jacobean drawing room filtering up the stairs.

'Oh dear, Justin, I don't think your father is too happy about our engagement.'

'I couldn't give a fizz, Ruby,' he said slumping down on the bed in exhaustion. 'He's never agreed with anything I do, but,' he grinned broadly, 'it's never stopped me doing anything. At least Sarah and Peter are on our side.'

'Thank goodness.' She kissed him. 'Now can I get you something bland to eat?'

Justin grimaced. 'Ask Mrs Blair to make it tasty, will you? This diet is going to kill me.'

'Anything other than bland food will kill you, and I don't want that now I have you back from the brink.'

He reached for her hand to have her sit beside him. 'I might have to go back to hospital for another transfusion, you know?'

Ruby nodded. 'We'll cross that bridge when we come to it.'

Lifting her hand to kiss it, he smiled. 'We're going to have that life we planned after all. We're going to be married and live our life in Italy!'

Ruby burst into happy tears. 'I just need to get you completely better first,' she said wrapping her arms around him. She turned when Thomas appeared at Justin's door, smiling at the look of confusion on his face.

'I'll leave you with Thomas now - he'll help you back into bed.' She kissed him on the lips and walked past Thomas, who was wide-eyed with astonishment.

Ruby skirted the Jacobean drawing room – the row beyond the door was intensifying - Charles Devereux was clearly unhappy. The staff in the kitchen fell silent when Ruby entered - word of her engagement had obviously circulated.

Joe gave her an encouraging smile, so too did Betsy, who had arrived in the kitchen a few minutes earlier.

Mrs Blair had returned from Mullion, and was now preparing a well-seasoned piece of trout with green beans and boiled potatoes for Justin.

'Are you really engaged to Mr Justin, Mrs Sanders,' Mary blurted out.

'Hold your tongue girl,' Mrs Blair scolded and Mary's chin trembled.

Ruby's face broke into a wide smile. 'It's all right, Mrs Blair - as to your question, Mary, yes, I am engaged to be married to Justin.'

'That's the most wonderful news, Mrs Sanders. Congratulations,' Betsy said.

Mrs Blair pulled her apron straight. 'Yes, well, let me also add my congratulations. But I take it from the racket going on in the drawing room - the family aren't too pleased about it!' She raised an eyebrow.

Ruby bit her lip. 'The Earl and Countess are happy for us, but, as you can hear…' she gestured towards the noise, which suddenly stopped, following the slamming of a door and footsteps quickly ascending the stairs.

'Lordy me - this place isn't going to be the same without you and Betsy. I don't know what we're going to do without you both!'

'Never fear, I have someone in mind to take my place,' she glanced over at Joe who nodded.

Juliet felt her heart implode realising that she meant Molly Johnson – Joe's old school friend!

'Here you go, Mrs Sanders,' Mrs Blair handed Ruby the tray for Justin. 'It looks unappetising, but it'll mend him,' she said with a nod.

As Ruby climbed the stairs with the tray, she could hear Mr Devereux in Justin's bedroom, so held back for a moment.

'I will not allow it - do you hear me?' Charles shouted, 'This *unsuitable marriage* will not happen! She is not good enough for you, and is far below your station in life. Good god man, I can't have a daughter-in-law who once emptied my chamber pot!'

'Ruby is a housekeeper, not a chamber maid,' Justin answered coolly.

'Stop splitting hairs, Justin. I didn't save your life so you could throw it away on some common gold-digger.'

'*I* pursued Ruby - it was not the other way round.'

'That may be, but she could see you had money. I've seen her type before – they're like parasites. You will regret it - you mark my words. Now I insist you give up this folly at once. God damn it man, you will not be able to hold your head up in polite society with *her* on your arm!'

'Have you *quite* finished, Father?' Justin answered angrily.

'Not until I know for sure that you will throw this woman over.'

'Enough, Father, you have insulted the woman I love and I will not hear another distasteful word from your lips about her.'

Charles growled under his breath. 'You always were wilful. To think I saved your life, only to have you waste it on that, that...*serving wench.* I was about to write you back into my will, but if you marry that woman, I warn you Justin, I will never see you again!'

'Good, I hope that's a promise. Now, get out of my room before you utter another despicable word against Ruby!'

Charles stormed out of the bedroom, and seeing Ruby standing there, he took a swipe at the tray she was holding and knocked it clean out of her hands. She shrieked in shock as fish, potatoes, beans and a broken plate splattered over the floor.

'Clean that up, wench,' he growled, as he made his way down the stairs.

'Ruby, *Ruby*,' Justin shouted in panic, 'are you all right?'

'Yes, I'm fine,' she said scraping the debris of his

dinner back onto the tray. She came to stand at his bedroom door. 'But I don't think your father is coming to our wedding!' They both burst out laughing.

*

Charles was back in the Jacobean Drawing room - his face puce with anger.

'Patricia, get your things, we're leaving now,' he demanded.

'Father, please don't go yet. Mother, make him see sense,' Sarah pleaded.

Patricia bristled with contempt for her husband. 'I am not leaving until I know my son is completely better.'

'We are not staying another moment in this, this - den of iniquity.'

'*Charles*, how dare you say such a thing? Apologise at once to Sarah for that dreadful remark.'

'I will not. She has allowed this *folly* to happen, and she condones it!'

'Justin is a grown man. He can make his own decisions in life – he's forty years old for goodness' sake,' Sarah tried to appease.

'Well, he needs to act like a grown man. Now come on, we are leaving.'

'No!' Patricia sat down on the settee and folded her arm defiantly.

Sarah was beside herself caught in the middle of this.

'If you do not come with me now…I'll….I'll.'

'You'll what, Charles - what will you do? Are you going to cut me off like you have our only son? If so, then good, I won't have to look at your pompous face over the dining table again!'

Charles Devereux flared his nostrils. '*I am leaving*, Patricia.'

'Goodbye then,' she said as she picked up a newspaper and started to read as Charles stormed out of the room and up the stairs.

Sarah blanched and looked at her mother - *would he leave*

without her?

Noting her daughter's consternation, Patricia said, 'Don't fret, my dear – he's full of hot air if things don't go his way. The house in Devon will not run correctly without me. He'll be back for me with his tail between his legs in a few days - if you don't mind me staying.' She gave a wry smile. 'Besides, I would rather like to get to know my future daughter-in-law.'

*

Mr Sheldon had arrived at the kitchen door to find the house in a high state of agitation. So, while Thomas was helping Charles Devereux out to his car with his luggage, Joe showed Mr Sheldon into his office.

'I need to interview Miss Gwyn,' Mr Sheldon said gravely. 'Ryan Penrose is keeping something from me and I need to know what it is if I'm to clear his name.'

Joe nodded. 'I'll fetch her then.'

Joe caught Ruby as she was returning from delivering another tray of food to Justin – this time intact. 'Are you aware that Mr Devereux has left us?'

'I am and good riddance,' she whispered. 'Pompous man, he was so rude about me - you should have heard it.'

'We did! We all came to the bottom of the stairs when we heard the shouting.'

'At least Mrs Devereux is on our side – I've just spoken to her. Do you know she wanted me to have dinner with them tonight! Can you imagine, *me*, the housekeeper, sitting down with the Earl and Countess de Bochym, while you and Thomas serve me! I swiftly declined, but,' she smiled, 'we're all going to Poldhu for tea on my day off.'

Joe put a comforting hand on her arm. 'There will be a time when you *will* sit down with the Earl and Countess, Ruby. I just hope I'm around to serve you, because it would be my ultimate pleasure to see you happily married and settled.'

'What a lovely thing to say, Joe. I hope that one day you too will find the happiness you deserve.'

'That won't happen if I become a jail bird. God, Ruby, with you gone, what on earth is going to happen to this household if *I* go to jail - and I will, if Ryan is charged with this so-called murder? I took him there - I may be on a ludicrous lesser charge of assisting him, but it will mean a prison sentence for me too.'

'I'm sure all will be well, Joe. The case is based on lies didn't you say. Truth always comes to the surface in the end.'

'I hope you're right. Talking of which, Mr Sheldon wants to interview Juliet. Can you spare her for a while – she knows the truth?'

'Of course, I think she is in the kitchen with Betsy.'

*

Betsy was revelling in some good news at last - Mr Sheldon had brought word that although her ma was still poorly, she was well enough to be brought to the hospital in Helston – the move was to happen later that day. Betsy was delighted, but when Ruby came to tell her that Mr Sheldon wanted to interview her, Juliet's face dropped.

'Do I have to go?'

'Mr Sheldon just wants to ask you some questions. I'll stay with you all the time, if you want?' Ruby placed a comforting hand on Juliet's shoulder.

Juliet felt her stomach lurch. 'If I have to go, would you mind if Betsy accompanies me?' she asked, glancing at Betsy, who nodded.

'Of course, whatever you want. If you need me, have Mr Treen call for me.'

Juliet stood at the door of Joe's office all a fluster - her palms felt sweaty and her heart was hammering in her chest.

Betsy put her hand on her sleeve. 'It'll be fine,' she assured.

Wiping her hands down her skirt, she took a deep breath and entered. Her eyes darted fearfully between Joe and Mr Sheldon, but they smiled gently, gesturing her to sit.

'Hello, Miss Gwyn,' Mr Sheldon steepled his fingers, 'now, I've spoken to Amelia Pascoe for the defence and also to your stepbrother Ryan and collated their statements, but the prosecution has a witness who swears he saw Ryan kill your stepfather.'

'George Blewett, you mean?' She almost spat his name out. 'He's a liar!'

He hummed. 'Well, I've looked at Blewett's statement - he claims that your stepfather was a hardworking, popular man, a good humoured chap, who liked to drink but not to excess. He said he took you and your mother under his wing when you were in dire straits. Blewett claims that Ronnie loved you like his own daughter, and was often eager to get home to you both after a long fishing trip. Blewett states that your stepfather had to throw Ryan out of the house when he developed an unhealthy interest in you! He says that when Ryan eventually stole you away, leaving your frail mother to cope without you, Ronnie was worried about your mother being left alone, because she was prone to falling and hurting herself. This is why he sought you out to bring you home safely. Blewett also claims that Ronnie knew bringing you home would bring him trouble, because he knew Ryan wanted you for himself, and would come to fetch you with the intent of killing Ronnie. It seems Ryan had threatened to kill him on more than one occasion!'

Juliet clenched her fists and hissed, 'They are lies, all lies I tell you. The only reason my poor ma fell and hurt herself regularly was because my stepfather knocked her down - he was a drunk and a bully. Yes, Ryan had threatened his father but in truth, Ryan hasn't got a bad bone in his body and he did *not* kill that monster. Ronnie was chasing me, he was about to - harm me, but he slipped and fell onto Ma's fish gutting knife. I saw it all happen. Amelia saw it too and Blewett was *not there* when it happened and neither were Joe and Ryan.'

'Would you be prepared to sign a statement to that effect?'

'Yes, of course I would, because it's the *truth!*' Juliet glanced wildly around the room, embarrassed at her impassioned outburst.

'Thank you. Now, Juliet, can you explain *why* Ryan threatened his father?'

Juliet felt her body begin to tremble. 'Because it was my stepfather who had the unhealthy interest in me, not Ryan, he threatened him to stay away from me!' She glanced at the office door, but had to clutch the seat of her chair to physically stop herself from running out of the room. She did not want to have this conversation.

Seeing her unrest, Betsy closed her hand over hers to settle her.

'Can you explain what you mean by an unhealthy interest in you, Juliet?' Mr Sheldon asked.

A pitiful cry escaped her throat. 'I…I…. no, I don't want to.' She wrapped her hands around to quench the sickness in her stomach.

'Miss Gwyn,' Mr Sheldon leaned forward, 'When Ryan gave a statement to me he refused to tell me why he was so intent on getting to you that night. I've questioned Mr Treen here who accompanied him that night and Ryan wouldn't tell him the reason either, other that you were in danger.'

'*And I was in danger.*' Her voice was choked with tears. 'Ryan came to my rescue because he is a good man. He….he knows what Ronnie did to me…..' She buried her head in her hands and began to cry like a baby.

Mr Sheldon gave her a moment, and then said very gently, 'Can you tell me, what exactly he did to you?'

Juliet lifted her tear-stained face – her body shaking like a leaf. 'Isn't it enough that Ryan knew something awful as going to happen to me?' she sobbed.

'Juliet, I cannot base a defence for Ryan on an assumption as to why he came to you that night. George

Blewett says that you, Amelia and your ma are all lying to protect Ryan.'

'Damn that man to hell! It is Blewett who is the liar!'

'Then let me prove he is. To all intents and purpose, the judge will hear that Ryan came with intent to claim you back, and to kill his father in the process. If I don't know the truth, Blewett's statement will be heard. Ryan will hang, and Joe will be imprisoned. They will both suffer for things they didn't do. Please, Miss Gwyn, tell me the real reason why Ryan felt it necessary to come that night to rescue you.'

Juliet glanced at Joe's pleading face and her body crumpled, as a great shuddering sob wracked her body. She felt Betsy's comforting arm around her shoulders, and a clean handkerchief was pushed into her hand. She shook her head. 'I'm too ashamed to tell you,' she mumbled into the handkerchief.

'You have nothing to be ashamed of,' Joe said softly.

She lifted her eyes to meet his, tears streaking her cheeks. 'Yes, I have, Joe - you have no idea. You'll despise me if I tell you.'

Joe leaned closer, careful not to touch her. 'Juliet, I love you, you know I do. I need to hear what your stepfather did, so I can understand your pain and perhaps help you.'

'Nobody can help!' She stood, knocking the chair aside and began to pace the room.

Joe reached out to her, but she pulled away as though he would burn her. He retracted his hand and said gently, 'Juliet, I rode with Ryan on that journey to Gweek and all he wanted to do was to get to you fast - to save you from your stepfather. He was terribly fearful at what might happen to you, and was distraught, and kept saying that he'd failed you again. He thought only of you during that journey, and his actions made him miss his own wedding to Betsy. You heard Mr Sheldon - Ryan will hang if the truth of why he really went to rescue you doesn't come out. Please, help him as he helped you.'

Juliet buried her face in her hands, and Betsy took her into her arms and looked at Mr Sheldon. 'I know you need to know, but please can we stop for now,' Betsy pleaded on Juliet's behalf, 'she's terribly upset.'

'No Betsy,' Juliet pulled away from her. 'It's all right,' she said wearily, 'I'll tell my story. I also owe it to you and Joe, because my secrets have hurt us all.

51

While Betsy brought her a glass of water, Juliet sat back down and took a few deep breaths. She took a sip, glanced first at Joe and then at Betsy, who smiled encouragingly.

She cleared her throat. 'It started two years ago,' she whispered - her chin involuntarily trembling. 'I was sixteen, my stepfather, Ronnie, had recently married my ma and soon afterwards he began to take an interest in me. It was subtle things, like squeezing against me to pass me, even though there was plenty of room to pass. He began to continually touch my behind, and if I was sat at the table sewing, he'd rest his hands on my shoulders, and if Ma wasn't looking, slide his hands down to touch my breasts.' She crossed her chest to deflect the thought.

Joe and Betsy exchanged a glance – remembering the incident in the tea room with Thomas, and indeed the time Joe had approached her from behind to hand her a letter - her extreme reactions made sense now.

'Did you not tell anyone, Betsy?' Mr Sheldon asked.

'No, I told Ronnie I would tell Ma about him, but he warned me that if I said anything to anyone, he would harm Ma badly. He'd already started to knock her around – I was fearful of him hurting her more. Every time his hand came near me, I could feel my skin crawl, and then one evening,' she faltered, and took another sip of water, 'he followed me upstairs when I went to bed. Fortunately, Ryan was still living with us then, and saw what was happening. He stopped that, and many more attempts that Ronnie made to enter my bedroom. Poor Ryan, he took many a thumping for his intervention, but he vowed he'd do everything in his power to keep me safe - which made Ronnie angrier with him. Realising Ryan would forever thwart his attempts to get near me – Ronnie threw him out of the house, telling Ma that Ryan had started to form an unhealthy interest in me. That is when my fear intensified.' She lowered her eyes and fiddled with her skirt - psyching herself to tell what happened next. 'He came to my bedroom in the middle of the night, warning me again what would happen to Ma if I called out. He lifted his nightshirt and....,' her lip curled in revulsion, 'he exposed himself to me. I shut my eyes, but he made me open them to look at him.'

Juliet felt her cheeks flush with embarrassment, but Betsy reached over and covered her hand with hers.

'As the days passed, his night-time visits became more sordid. He stripped completely naked in front of me, and, oh god!' She paused when she felt the bile rise in her throat and took another sip of water. 'He would hold himself and climb onto the bed to... to touch my face with his...' Her shoulder rose to hide her burning cheek. 'I was made to watch what he did to himself. I was made to watch until his face contorted grotesquely and his *filth* splashed over me. Oh, god! It was horrible!' She shook her head to rid herself of the memory, but could not look at Joe - not now he knew she was dirty! 'This went on for a long time - the only respite was when he went off on one of his fishing trips. I was at my wits end - I dared not tell Ma, in case he hurt her bad. Ma noticed of course that I was suffering from some malaise - and asked me on many occasions if I was sickening for something, but I could not tell her. I was too frightened, and far too ashamed. It was then I decided to take my own life.'

Juliet looked down at her hands which were folded on her lap.

'I know it's a sin to even contemplate suicide, but I had no option. I chose a time when Ronnie was away fishing and Ma out shopping, but providence brought Ma back home having forgotten her purse, and she caught me putting the bottle of rat poison to my mouth. Then the whole sordid affair came out. Poor Ma, she was shocked to the core, and called on Ryan to put a lock on my door immediately, they decided between them that they must try to get me away from the house. So, Ryan borrowed a horse and wagon and took me to all the big houses in and around the Lizard, to try and find me a position as a maid somewhere. Unfortunately, no one was hiring at the time, but we left my details and Amelia Pascoe's address at all the big houses just in case something came up. When Ronnie came home and found my bedroom door locked, he did, as he'd threatened, and took his anger out on Ma. I could hear her screaming in agony, and from then on, there was not a day passed that she did not sport some awful injury for her intervention.' Juliet fell silent for a while, reliving the horrors of living in that house.

'So, after that you came to work here?' Mr Sheldon asked gently.

Juliet shook her head. 'I didn't come here until,' she paused, 'after the very worst thing had happened.'

Suddenly the thought of telling them made her body tremble. She reached out and grasped the edge of the desk recognising the familiar feeling of panic rising. Her heart began hammering and her breath came in deep sharp desperate rasps.

'Take your time. Take deep breaths, Juliet,' Betsy said gently putting her arm around her. 'Come on, deep breaths.'

'Yes,' Mr Sheldon reiterated, 'take your time'

It took a few minutes, but when eventually her breathing calmed, she let go of the desk and her eyes flickered up to Mr Sheldon. 'I'm so sorry,' she whispered.

'Nothing to be sorry about, Juliet, if you're able to continue, you must do so in your own time.'

'It was the beginning of May,' she spoke into her lap. 'We thought Ronnie had gone to get the boat ready to sail on the tide. It was a huge relief when he went away – at last we could relax and Ma's injuries would heal. But we were wrong - he came back.' Her body gave an involuntary shudder. 'He must have seen Ma was busy at the back of the house pegging washing out because he sneaked in and grabbed me. I screamed of course, but he dragged me upstairs, threw me on the bed, searched my pocket for my key and locked the bedroom door.' She stopped for a moment reliving that dreadful moment. 'He ripped my clothes open from top to bottom, and then he started to strip,' she whispered, 'I can still taste the vomit that rose in my throat from the stench of him as his fat, sweaty, grotesque body loomed towards me.'

She saw Joe shift uncomfortably and thought. *How you must despise me now.*

'I tried to cover my breasts with my hands, but he grabbed them away and forced me to touch his, his,' she shook her head. 'He would not let me go - he made me hold it.' She turned to Betsy. 'I can't get the feeling off my hands. You've seen me try, Betsy, haven't you?' she cried. Betsy nodded. 'I scrub and scrub, but I can't rid myself of that horrid feeling.' The thought made her frantically rub the palms of her hands down her skirt, trying to rid herself of the terrible feeling she'd so diligently tried to suppress.

Betsy closed her hands over both of Juliet's to stop them moving. 'Breathe deeply again, Juliet,' she said softly.

The room had fallen silent, and Juliet felt her throat constrict as tears trickled down her face. 'He, he let go of my hands, and straddled me – crushing me with his weight. I could hear Ryan battering my bedroom door with something. Ma had fetched him, but he couldn't get in. When I heard him, I screamed for him to help me, but Ronnie put a hand to my throat and pressed until he nearly choked me, and then all I could feel was a terrible searing pain between my legs.' She lifted her tear-stained face to Betsy. 'Ryan broke the door down, but it was too late,' she shook her head and dropped her voice to a whisper, 'it was all too late. Ryan was so angry - he dragged him off me and punched him so hard in the stomach Ronnie vomited. I remember Ma covering me up, rocking me gently like a baby, but I just felt numb, but for the pain of where he'd been. She took me to Amelia Pascoe's cottage for safety, and then we heard the bell in the boatyard calling the fisherman to the boats which were sailing on the tide. From Amelia's window, we saw Ryan punch and kick Ronnie out of the house, flinging his clothes after him. But as he stood outside the house getting dressed, he was shouting profanities and vicious threats to us all.'

Juliet stared skywards for a moment - spent and weary that the worst of her story had been told. Taking a deep breath, she said, 'Amelia was very kind. When she found out what had happened. She put me in a hot bath of vinegar to try to flush his filthy seed out of me. It worked, thank god, but it was too late, I was ruined.' She closed her eyes and tears trickled down her cheek. 'Amelia arranged for me to go and live with her sister in Gunwalloe who had a boarding house there. Ryan took a job in Penryn. He wanted Ma to go with him, but she was determined not to leave the house she had once shared with my father. They decided on a story Ma was to spin to Ronnie - that Ryan had taken me away, up country. That way, hopefully he wouldn't come looking for me. Ryan swore he'd keep what happened to me a secret until his dying days. I was a fallen woman - no one would have employed me if they knew. I would never have got this job here if they'd known. Well,' she said forlornly, 'you all know my shame and ruin now!'

Mr Sheldon nodded sympathetically, and then Juliet chanced a glance at Joe – she could not read is face, except that he looked pale and drawn.

'Thank you, Miss Gwyn. You're a very brave young woman. Your statement will help this case enormously, but rest assured - I will only use what you've told me, in court, if I absolutely have to. Now I know the facts, I think I can get this case quashed.'

Juliet nodded sadly.

'May I take Juliet outside for some fresh air, Mr Treen?' Betsy said.

'Of course,' he said stiffly and turned to the lawyer. 'Mr Sheldon, now you have what you needed, let me show you out.'

Juliet watched as Joe left the office without a backward glance to her, and then dropped her face into her hands to cry.

'Come on now, Juliet. It's done – let's go outside.'

Because Juliet was visibly distressed, Betsy grabbed their coats and led her outside via the laundry room.

'My life is finished here – they won't keep me on,' Juliet cried as they sat on the wall.

'Of course they will. I don't believe Joe would tell anyone. Everyone looks after each other here, as you saw when Trencrom molested me.'

'But the shame…'

'You're a victim, Juliet – there's no shame in that, and you *are* brave. Mr Sheldon needed that evidence. He knows now why Ryan came to your aid – and it was not to kill your stepfather – though I think I'd have flipping killed him if I'd have been Ryan,' she added. 'Perhaps now you've shared your story with us, you could maybe move on from this?'

'And do what?' she asked wildly, 'I could never let another man near me – the thought is just too horrible.' She lifted her stricken face to Betsy. 'Oh, no, I haven't put you off marrying, have I, with what I've told you?'

'Of course not - well,' she rolled her eyes, 'if I ever get the chance to marry, that is.'

'I'm so sorry for that,' she said truthfully. 'But can I ask? weren't' you worried about…you know…seeing Ryan, without….'

'Without clothes?'

Juliet nodded and grimaced.

'I was understandably nervous about the wedding night, but being married is about discovering each other. I was rather looking forward to knowing every single part of Ryan's body.'

'Oh, Betsy,' Juliet shook her head, 'how could you?'

'Because I love him! Juliet,' she put her hand over hers, 'what you witnessed was a horrible, stinking monster.

You'll *never* be exposed to anything like that again. He's gone, and dead for his sins - you must try to let what he did to you die with him.'

'I don't think I'll ever erase that memory.'

'Perhaps not, but a good man would show you that it's not horrible.' Betsy squeezed Juliet's hand. 'I've no experience of what it's like to be properly intimate with anyone yet, but to be with someone you love, someone who will take care of you and be tender with you…well.'

'I could never,' she shuddered, 'you know, never…be with another man.'

'Never say never, Juliet. I remember Jessie telling me that Sophie Trevellick was once married to a hateful man, but she took a chance on Kit Trevellick and look how happy they are!'

'I would be terrified at seeing another naked man.'

Betsy laughed gently. 'I'll let you into a little secret. I came across Ryan in the woods, washing himself once. He was completely naked – I saw everything!'

Juliet gasped horrified. 'Did you run away?'

Betsy broke into a wide smile. 'No, I couldn't take my eyes off him – he was the most beautiful thing I'd ever seen.'

Juliet's mouth turned down. 'Even his….'

'Especially that! Look, Juliet, Trencrom tried to spoil things for me. His hands went where they should not have gone, and yes it still makes me shudder, but Ryan's touch would have taken that horrible feeling away, I know it would. You have to let someone heal you of this disgust. Let Joe into your life. He'll be tender and patient with you - I know he would.

'It's too late for that.' She gave a deep tremulous sigh. 'You saw his face when he left that room. He was disgusted in me, and I *have* been used.'

'*No*, he was not disgusted in *you*! He was disgusted, as I am, in what that man did to you. And as for being used – you're no more *used* down there than you would be if you'd been widowed – and lots of people remarry again.'

Juliet was not convinced. 'There is another problem too - Molly Johnson is going to be asked back to be the new housekeeper. You saw them together – she and Joe have known each other for years, so he'll probably marry *her* now!'

Betsy grasped her hands. 'Juliet, when will you realise, *you* are Joe's heart's desire. Come on, I'm freezing out here. Do you feel up to a cup of tea?'

Juliet nodded. 'I'll just go and wash my face.'

She climbed the stairs to her attic bedroom with a heavy heart, but when she opened the door, she found a vase of alstroemerias on her bedside table, and an envelope beside it. With trembling fingers, and blurred eyes, she read:

I love you, Juliet, now and forever more. Joe x

52

Betsy left Bochym before tea time. She walked back to Poldhu along the fields where Ryan had taught her to scythe, then past the stile where they had secretly courted, and the woodshed where she'd seen him naked! The evening was drawing in when she reached the church where she should have been married three days ago, so she hurried past, feeling the cold wind bite.

Bringing the fire back to life in the cottage, she picked up the unopened letter that she'd received from Ryan that morning. A few hours ago, she was unsure if she wanted to read it, but now, after Juliet's confession - she was ready.

My darling, Betsy,

I am so very sorry to have let you down so spectacularly. You know that I would not consciously have hurt you for the world. I love you, Betsy - I love you with all my heart. I can't even explain to you why things happened as they did - it is out of my control. Juliet, as you probably already know by now, is my stepsister, and for reasons I cannot divulge, I felt duty bound to keep her safe. The night Juliet was taken - I completely lost my reason with worry. I knew who had taken her and why. There was only one thing on my mind and that was to rescue her. Not being there to stop her being taken in the first place made me feel that I had failed in the one thing I had promised her — to keep her safe. Consequently, because of my actions, I failed in my other promise, which was to make you, my wife. Although I have not been able to give you the reasons for what happened, I beg your forgiveness, for I never meant to hurt you or keep secrets from you. The secrets I kept were not mine to tell, you see, they are Juliet's, and are too painful and private to share with anyone — even you, my love. I truly thought I would rescue Juliet on Friday night and bring her straight home to Bochym. I never dreamt that my actions would end up letting you down so dreadfully. When I sat in my cold cell on Saturday morning, knowing you were getting ready for our wedding, it broke my heart. Before Joe was released on bail, he asked if I would do it again, knowing what I knew now? The answer would be yes —

my conscience would never let an innocent woman flounder. Perhaps one day Juliet will confide in you, and you will understand.

Rest assured, Betsy, I have not committed the heinous crime I'm accused of. I am not a murderer! I'm just someone who tried to help someone else. I am to be moved soon to stand trial, but have secured a pass that will enable you to visit me in Helston on Monday. Please come, and wear the blue ribbon in your hair – the one I gave you at harvest supper, and then I will know I am forgiven. If my trial goes against me and I must meet my maker, I beg you, Betsy, don't let me die without gaining your forgiveness.

Your ever loving, Ryan.

With tears in her eyes, she opened the drawer and picked up the blue satin ribbon. Her shoulders heaved as she rubbed it between her fingers, before putting it back in the drawer.

*

As the slow creeping darkness of evening loomed in Ryan's cold, gloomy cell, he finally lost hope that Betsy would come visit him that day. He knew the tea room was closed on Mondays, and was sure she'd received the letter today by second delivery. He'd been full of optimism that she would visit – if only to shout at him for letting her down so spectacularly. Every footstep down the stairs leading to the cells, every voice heard above, lifted his heart, only to be crushed each time. He sat with hunched shoulders - his hands clasped together in a penitential pose. Perhaps it was best that she had not come - he'd been in the same clothes for four days and had not shaved. He rubbed his hands over his stubbly chin and though he'd washed, the acrid tang of sweat on his clothes – the residue from his fast dash to Bochym on Friday night - was clearly evident. He'd never felt more wretched. At least he had some warm clothes and something to read in his isolation. Not allowed to visit - for chance they colluded with the evidence, Joe had sent warm socks, a jumper and a couple of Charles Dickens novels with Mr Sheldon. The books were not the most uplifting of reads, many of the characters resonated with his predicament, but he was grateful all the same. When the food, which passed for supper, arrived Ryan felt a familiar sense of loneliness and a visceral sense of foreboding looming. He looked up at the tiny prison window and whispered. 'Goodbye, my darling, Betsy.'

*

While Betsy was half way through her first shift at the tea room on Tuesday, and still fighting the demons resulting from the contents of Ryan's letter, Juliet was at the hospital visiting her ma.

Rosemary Gwyn was strong enough to grasp Juliet's hands tightly, though still dreadfully pale and speaking in raspy breaths.

'It's over, Juliet – he's dead, at last! I rue the day I brought that man into our home. I had that nice Mr Sheldon here first thing this morning and I've given him my statement. Hopefully it will get those poor boys off the hook.'

'Will you be in trouble for what happened though, Ma?'

'I don't know, love - Blewett is making trouble as usual.'

'I know – hateful man.'

'We shall have to see. Now, tell me, how *you* are? Are you settled back into manor life? Tell me all about it.'

*

Mr Sheldon drove into Gweek later that cold, crisp afternoon. It was only the second time he'd been there and it struck him how busy the port was for such a small place. There was a constant stream of wagons leaving the boatyard, all loaded up with goods that had come in with the mid-day tide. He paused for a few minutes on the stone bridge, looking at the mud flats left behind after the Helford River had retreated back towards the open sea. Apart from the ships on the dock, the opposite bank was also littered with smaller vessels of various sizes, tied up and leaning drunkenly on the black muddy shore, some were in a bad state of repair and an air of decay emanated from them.

He looked towards the Blacksmiths - the clanking of hammer on anvil, told him the proprietor was in residence. He'd been warned as to Blewett's character, but Sheldon had come across more unpleasant people than he could shake a fist at. Blewett did not faze him.

The hammering stopped when he walked through the door and Blewett scowled at him.

'Good morning, Mr Blewett. My name is Mr Sheldon. I am a lawyer.'

Blewett narrowed his eyes. 'I've already spoken to my lawyer, Mr Goodman.'

'Yes, I need to speak to you, regarding the statement you gave my learned friend.'

Blewett spat on the ground. 'I've said all I'm going to say until I get to court.'

'All the lies you've told you mean?'

Blewett bared his teeth. 'I know what I saw. Ryan Penrose never liked his father – he came here to kill him, because my friend Ronnie had taken that daughter off him and brought her back under his protection.'

Mr Sheldon laughed sardonically. 'I know quite a bit about your *friend's* character, *and* what he planned to do to Miss Gwyn, and so, I suspect, do you! You're no better than Ronnie Penrose, and I know you're *lying* about what you saw. Your lies would send an innocent man to his death, a man who was trying to keep a woman safe from the likes of your disgusting friend.'

Blewett snorted.

'I have a doctor's report to say Rosemary Penrose's chest injuries were the direct result of the handle of a knife she was holding, hitting her ribs from the impact of a heavy load falling against her. In other words when her husband slipped and fell on it! I also have three signed affidavits saying that you were not present in that room at the time of Mr Penrose's death, and that the death was an accident.'

'What the bloody hell is an affo david?'

'An affidavit is a written statement from individuals which is sworn to be true. But truth is a word you seem unfamiliar with.'

Blewett curled his lip.

'Do you know that it is a crime to lie under oath, Mr Blewett?'

Blewett shifted uncomfortably. 'I wasn't under oath when I told Mr Goodman what I saw.'

'No, but you *will* be under oath in a court of law. To lie under oath is to commit perjury.'

Blewett shrugged. 'I don't know what you're talking about.'

'Let me put you straight then. Lying under oath in a court of law, or making a false statement after taking the oath, is an offence under the Perjury Act 1911. Anyone found guilty of that crime could be imprisoned for up to five years.'

Blewett visibly blanched.

'Rest assured, Mr Blewett, I am very good at my job, and I *will* expose you to be a *liar*. I suggest that you give this a great deal of thought, and the sooner you speak to my learned friend, Mr Goodman, and withdraw your statement, the sooner *you* can get on with your life without the threat of prison hanging over you.'

*

On Wednesday morning, and despite Ruby's protests, Justin insisted on getting up to take breakfast with his family, and try as he might to persuade her, Ruby would not sit down with them.

'You'll have to when we're married,' he teased.

'And I will, when we're married, but at the moment, I've work to do!'

He picked up her hands to kiss them. 'It's your day off, Ruby.'

'Yes, but I am seeing Molly Johnson again about

replacing me.'

'Ah, good,' his eyes twinkled, 'and then I'll have you all to myself.' He kissed her on the lips at the dining room door and went in. Just as he sat down to a breakfast of scrambled egg and black tea, Thomas came to inform the Earl that he had a telephone call.

When Peter returned to the dining room, he grinned and slapped Joe on the arm. 'Good news, Treen. The case has been thrown out and all charges dropped against you and Ryan. Mr Sheldon has made that Blewett fellow see sense.'

'Oh, thank Christ for that!' Joe said, suddenly realising what he'd said. 'I do beg your pardon for my profanity.'

Peter roared with laughter as he filled his coffee cup. 'Think nothing of it, Treen, but it's Sheldon you need to thank, not Christ!'

'Ooh! I wonder if Betsy has heard the news. If not, we'll let her know when Mother and I take Ruby out to tea at Poldhu today,' Sarah said happily.

*

In Helston jail, Ryan looked up as footsteps came down the stairs towards the cells. He stood up when he realised the key had been inserted into the lock on his door – they must be moving him today. His jailer grunted for him to collect his things and follow him.

At the desk upstairs, his coat was pushed into his arms. 'You're free to go,' the sergeant said gruffly. 'Go on, get out of my sight, and don't let me see you back here!'

Ryan walked out of the gloom of the police station blinking furiously in the bright sunlight. Pulling on his coat against the chill of the day, he looked up when he heard the toot of a car horn, to find Mr Sheldon waiting for him.

'Have I made bail?' he asked, when Mr Sheldon shook his hand.

'You've gained your freedom, Ryan. All charges have been dropped.'

'Oh, good god!' He raked his fingers through his filthy

hair. 'Really?'

'Really! Now, where would you like me to take you?'

*

Ruby nervously patted her hair in the bedroom mirror, a few moments before she was to leave to go to tea with Sarah and Mrs Devereux. She wore the outfit Justin had bought her – though the scarf he'd tied around her head in Lamorna was now draped tastefully around her neck. She wanted to make the best possible impression to show Mrs Devereux she would be a suitable wife for Justin.

When she came down the back stairs, everyone from the kitchen was waiting in the corridor, and a ripple of delight followed seeing her so finely dressed. Justin was there too, and he stepped forward to proudly take her hand, on which she wore her ruby engagement ring. He kissed the back of her hand in front of everyone, before leading her to the drawing room.

*

After Mr Sheldon very kindly dropped him off in Cury, Ryan knocked tentatively on Miss Taylor's boarding house door, bracing himself, fully expecting her to throw his belongings at him when she saw him.

When she opened the door, Miss Taylor gave him a serious look and stood aside to let him in.

Ryan stood in the hallway, unsure of himself as she shut the door behind him.

'Well then, I'll put some water on so you can have a bath and get changed. There will be dinner on the table for you within the hour.' She put her hand on his coat sleeve and smiled. 'Welcome home, Ryan.'

*

When the trio arrived at the tea room at Poldhu, congratulations were showered upon Ruby for her engagement.

'I'm so happy about your news,' Ellie said admiring Ruby's engagement ring. 'We've known each other a long time, and I can't think of a nicer husband than Justin for you. How is he by the way?'

Ruby glanced at Sarah and Patricia. 'He's a very difficult patient. He got out of his bed this morning, insisted on taking breakfast downstairs, when he should be resting! I also have no doubt that he's locked himself in the attic now we're out of the way. Goodness knows what he's painting in there!'

Ellie shot a furtive glance at Sarah, but fortunately did not give away the secret Sarah had shared with her!

As they settled at a table, Sarah smiled at Betsy who was poised ready to take their order.

'Have you heard the good news then, Betsy?'

'My lady?' She tipped her head.

Sarah smiled and touched her gently on the sleeve. 'Ryan will be released from jail today - without charge!'

'Oh!' Betsy dropped her order pad and rubbed the back of her neck with her hand – her mind suddenly in turmoil.

Ellie picked up the order pad and said softly, 'Perhaps you should go home to wait for him, Betsy. I'm sure he'll come straight there, and Meg and I can manage.'

'Yes, thank you, Ellie,' she said hesitantly.

*

After tidying herself, building the fire up and plumping the cushions on the fireside chairs, an hour passed, and Betsy sat at her kitchen table nervously drumming her fingers. Would he come and see her, or would he be unsure of how to judge her feelings for him following her failure to visit him in jail yesterday? Perhaps he would not forgive *her* for her seemingly *lack* of compassion! She stood and paced the room for a while, but when a couple of hours had passed, and still, he had not come, she took her coat from the door peg, pulled on a pair of gumboots and stepped out into the cold November day. Taking the path to the water's edge, where, Jessie had assured her, all problems could be resolved, she watched the wintery sun as it sat low in the sky.

She closed her eyes to make a wish and then felt a

familiar pair of strong arms encircle her.

'I've been sat on the dunes for a while, debating whether you'd want to see me or not, and then I saw you walk down the beach with my ribbon in your hair. Dare I believe that I'm forgiven?'

Betsy tipped her head back and sighed. 'Yes, Ryan, you are - as long as you forgive me for opening your letter too late to come to you yesterday.'

He kissed the nape of her neck and she turned around in his arms to gaze at his strained pale face.

'I'm so sorry, Betsy,' he whispered, 'the wedding - the secrets, I wish I could explain, but I…..'

She silenced him with a gentle kiss. 'Juliet has told me all the secrets.'

'Oh! Thank god!'

She felt his strong body relax in her hold. 'I know now, that you are truly the best of men, and I'm sorry I doubted you.'

'I'll never keep anything from you again,' his voice quivered slightly.

'You had better not!' she said, kissing him more passionately this time.

'Shall we go and see the vicar after evensong - to see when he can marry us?' he asked tentatively.

'I think we should, because I'm not sure how much longer I can wait for you to be my husband!'

53

New Year's Eve

Ruby stood in Sarah's bedroom while Lowenna, Sarah's lady's maid, was putting the finishing touches to flowers and clips which held the de Bochym heirloom antique veil in place. Ruby wore an A line wedding gown of flowing ivory silk and lace. It was long-sleeved, high-necked and encrusted at the bodice with tiny pearls. The dress had come from an exclusive couture house in London, purchased whilst on Ruby's first ever shopping excursion to the capital with Sarah and Patricia. It had been bought and paid for by Patricia as a wedding gift, "only the best for my soon-to-be daughter-in-law" she'd declared.

Under her gown and antique veil, she wore something borrowed and blue - her silk stockings were tied with the blue ribbons she'd given to Betsy for her wedding day. Betsy, herself, had been glowing with happiness from being newly married to Ryan when she had loaned the ribbons back to her.

'I hope you are as happy as we are,' Betsy said.

Ruby smiled to herself - she had no doubt in her mind that she would be.

*

Downstairs the manor was buzzing with the excitement of the day - extra staff had been brought in to serve the wedding breakfast, so that all the Bochym staff could attend the wedding. They were overseen by Molly Johnson, the manor's new housekeeper. This kind-hearted woman, who had slipped so perfectly into Ruby's shoes, was relishing this day - eager to prove her worth in her first large function at the manor since taking over the post. Neither Sarah nor Ruby doubted that the day would be a triumph for her.

*

Justin's good friend Lionel - whose cottage they had

borrowed in Lamorna - had come down from London to be his best man. They'd spent the night in the Dower Lodge so as not to see the bride – the last thing they wanted was any more bad luck! Justin was fidgeting alarmingly in his stiff morning suit as he climbed into the car to take them to St Winwaloe's Church in Church cove.

'Good god, I've never been so uncomfortable,' Justin declared, pulling at his neck tie.

'I'm sure Ruby is worth the discomfort,' Lionel slapped him on his back.

'I know she is!' he grinned.

*

Sarah handed Ruby her bouquet and she turned in astonishment to look at herself in the mirror. Gone was the dowdy housekeeper and there in her place stood someone Ruby could hardly recognise. Sarah stood behind her, as did Patricia Devereux - her husband Charles being rather conveniently 'away on business'. They were all smiling with delight at the image before them.

'You look beautiful, Ruby,' Sarah said, 'So, we will leave you in the capable hands of Peter, your soon-to-be brother-in-law to escort you to church and walk you down the aisle.'

'I think I'm in some sort of dream!' Ruby laughed. 'Who would have thought three months ago, that his Lordship would be walking me down the aisle to marry the brother of a Countess?'

'Well, dreams do come true,' Sarah smiled, kissing her on the cheek. 'Oh, before we go, my brother has left something for you – a wedding gift.' She gestured to the large oblong object in the far end of the room covered with a dark cloth.

Moving towards it in a swish of silk and lace, Ruby lifted the corner of the cloth and the smell of oil and turpentine permeated the room.

'Oh, my goodness!' she gasped in astonishment - her hand clasped to her heart. The life-size image Justin had captured was of her, on the coast path above Poldhu Cove – a place and time where she'd first experienced the joy and freedom as an artist. Her hair was down and softly tousled, her white cotton blouse lit the painting with a startling luminescence. She was outwardly smiling with joy holding a paint brush in hand with an easel before her.

'The way Justin captured the love in your eyes for him, makes this truly a love story in oils,' Sarah whispered over Ruby's shoulder. 'He caught the very essence of the free spirit within you – something no one else had ever been party to before.'

'Yes,' Ruby breathed. 'I had no idea he was painting it, did you?'

'Yes, I saw it the day you finally declared your love for each other – that dreadful day we thought we were losing Justin. I was confused when I saw you together - I didn't know what to make of your relationship, but when I took your keys to unlock the attic door and saw this painting, I knew then how very much in love you were with each other. I cannot tell you how happy I am that my darling brother has finally found someone to love. It is my joy to be welcoming you into this family today.'

*

Joe and Juliet were the last of the staff waiting for the carriage to return to take them to church.

'I'll just get my hat, and I'll be ready,' Joe said.

When he opened his office door, he noted that the familiar smell of leather and furniture polish was mixed with the unmistakable fragrance of paperwhite narcissus. His gaze fell onto his desk where several delicate stems of flowers were. He walked slowly around to stand in front of his chair. A small vase of the flowers stood by his inkwell, and a stem lay on his writing pad next to his spectacles. With his knowledge of flowers, he knew narcissus represented new beginnings. His heart caught – only one person could have done this. Could he dare to dream, that at last, there was hope? He smiled as he put his hat on and buttoned up his coat, and when he emerged from his office, Juliet was standing there – waiting. Neither spoke, but her eyes told him that she trusted him. Very tentatively she linked her slender arm through his, and Joe, in turn, tenderly folded his hand over her fingers. He smiled down at the woman he loved. A New Year was coming - It was time to follow a new path in life.

BOCHYM MANOR

Please note, Bochym Manor is a private family home and the house is not open to the public. They do however have holiday cottages available via Cornwall Cottages.
Take a look at Bochym Manor Events on Facebook and Instagram for more information.

If you enjoyed The Path We Take, please share the love of this book by writing a short review on Amazon. x

Printed in Great Britain
by Amazon